AF419118

BOOK ONE OF
SOMMERS IN LOVE

A NOVEL

Sommers in London

MEENAH

AYNEVOL PRESS
BOOKS

Book cover character illustration by Umaimah Damakka
(IG: @coloured_braids)
Cover design by Meenah
Cover copyright © 2025 Meenah

ISBN (Ebook): 979-8-9994940-0-9
ISBN (Paperback): 979-8-9994940-1-6

First Edition: September 2025
Published by Aynevol Press Books / Printed in the United States of America

CONTENTS

AN EXCERPT FROM MEENAH'S NEXT NOVEL

For Hamza Ayyub ibn Assad Ahmed

You said, "Don't watch the sun,"
but he can't take his eyes off a-her.
& if all skin 'nd bones ache for warmth,
is it wrong the moon crawled to her?

AUTHOR'S NOTE:

This story touches on sensitive topics such as healing after a toxic relationship, coping with the loss of a loved one, and experiences with racism and Islamophobia. If these themes are difficult for you, please read with care.

And also know that I wrote this book in search of a happily ever after. If you share that hope, rest assured you'll find one here.

PROLOGUE

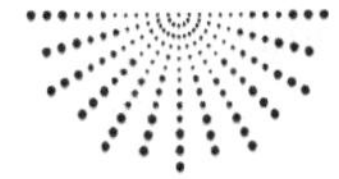

THIS WAS FATIMA'S WORST NIGHTMARE INCARNATE. FATIMA Sommers reread the airline on her plane ticket—American Airlines—and compared it to the one in front of her on the wide banner at the check-in desk—also, American Airlines.

No. Nein. Non. This wasn't happening.

"What do you mean this is the wrong airline? Look, it says American Airlines right here," Fatima insisted, pushing the ticket toward the blonde woman behind the counter.

"I know, dear," the agent said, taking two steps back and straining a smile. "But British Airways operates it, so you'll just have to check in there," she tittered, quickly double-checking the ticket before handing it back. "But I'd hurry if I were you. This is your flight reservation, not a plane ticket."

"Meaning?" Fatima stared at the small paper in her hand.

"Run."

Fatima was a twenty-year-old English major whose primary responsibilities at school focused on reading analytically. The last thing she wanted to believe was that her downfall of the day would be rooted in reading comprehension. She quickly picked up the handle of her suitcase and sprinted like a just-born giraffe in the face of danger, searching for the sign to British Airways.

Fatima had never been outside of the US or navigated an airport at all before—much less alone—but she believed she'd done enough research on the matter. Ever since she'd been approved for her university's European Immersion Program the spring semester of her junior year, her phone and computer search history had become a barrage of questions she couldn't ask the representatives of her cozy little PWI, like:

1. Black people in London?
2. Black people in Europe?
3. Where should you go if you're Black in Europe?
4. Where shouldn't you go if you're Black in Europe?
5. Should you just not go to Europe if you're Black?

To their credit, Fatima was advised to arrive at the airport with at least three hours to spare, which gave her time to course correct after arriving at the wrong airline in the wrong terminal.

She made it to the airport train just as the doors were sliding shut and hurried inside right before it lurched forward, fumbling around for her phone as it rang frantically in her jeans pocket. Fatima let go of her hand on her suitcase in favor of the one holding the pole to find Sadiyah Mitchell, her best friend, who she'd soon be rooming with in London, FaceTiming her.

"You good?" Sadiyah asked, all freckled, warm almond skin and bright, brown eyes. She immediately pressed Fatima for her most current status update, most likely with no thought to actually saying hello, which made sense since she'd always been more "together" out of the two of them. Never needing to be checked up on and constantly checking in on everyone else.

Fatima, unfortunately, needed this sort of delicate surveillance. "I'm about to miss my flight," she groaned. Then, quickly placing an AirPod in her ear so she wouldn't annoy the others on the train with her call, she moved her suitcase in front of her, wedging it between her body and the pole after it began to slip away.

"You're- wait," there was a rustling sound in the background. Fatima watched as Sadiyah shifted around before comfortably sitting back down in her chair, already checked in and waiting to board her plane. "What happened?"

"I went to the wrong airline," Fatima summarized in a low voice, anxiously checking the digital marquee above her to see how close she was to her stop. She still had a little ways to go.

"Fatima, wallahi," Sadiyah swore to God, an anxious tinge beginning to color her voice. "What am I going to do with you? You tryna leave me alone with Mary Poppins?"

Mary Poppins was the immediate nickname Sadiyah had deemed for their soon-to-be host mom, Louisa Thompson, after receiving a picture of her alongside a core list of dos and don'ts for her home, like:

Do: recycle correctly and eat with her family the mandated three times a week (per university housing guidelines).

Don't: do anything else (this portion was far too long to memorize, ranging from red zones of where they couldn't go in her home to a twenty-four-hour bathroom schedule breakdown between her family and them). Breathing, Fatima was sure, was definitely optional.

"Girl, loosen your hijab," Fatima tsked, grinning. "I'll make it," she assured her just as an incoming call came in from Javier, her high school sweetheart of a boyfriend, who'd been sweetly ignoring her for the past week leading into her trip. "Javi's calling. I gotta take it."

There was a short-lived pause before Sadiyah responded. "Says who?"

Sadiyah was well aware of Javier's habit of disappearing whenever Fatima needed him. Fatima had made the mistake of venting to Sadiyah about how he'd iced her out after their graduation because a friend of his said high school relationships never last. And because Javier was just as susceptible to everyone as she only was to him, he listened and left her without any notice that he'd enlisted in the military to join the Navy and would be headed away for boot camp.

There was no letter, no carrier pigeon, just radio silence for weeks that was most likely only broken because he'd ended up stationed (conveniently) near her university.

Remembering that made something in Fatima's chest tighten and pull apart.

So, knowing this history and seeing that it'd remained unchanged didn't help Fatima's campaign to redeem her relationship in her friend's eyes. Sadiyah, for all intents and purposes, couldn't stand Javier. Aliens on Mars knew she wasn't a fan of Fatima's boyfriend. Sadiyah didn't like how Fatima, as she put it, "allowed him to isolate and toy with her." But Fatima knew that wasn't the case. She knew Javier needed her, especially after their car accident at the end of her sophomore year.

After that day, and entirely against military protocol, Fatima became a decorative fixture in his room every weekend at the barracks. She made sure he slept well, got to work on time, ate properly, had his hair braided just the way he liked it, and that she was always a call away if he ever needed her, whenever she wasn't around. Sadiyah said she was being his mother, and Fatima brushed her off because how could she know what it took to be a good girlfriend when she'd never been one at all?

Sadiyah didn't date. Her hand had faithfully held onto her Quran her entire life. And much to Fatima's parents' dismay (though they hadn't exactly voiced this thought to her, it was just something she felt that hung swelteringly in the air between them), Fatima had put hers down, exchanging it for Javier's hand instead. And maybe that wasn't her best decision. Maybe in moments like these, she wished she'd tried harder to be more like her friend, who still wore her hijab, prayed, and did everything Fatima convinced herself was just too hard.

Maybe loving someone who refused to let you was harder.

Fatima took a deep breath, not willing to get into all of that while his call was still ringing and they'd hardly spoken in days. "I'll call you back," she promised, not wanting to explain her reasoning any further because she knew there wasn't any reason when it came to her and Javier. Just the bone-deep, unexplainable love she held for him.

Sadiyah sighed. "Be smart," was all she'd said before Fatima hung up to answer Javier's phone call.

"Bueno?" Javier asked, his voice low and silvery, speaking as if everything between them were normal.

"I am now that I'm talking to you," Fatima told him warmly, playing along.

"Hm," he muttered. "I'd believe that better if you weren't leaving me."

"Who's leaving you?" Fatima tried to be funny about her response, although she was only getting more anxious as she waited to get off the train.

Javier pretended not to hear her, though. "I told you that you should've taken the semester off. Sounds like you're just wasting time we could've spent together instead."

Fatima reflexively let out a full-body sigh, trying to ignore the unsettling pressure of her heart churning over in her stomach. A semester abroad was inarguably the main reason why Fatima wanted to go to college in the first place. Javier knew this. He knew she'd tallied up all of her requirements and organized each year to align with her goal of eventually going abroad, all *Eat, Pray, Love*-like. She had a plan. The plan was working. And yet, here was Javier, faithfully determined to unsteady her course.

"Baby. . ." Fatima's voice trailed off, not knowing what to say that wouldn't turn things sour.

She knew Javier liked having her around more than usual, especially after their car accident. Sometimes, his closeness was a good thing. Other times, she felt the weight of his Honda Civic smashing into the guardrail. Smelled the acrid scent of burning oil. Saw his head crashing into his driver's side window. Heard herself yelling for him to wake up.

But since a car crash isn't exactly the best thought to have before shipping yourself off to a foreign country in an aluminum-covered can, Fatima refocused her attention on her baby giraffe sprint to what she hoped would be the correct airline once the train doors opened instead.

"What? I'm gonna miss you, is all," Javier blandished. "You're going away for four months, Ti, and everything's already changing. Now I have to text you over this WhatsUp app just to hear from you while you're gone."

"Whats*App, baby,*" Fatima corrected with a small smile, dry heaving as she sifted through the overhead signage, heading for British Airways.

"What. Ever. Ti."

Fatima could nearly hear Javier rolling his eyes as he spoke. She pretended she couldn't. "It'll be over before you know it."

"Yeah, I guess," Javier muttered. "Think you'll miss me? Or you gonna get with some *bloke* once you get over there?"

"You do remember you're my boyfriend, right? Why would I waste three years with you like that?"

"You're crossing international waters, baby. That changes things, you know?"

Fatima stopped walking once she'd found British Airways and reached the end of its line. There were five people waiting ahead of her. "For who?"

Javier just chuckled, an awkward sound drifting over their sudden awkward tension. At that moment, all Fatima could concentrate on was what he'd told her last week during her winter break: that he missed her and that he was also cheating on her with some girl named Bea. Well, technically, he hadn't *said* cheated. *Technically*, he'd said Bea invited him to hang out with some mutual friends, but he declined because he didn't want Fatima to feel uncomfortable about it.

Problem was, Javier Antonio Díaz didn't have friends. He'd cut them all off after their car accident because he didn't "need their pity." He just needed Fatima. All the time. And so he clung onto her like a stuck zipper on a jacket because he knew she'd always feel too guilty to remove it.

Still, when Fatima allowed herself to think of what he'd said about Bea, she'd found that she'd developed a tedious habit of paying too close attention to even the commas in his sentences. She'd learned that careful words and punctuation were Javier's way of telling her the truth when his completed sentences did not.

Fatima knew he'd already spent some time with whoever this Bea was. And that she was the only "friend" involved during their visit in question. But, like always, she couldn't bring herself to say anything about it, choosing his lies and half-truths over facing a reality she wasn't ready for.

"For us, actually, Princessa. I was thinking about it. You know, I don't want to hold you back while you're over there. I think we should take a break, don't you?"

Fatima blinked skittishly. What he was saying made absolutely no sense to her. "Where is this coming from, Javi? Why would we. . ." she couldn't get herself to repeat what he'd told her, "do *that?*"

"To help us grow and remind us why we're together in the first place."

"And why is that?" She wanted his answer. She wanted to understand why he was doing this when she was just about to get on a plane and couldn't fight back.

"You not knowing why we're together is exactly why I'm saying this, Ti," he'd explained as if he weren't crushing her whole world under his thumb like it was nothing. Fatima knew why she was with him, though—it was because she loved him. Full stop. She just wanted to hear that he felt the same. "I think you're incredible and I have love for you, I do, but I think we need some space. I need to spend some time on my own while you're out there doing your thing, you know?"

"What do you mean you *'have'* love for me?" The word scratched against her throat like sandpaper as she tried to match the clarity in his voice by whisper-yelling. But then two groups ahead of her turned around to her with widened eyes, and Fatima sensed her near glass-shattering pitch.

She apologized, bowing her head repeatedly. It was quiet for a moment before Javier responded, though, not in answer to her question. "Is it possible to feel so close to someone and miles apart at the same time?"

"Huh?" Fatima hiccuped, not knowing what he'd meant. Or what to say.

Javier spoke for her. "We'll have a break for a little while. 'Kay, Ti? I'm going through a lot right now, and I know you've felt like we've been out of sync, too." He was wrong. She didn't. She felt like he disappeared from her whenever the fancy suited him best and like she could breathe again only after he'd returned. Now what? "I don't see how we'll get any better with you not even being on the same continent."

A lump formed in Fatima's throat. "Sometimes you act like you can only love me if I'm right in front of you and—" *it's suffocating.*

She stopped talking before that panicked, unfamiliar part of her could sell her out.

"You're out of my league, Ti. And I feel like you deserve more than the little I can give you right now. I need some time to be better for myself so I can be better for us- you," he amended lazily, "you know?"

The line stirred awake, and Fatima rolled her suitcase along with it.

"Ti? Ti, you there?"

It took Fatima longer than she'd care to admit before she said anything. Fatima always wrestled with a greedy affinity she had solely in place for Javier, but something about his waiting to do this until right before she left the country unsettled her.

"Fatima," she corrected him. Ti was for friends, family, and boys who said they loved her and meant it.

"Fatima?" He rarely called her that.

"My name," she cleared her throat, steeling her spine however briefly, "to you, is Fatima."

"Fatima," he sighed, giving in. Or maybe he was just that ready to leave her. This wasn't the Fatima he was used to. This wasn't the Fatima *Fatima* was used to. But she was upset right now. She'd come down soon enough. So would he. And then things would go back to normal like they always did. She was sure of it. "I hope we can talk about us again sometime."

Fatima held her breath. She was feeling everything at once and couldn't decipher which of them to grab onto. She fixed her glasses over the bridge of her nose. What a send-off. "Okay then."

Fatima hung up before allowing herself to be disappointed by whatever he would've said next. She looked up as a plane took off to who-knows-where, annoyingly contemplating what would've happened had she just given in to him. Had she just skipped her flight, thrown in the towel for the semester, and spent her time wrapped in his muscle-roped arms, the color of honeyed sand, as they enveloped the deep brown of her own. She could almost feel the curls that sprang in coils atop her head whenever he hugged her. Could almost smell his familiar scent of sage and cucumbers.

But none of that was happening now. Fatima sucked in a breath and slipped her phone into her pocket, the weight of it like a brick anchoring her in place as she rubbed her eyes with the backs of her palms in a desperate attempt to center herself.

"Miss?"

She blinked out of her trance to find that everyone ahead of her was gone now, and the representative was waving for her to come forward.

"Hi," she told him, nearly choking on the sob tiptoeing up her throat. "I'm checking in for the flight to London."

The representative, a man with short brown hair and a curious look, took her ~~ticket~~ flight reservation and began typing away on his computer. Every tap was a tighter squeeze on Fatima's chest, like the way those blood pressure monitors feel at the doctor's. She fidgeted with her box braids anxiously, tightening and retightening her ponytail as she waited.

It took what felt like a lifetime before the representative looked back at her with a careful smile. Fatima was still sniffling, attempting to not full-on wail, despite being sure her chest was in immediate danger of caving in on itself.

She was busy discerning how she'd survive before it finally broke, or at least until she could make it to a bathroom stall so she could keel over in peace, when the representative said, "You would've missed your flight had you gotten here just five minutes later. Glad you made it. Let's get your bags checked in now, huh?"

Fatima wasn't the type to cry in public. She thought that was a luxury reserved solely for the overly dramatic and needlessly disruptive. But she'd had a day that wasn't even close to over yet. So, somewhere, caught between the relief of finally being checked into her long-awaited trip to London and the shock of her newfound supposed singleness, Fatima Sommers began to bawl. Overly dramatic and needlessly disruptive before she could even make it to TSA.

PART I

And then, along came you.

CHAPTER ONE

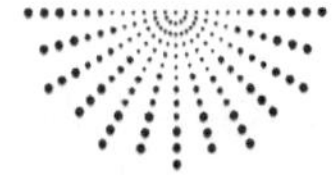

ONE WEEK LATER

THIS WAS IYAD'S WORST NIGHTMARE INCARNATE. IYAD AHMED hurried away from Euston Station, working through the bustling morning crowd of anxious travelers, their eyes glued to the departure board rapidly updating its schedules and destinations. He was late.

He knew he was going to be late ten minutes before his class had even begun, so it didn't make much sense when he took out his phone to check the time again. But Iyad was either incredibly optimistic or had a deep affinity for torturing himself, so he couldn't help it.

Usually, Iyad was better about his time management—but those times, he wasn't at the mercy of his cousin, Mo. Today, Mo took his sweet time showing up for his shift to watch over their family's store, Ahmed Azyaa, so Iyad was left to cover for him. Again.

"Before you start," Mo began with that dumb grin of his, shrugging off his black puffer jacket and exchanging salams once he'd made it to the shop. "Mans was late for good reason." He sat down on the aged wooden stool, with Islamic books lining the wall behind him.

"What's the 'good reason' this time, Mohammad?"

Iyad always called his younger cousin by his full name whenever he'd bothered him, which was often. Mo was often in his own world, making up the rules as he went along. Iyad used to be like that, too. Before. In his own way.

"I almost got hit by a double-decker," Mo gawked, and Iyad raised an eyebrow.

"You used that 'good reason' two weeks ago after the bus almost hit *me* while *you* were on FaceTime." Iyad's jaw set into a tight line.

"Right, that was you," Mo said under his breath. Then, louder and somehow wholly undeterred, he said, "And I'll keep using it until the shock wears off. Did you know that every time I blink, I see my life flash before my eyes?"

Iyad sighed, slipped into his jacket, then picked up his rucksack. The store wasn't busy that morning, but The Strand outside was already restless. He watched pedestrians in hats and scarves go by, braving the January cold, and prepared to do the same.

"And did you happen to count how many times I've covered for you in all of that flashing?"

Mo's grin widened. His teeth gleamed white against the wheat brown of his skin. "Ah, you want a tally of how many times you've played hero?"

"Nah, man, I'm not sure you can even count that high," Iyad countered with a wry grin. Glancing at his phone, he noticed how much time had passed. "Oh my days, I've got to go. Don't burn the shop down while I'm gone, yeah?"

Iyad had already darted outside to the snow-covered city, rushing past a rack of abayas before Mo could try and weasel his way out of his own shift. Now, Iyad found himself running late for his English History class, as he was forced to trail behind two girls, obviously tourists, who were somehow taking up the entire pavement.

"Yallah," he muttered, silently urging the girls to pick up the pace as they crossed the street to Tavistock Square.

Iyad lowered his head and stashed his phone in his pocket, warming his hands there. Beyond the girls, he was the only one walking along the path of terraced homes, headed for his class today at LSHS, London School of Historical Studies, so he thought it best to give them as wide a berth as he could, but they weren't making it easy.

It was evident they were lost, which, for one, wasn't all that far-fetched, considering even natives got turned around in London. But these girls seemed less lost and more confidently hopeless, stopping, slowing, and searching for whatever marker they needed, their eyes darting around like the frantic wings of a hummingbird.

Before they saw him.

The one in the hijab saw him first. Not like when she'd just happened to see him while looking around and most likely cataloged him with the rest of the scenery, but like she'd finally found Waldo. Like, that *aha!* moment after you'd been looking at the same image for too long, only to find he'd been there since the first glance. She looked at him, now on maybe her fourth scan around, and then nudged the one with the long braids, who looked back at him and

frowned?

Why did she frown at him, and why did it bother him so much that she seemed so. . . disappointed? Why did he feel his heart begin to match the pace of their steps, quick and chaotic as they looped their arms together and hurried away like frightened mice in daylight to get away from him? Iyad wanted to stop them. He wanted them to know he wasn't some wasteman waiting for a chance at unsuspecting girls—he was just late to class, and they were just in the way.

He rubbed the back of his neck as the girls disappeared from view, an unconscious nervous habit he'd had ever since he could remember. Figuring he'd lost the chance to explain himself, Iyad charged it instead, ducking inside of LSHS before he lost his nerve entirely and gave up on the day altogether.

THE MUTED HUM OF CHATTER AND LAUGHTER SEEPED THROUGH the closed door as Iyad approached his classroom. With a deep breath, he pushed it open and sat down at the far end of the class while his professor, Tom, continued speaking.

"—work on your final group projects, which shall account for half your grades for the term." Tom was saying in his weighted Cockney accent. "You'll be delving into a piece of history of my choosing, creating a presentation that not only showcases your understanding, but also answers the age-old question: 'Where does our past fit into our present?' All right?"

Tom drummed his fingers on the tabletop, explained the project's specifics, instructed the class to pair up, and then asked them to come to him for their individual assignments once they were done. Iyad didn't move. He was in his last year at Willowmere University and had spent all three of them alienated from everyone else, even before his time there had begun.

That was shortly after his dad died. Iyad took a gap year before university to "find himself" as his therapist had suggested, like he was some well-to-do kid with too much time on his hands. Meanwhile, Mo lapped him in school and graduated first.

Most days, Iyad didn't care how his choices left him alone more than some would consider "healthy." That's what he told himself, at least. Still, self-imposed isolation in any form was quite inconvenient in times like these.

Iyad leaned back in his seat, scanning the room to see who might be left without a partner as everyone scurried around the class, getting their tasks from Tom and organizing amongst themselves. Just as he realized Tom must've miscounted how he'd split up the class since there wasn't anyone left to pick from, the door flung open and two familiar brown-skinned faces swept through: Braids and Hijab from outside on the pavement.

"Sorry we're late, Tom," Hijab announced with an. . . American accent? Were *these* the Americans Tom was leading the orientation he sent that email blast about? The one that said he'd have to move their first week of classes to condensed lectures so he could lead his time with them as well? Must've been. Hijab already seemed familiar with him.

"Yeah, we couldn't find the sign for Tavistock, and then we had some trou—" Braids chimed in, also definitely American, her voice carrying a touch of a Southern drawl drifting throughout her words. She stopped explaining, as for the second time in less than an hour, she locked eyes with Iyad.

"We had some trouble finding the building," she continued, her smile faded, obviously uneasy at the sight of him.

But Iyad was thunderstruck. This girl was beautiful.

And with the knowledge that he'd already ruined any chances of making a halfway decent first impression on her, he suddenly wanted to throw himself out of the window.

"No worries, ladies," Tom reassured them. "You've actually arrived just in time for our day out. Class, this is Fatima and Sadiyah, our exchange students for the term from the States." Braids and Hijab, now Fatima and Sadiyah, nodded at the class as Tom clapped his hands.

"Ladies, I've just completed assignments for our group project. We'll go over the details together momentarily, but you'll be working with. . ." he surveyed the class. Iyad thought he might've imagined the faintest smirk settling across Tom's face when their eyes met. "Mr. Ahmed."

CHAPTER TWO

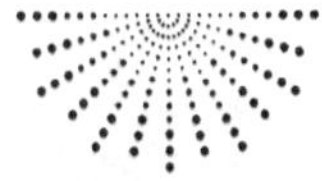

"Ti?" Sadiyah mumbled, scanning for the Tavistock Square sign again. It was their first day of classes, and they were already late since they had absolutely no idea where they were.

Fatima rolled her eyes away from the erratically changing map on her phone that was doing a fantastic job of getting them absolutely nowhere. "What, Sads?"

"You could drop the bass in your voice."

"You could tell me what you want," Fatima spoke curtly. She'd been fairly moody lately, as one becomes after having their heart stomped out, and Sadiyah had unfairly spent their last week of orientation on the receiving end of it. Which, Fatima knew, wasn't right. Especially being that although Sadiyah's stance on Javier had long been made clear, she'd held onto Fatima as she cried and explained what'd happened before her flight, the second they'd found each other in the airport with no inhibitions.

"Don't get mad at me just 'cause—" Sadiyah started, then shook her head because she was so good at being good, before she looked around them again. "That guy back there is following us," she muttered.

Fatima jerked her head around. Oh. *Oh.*

She'd been so tangled up in her head until then, recounting her last conversation with Javier and rearranging it with better comments on her behalf, submitting to her funk. She wanted to blame the way she felt on Javier or the weather and her surroundings, since everything around her was loosely some replica of what she'd seen before in varying shades of beige, green, and black under the grayest sky she'd ever seen. It was all very bleak. And she felt very bleak. Until she saw him.

He looked just as bleak as she felt, meandering slowly behind them in all black. He was tall and built like a football player with his dark hair cut low, skin the color of coffee before creamer, and a beard as dense as a forest. Still, the man was uncharacteristically handsome—good.

On the other hand, kidnappers and killers are often quoted to be uncharacteristically handsome too, at least the ones who get the movies made about them—bad.

They stopped? He stopped.

They slowed? He slowed.

And Fatima and Sadiyah were the only ones on the sidewalk with him then. How convenient.

"Why did you *look* at him?" Sadiyah groaned, linking arms with Fatima and hightailing it to anywhere-but-there.

They waited five minutes in front of some random building, catching their breath, before they figured he'd be gone and headed back. And he was. Until he wasn't. Until they found him again at their same destination in the form of a classmate. There, they'd been assigned a group project with him on King Henry VIII, famously known for the mistreatment of his wives, right before they left for their class outing—a fun development.

Fatima sat up as the train slowed to a stop on their way to Windsor. She and Sadiyah were the only exchange students in a class full of natives. They started a week late, having attended orientation with Tom, where they toured staples like St. Paul's

Cathedral, Tower Bridge, and Buckingham Palace. Tom looked like Spencer Reid from *Criminal Minds* when his hair grew out in the later seasons, and especially reminded Fatima of him when he fixated on retelling his country's history.

His excitement was something that made Fatima happy she'd looked forward to this class. It was notably harder since most of this information was new, but she and Sadiyah had welcomed the challenge since it meant guided tours, meeting Londoners, and was only for two days out of the school week. The other three days, Fatima and Sadiyah spent at their internships. Sadiyah had scored a Biotechnology and Life Sciences internship with Briarvale University, while Fatima would be a Fiction Editorial intern at Aynevol Press Books in Soho. These were good things. Being here was a good thing.

Being on the train, as Tom finished explaining the project while Kidnapper/Killer (technically, Iyad Ahmed) sat somewhere behind him, though, she wished she could take it all back. And she hated that. But her body was anxious. And she hated that even more.

"Alright, I'll say it," Sadiyah announced once they'd arrived at the station and made it onto the platform. "You know we'll have to talk to him eventually, right?"

"I'm aware," Fatima said, folding her arms. She glanced around Windsor Royal Station, taking in its beautifully high curved ceiling and stores. "But no men today. I'll short-circuit."

"You exaggerate."

"You wanna find out?"

They followed Tom as he gave another one of his excitable historical lectures, discussing how Henry VIII and his third wife, Jane Seymour, were buried in St. George's Chapel at Windsor Castle, the oldest and largest inhabited castle in the world, and so on.

Walking around Windsor was like Fatima had stepped into one of those storybooks she used to read growing up. Except, it was rearranged like in *Shrek,* where it was just as plausible to see a typical royal queen as it was to see a talking donkey.

Fatima distracted herself in what she referred to as Fatima-land, where she was physically in front of a castle but mentally in the military barracks with Javier miles away. Then Iyad crossed by, looking their way through heavily lidded eyes that threatened to swallow her whole, and briefly, she was distracted in a completely different way. She turned around. A handsome face would be the end of her one day, for sure. But not today.

Once they were inside Windsor Castle, her group was advised against photography and given a handheld audio device with headphones to guide them during their walkthrough. Quietly. Translation: shut up, listen, and look. She was all too happy to oblige.

Fatima walked along the regal floors, gazing at the statues and the hanging crystal chandeliers. She took out the orange notebook she'd bought before classes began, flipped to the first page, and dated it with a heart. One thing Fatima always loved was filling up a notebook, and this one would be no exception, if she could help it. If she could just get her mind to shut up. Listen to the guide. And look at the royally designed patterns on the walls and fabrics around her.

Everything could be so simple. Yet, for some irritating reason, she couldn't help but notice him, completely unfazed by them, as he looked at a painting of a uniformed man atop a horse.

"You know," Sadiyah was practically purring as she wedged herself between Fatima and Iyad, blocking Fatima's line of vision. "It's rude to stare."

"I'm not staring." Fatima lied. "I'm thinking."

"About riding that horse with him or him holding you as y'all slow dance in this drawing room?"

Fatima rolled her eyes, letting them linger on the gold fili-gree ceilings above her. "About how we were running away from him barely even two hours ago. Now, we have to work with him, and he can't even say 'Hi?' 'Sorry, I scared you?' 'Truce?' *Nothing?*" she gawked a little too loudly, and someone in the room shushed her.

Defensively, Sadiyah immediately swiveled her head around, searching for the culprit, but the coward remained hidden. "To be fair, we didn't say anything to him either," she conceded.

"So you're saying you're on his side," Fatima summarized.

"I'm saying we were just as quiet," Sadiyah doubled down.

"Well, say something else," Fatima muttered, dragging her shoe on the ground like a child.

"Pouting doesn't look good on you."

Fatima rolled her eyes. "Can't you see that we're the victims here?" She thought this much was obvious.

"Of being late to class?" Sadiyah clearly disagreed.

"Whose side are you on?"

"You gonna be like this the whole time?"

"Like what, exactly?"

"Like someone ruined your Corn Flakes—"

"Of all the cereals to choose from, that's what you go with?"

"—specifically, Pretty Boy," Sadiyah continued, ignoring Fatima's feeble attempt to change the subject. "Iyad is not Pretty Boy. He's just *a* boy that we have a project with, Ti. Quick and painless. You don't have to paint him out as a villain already."

Easier said than done.

"He has a name," Fatima muttered. She didn't have a good argument in Javier's defense ready then, but she did know his name wasn't "Pretty Boy"—even though Sadiyah exclusively acted like it was—"And he's going to come back," she smiled flatly. "We have, what? A five-hour time difference, right? He probably just hasn't had time to talk to me yet. He could be sleeping right now, for all we know."

"You said he was an early riser and it's. . ." she checked her phone, "already past ten in the morning over there?" Sadiyah hedged.

"You know what I mean," Fatima kissed her teeth. "He most likely just had a long night yesterday, or maybe he's on duty now." She could hear herself going in circles. Fatima was sure he wasn't on duty because she was sure she knew his schedule. But not so well with added factors, added girls, added Beas. "Or, like I said, he's sleeping."

"Or, he could be living his life like you should be living yours, Ti," Sadiyah told her gently. "My mama said a person is just a person at the end of the day, ukhti, skin and bones." *Ukhti. Sister.* "That boy text you, cool. Don't text you? Better. We're in *London*, Ti."

"I—" Fatima hesitated.

Sadiyah moved them near a wall, cornering Fatima so that all Fatima could see was her. "Breathe, ukhti."

Fatima hadn't noticed she was hyperventilating, blinking rapidly, and failing at fighting off tears. She felt hot and disgustingly visible.

"*Breathe,*" Sadiyah repeated, unaffected. "In through your nose. Out through your mouth." Fatima did. "It's just a project. He's just a boy. Skin and bones, right?"

"It's just. . . I, ugh." Fatima felt like she'd been running for miles nonstop. "I thought he loved me, Sads," she admitted in a whisper.

"I know." Sadiyah thumbed away a tear from Fatima's cheek.

"He wasn't supposed to be like that," Fatima told her.

And Sadiyah never responded.

Later, when Fatima and Sadiyah were on their way to their homestay after an hour-long Underground train ride back to Louisa's, it began to rain.

"The forecast said it was just going to be cloudy today," Fatima grumbled, rain falling in cold droplets against her skin.

"*Just* cloudy? In London?" Sadiyah pulled up her hood and

zipped her coat. "The place known for leaky skies and falling bridges?" she jeered.

"You think you're funny," Fatima said, the corner of her lips raised. Then she sighed, plucking a few braids from the velcro closure of her coat as they walked.

"Of course, I do," Sadiyah smiled.

Fatima barely heard her, though. She was distracted again, looking around their neighborhood at the aged buildings that looked like historical artifacts preserved for centuries. The older men wore gloves and newsboy caps, and kids moved around them in school uniforms, all deceptively fast. Or maybe, in hopes of not getting lost again, Fatima was just moving slowly.

She had a lot on her mind. Fatima had spent the whole commute back from Windsor compulsively categorizing a pros and cons list of her relationship when she had it—convincing herself that, in some way, she still did.

Javier called it a 'break' instead of a breakup, which was more of a gray area than anything, considering this wasn't the first or second time he'd "broken" things off between them. Fatima was used to him leaving as much as she was used to him coming back.

Con.

Con.

Con.

Admittedly, there wasn't much to report on the pro side.

"Ti," Sadiyah waved a hand in front of Fatima's face, bringing her back to where they were now: the driveway to Louisa's brick townhome.

"Huh?"

"You think we're having pot pie again?" she asked, taking out her keys as they made their way up the driveway.

"Depends," Fatima blinked, tongue-in-cheek, thinking of how that'd been their last three dinners there already, as she waited for Sadiyah to open the door. "What's the forecast say?"

"I'm gonna leave you outside with the foxes," Sadiyah threatened. They'd grown accustomed to seeing the red canids running around like they owned the place.

"I'm gonna leave you inside with Mary Poppins."

Sadiyah quickly opened the door and pulled Fatima inside. "Don't you even think about it," she warned, since by now, they'd firmly decided they didn't like their homestay.

They both found Louisa to be entirely too nosy and critical for someone who'd independently decided to host strangers in her home. She'd taken the lock off their bedroom door after their first night without telling them, and often passive-aggressively complained about their "hedonistic Americanism." And though Fatima and Sadiyah had very politely requested that she stop, Louisa had made a habit of frequenting their bedroom to move things around under the pretense of needing to "hoover" while they were away. Really, she just needed an excuse to snoop on them. The girls had discovered quickly that Louisa had a habit of moving their things around as proof.

This in mind, Fatima laughed, knowing Sadiyah meant what she'd said. "You started it."

Once it was time for dinner, Fatima and Sadiyah headed downstairs from their room, where they were having—surprise, surprise—pot pie.

"How was your day, darlings?" Louisa asked, her voice like quicksilver as she carved into her dish.

Fatima glanced at Sadiyah; they both knew their homestay dinner conversations often followed the reverse order of seniority, and since they were the last to join the ranks, the girls were always the first called on to speak. Louisa's eleven-year-old son, Artie, was second, followed by her husband, Paul, a white-haired businessman who rarely ever gave any conversation the time of day, and finally Louisa, who then proceeded to give a lot of it. Knowing this, that must've been why Sadiyah had effectively stuffed her mouth with chicken and creamed vegetables while Fatima hadn't so much as lifted her fork yet. Traitor.

"Oh, it was nice," Fatima said primly. "We went to Windsor. Saw the castle and St. George's Chapel."

"Ah! You went to church. How lovely," Louisa trilled. "I hope you both enjoyed it. Maybe even learned something. . . new." Louisa's eyes lingered a little longer on Sadiyah, who, for a brief moment, seemed to almost shrink beneath the folds of her hijab.

"Yes, we did. I loved all the paintings and the gold. Things are so different here than in the States," Fatima went, steering the attention away from her friend before sprinkling a few drops of hot sauce onto her pie, and digging in.

"Oh, bless you, I'm sure it is. What with all your bald eagles, baseball, and such," she barbed.

Or at least, Fatima took it as a barb as she and Sadiyah had quickly begun to with most things Louisa said since they rarely ever came across to them as friendly. Fatima knew she might not have immediately understood everything Louisa said because the dialects were different between the US and the UK. Still, she figured "bless you" had to be an earlier form of "bless your heart." And since Fatima grew up in the South, she knew that phrase, at least, wasn't a compliment.

"I've never seen either," Fatima acknowledged. "Funnily enough."

Louisa smiled, just about to turn her attention back to Sadiyah, somehow still filled up with pot pie, when Artie piped up.

"You've never seen a bald eagle or baseball?" he asked. Artie was usually quiet around Fatima and Sadiyah, which was understandable, given they hadn't been there for long, and he probably wasn't used to them yet. Still, it was nice to have his interjection.

"No, sir," Fatima smiled. "Never seen a bald eagle, and I've never been interested enough in watching a baseball game. I have seen a base*ball,* though," she said, suddenly feeling the need to clarify.

"Wow, I thought you all only watched baseball," he said, dumbfounded as he adjusted the tie on his school uniform. "You know what I would do if I went to the States?"

"What's that?"

"I'd go see Spider-Man and ride on one of those yellow buses."

Sadiyah put her fork down; her mouth suddenly on E. "A school bus?"

"Ah, so it's *just* for school," he gawked, brushing his brown side-swept bangs from his face.

Fatima stifled a laugh.

"That we do," Sadiyah nodded.

"That is so cool." He jumped up from his seat a little.

To be fair, Fatima was just as in awe of the red double-decker buses as Artie seemed to be of the yellow ones back home. But still, a school bus? Fatima almost quirked a smile at that being the peak of his US excitement.

"I'll tell you one thing, my good sir," Sadiyah promised, "Spider-Man is way better than the buses," she finished, which quickly launched them into a conversation over who is the best superhero and why—Sadiyah not giving up on Spider-Man being the only valid answer.

Fatima never knew why Sadiyah knew so much about comic book-related issues. Sadiyah never liked to get into that, but Fatima was glad the information proved helpful for them now. Especially when it gave her time to fixate again quietly.

Fatima had always been an overthinker. Overthinking was

just one of those things she excelled at. Why's the sky blue? Why's grass green? Things like that.

But now her thoughts had become more. . . targeted. More Javier-centered. Like, why had he turned off his shared location setting?

Where was he?

Who with?

Silly little things like that.

CHAPTER THREE

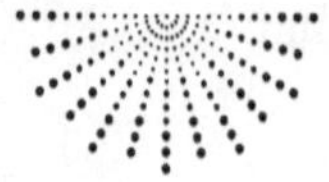

"Aynevol Press Books, you've reached Claudette Anderson's office. This is Fatima."

Fatima had never met Mia, a prominent literary agent in Claudette's inner circle, but in her first three days of working in Editorial at Aynevol, the majority of the phone calls had been from her.

"You'll let Claude know I'll be sending the updated draft promptly, okay?" she ordered. Mia was a French woman with a delicate lilt who talked quickly and demanded things even quicker.

Fatima hummed as Mia continued speaking, pressing the pen's clicker up and down against her desk before flipping to a new page in her notebook to jot down what Mia needed to discuss. She ended the call, promising to pass along her messages.

Glancing up from her desk into Claudette's office, Fatima observed her beleaguered editor hunched over her keyboard, ginger brown hair fanned around her chestnut skin. January, Fatima discovered, ushered in a Herculean workload for the department. Claudette's desk was piled high with manuscripts at different stages of editing that she teased Fatima would be joining in on soon enough. For now, Fatima had essentially been handling administrative tasks, such as making phone calls and updating the office's media list.

Trying to complete the media list would've been a more apt description, though. For the past four hours, Fatima had been a dedicated part-time student of YouTube University, looking up tutorials to try and figure out how to manage the Excel sheet she'd been given after pretending to understand Claudette's rushed explanation of it. It'd been assigned on Tuesday, her first real day in the office, where she'd found she needed the project done by the end of the week. Today, Friday, that meant the end of the day. So now, her reputation rested on the progress of a four-page spreadsheet she was still struggling with.

"Fatima?" Claudette called. She was in her late twenties, but spoke with a smooth competence that made men even twice her age stop and listen. Fatima was no exception.

"Coming," she answered.

Fatima rose a little too swiftly and stumbled, suddenly feeling dizzy. She made sure she had Mia's notes in hand as she stepped into Claudette's office and found her boss trancelike behind her desk, scanning her computer screen before distractedly fanning Fatima over to the armchair across from her. Fatima obliged, settling into the seat, and looked around the office as she waited.

Claudette's office seemed to laugh at her in the silence. The desk alone had just enough lovey-dovey innards of a Valentine's Day card that Fatima would've felt justified had she vomited at the sight of it: pink heart Post-its, a heart-shaped glass bowl of individually wrapped pink communal chocolates, and a bouquet of fresh red roses.

She took out her phone instead of fixating any further. Dust balls shot out of the speakers, letting her know there weren't any messages from Javier taking back his opposing stand against her. Not yet, at least.

"Have they messaged you yet?" Claudette asked, unbidden.

"What?" Fatima put her phone away, and Claudette considered her for a moment before shrugging.

"Nobody checks their phone that much unless it's for some result. Most likely, a job, a doctor, or someone they're into. So which is it?"

After already meeting Claudette at Tom's luncheon for internship advisors to meet their advisees last week and getting to know each other throughout this one, Claudette and Fatima quickly fell into a more familiar territory than a strictly business one, that'd been cemented by their shared admiration for Black Arts Movement artists like Sonia Sanchez, James Baldwin, and Amiri Baraka. Fatima liked how self-assured Claudette was. How she was always cool and didn't seem like she'd lose herself just because a boy told her he didn't want her anymore.

But that was also, unfortunately, the exact opposite of Fatima at the moment, so she changed the subject. "Mia called again. She says she's sending over a new draft and wants to talk when the edits are done."

Claudette shifted forward onto her desk, supporting the weight of her upper body on her intertwined palms. She tutted grandly at Fatima's redirection, but allowed her to go over everything Mia had just called for Fatima to detail with Claudette instead.

Claudette nodded as Fatima spoke, before her eyes settled on the stack of manuscripts resting at the edge of her desk. A sly look crept across her face as Fatima finished, her voice soft and syrupy when she asked, "Ready to take the training wheels off?" She reached for her glasses and used them to push her hair back.

Fatima's eyebrows lifted. "You're serious?"

"They pay me to do more than sit pretty and joke around."

Claudette had one gold tooth on the left side of her mouth that flashed when she grinned at Fatima.

Fatima sat up, pin-straight, and returned Claudette's gaze as confidently as she could. "I'm game."

"Lovely," she responded, vanishing behind her computer screen for a moment, suddenly clicking away. "And I see the media list is progressing well." Claudette peered at Fatima, who tried not to seem so surprised by this feedback, before she disappeared again behind the screen.

"The novel is called *Control,* so you know," she went on. "I've already completed the first two rounds of editing, so you'll be helping to bring up the rear starting next week. How do you feel about, what? Five chapters to start?" She didn't pause to see if Fatima had any uncertainty about it. "I'll walk you through the copyediting process then."

"Definitely, I do that all of the time back at school," Fatima affirmed and adjusted herself in her seat just as the air in the room began to thicken around her.

Claudette reclined in her desk chair without responding. Fatima couldn't help but sink further into hers. "Alright?" Claudette probed, studying Fatima with curious brown eyes.

Fatima shrugged. Usually, she was much more talkative around Claudette, but tomorrow would mark two weeks since she'd heard from Javier, and suddenly—frustratingly, unprofessionally—it was all she could think about.

"I'll ask again," Claudette prompted. "Job, which will hurt my feelings since you're already here. Doctor. Boy. . . or girl—I don't judge, but I am banking on the last option since you've been mugging off my roses ever since you got in here."

"My ex," Fatima blurted, hearing his familiar calloused voice in her head.

Is it possible to feel so close to someone and miles apart at the same time?

Fatima pulled at her shirt sleeve. "He broke up with me right before I got here."

"That bastard," Claudette cursed.

"But he'll be back."

"Do you want someone who could ever leave you at all, even to come back?" Fatima wasn't ready to know her answer to that question, and thankfully, Claudette kept talking so she wouldn't have to try and find it. "Is there a character from a love story you really love?"

Fatima's answer was instinctual; happy to think about anything else. "Not so much a love story in the technical sense, I guess, but *Star Wars*. Anakin Skywalker."

"You mean Vader?"

"Well," Fatima halted, "I guess him, too."

"Why them, then?"

"Because," she stretched the word out like old gum, "Anakin or Vader, everything he did was because he cared enough to do so."

"Please elaborate," Claudette fielded, sounding like one of Fatima's English professors.

"Well," Fatima thought it over. "Anakin wasn't taught how to deal with his emotions because Jedi aren't meant to have them in the first place, but he did what he wanted. He married his wife, Padmé, in secret, but was always loud and obvious about his love for her. So, if someone messed with her and he wanted to start a war over it, he did. And I liked that he cared enough to do *something*, you know?"

"As opposed to?"

"Giving up," Fatima highlighted. "If he said something, he meant it. It wasn't 'actions speak louder than words' with him because they were synonymous. His words *were* his actions. And that's why I was looking forward to this internship. I was excited about helping to create worlds like that," she continued. "Before. . ."

"Nonononono," Claudette rushed before Fatima had the chance to complete her thought. Or start to cry. Again. "Forget him. Forget 'before.' What's the most impactful part of a story?"

Fatima would've gotten whiplash if she focused on how sharply Claudette could cut the corners of a conversation. "The climax?"

Claudette folded her arms across her chest, pushing. "Why?"

"Because that's where all of the action is."

"So that one part of the story is what you look forward to? Then why not just stop there?" Fatima couldn't think of an answer, and when enough time had grown into a chasm between them as she thought it over, Claudette persisted. "Think about it. Sometimes the action is the impact, the climax. Sometimes the action is the ricochet, the falling action," she explained. "It just depends on your perspective, do you know what I mean?"

"You talk about fiction like it's real," she mumbled.

"Contrary to popular belief, I like to think fiction *is* real. That's why we have these books to begin with—since most of our authors refuse to go to therapy," she smirked. "They choose a random climactic point in their life and stretch it to its furthest point of possibility, which is why it's so highly sought after. That's why we have your Anakins, or even your Vaders, who give you so many possibilities. Your 'yeses,' your 'one days,'" she surmised.

Fatima twitched her fingers as her lungs pushed and pulled for air. "But if it's your life, instead of just words on a page, how do you know what part of the story you're in?"

"You don't." Something in Claudette's expression changed. She flinched, just barely, and just for a moment, Fatima saw herself reflected. "Everything is a combination of yours and someone else's story connecting and diverging over and over again. You have no control over it, and it doesn't matter if it's on a page or happening right in front of you. You just have to know not to let it take over," she wagged a finger around and grabbed one of her Post-its. "You know what? I know what you need."

"What's that?"

"Revenge."

"You listen to those murder podcasts on the tube, don't you?"

"Yes, but this isn't that," she sneered. "This is your next assignment. Due by the end of the day. What's your ex's name?" she scribbled onto the sheet, then scratched it out. "Actually, never mind that, I don't want to know. I'm only concerned with you finding what part of the story he served as for you."

"And I do that by getting revenge?" Fatima questioned.

"Precisely," Claudette mused. "You're going to write a revenge list of things to accomplish without him and his influence before you leave London, so that when you audit your memories once you return to the States, you'll know you didn't waste your time while you were here. That way, you can see how necessary he is to your life's story.

"And *when* you see that the plot still moves on without him, you'll understand that his purpose was just for your character development. You'll realize you're past that hyperbolized need for him, and then you won't think of him the way you do anymore," she made a face. "Give your love a chance to change into something fathomable—or get back with him, what do I know?" she shrugged.

"Claudette!" Fatima blurted, surprised.

"Joking," Claudette winked, then handed her instructions across her desk.

Fatima leaned in to grab it, trying to figure out just where exactly Javier fit into her life if it were a book. As far as she could tell, he was strewn across every page. And that, she knew at the very least, wasn't healthy. "So I'm writing a list of resolutions?" she asked.

"Resolutions, revenge, same bother. I don't need to see it, but I will need your word that you'll write and commit to it."

"Okay," Fatima agreed.

Claudette narrowed her eyes unbelievingly at Fatima, which managed to steal a small laugh from her.

Fatima drew in a deep breath, knowing already that Claudette wasn't someone she could easily get over. "I promise."

At six o'clock, Fatima exchanged her booties for her Sambas when her shift was over and she was about to walk to the Underground station to get back to Louisa's. On her way out, she knocked on Claudette's open office door, fanning her tiny inventory of vengeance, penned in black ink on the reverse side of Mia's laundry list.

Claudette looked up from the paper she'd been marking on her desk and beamed like a proud pageant mom witnessing her child claim the top title. "And I have your word about this?" she asked.

"Bond," Fatima spun around on her heels. "Enjoy your weekend."

"Cheers," Claudette called behind her.

Note completed, Fatima had written, only:

Have fun.

CHAPTER FOUR

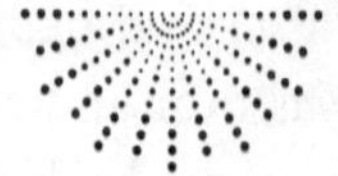

Iyad had one thought as he stepped into Tom's office: change the man's mind.

According to the syllabus, time would be set aside to work on their group project today. According to Iyad, Iyad Ahmed didn't *do* group projects. Especially not with two Yankees he'd already scared off without meaning to—and who probably knew next to nothing about English history at all.

"Tom, I, erm—" He was scattered. Again, Iyad had only come there with one thought. He had only a vague concept of a plan, rather than the whole kit and caboodle.

"Talkative as ever, Mr. Ahmed." Tom looked up from his computer and shifted toward Iyad. "What can I do for you?"

"I'd like to do the project alone," he grunted.

"How paradoxical," Tom scratched his head, unfazed by Iyad's squirreling about. He turned to retrieve a laminated binder labeled "ENGLISH HISTORY," flipped a few pages, then rotated his main copy of the project guidelines to face Iyad. The paper hung between them like a strange appendage. "To want to do a group project," he said, pointing to the assignment's title— *PAST TO PRESENT (PARTNERED)*—"alone."

"I know we're meant to do this with others, Tom," Iyad scowled, although no amount of glowering ever seemed to disarm the man. "They're tourists, though, and you've given me *two* of them when everyone else is just in pairs. I'll be a tour guide explaining every little detail the whole way through."

"Oi, and you figured this out about them through extensive conversation, I presume?" Tom squinted. When Iyad didn't engage, Tom pursed his lips and took a deep breath. "Look, they're clever girls and you're taking the mick. At least give them a chance."

"Tom—" Iyad bargained.

"Tom, we can get it done ourselves if it's that deep."

Iyad immediately recognized that voice without turning around. It wasn't as gentle or sweet as he'd first remembered it. It was hardened now by words that, along with his foot, seemed lodged somewhere deep in his esophagus.

"Cheers, Fatima. You're both here early for our check-in. Anyway," Tom chuckled, disgracefully unconcerned. "All is well, your—" he looked to Iyad, then back to the girls, practically crowing, "—*tour guide* just wanted to be sure he wasn't holding the two of you up. That right, Mr. Ahmed?"

Iyad rubbed a hand over his beard. Despite his mocking, Tom had arrived apropos, setting Iyad up for some level of success with their growing negative perception of him, although Iyad seemed intent on losing out.

He turned to the girls and proclaimed, in an incredible display of camaraderie, "Getting all the details. Rather not be held up." Then, he slid past them quickly, doing his best to avoid Fatima's wide brown eyes that angled ice picks and daggers at him, while Sadiyah stood beside her, blades just as sharp and fixated.

Great.

· · ·

As promised, Tom allotted the last quarter of the class to none other than his beloved assignment.

Iyad, indignant at his failed attempt to put the 'I' in team, didn't make an effort to join the girls at first. He studied them from his seat instead. Fatima, he gathered, wasn't much of a talker. She only ever spoke to Sadiyah, Tom, and that notebook she was currently hunched over, penning away whatever they were rattling on about.

Iyad had never been so jealous of an inanimate object, let alone sheets of paper, before. But ever since Kidnapping-gate, when Fatima had first fixed those doe-like eyes onto his, he found himself increasingly intrigued by her. He found himself curious about what was on her mind. What she was writing about. Any little scrap that meant he knew anything about her at all—apart from her probably already hating him over what they'd overheard earlier.

Rather than get up to rectify any of this, Iyad decided to look busy by scribbling down whatever facts he remembered about King Henry VIII and considering which aspects of him might be viable for a more modern setting. He never got far, ending up trying to come up with a way to explain his second major misunderstanding with the girls instead. He felt the age-old "It's not you, it's me" excuse wouldn't work with either one of them.

Focusing on Henry again, Iyad figured that if he could come up with something decent to say about the less-than-decent man, then he could at least back up what he'd said in Tom's office about knowing more English history than they did. The way he saw it, he'd have something smart to mention once he got over there that wouldn't make them want to run away again.

Running away was something Iyad knew too well because it was something he'd gotten too good at. After his dad died, his mom had made him see a therapist for a little while, who probably would've said Iyad was still exhibiting his symptoms of grief through methods of avoidance. Then she'd discuss healthy coping mechanisms to better support his ongoing healing.

Iyad knew his therapist meant well, but he could never get her to cosign his indifference toward the healing component she spoke so diligently about. Really, for the idea of being healed at all. Everyone always made it sound like a stand-in for forgetting, like a cut that disappeared instead of scarred over. Iyad didn't deserve to forget. He didn't deserve anything other than a lasting mark to serve as a reminder of what he'd done. His dad passed from a sudden heart attack because Iyad couldn't get his act together. So, what right did Iyad have to move on?

After enough time had passed, Iyad finally strode over to the girls. "Hello," he said, meaning the word as an olive branch, like, *We're not cool, but let's be cool. Cool?*

Fatima didn't look up from her notebook when she responded. "Is His Majesty ready to grace us with his presence?"

Sadiyah snorted.

Iyad scrunched up his face and ran a hand through his beard as he sat down. Fatima, evidently, had her reservations about him laid out and color-coded. For some reason, Iyad found himself wanting to change that. He looked between her and Sadiyah, and chose to start again with the safest response, "As-Salamu Alaykum," he nodded, greeting Sadiyah.

The girls shared an unconvinced glance, and Iyad remembered he wasn't wearing any obvious Islamic markers for them to know he wasn't just saying it to say it. "I'm Muslim," he vouched for himself like he was trying to be let into some secret society.

"Wa Alaykum As-Salam," Sadiyah returned. She even looked moderately impressed before morphing back into her steady Anti-Iyad stance.

"So, introductions first," Fatima began, checking her phone. "I'm Fatima. That's Sadiyah. You're Iyad. Introductions over, let's begin," she glided her pen over the opened page of her notebook before continuing. He would've been lying to say something didn't spark a little within him, knowing she'd already known his name.

"Sads and I were considering talking about King Henry VIII from a familial perspective since politics seem too easy for a king. From my understanding, his personal life was riiich," she looked up with a soft grin that quickly deflated. "I'm interested in him as a husband and by proxy, a father to his daughters, since he wanted a son so bad," she went on. "What do you think?"

What did he think? Iyad thought that even if he'd barred the backlash of the conversation they'd walked in on between himself and Tom earlier, this was the most he'd ever heard her speak. Against his understanding, Iyad didn't care that it was about an old king who was probably a terrible husband and father, too. He just cared that they were words. At all. To him.

"Sounds good," he flipped through his notes, although his mind was blank, his throat was dry, and his heart was racing for some odd reason. Was this the beginning of a heart attack? Should he make an appointment with a doctor? He made a mental note of his symptoms to check against WebMD later.

"We were thinking of going to Hampton Court Palace, too. Tom said Henry lived there, but he's not sure if we'll have time to visit as a class," Sadiyah added.

"Did you want to come?" Fatima asked.

Was that a trick question? Was she already warming up to him without him having to do any grand gestures? Any blind heroics? Did he want that? He decided to roll with it and find out.

"Sure," Iyad said, trying to sound cool and like he wasn't absolutely buzzing on the inside. The feeling truly didn't make any sense to him. But it felt good. So, he wouldn't let himself question it. Not yet.

But then Sadiyah decided to ruin his concentration. "Do you have any actual ideas to contribute?" she posed, waiting.

"Times up," Tom went just before Iyad could say anything. Saved by the bell. "See you all next week."

Almost as soon as he'd said it, the girls were gone, and Iyad didn't have either one of their numbers to organize anything or know when they wanted to go to Hampton Court. Quickly, he gathered his things into his rucksack and hurried out behind them, catching up right as they were about to leave the building.

"Fadiyah, he sputtered, accidentally combining their names into connected gibberish.

Fatima and Sadiyah's heads whipped around to him, eyes wide.

"You're running up on us *again?*" Sadiyah questioned, arms akimbo.

"Nothing gets past you," he challenged automatically, and she seemed amused enough to leave him alone for a few beats. He took them graciously, angling his body around them to open the front door. "Apologies, by the way. It looked a lot worse than it was."

"What did?" Fatima asked him because, of course, Iyad had options to choose from. He decided it was safest to answer chronologically.

"The first day. When you both ran from me."

"You gotta admit, that was a bad look on your part," she told him honestly, following his lead down the stairs.

Iyad nodded. "You're right."

Fatima took her phone from her pocket and swiped around before putting it away, immediately continuing to question him. "Why didn't you just pass us if we were in your way?"

"You both were taking up the whole pavement, and I didn't want to scare you," he answered, looking back toward LSHS as they headed toward the Underground.

Technically, Iyad didn't live too far away from the school

and didn't have to go into the shop until later. So there was no need to walk with them all the way back to the train station. He just needed their phone numbers, then they could all go on about their days. But something about talking to Fatima was different. It didn't leave him nauseous the way he usually felt when speaking to people—even his family—after his dad died.

Most social interactions since then often led to anxiety attacks that turned his veins to stone. With Fatima, though, Iyad felt his body begin to exhale. He wanted to investigate the anomaly of how calm he felt around her a little while longer.

"So, to be as least threatening as possible. . ." Fatima persisted, adjusting the arms of her glasses. "You did the most threatening thing?"

He lifted both his arms in answer. "Hence my apology."

"'Hence,'" she copied him, grinning lightly. "Anyway, if you're really worried about the project, we won't hold you up. Here," she handed him her phone. "Let me have your WhatsApp and I'll hit you up later so we can figure out what we're doing."

Iyad entered his contact details and passed the phone back after they'd crossed the street into Euston Square. She tapped around a little before putting it back in her pocket.

"And, uh, sorry about what you both overheard, too," Iyad rubbed the back of his neck, finishing up in atoning for his now hopefully stagnant line of offences. "I've just gotten real used to doing things on my own, is all."

For a moment, Fatima regarded him as if she were giving him time for further explanation, her features softening like a rip current gently subsiding. And he didn't know her at all, but the calmness of the movement made him want to tell her more. He wouldn't, of course, but for once he wanted to say something, at least.

"You're apologizing a lot," she remarked eventually.

"Twice is too much?" He canted his head. When she didn't

reply, he went on, "I was told to apologize when it's due. That a bad thing?"

"Not at all, Tour Guide," she smiled, glancing at the ground and sweeping a braid behind her ear. "Just not used to it."

"Get used to it then," he told her automatically before processing what he'd said when he caught Sadiyah smirking. "I mean, because I'll be around some," he explained. "F- For the project."

Fatima didn't say anything, just smiled, and Iyad instinctively bit his tongue to keep himself from smiling, too. "By the way," he said, his gaze shifting between her and Sadiyah when neither of them said anything. "How long is this 'Tour Guide' thing gonna stick?"

"We still 'tourists'?" Fatima motioned air quotes around the word, still smiling at him. There was a single dimple indented on her left side. Iyad thought it was cute. Small, like her.

"Fair enough," he conceded, raising a hand as they all milled into the station.

"You headed to the trains, too, TG?" Sadiyah narrowed her eyes at him.

It took him a moment to make out that TG was short for Tour Guide. And then another to realize Sadiyah was trying to rush him off. Or, to figure him out—Iyad couldn't quite make heads or tails of her just yet.

Scrambling for an excuse that wouldn't reignite Kidnapping-gate, he pointed upstairs to Leon.

"I came for some chips," he cleared his throat, glancing back over at Fatima. "Well, you've got my number," he stalled. "Message me whenever. See you both next week."

"Bye, TG," Fatima responded, taking her phone out again.

Iyad nodded, understanding he'd lost her attention. He started to finally turn around when a burly gray-haired man flew past him. The man, holding a briefcase in his left hand and a cell phone in his right, not only sped past him, but then proceeded to knock right into Fatima, sending her straight to the ground like a bowling pin.

"YOOO, what the fu—" Sadiyah snapped, reaching down to help Fatima up. The man turned back to them, waving the hand holding his phone at her as if he hadn't been the one who'd just knocked her down.

Iyad was heading for him before he could think to stop himself.

"Sir," he stepped in front of the man, putting a firm hand on his shoulder to get him to stop walking. The man looked like a character Roald Dahl would've drawn, with clumps of wiry gray hair spilling from his pallid-toned ears, and lines etched deeply across his face. "You shoulder-checked her back there. You alright?"

"Get off my back, man, it's not like I've killed her," Dahl's Doodle snapped before looking up at Iyad. He swallowed nervously once he had, although he immediately tried to seem indifferent and steamroll past Iyad, too.

Unfortunately for him, Iyad and his therapist had discovered that weekend rugby was his best healthy coping mechanism, which meant that despite not having played for a few months, he continued to go to the gym regularly. So, Dahl's Doodle was going to have a way harder time trying to manhandle Iyad than he did with Fatima.

"She shouldn't have been stood there in the middle of the path!" The man whined like a child not ready for his bedtime.

Iyad wasn't sure if his argument was meant to be an explanation or an accusation. Most likely both. He steadied himself and glanced past the man to get a glimpse of Fatima. She was standing by then and looked okay enough from a distance, but there was a Boots pharmacy nearby. Maybe there was something he couldn't see that needed patching. Maybe—

He needed to find out, and Dahl's Doodle wasn't doing anything to help expedite the process.

"You should apologize to her, Big Man." Iyad only used one hand against the man's shoulder to ground him in place.

"I- *why?*" the man spluttered.

"Careful," Iyad sighed more to himself than the man, noticing people beginning to watch and that, right or not, this situation at first glance looked a lot worse for him than for Dahl's Doodle. "You had plenty of room to go around her," he explained slowly. "Don't get carried away because I'm being nice now, mate, yeah?"

"She—"

"I'm losing my patience. Go now," he muttered lowly, the words coming out like a King's Guard command.

The man tripped on his Oxfords as he abided.

Iyad returned to the girls then. Sadiyah's arms were folded, and her head was cocked to the side, squinting at him as if he were a book and the words were too indistinct to make out.

"You alright?" he asked, impulsively scanning over Fatima for injuries. She seemed fine enough.

"Yeah," Fatima answered, her eyes meeting his.

Iyad felt a gentle tug in his chest, and his heart cartwheel when she spoke to him, which didn't feel too healthy. Arrhythmia, maybe? Indigestion?

"You know what? Maybe it's good we're working together," he pointed out. "The city's full of foolish geezers like him."

"And you think we need a big, strong man to protect us?" Sadiyah contested.

"No, I—" He must've looked ridiculous. He was practically power posing like some self-involved superhero idiot in front of them.

"She's kidding, Iyad," Fatima apologized and swatted at Sadiyah, who jumped out of the way, laughing at his expense.

"Thank you for your service," she gave him a two-finger salute. "Really."

"For you, anytime," Iyad grinned down at her. It wasn't out of his nature to help someone if they needed it, but something about knowing it was for her made doing so feel different. "For you, maybe," he joked to Sadiyah, and she laughed before they left, melding in with the bustling crowd of the station around them.

CHAPTER FIVE

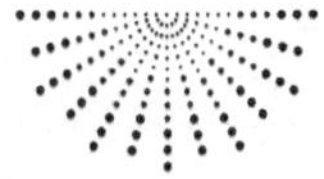

"'Scuse me."

Fatima scrunched her eyes over her phone as Sadiyah pulled her to the right side of the escalator, headed deeper into the Underground station, so the woman behind them could walk down the left.

"Tighten up," Sadiyah told her.

Fatima didn't know what she was talking about. "What?"

"Are you *trying* to get dropped again?" she asked as the woman passed them, and Fatima finally understood what was going on.

In answer, no, she wasn't. Truly, she wasn't. But Fatima was trying to see if Javier had finally come to his senses yet, and wasn't all too into the idea of what sounded to her like being blamed for what that man had done to her. "You're saying what happened just then was my fault?"

"I'm saying," Sadiyah let her gaze dip down slowly to Fatima's phone, then back to her, repeating sternly, "Tighten up. I know you're still checking for Pretty Boy."

"I'm not." She was.

"You are." She knew. "It's kind of impressive, though."

"What?"

"That you're not thinking about Iyad *at all* after that."

Technically, that wasn't exactly true. *Technically,* Fatima had been thinking of Iyad *some.* A flash of a teasing grin. Soft brown eyes. A quick swipe at his beard. Head. Shoulders. Knees. Toes. But what did she look like confessing to that bored housewife daydream while still trying not to go stir-crazy waiting on the inevitable return of Javier?

"You're talking about the caveman stunt?" Fatima inhaled, doing her best to sound nonchalant as they stepped off the escalator. "He's just being nice because he feels bad—you heard all those times he apologized on the way over, right?"

"Didn't you say you wanted him to apologize, though?" Sadiyah countered, continuing before Fatima could respond. "And anyway, is 'just being nice' looking like he might kill a man if you asked him to?"

"As I said: Cave. Man." She rechecked her phone. Maybe this was getting to be a problem. "You want me to give him a gold star or something?"

"That lover girl gene is hard to kick, ain't it?"

"You're not, though," Fatima muttered, looking for the sign that led to the Northern line train.

"Funny," Sadiyah observed thoughtfully, unzipping her coat and draping it over her arm. "My daddy said the same thing," she finished, playing her trump card that her dad had abandoned her family just before she left for college, and that she hadn't heard from him since.

Fatima let her win for the time being as they headed onto the Northern line platform, asking, "Why are you on his team anyway?"

"Iyad's?" Sadiyah clarified as if there were ever a world where Fatima could've meant Javier.

Fatima nodded, glancing from the countdown clock above them to a rat eating what appeared to be a Doritos chip down on the train tracks. It scurried away just as the tube roared into the station, and they boarded, settling into the bright blue, patterned seats. Just a couple of stops until they'd be back at Louisa's.

"I'm not," Sadiyah said finally. "I just know he likes you and that I'm *very* against Team Pretty Boy."

"Aren't you supposed to be Team No Boys?"

"I adjust for my audience," she explained knowingly, pulling out her phone to play one of the no-WiFi games she'd downloaded just for their train rides.

"Ha. Ha," Fatima sighed. Before she lost her nerve, she muttered, "You really think he likes me, though? Iyad?"

Despite what she'd initially thought of him, it wasn't the worst thought in the world if he did. Iyad was quiet in class, unreadable. But he was different when they left. He was confident, funny, and so very handsome, even before what'd happened with that man.

Unfortunately, Fatima was already taken, though. Kind of. She thought. She hoped.

But it couldn't hurt to look.

"How hard did you hit your head when you fell?" Sadiyah asked.

Fatima shot her a glare. "Why do I put up with you?"

"Because you have great taste," she winked. "For real though, I think he does? He kept looking at you in class, and I think he was flirting when we were headed to the station. Only competition you might have is ol' dude that bum-rushed you."

Fatima leaned her head back in her seat, fighting a sneaking grin as she considered this.

"I like him, too," Sadiyah added. "I mean, he's a step up from Pretty Boy, at least."

Fatima fixed her eyes on the tube's ceiling, not even registering Sadiyah's newest jab at Javier. She was too busy thinking of Iyad's broad shoulders and full arms. The way it took him barely any effort to hold that man in place. The way his eyes, low and daring, seemed to soften as soon as they met hers. Of course, that last part was likely just her overactive imagination. Ahem. Purely hypothetical. And besides, Fatima didn't want him. Again, she *had* a man.

Still, she asked. "Why?"

Sadiyah didn't look up.

They hadn't been in the city long, but they'd quickly gotten into the habit of talking as little as possible on the Underground trains because of the less-than-subtle glares they'd get if they didn't. But this was a conversation that needed to be had.

"He's Muslim," she breathed.

"So?" Fatima asked, although she already knew the answer.

She knew there was a part of Sadiyah who saw this as an opportunity for Fatima to return to being a Muslim again. But she wasn't going to do that. Not for a man. If she ever decided to practice again, it'd be because *she'd* decided to. She knew herself well enough to realize she'd already lost who she was for one man—and was still paying the price for it—so she wouldn't repeat the same mistake again.

Sadiyah gave her a wary look, then returned to her game. "I know a man is supposed to be good to you in Islam. Despite what people may think, it's a fact," she shrugged. "You should be with someone who at least has that guideline down, I think."

Oh. There Fatima was, thinking the worst of someone who only wanted the best they knew to hope for her. Fatima took out her phone, feigning the same indifference as her friend. "You're sweet."

"On you? Not at all, Tweedledee," Sadiyah smirked, nudging Fatima's side. "Just stating the obvious."

THIS WAS NOT GOOD. THIS WAS, IN FACT, BAD. THIS WAS VERY, very bad.

Fatima was no stranger to being distracted. To "Fatima-land," so to speak. When she woke up, she'd get sidetracked looking for her glasses because she was scrolling through her social media. When she was in the middle of a conversation, she'd lose focus because she was thinking of ten other things she wasn't doing. Now, when she was missing one boy, she was (moderately) distracted by another.

She'd never been distracted like this before, though, and she couldn't figure out if being so was wrong of her.

Fatima slipped out of her socks and let them get lost under her covers. While Sadiyah was in the shower, she was rewatching the third episode of *Star Wars*, trying her hardest to distract herself from her latest diversion.

Hours had passed since everything went down at the train station, but Iyad was still weaving his way through Fatima's mind. On one hand, he had just done her a simple kindness that was without a doubt within his physical wheelhouse to do so. On the other hand, it was a simple kindness he didn't *have* to do. But he did. And it was the fact that he'd done that, and that she wasn't so sure if Javier would've, if in the same situation, that was currently making her lose her head—just a little.

To get herself back under control, Fatima decided to send Iyad a quick text so he'd have their contact information and then she could move on for the time being. At least for a few hours. Minutes. Seconds. Fatima unlocked her phone and opened it to a new message prompt. She added Sadiyah and Iyad to a group chat, then hesitated, feeling some restless mix of guilt and anxiety spinning inside of her.

Would she feel bad if Javier were acting the same way as she was right now? Did she have the right to care? To be thinking about him when he'd told her not to? Fatima knew Iyad wasn't a monster; he'd disproven her theory quite impressively. But even still, shouldn't Javier still take precedence?

She couldn't tell.

Maybe Sadiyah was right that she needed to tighten up. Focus on herself in this new country and get herself way under control.

This would be the way they got that ball rolling. She pressed 'send.'

Ti:

you're still game for hampton court, right?

Fatima decided that she was only starting this group chat as a formality. She labeled the group chat tourists & tg and then formally swapped the contact photo to the meme of the three Spider-Men pointing at each other. After, she returned to watching the movie with her phone still in hand, satisfied to be regaining some of her reasoning. To be "tightening up." To know that there was absolutely no connection between herself and her hair-brained thoughts of Iyad. They were indicative of a minor concussion, at best. A stupid crush, at worst, that she'd purge from herself soon enough if that were found out to be the case.

Fatima rationalized that she was only starting this group chat for brevity's sake. It wasn't like she was trying to have a conversation; she hadn't even said hello. Fatima was just trying to make sure he had her—

Iyad:

I wouldn't be a good "TG" if I weren't.

Fatima must've lost her good senses in the fall back at the train station because there was no way, no conceivable manner, in which time stopped and sputtered like that after reading something so benign. If it was, then she had a bigger problem than a concussion.

Suddenly, Fatima remembered the same dancing butterflies from when she'd met Javier and where they'd led to. She was feeling them again now. A nervous little pitter-patter starting up inside of her, echoing what her Spanish professor would say when she'd get frustrated with her conjugations back at school:

Ten cuidado. Be careful.

CHAPTER SIX

tourists & tg
WED, JAN 23 AT 19:31

Ti:

you're still game for hampton court, right?

Iyad:

I wouldn't be a good "TG" if I weren't.

And who is this, btw?

Ti:

fatima

Iyad:

You're still feeling alright?

Ti:

gonna plead your case to tom again if i say no?

Iyad:

'fraid not.

Sads:

So we're stuck with you?

Iyad:

'fraid so.

tourists & tg
FRI, JAN 25 AT 17:54

Ti:

hey tg, what's a good dinner spot?

Iyad:

Ever heard of Nando's?

Ti:

if it's the one from the 1d fanfics, yes. if not, then idk.

Iyad:

Slightly wounding that that's how you know it, but I'm sure that's the place.

Sads:

Oh no, Ti. You've wounded him.

This is how you repay him after he beat that man up for you???

Iyad:

Beat him up? Hardly. 😄

Ti:

you're right, sads.

and he's been so humble about it.

Sads:

Not all heroes wear capes.

They just wear all black and pretend to kidnap you.

Iyad:

Oh my days, we're back to this?

Ti:

looking like vader coming down a hallway.

Iyad:

I'm not sure Vader would've let that bloke go, though. 😂

Ti:

especially if it had anything to do with padmé.

Iyad:

You fancy yourself Padmé?

Ti:

not at all.

you let him go.

Sads:

LOL

Ti:

tourists & tg
SUN, JAN 27 AT 9:48

Iyad:

Did you lot try Nando's?

Sads:

Yeah. Other than Ti reliving Wattpad stories the whole time, the chicken was good.

Iyad:

I'll consider that a win.

Also, mind holding off on Hampton Court until sometime next month?

Sads:

Yeah, we don't have time between class and work during the week for it right now anyway.

Iyad:

Work?

Ti:

well, internships where we work for free, lol.

i'm at aynevol editing books, and sads is in the labs at briarvale uni for biotech.

Iyad:

Impressiveeee.

I work at my family's clothes/book shop.

Ti:

what's it called? we'll look it up.

Iyad:

Ahmed Azyaa (it's on The Strand in Covent Garden).

Sads:

Ti!!! It's the motherload!

Ti:

i see it. i'm right beside you!

Sads:

Hijabs! Khimars!!! Abayas!!!!!!!

Faints

Iyad:

Sads:

We're coming over ASAP!

Literally running there right now!

Iyad:

Okay!

See you both then.

Ti:

see you, vader.

CHAPTER SEVEN

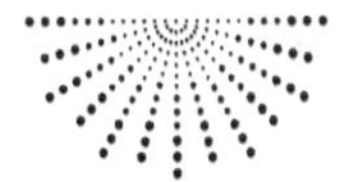

"VADER?"

It was a good thing Iyad hadn't been discussing anything truly confidential, because secrets had no home where his cousin Mo was concerned. Iyad took his phone from the top of the till drawer and slipped it into his pocket, not allowing his cousin to see more. As he did so, he noticed a little girl in front of him, staring in his direction.

"It's just a group chat for school," Iyad explained gruffly, shooing Mo back to his (supposed) task of restocking the shop floor with more scarves. He returned his attention to the girl, she couldn't have been more than three years old, and thought that maybe she needed something, when he realized her line of sight was trained directly on the container of candy in front of him. "You want some, miss?" he asked. Intentionally curious, audibly annoyed.

The girl's eyes widened as she began to back away. Something about Iyad these days often had that effect, even when it was the exact opposite of his intentions.

"I reckon she does," Mo quickly intervened as he came behind the counter. "As-Salamu Alaykum, akh"—brother—"Can she have a one?" he raised his voice for the girl's father to hear as he held up a Cadbury bar.

After getting his approval, Mo handed the chocolate to the girl, flashing her a winsome smile that she quickly matched, then took hold of the candy and ran back to her dad.

"Mmm," Iyad conceded, done with manning a position that forced him to speak when his voice was less than wanted. He let Mo take over, switching to restocking the scarves his cousin had set down instead.

This wasn't out of the ordinary. Since his father's death, sometimes Iyad would open his mouth, and all the wrong things would fall out. Talking didn't come easy for him anymore; it felt like pushing breaths out that he didn't have to waste. So, for the most part, he stopped everything: talking, being, and nearly even existing.

Initially, Iyad didn't want to deal with anything. He avoided the shop entirely unless it was just him and Mo because Iyad didn't have the stomach for being near his uncle, his father's identical twin. And without ever talking about it, they'd managed to rearrange things so that Iyad and Mo handled the shop while his Uncle Hassan dealt with the paperwork behind the scenes.

It all worked out well enough on the surface for them. Doing things this way allowed Hassan more time to dedicate to their business matters, sparing him from constantly juggling responsibilities between managing the storefront and handling everything else. Before, that was the norm for him and his brother—Iyad's father—since Iyad and Mo rarely ever bothered to show up there.

Before, it wasn't on purpose. It was fun. It was being eighteen and not wanting to deal with their family's workload. Now, Iyad was twenty-one, and it was the warm glow from the lanterns overhead that gave him headaches. It was the wafting scent of fragrances like sandalwood and myrrh from the brass incense burners throughout the store that made him nearly throw up.

Iyad's therapist told him that sometimes, grief heightens the senses, and that it would be on him to confront the store altogether when he was ready. But he'd forced himself to come around in that way. To man up. What he needed now was to come to grips with even looking at his uncle for anything longer than three seconds without coming apart at the seams.

That confrontation was still well underway.

"Sooooo. This school group chat is coming here. Today?" Mo pestered, back at Iyad's side.

Mo and Iyad's dads were twins who raised the two of them as if they were also identical. Despite Mo's complexion being a good few shades lighter than Iyad's, the two seamlessly fell into the role themselves, which never bothered Iyad when they were coming up.

But then, when you're forced to see your father's beard gray on someone else's face, sometimes it's hard to think about family roles and ties and all that. Sometimes, it was hard not to just be angry with his uncle for breathing at all, while his father couldn't anymore. Most times, it was hard for Iyad to remember that must've been everyone's trouble at some point or another with seeing uncle, especially for Hassan, who still had to look himself in the mirror, and see more than just himself looking back.

"Why are you so nosy?" Iyad glowered.

Mo smirked. "Why aren't you answering?"

"They're just coming to look at the shop for a bit." Iyad relented, filling up the wall with the last of the scarves he had in hand.

"Ah, so extracurriculars. . ." Mo trilled, annoyingly cheerful.

"Ah, nothing," Iyad mimicked, turning to face him. "You know me."

Mo hummed in agreement, starting to drift off to some

other task. Iyad knew Mo had the attention span of a squirrel on a walnut tree. Most days, that didn't bother him since his social life was less than fruitful enough to interest even himself, much less his cousin, who was always getting into something or other. But this time, Iyad finally had more to say.

"I did get into it with a guy over one of them, though." Iyad blurted out, following Mo back to the till.

"Really?" Mo's eyes lit up, and it was a shame how much that ignited Iyad.

"Yeah, her name is Fatima. This guy ran into her over at Euston, but then he got all scared when I confronted him about it," he explained smugly.

"Probably thought you were Thanos," Mo trumpeted, clapping Iyad on the shoulder. He knit his eyebrows together. "And this is just a school ting, fam? Nothing else with this. . . Fatima?"

"Fatima—" Iyad's phone pinged, interrupting their conversation. He picked it up fast, but it was just an email. Not her.

"Fatima, what?"

However, that familiar gentled Southern lilt. . . that was definitely her.

Iyad turned and looked at her as if she'd just asked him if trees could swim. "I'm going to have to get you lot a bell."

THE LAST THING FATIMA WOULD'VE ADMITTED WAS THAT SADIYAH wasn't the only one looking forward to going to Ahmed Azyaa. Especially to the boy she'd just walked in on with her name already in his mouth. Apparently, he couldn't be trusted with such knowledge.

"Fatima, what?" she repeated sternly. She was overcompensating, but she felt like she had to. When had it ever been good to walk in on someone in the midst of talking about you? Especially with Iyad, who already had a questionable track record after she and Sadiyah had caught him trying to get out of their project with Tom.

"We were talking about Euston," Iyad answered finally, and Fatima's instinct to think the worst eased almost immediately. Weird. How quickly she believed him.

"Oh," Fatima sighed, turning her attention to the man behind the counter next to Iyad. "Yeah. He scared the poor guy half to death."

"*Poor?*" Iyad exclaimed in that low, whisky-neat voice of his.

Fatima almost fell for it. She nearly gave him a gold star, cookie, and the whole dang cake before she caught hold of herself, deciding to joke instead as her last layer of defense. "You got a big head, don't you?"

Iyad's eyes widened. "Huh?" he sputtered.

"It's not your fault," Fatima sympathized. "I feel like most guys whose beards connect have big heads. Show-offs, you know?"

"She's moving mad." The guy beside him didn't even try to hold back his laughter. "I'm Mo, by the way. The show-off's cousin," he snickered.

"Fatima." She smiled and nodded, then glanced at Iyad, who looked like he'd just discovered life on Mars. Good. Balance restored. She tilted her head back to Sadiyah as she sifted through a rack of abayas behind her. "That's Sadiyah over there."

"I'm surprised you two made it," Iyad said, back to himself. "Thought you would've gotten lost on the way."

Fatima's nose crinkled. "Sads warned you that she was excited."

"Yeah. I could tell by all the caps she messaged," he simpered.

"She was right to want to come, though. This place is beautiful." Fatima tapped the counter, looking around. "What does it mean, by the way? Ahmed Azyaa, how do you say it?"

"Ah-med Az-zee-yah," Iyad enunciated slowly. "My dad named it. Ahmed is our last name and means 'praiseworthy.' Azyaa means 'fashions.' Not to say our fashion is praiseworthy," he clicked his teeth. "But it *is* good," he finished, eyes locked directly on hers like he was almost daring her to look away.

She did. Feeling giddy like a schoolgirl. Weird.

"I love that this is a family operation," Fatima continued. "Your dad around? I like words and things, it'd be cool to see how he landed on the name over his other ideas."

Mo and Iyad darted a wary look at one another before Iyad changed the subject. "Are you going to look around, too?"

"Maybe not," she spoke haltingly. "I'm not sure I'm your target audience."

"What do you mean? It's just clothes and books," he questioned.

"Yeah, I don't know. . ." She did. "Ever since I stopped practicing Islam, I've just felt. . . I don't know." Again, she did.

"Inshallah"—God willing—"you'll figure it out," he said, his voice so quiet that if Fatima hadn't been inching closer throughout their conversation, she probably wouldn't have heard him at all.

Fatima felt the tension fade from her face and shoulders when he spoke to her. She liked that she didn't feel herself overthinking with him. That something about him felt easy. Like they'd already known each other somehow. Which was precisely the opposite of what she needed to be thinking about a man at the moment.

"Yeah, well," she interjected, clearing her throat. "I gotta check in on Sads." Fatima glanced at Sadiyah, then turned back to Iyad, her words slipping out before she could think to stop them. "Coming?"

He was by her side in seconds.

They found Sadiyah speaking to a man who looked a lot like

Djimon Hounsou, while picking between a black and gold pashmina and an olive green jersey scarf, once they'd reached her.

"You leaving with the whole store?" Fatima teased Sadiyah, in seeing how she'd somehow managed to expertly hold a bucketload of fabric in the crook of her arm, and keep looking for more things to add on.

The man standing next to Sadiyah laughed. "She might just. I tried to come over and give her a hand, but she said that this is part of her process?"

Sadiyah nodded intently. "I have to hold them to know which ones I'm leaning more toward," she clarified. "I'll downsize eventually, but I also have to send these pictures to my mom so she can see her options and help me decide what I'll get, too."

Fatima bit back that familiar tinge of jealousy she felt every time Sadiyah mentioned how easily she bonded with her mom about anything Islamic. It was part of a bond with her own mother that she hadn't expected to miss so much.

"Also, Sadiyah, I'm sure you know, but Fatima, this is my Uncle Hassan. Mo's dad," Iyad spoke up, and it was the first time he ever sounded small to Fatima.

"Yes, it's nice to meet you." Hassan placed his hand over his heart to greet her. "I hear my nephew will be showing you around the city for class."

Fatima grinned at Iyad. "Yes, we're his personal tourists."

"Then you're in for a proper time." Hassan's eyes creased when he smiled, and for a fleeting moment, she saw Iyad reflected.

About fifteen minutes later, they made it back to the register with Sadiyah's top picks that included the black and gold pashmina she'd chosen over the olive one, a cornflower blue one that looked like moving water, and a pink khimar with a matching dress.

"You girls have plans after you leave here?" Hassan asked.

"We're going to look around for somewhere to eat," Sadiyah answered.

Fatima pretended she didn't notice when Mo elbowed Iyad's side. "Yad knows these ends well," Mo announced. "Plus, he was just about to head out anyway, so he can show you two around."

Sadiyah narrowed her eyes unbelievingly. "You can come, TG," she leered amusedly, moving to tap her phone against the card reader.

Hassan covered it. "On the house," he told her. She raised a befuddled brow, and he smiled, "Looks like you'll be too busy paying my nephew, anyway."

Iyad snorted. "I'm expensive, by the way."

Fatima sank her teeth into her lower lip and steadied her breath, forcing the budding tinge at the ends of her mouth to stay in check. "We need a free tour to see if you're worth the trouble first."

"Livewires, these two," Hassan chuckled, then slipped a jersey black hijab into a small, deep green paper bag beside Sadiyah's larger one that said *Ahmed Azyaa* on it in golden script. He nodded to Fatima. "For you."

"Oh, I don't—" she started, but was cut off.

"Thank you," Sadiyah picked up the bag and handed it to Fatima wordlessly. "For both of us," she said, cueing Fatima to at least look grateful.

Fatima forced a smile. For a brief moment, she allowed herself to think of a time when being offered a free hijab would've excited her. A time when she would've come into this store and gone through the racks right beside Sadiyah, debating between the extensive lineup of materials and colors. But then, rather frustratingly, she remembered that time wasn't now. And that she didn't think this time was a good one to explain that. So, she gave in, accepting the bag as graciously as she could, and headed to the door with Sadiyah.

When Iyad caught up behind them, he found her staring in

stunned silence at the growing downpour outside as she thought about how the sky was so blue maybe just two minutes before then. Well, a faded version of the color. But still. Blue was blue, and not gray and torrential.

"Welcome to London, Yank," he grinned down at her, going into full-on Tour Guide mode. "The wind is just going to knock an umbrella back for now, so we've got to make a run for it." He opened the door and stood outside, holding it for them despite the cloudburst that left him at the mercy of. "Hope you like the rain."

CHAPTER EIGHT

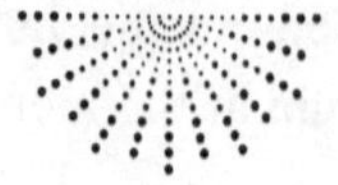

To be clear, Fatima did not like the rain. She didn't like it the first week it rained, or the second, or the third. Regardless, London. Kept. On. Raining.

She figured it wasn't as intolerable running behind Iyad, though. At least he knew where he was going as he owned up to his "tour guide" role while the raindrops continued to fall. He took them to a '50s-inspired American-style restaurant called The Diner that felt like walking back in time. Fatima wasn't sure if the fifties were a time she wanted to walk back to, but after they'd ordered their food, the question itself was a good enough thing to focus on.

"Before you two start," Iyad shrugged out of his jacket from his side of the booth across from them. Fatima glanced at him, trying to seem unaffected, but it was harder to convince herself of that when she was also busy trying not to notice how big his arms were. "This place was the closest and the food isn't bad, either. We're not here *just* 'cause you're Yanks," he smirked.

"I'm going to hold you to that," Fatima said as she took a sip of her tea. She was cold and wet, but she had a burger on the way, so there was that. "If not, you'll have to take us out again."

"Careful, there," he returned morosely. "I might think you like having me around."

Sadiyah snorted on a laugh.

Fatima swallowed hotly. "Keep it up, chinstrap," she deflected. He had a wonderful beard.

Iyad laughed out loud. "You're funny, I'll give you that."

"You can't *give* it to me," Fatima didn't hesitate, which was good, because it meant she was in control of her facilities again. "I'm hilarious. Props for noticing, though," she grinned, to which he grinned back, and her facilities, subsequently, weren't as facilitative anymore. So, she checked out and into Fatimaland.

Fatima nodded along in her daze to the fragments of conversation she'd picked up between Sadiyah and Iyad about Sadiyah's work at her internship and Iyad's other classes, primarily in. . . what was it? Business? Yes, business and marketing tactics ultimately intended for the development of his family's shop. He was mainly taking their class because his program required one course from another discipline to gain an outside perspective and better round out his studies.

She sighed and took off her coat, finally warmed up. Fatima tried to concentrate on their words, pushing aside the little insignificant distractions—like her reflection in the silver napkin dispenser on the table. *Was my sweater this linty when I left Louisa's?* Fatima started to round up all the rogue stray purple fuzzies, falling deeper down the rabbit hole when she felt her phone vibrate in her pocket.

Javi:

You good?

Fatima quickly locked her phone so Sadiyah couldn't see the message, thinking and overthinking about what those two words could mean. Clearly, Javier was thinking of her. That had to be a good sign. But what did it mean that he was thinking of her and she hadn't been thinking of him?

Just before Fatima could lose herself in yet another round of Javier-filled confusion, Sadiyah nudged her under the table, abruptly breaking her train of thought.

Sadiyah was one of the few people on the planet who didn't seem to get bothered whenever Fatima got absorbed in her own head. With Sadiyah, something Fatima had affectionately been told many times was a wonderfully aggravating trait of hers, was really just a side-effect of her being so creative. Sadiyah's logic dictated that anyone who said otherwise was likely too minute a person for Fatima anyway. And, of course, Fatima believed her. Sadiyah was often right about these things.

Especially that pesky soft spot Fatima had for men who couldn't love her back.

Javi:

Haven't heard from you.

"—Ti's been working on a book that might actually get published," Sadiyah was saying.

Fatima was busy trying to come back down to earth. What was going on? She'd started texting back before she could stop herself, and before Javier inevitably did.

But then. It occurred to her that Sadiyah and Iyad had found their way to a conversation that ventured into Fatima's interests, and Iyad actually looked. . . interested? She put her phone down and eyed him suspiciously.

"What's it about?" Iyad asked.

Well, this was different.

She glanced from her phone, and then back to Iyad, responding slowly, "I've been editing this story about this girl who's in high school, and is struggling with her mental health. I'm not too far into it, but so far, I can tell that she puts way too much stress on herself to be close to perfect like her friend, this big shot football quarterback—" she stopped cautiously, flashing a smile at Iyad. "The American one. Football. With your hands and not your feet."

"Figured," he responded, completely deadpan, but then he ran a hand over his beard, and Fatima knew she'd caught a hint of a smile.

Fatima tucked a braid behind her ear. Iyad still didn't seem bored. It wasn't like she wanted him to be, but she couldn't understand why it even seemed as if he'd perked up some. "Basically, it's about a girl who's growing up and learning to accept herself, which is cool because there aren't many Black mental health books out there. Especially in fiction, you know?"

"I don't," he said, and Fatima felt her stomach twist into fisherman knots. "But I think it's important to be bookish that way, you know?"

She didn't. What he'd said sounded like a good thing, but 'bookish' could mean what it meant. Alternatively, it could've also meant something slick. Fatima was used to men being slick.

She frowned because she couldn't help it. "Meaning?"

"Erm," he rasped, just as the food was brought out to the table. "You're helping things that matter, things that some of us don't even realize we don't have, to be brought to life. I think that's cool."

Thump, thump, thump.

Fatima felt a rabbit hop inside her ribcage. She didn't know what it meant that it was for the boy in front of her, and not the one she'd known for years that she still hadn't responded to. She told the feeling to go away. Just because Javier didn't like this one thing about her that Iyad seemed intrigued by didn't mean that she should, in turn, feel things for Iyad.

Right?

THE RAIN AND HAIL HAD CLEARED ONCE THEY LEFT THE restaurant, the previously gray sky shifting to a clear blue, almost as if it had completely forgotten the downpour that Iyad was forced to hurry the girls through just an hour before.

"Alright, TG," Sadiyah said wryly, clapping her hands as they stepped back onto the pavement. "Time to make yourself useful."

Right on time, Iyad forgot everything he'd ever known about Covent Garden. "Oh, hush," he muttered to her, standing there with his hands in his pockets like an oaf. "I'm trying to be nice, and you're chatting rubbish."

"Is that right?" she asked with a crude English accent and a teasing grin.

"Is that right?" he mocked her back dryly. "Come on, then."

If Iyad were paying attention, he would've noticed Sadiyah's knack for working his nerves and Fatima's talent for not coming remotely near them. He knew from their class with Tom that they liked taking pictures. So, he took them to Neal's Yard because it was colorful. Then, they went to Floral Street, where he took what must've been hundreds of photos in front of the telephone booths and flower carts. They kept nagging him to help them reach their impossible level of perfection as he held their bags and took their pictures, though the photos mostly featured a rotation of the same three poses—four, if he was pushing it.

Still, something about every grin Fatima sent his way was the slightest bit overwhelming, even if it was actually for the camera he was holding. In any case, he was glad to have seen it at all.

"I'm a little jealous you got to grow up here," Fatima said, following his lead as they walked.

Iyad just grunted in affirmation because he didn't know what'd slip out if he let himself speak. There was a part of himself that wanted to tell her he was jealous of her, too. Of the way she looked at what he saw every day as if it were something cosmic. Of the way there were moments of being around her where he felt like himself again.

Maybe it was all purely chemical. Maybe it was just dopamine and other deceptive materials that made him look at her like a lovesick puppy. Maybe it was his own selfishness that nearly begged to keep tagging along for his own gain, because what did he have to lose anymore?

He'd never tell her that he felt. . . something toward her. She'd be on a plane back to the States soon enough, and this would all fade into a distant memory for both of them.

"I was thinking that since you're a professional, innit?" he explained, neglecting his previous thoughts by bringing the bookish girl to the bookstore. "You might enjoy this?"

"You're joking," she cocked her head to the side, staring at the books through the window.

Iyad's eyebrows rose. "In a bad way?"

She jerked her head up to him, her eyes shining like sunlight over a lake. "The best way."

Iyad couldn't help it—the sudden breathlessness he felt just by looking at her. He wanted to say something, anything, to make this moment stretch on for miles.

But, of course, he could always count on Sadiyah to ruin it. "We headed in?" she cleared her throat, eyes narrowed in question, as Iyad was reluctantly pulled from his Fatima-filled haze. "Or what?"

Once inside, Iyad quickly got the feeling he'd locked himself and Sadiyah in there for the rest of the afternoon. He wasn't complaining, though, because being there meant being with

Fatima. And he wanted to be around her as much as possible, for research purposes. To figure out what it was about her that made the miserable creature always screaming inside of him begin to quiet.

"You're not a big reader, right?" Fatima asked him, and in his peripheral vision, he saw Sadiyah veer off a little ways away from them to thumb through the manga section.

Suddenly, Iyad felt incredibly ill-prepared and unequipped for semi-alone time with her without an immediate buffer. "Not if I don't have to," he admitted grudgingly, shoving his hands in his pockets. Fatima nodded, slowly walking through the romance section. He followed her lead this time.

"Same, honestly. I'm reading this book named *Queenie* about a girl getting over a bad breakup," she stopped like this was the first she was hearing of the book's contents, picking up a yellow book and turning it over in her hands. "I haven't read for myself in ages."

Standing beside Fatima, Iyad realized, carried a slightly dizzying effect for him. He waited as she read the book's dust jacket, watching the lines crease across her forehead as she furrowed her brow in concentration.

"What got you reading again?" he asked once she'd finished.

Fatima lifted her chin to him. "You know what? I have no idea. I was walking past a Foyles not too long ago when I saw a pink book with a girl who had box braids on the cover, and then, bam, it was in my hands. I might get this one, too, but I can't focus for some reason to tell if I like it or not," she laughed softly, putting the book back with its pile.

"Me holding my breath so you didn't have to hear my Vader breathing didn't help you at all?" When Fatima stared at him in silence, he added, "That was a joke, you know? Vader? From the group chat?" he stammered.

"I know," she said, a barely-there smile at the corners of her lips. "I just thought you needed a moment to hear how corny you sounded."

"Corny? Me? I'm the king of comedy," he guffawed.

"I know who the Kings of Comedy are," Fatima told him archly. "I don't think you made the cut, big dog."

"Oi, I did, though," Iyad shot back.

"King of Comedy," she giggled. "You're cute."

Iyad pursed his lips. "I am?" he asked, as a satisfied grin spread across his face without much, if any, concern about being seen. Immediately, he wanted to know what she'd meant by that. Had she meant to say that? Did he want her to mean to say that?

"You know that's not the way I meant it." She tugged at one of the braids hanging in front of her face, whirling it around her finger, and Iyad found himself thoroughly distracted by trying to determine the exact shade of brown her eyes brightened to when they caught the light as she stood there.

He leaned in. Just barely. Just to see. "But is it true?"

Copper. That was the color. Bright like the element itself. He kept his eyes fixed on them just to be sure.

"Is it—" Fatima muttered, then snorted mildly and changed the subject, stepping back some. "Anyway, I was thinking we could make up a story for our project. Like historical fiction from Henry VIII's, one of his wives', and a daughter's point of view," she explained, a hint of an edge calcifying her voice. "Sound good?"

It didn't. Iyad didn't care about the project. He cared that she was hardening up again. Iyad was a brick wall himself, so he could easily recognize when he was on the other side of someone else's.

"So, you're saying," he smirked, all of a sudden hungry to hear her laugh again. "I am your father," he said, giving his best Darth Vader impression for good measure.

Fatima put her hands on her hips. "You are dumb," she said in her own Darth Vader voice, quietly giggling to herself—which, in that moment, was good enough for him.

CHAPTER NINE

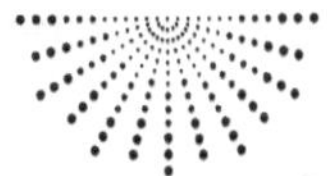

When Fatima's phone vibrated on her desk, she felt her whole body shake with it, thinking it was another text from Javier. She reached for it, curious to see what he'd said, and found the alert she made for her extended sitting periods in the office instead:

Drink some H2Omg.

Fatima had been texting Javier for almost a week now whenever he'd randomly pop in and say hello. Neither of them had mentioned their last phone call, though, which was driving Fatima insane because she wanted to know who she was texting. Javier, her boyfriend. Or Javier her... friend?

She turned the alarm off and got up to stretch. Fatima only set the alarm because Iyad kept saying her headaches and dizzy spells were because she hardly ever drank any water. But it wasn't like it was entirely her fault. Fatima just found the water quality in London to be abysmal. Still, she was becoming increasingly dehydrated, so she silently followed his instructions anyway.

Fatima left the office and walked to the community center. When she first found out she had an editorial internship, she couldn't imagine anything further than her round-table classrooms back at school for what the space would look like. This office was better, though. It was spacious, modern, and overlooked Soho through its full windows, where people were moving about on the street below. She headed to the kitchenette and grabbed a bottle of water from the fridge, practically inhaling it.

"Nipped off for a run, have you?" Claudette asked, appearing almost from thin air.

"L—" *Inhale.* "O—" *Exhale.* "L—" *Inhale.* "Claudette," Fatima heaved, catching her breath. "Iy—" Fatima began, but she caught herself just as she was about to ramble on about Iyad's bootleg doctor's advice. Why was she about to tell Claudette about Iyad's bootleg doctor's advice?

Hold up.

Why was she *thinking* about Iyad's bootleg doctor's advice?

"Hmm?" Claudette asked, preoccupied with pouring herself a cup of tea.

"Eey—" True to life, Fatima couldn't think of one helpful word to replace his name with. *Eerie. Eelgrass. Eeyore. Eey—* "yup?"

Fatima desperately tried to return to mindlessly devouring the water, embarrassed by her terrible cover-up, but she'd quickly found she'd already done that. She threw the bottle into the recycling bin, then looked back at Claudette, who was dressed in all black today, like most Brits tended to do as well, as far as Fatima could tell.

"Eeyup?" Claudette questioned slowly, arching a curious eyebrow at that.

"Yup," Fatima answered, deciding to embrace it. She didn't know why Iyad was suddenly becoming relevant outside of situations where he was immediately present, but she wasn't going to give in to contemplating it all willy-nilly. "Eeyup. Yeehaw. Howdy do. Et cetera. What's up?" Fatima tried to act like these were everyday things she said, although she'd never been in a situation where she'd ever genuinely said any of those at all. Regardless, Claudette's wheels were always turning, so it didn't take much work to get her refocused.

Thank God.

"Well," Claudette started, leaning her hip on the granite island table in between them, "How is the editing coming along? I've been meaning to tell you that Mia and the author send their love about your notes."

"Really?" Fatima faltered, swallowing the phantom lump in her throat. Her chest tightened at the affirmation.

She knew of Mia to some extent. Fatima had dozens of brief phone calls and emails with her, the contents of which she immediately volleyed to Claudette. So, it was good to have something directed to her for once, but *Control*'s author?

The author was a complete mystery to Fatima. Fatima didn't know anything about her except that she was super secretive, from the States, and went simply by "m." Any feedback from her at all felt official, like when a verified account engages with your social media. But come to find out that the feedback was positive? She was floating.

"Of course," Claudette said firmly. "And never doubt yourself, it's unbecoming," she finished, big-sisterly drilling her unshakeable self-confidence into Fatima.

"Duly noted, Sarge," Fatima saluted. Claudette could be intimidatingly pragmatic at times, and it always helped to speed up Fatima's return to herself. Honestly, she reminded her of Sadiyah fairly often. "Oh, while I've got you. I also wanted to ask if it's normal for a project to start to feel so personal? Like, in a way, you become a little possessive over the story, even though you're not its actual writer?"

Claudette's smile was hushed and delighted. "Very. Sounds like you're enjoying yourself, I'm glad. There was a point when I wasn't sure if I'd given you the right assignment. What, with Elle, your titular character struggling so inwardly to embrace her. . . challenges, you know? Parallels between the two of you, and such."

'Parallels' being the operative word there.

Claudette was right, though. There were certain parallels at play between Fatima and Elle, two Black girls who couldn't seem to make heads or tails of themselves. Elle wrestled with anxiety that she chose to ignore to the point where she tried to act like she didn't feel anything at all. Reading the story, Fatima was realizing how both she and Elle put so much weight into thoughts and opinions that weren't their own, that those co-opted ideals eventually took over altogether.

For Elle, she completely lost it. Lost control. And, the losing control bit was the part that terrified Fatima. Of knowing what could be beneath her surface. Maybe that's why Fatima felt so protective of Elle the more she worked on her story, connecting dots from Elle's life to her own with a red string. Parallels. And such.

"Oh, sure," Fatima tsked, cautiously side-stepping any further revelations that might make her ribs ache even more. "You picked me because I'm the only one here who's been to an American high school."

Claudette, Fatima discovered, was deeply posh. Sometimes, she didn't even have to say anything because there was still this regal air about her. She smiled beatifically at Fatima, not outright agreeing with anything, but still agreeing with everything. "Don't forget to remind me that I set aside fifty quid for your lunches each week starting today," she veered.

"Really?" Fatima gasped like she'd just won the lottery. Something inside of her lurched forward because never once when an internship was labeled as "unpaid," did she find a gray area with a little lunch stipend attached to it.

Claudette Anderson was a sheer force alive.

"What did I just tell you about doubting yourself?" She cut her eyes. "But yes. It's actually quite selfish on my part. Watching you eat crisps and juice for lunch has truly been a depressing feat for me." Claudette winked and shifted on her heels to saunter back to her office. "Lunch is in an hour. Don't forget to eat something!"

"STOP EATING ALL THE FOOD, YADDY!" IYAD'S MOM, FARAH, swatted his hand as Iyad shamelessly took another golden plantain from the kitchen counter he'd grown up swiping food from.

"I'm checking to see if they're poisonous," he told her, feigning innocence as he bit into the fruit. "I'm doing you a favor."

"A favor," she repeated, fighting back a smile as she poured extra gravy onto Iyad's plate of oxtails with fried plantains and rice and peas. "I forget how helpful you are."

"Always happy to remind you."

Farah nodded and went back to tending to her oxtail stew. Since his father's passing, Iyad made a point to come home at least once a week. He led their afternoon-to-night prayers. They had dinner. Watched a film. Wash. Rinse. Repeat.

"So, my son," Farah tapped his nose, then adjusted her loose black hijab over her shoulder. "You haven't filled me in on a certain pair of ladies you've been spending time with."

"*Spending time?*" Iyad wheezed, hurrying over to the living room to position the TV trays in front of the sofa before Farah could tell him if his brown skin blushed red.

"Yes, your uncle says he met them at Azyaa. 'Lovely girls,'" she mimicked Uncle Hassan's deep voice as she brought the plates over.

Coming home to the warm, familiar aroma of his mom's home-cooked food was something Iyad had begun looking forward to. This conversation? Not so much.

"No, I- erm. We have a project for school," he mumbled.

"Hmm," she trilled, setting the plates down.

If Iyad hadn't known Ahmed family lore so well, he would've been surprised about the little game of telephone that'd gone on behind his back. But he did know their canon, and he knew exactly how close they always were, despite how fast he'd run away from them, grief-stricken and raw, three years ago.

Had this been then, it would've made complete sense to Iyad that Hassan had blabbed. Iyad was just a little surprised he'd done so now, when things were so different between himself and his ~~father's reflection~~ uncle.

Iyad plonked down onto the sofa and picked up his fork, already knowing he didn't have a prayer of enjoying his meal if he didn't tell his mother—who was probably some high-level interrogator judging by how expertly she could extract information from him while barely breaking a sweat—what she wanted to hear.

He put the fork down.

"Hmm," she repeated, taking her seat and retrieving a piece of fabric and thread. She rarely ate while the food was hot anymore. Now, she spent a decent amount of time finishing up on projects for the store, sewing dresses, scarves, and things to sell there—something she started after losing his dad. Biding her time. Noticing new little antics like that made it hard for Iyad to ignore how much he hated her being home alone now.

"We're presenting on Henry VIII," he gave in, answering because, of course, he did. "And I've been paired with the only Americans in the class, Fatima and Sadiyah."

"Who just *happened* to come by Azyaa?"

"You sound like Mo," he sighed.

"Mohammad," she corrected briskly," has good sense. Some-times." Farah teased, stabbing her needle into the blue-gray fabric on her lap. "So anyway, Fatima and Sadiyah. . ." she prompted.

Iyad blew out a breath. "I mentioned the store to them, and Sadiyah wanted to visit, that's all," he said, hoping to move the needle of their conversation in his favor some.

But if Farah were a fish, she wasn't biting. She set the cloth aside, studying him thoughtfully. Sometimes, Farah took the saying "think before you speak" as less of a gentle nudge and more of a requirement for conversation. She carefully thought through her words, rolling them over like the oxtail she'd slowly braised, and he still wasn't eating.

"And this. . . Fatima?"

"Is just the other one?" Iyad attempted to spin a bright lie, but once again, Farah didn't take the bait. He sighed because his mother was too exceptional a woman to deceive and because, although he didn't know much about Fatima, he was well aware she wasn't *just* anything. "I'm not sure," he finally said.

Honestly, Iyad wasn't pining after Fatima, but he also couldn't figure out what he *was* doing. All he knew was that there was this pretty, pint-sized girl with long braids and one dimple when she laughed, and that he liked it when she laughed. And that he wanted to keep making her laugh.

But he wasn't about to say any of that, so he stuck with the facts. "She's nice. . . sometimes, smart. . . ." Then, when he saw the way Farah's face lit up, he cleared his throat and diverted, "kind of rude."

"Which is why you showed her around Covent Garden?" Farah asked cheerfully.

"Which is why I showed her *and her mate* around Covent Garden," Iyad clarified, as if his clarification would've even mattered to whatever she was already getting at.

"You hardly take *yourself* anywhere," she mimicked his flustered tone. "Much less *around* it," Farah narrowed her eyes, then turned back to her stitching. "I'd like to meet your future wife soon," she told him, fanning him off like a queen who was done with their conversation.

Iyad shrugged because he'd been done with it from the start. He wasn't even surprised she'd mentioned Fatima as his future wife. Any girl would've been considered that if his mom had anything to do with it.

Farah wouldn't understand that Iyad was solely on a mission, so he wasn't going to explain it to her. He had no intentions of getting close to Fatima, of getting close to anyone any time soon, for that matter. Iyad didn't have too many fears, but he was terrified of losing someone else. So, he maintained the position that there was no endgame beyond a completed project and her returning to the States once her term was over. If, in between that time, he ever felt, even for an instant, able to catch his breath after years of holding it, he'd dismiss the feeling as nothing more than a fleeting, happy coincidence.

Iyad picked up his fork again and speared it through an oxtail. Finally. He pressed play on his pick of the night, the movie for the third episode of *Star Wars*, because a certain bookish girl said it was her favorite, and he wanted to rewatch it so he could chat with her about it sometime.

Not that he was thinking of bookish girls, of course.

CHAPTER TEN

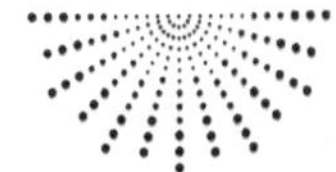

EVERY MONTH, FATIMA AND THOSE IN HER ABROAD PROGRAM received their stipends from Tom. January's allocation had barely moved an inch from Fatima's bedside nightstand, apart from a quick money handling USA vs UK session between herself, Sadiyah, and their host brother, Artie, one bored afternoon. And before she could figure out what to do with it, she was already being handed her next installment.

"Right. Here's your February supply, ladies," Tom handed Fatima and Sadiyah their cash-filled envelopes after they'd entered Kew Gardens for class. "Don't spend it all in one place," he winked before leading the way to the Marianne North Gallery up ahead of them.

Tom guided the group through the garden's manicured lawns and flowers, sharing historical facts, such as how King George III and Queen Charlotte used to spend their summers on the grounds of Kew Palace. Fatima looked around, wondering how it would've felt for her to spend a summer somewhere so grand, and repetitively.

When they made it to the gallery, Iyad glided their way as soon as she and Sadiyah sat down on one of the benches outside, his face a mixture of confusion and intrigue. "As-Salamu Alaykum," he nodded to Sadiyah. "Tom your guys' dealer or something?"

"Wa Alaykum As-Salam, nosy." Sadiyah greeted him back, then added, "Can you stand more in front so no one sees us put the money in our wallets?" motioning for him to stand guard.

"I beg your pardon?" Iyad shot her a glare that, to Fatima, was about as menacing as a cartoon bear in a top hat. Still, he moved directly in front of them, widening his legs and squaring off his shoulders as if he needed to make himself seem any larger. She wasn't complaining, though.

He cooly looked over at Fatima through his long, shadowy lashes. "Hello, there."

If Fatima had even an ounce of self-respect, she would've been at least a hair more skeptical of him because something was off. He was being nice, and she wasn't—at least, not enough. So, despite every kind thing he'd already done for her, she told herself to remember that he still was a man, so he still was dangerous, and could still hurt her.

She didn't know how just yet, but that didn't change the fact that the potential of it happening remained.

"Hey, Vader," Fatima rallied, zipping up her purse and mentally scolding herself for getting distracted by the rhythmic bobbing of his Adam's apple. She hopped up from her seat with a jolt, pulling herself together. "Tom isn't our dealer. He was giving us our monthly stipend since he's also our program coordinator."

"Oh," Iyad huffed out a breath, putting his hand out.

Instinctually, her hand jumped up. She had to clasp hold of it with the other to keep herself from reaching out for his. "What do you want me to do with that?" she asked tentatively.

Iyad grinned.

Fatima gripped her hands tighter.

"I want my cut," he said.

"Y- your cut of what?" Fatima stammered.

"Your stipends for my Tour Guide services, of course," he teased, finally putting his nuisance of a hand away.

"Ha. Ha," she clapped dully, doing a terrible job of ignoring whatever caterpillars inside of her that decided to go rogue and turn into fluttering butterflies right at that very moment. "I don't think I have enough for you, Yad," Fatima said, and then immediately kicked herself for giving him an unauthorized nickname.

Iyad only raised an eyebrow, and Fatima, being Fatima, tried to mentally list equations in her head that'd successfully allow her to time-travel back to at least ninety seconds ago so that she could say anything other than what'd spewed from her mouth before.

But alas, Fatima rearranged sentences, not numbers. So, she found herself trapped in the same time continuum with an adorably disturbed-looking man in front of her. Until he wasn't. Until his frown was replaced by a mischievous grin that said, simply, *gotcha!*

"I'll take it," he decided. "If I can call you, Ti."

Fatima's only solid move to mask her lapping humiliation was to agree. "Okay," she said quickly, looking down because he already had too much of an upper hand at the moment.

"Okay," he agreed. "Sadiyah's waiting for you." Fatima glanced up to find that Sadiyah had somehow slipped away and was waiting, not-so-patiently, at the gallery's entrance. "Ti," he thrummed, and Fatima quickly got up, maneuvering around his mammoth frame to make her escape.

"Way to thug it out, Tweedledee," Sadiyah needled impishly when she reached her.

Fatima pretended not to hear. Distracted the moment her phone buzzed again.

Iyad hadn't been to Kew Gardens in years. He also didn't care much for either flora or fauna. He was, however, very interested in how genuinely intrigued Fatima seemed to be in everything around her. How she seemed to. . . care. So much. Even in a gallery with photographed flowers—which he found to be redundant, given the literal flowers outside—she still looked at the collection as if it were commissioned just for her. Which made him realize it'd been a while since he'd cared about anything at all.

There was an exhibition inside showcasing visitors' plant memories, with their handwritten letters securely fastened to the wall, each against a map of the world to show humanity's interconnectedness through foliage. Iyad saw Fatima write down her own submission and leave it on the table instead of slipping it into the little wooden box for review before heading out with Sadiyah, most likely because she was too preoccupied with something on her phone. Instead of pointing that out to her, Iyad, the helpful lad he was, resolved to put it away for her. He decided—for gentleman's sake—to:

1. Put the slip of paper away. That was it. That was all. That. . . also did mean he'd have to

2. Pick up the paper. And in doing so, was it really his bad that he saw the thinly written words scrawled across the page? He'd argue that happening was purely coincidental.

3. *Entirely* coincidental, actually, that he'd managed to read some of those words detailing how she and a best friend went to a sunflower field at the start of every school year while the flowers were in bloom.

But then, he kept reading. A little less coincidental.

The letter said they'd gone in their first and second years of university, and she missed the third on account of a bad car accident and spending too much time looking after someone else. A boyfriend. She had a boyfriend? Regardless, the best friend (who he was sure was Sadiyah) made a point to bring some of the sunflowers back to their dorm so Fatima could still feel like she'd gone there in some way.

Sometimes, it said, *I wish I did.*

Iyad folded the sheet of paper and slid it into the box. He headed outside, following the group down the trail while wondering how best to atone for the more than needed information he now knew. Maybe Sadiyah was right. Maybe he was just a tad bit nosy.

"Anyone here like Scooby-Doo?" Tom was saying, gesturing at an ivory-stoned statue of a greyhound perched upright on its hind legs. Most of the class raised their hands. "Well, bang on," he remarked. "This is the White Greyhound of Richmond. He's one of the ten replicas of the original collection of the Queen's Beasts. Funnily enough, some believe he might've even been the inspiration for Scooby-Doo," he added, mouth agape in comical surprise.

"Now, about Palm House," Tom spun around, and Iyad tuned him out as soon as the sloshing sound of his waterproof parka against his rucksack reached Iyad's ears. One thing or another about the building being a rainforest glasshouse and blah, blah, blah. All he knew was that it was immediately humid inside.

"So," Iyad said slowly, catching up to the girls as they cruised past the tropical plants, palms, and things spreading across the entire garden. "How long have you lot been friends?"

"Since the first day of college." Fatima leaned her head over to see the waterfall up ahead of her. "We were roommates. She was obsessed with me."

"Oh, shut up," Sadiyah made a face. "*You* were obsessed *with me.* Let's be clear on that, you gnome."

Fatima cut her eyes. "Height jokes? Really?"

"Gnome says what?"

"What?"

Iyad resisted a smirk. "Was she there when you got in that car accident?" He had no intention of wondering that aloud, but honestly, he was curious. . . and he wanted to see if that would lead to information about whether Fatima truly had a boyfriend.

"Iyad Ahmed," Fatima spun around to him with the same severity his mother did whenever he'd messed up—and he definitely had. But all he could focus on was how his name sounded coming from her, the way the word relaxed more than he could himself, on her tongue. He wanted to hear her say it again. "Did you read the letter I wrote in the gallery?"

"I'd like to say no," he wavered, rubbing the back of his neck.

"But, then you'd be a liar, and that's worse than a snoop," Sadiyah scowled, shifting a prying glance between the two of them. "What am I missing?"

"Fatima left her paper back at the gallery on the desk, and I saw some of it when I turned it in for her, that's all," Iyad explained quickly. "But don't feel pressured to answer," he told her.

Sadiyah shook her head knowingly, loudly whispering to Fatima, "He got a problem minding his own business, or something?"

Fatima only shrugged. After a little while, she sighed and said, "No, it's fine. My ex—" *Ex.* So, she didn't have a boyfriend. Not that he cared either way. It was just a good data point to have on file. "It was raining one day, and he was busy being mad at me for taking too long to be ready for this secret date he had planned—"

"Because you were. . . ?" Sadiyah prompted.

Fatima groaned in frustration. Or maybe that was anger? Why did he have to read that letter?

"Taking a final," she finished. "It was on about forty Medieval books, and I'd only somewhat read one of them. Passed it, though." Fatima looked up at him with those wide, expectant eyes of hers. He took a breath, forcing himself to calm down by focusing on the cast-iron staircase behind her. "Anything else?" She spoke as if he were a lawyer in charge of her deposition.

So, he responded with an answer that matched the gravity of said situation.

"Did he take care of you, too? Like you said you took care of him."

Fatima swallowed and bounced up on the balls of her feet a few times. She looked down at her notebook and then over to Sadiyah, who pressed her lips together and then got very interested in the ferns around them. "I'm guessing you read the whole paper."

He nodded earnestly, because what else could he do then?

She took a deep breath, and Iyad wondered if she was trying to photosynthesize her thoughts like the plants around them. "I'm sure he thinks he did. Effort means. . . different things to different people, you know?"

"That's why you broke up with him, then?" Iyad pieced together. "What he thought was effort wasn't enough?"

Fatima shook her head. "He broke up with me, actually," she murmured, rolling her phone around in her hand. "I think."

"You. . . think?"

"Well, he said 'break.' Not 'break up.' Plus, he started texting me again—"

"Hold up," Sadiyah gawked, dumbfounded. "You've been texting Pretty Boy?"

"So there's a difference," Fatima firmed, ignoring Sadiyah. "I think."

Iyad was sure that Fatima was incredibly bright and thoroughly talented, but it was interesting to see her blind spot so clearly. "What does he talk to you about?" he posed, gently. "If you don't mind me asking?"

Fatima looked between him and Sadiyah, then took out her phone and said, "Here. It's not all that bad."

Sadiyah quickly took the phone, holding it between them so they could both see. "'Javi,'" she read aloud. Iyad tried not to grin at the way Sadiyah rolled her eyes after saying his name. He would've done the same if he had any right to. "'I can't wait till we get back together...' 'I think about you every day...'" She stopped scrolling. "Wait." Sadiyah stopped scrolling and fake gagging as she read the most recent messages where Fatima said:

I love you.

And Javier responded with:

I know you do, but you don't have to keep telling me. Quit trying to force me into getting back with you.

If Iyad hadn't witnessed it himself, he wouldn't have believed how fast Fatima snatched her phone back. She didn't meet their eyes once she had it back in her hand, now tucked securely under her folded arms. Fatima held herself together like she was afraid she might shatter. Iyad found himself with the same hesitancy.

"Sometimes, it just is what it is, you know?" he hedged softly, running a hand over the back of his neck. "There is no break. You're either on or you're off. You love or you don't. You're here—" Iyad swallowed. He could feel his eyes bulge over three words his mouth wouldn't let him say. He didn't like that. His eyes were moving around more than they'd probably ever done so in his life, and he kept cracking his knuckles, too anxious to speak or say anything.

Fatima was talking about her ex, and now here he was, thinking of his dad, somehow, while trying to help her. It made him think of how his therapist used to tell him he had trouble grounding himself when his thoughts carried him away like a balloon on a string. Made him wonder if that made Fatima a loose branch, cleaving him open without trying.

"Or you're not," he continued after clearing his throat. "And particularly with you, who I get the feeling loves hard, you've got to put yourself first, and think of men afterwards, like meat. 'Cause once you go spoiling us, we get rotten."

"You speak in absolutes just like a Sith would, Vader." She blinked through glossed-over eyes.

"You should, too. When it comes to men, at least. No yellow lights, you know? Just red and green sabers."

"What color is yours?" she asked him.

He smiled at her, cautiously thinking of what to say next. "That's not on me to tell," he said, offering a small smile. "Ti."

HALF AN HOUR LATER, FATIMA WAS STANDING OUTSIDE OF KEW Palace. She was going out of her way not to focus on how embarrassing it was to have let Sadiyah and Iyad read those stupid texts, after having forced the last one Javier had sent her this morning out of her mind.

If she'd remembered what he'd said instead of dissociating from it—an unfortunate skill she was far too good at—she wouldn't be in the mess she was in now.

"What do you think of this?" Iyad asked, handing Sadiyah her phone back after taking pictures of her and Fatima in the Queen's Garden.

Sadiyah held the phone between them. She was very specific about how she liked her pictures taken, and for some reason, Iyad was very good at carrying out her vision. He held their bags so they didn't touch the ground, didn't rush them, and never even asked for any of his own, since that probably defeated the whole tall, dark, and brooding thing he had going on.

Sadiyah flicked through the photos, zooming in on each one. "I like them," she nodded, going from far off and unfocused to unilaterally business-like. "Looks like we're outside of The Grand Budapest Hotel, or something."

"Yeah, just veryyy red," Fatima pivoted, walking a few steps back to study the house again as it beamed brightly under the high afternoon sun.

For a moment, her eyes drifted over the maze of greenery around her as a flock of tweeting birds flew by. It was nice being around so much plant life. Walking around London sometimes felt like she was either in some modernized Renaissance fair or maybe something a tinge more stately and regal, like Hogwarts. Still, the scent was consistently petrichor-coated cigarettes and roses wherever she went. Kew Gardens, though, just smelled like roses.

"Ray-yid," Iyad mocked her accent teasingly. "Yank."

Fatima glanced at Iyad, bemused. "You know, I was gonna let the 'Yank' thing rock, but what's up with this Revolutionary War-era joke?" she quipped. "Redcoat?"

Iyad snorted a laugh and cocked his head to the side, smiling as he repeated her in that deep rasp of his, "Redcoat?"

"Or do you prefer Knight in Shining Al-loo-min-ee-um?" Fatima drawled the English pronunciation of aluminum out with a smirk.

"That so?" Iyad exclaimed, a glint in his eye. "You think I'm a knight?"

"I th- You- Um. . ." she stumbled and shut up before her

mouth could betray her into saying something else she wouldn't be able to take back.

He just watched her, delighted and taunting.

"Whatever," Fatima grumbled, redirecting. "Also, back at the Palm House, when we were talking about my ex, were you talking about—" *yours?*

"You know," Iyad interrupted sharply. "I should talk to Tom to see if he knows how I could be officially knighted."

"Iyad, did something happen—" Fatima tried, but he cut her off again.

"No, you're right." Iyad's smile was bright, but that same gleam didn't reach his eyes. "If it's anything that deals with a history book, *of course,* Tom knows about it."

"Yeah. . ." She squinted, noticing the pleading look in his eyes, but she couldn't bring herself to stop. "Iyad—"

"Don't worry, Ti," he waved his hands between them. "I promise not to forget about the little people when I come up."

Fatima couldn't help but wonder how long he'd been playing this role of being okay, how long it took him to get so good at it. She figured the only way he would know exactly what to say to her was if he was going through something of his own, too. It was suddenly imperative to her that he knew he could talk to her.

"Iyad- wait,"—but then she processed what he'd just said—"'*Little* people?' You're that full of yourself?"

"No, you're just that little," he winked, putting a flat hand in the space above his head, then hers. "I mean—"

No. He was trying to distract her. Fatima cleared her throat. "Iyad, if you ever wanted to talk like you let me—"

But maybe this was a selfish way to go about it. Maybe she saw that he was in pain, and some part of her knew it was easier to focus on someone else's rather than her own.

"Fatima, please," Iyad drawled, his jaw flexing before his body went all stiff.

Fatima studied him for a moment and, after what felt like an eternity, could only fit out, "Iyad—" For some reason, she couldn't stop calling his name.

"The last thing I want to talk about," he stopped her, looking askance, "after speaking about your shoddy ex, is my dead dad."

Fatima's mouth turned into the shape of the letter 'O.'

"And I know you didn't know about it, so that's not your fault, but couldn't you tell I didn't want to *talk?*" Iyad's tone was desperate, nearly whining. "I've barely talked to anyone about it in three years, and I want to keep it that way—that alright with you?" He didn't wait for her response, stalking off down the trail before she could say anything.

Fatima's mind glitched in that instant. She felt herself lunge forward to follow before she could even question why or whether she'd given her brain the order to send her body chasing after him. She didn't like being the one left behind. Especially this easily.

"Not now, Ti," Sadiyah said quietly, grabbing Fatima's hand to pull her back.

It didn't matter, though. Iyad was already long gone by then.

CHAPTER ELEVEN

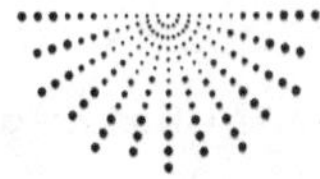

Thankfully, he just had Tom's class on Mondays and Wednesdays, and since it was the end of the week now, he was in the clear from dealing with the ramifications of what'd happened at the start of it with Fatima until the week circled 'round again. Iyad immediately pushed the Tuesday afterward from his mind, where he didn't reach out to her to recap his momentary loss of composure, and then purged the thought of Wednesday's lecture, where he'd completely ignored her in class.

It was like when they'd first met. Dull and stale. Fatima had been quieter than usual, somehow, or maybe it was just the absence of her speaking to him that made him feel that way. Still, Iyad said nothing. By today, Friday, he'd begun to understand that, eventually, he'd have to talk to her because of Tom's wonderfully carnivorous assignment. But he'd hold that impending meeting off for as long as he could until then.

"Shi—" Iyad muttered, catching himself after tripping over a misplaced wooden crate on the ground.

He was at Azyaa, back in the stock room as the shop stirred just outside the door. Iyad switched on the light and waited for a second as his eyes adjusted to the sudden brightness. Then, he bent down to pick it up and slid it onto the top of a nearby rack, just as the door behind him swung open.

"Yad?" Hassan surveyed. "It's a full house. What are you doing back here?"

Iyad turned around, quickly forgetting what he was searching for. He had a hard time focusing whenever his uncle was around, and found himself training his gaze right beyond him, watching as Mo checked out a customer until the closing door shut him out of view. "Sorry, Unc—"

"You alright?" Hassan interjected.

Iyad shifted uncomfortably. "Pardon?" he managed to croak out as the silence of the room returned, demanding Iyad remember his words; remember to say anything. But three years of space between them still didn't feel like long enough.

Following his dad's passing, Iyad and Hassan had fallen into a steady and unwritten rhythm of being seen and not heard. Iyad thrived on the allowance of that space. Something there never seemed to be enough of, being that Hassan had this annoying habit of always trying. Of constantly reaching out again and again, despite the way Iyad recoiled each time before he could even make contact. For some reason, just Hassan asking how he was felt like an attack. Felt like Fatima back at Kew Gardens. How she'd blindsided him and he'd pushed her away on instinct.

"I asked if you were alright." Hassan sighed. He did not thrive on space. And years of barely speaking to his nephew, who'd practically grown up as his own son, were evidently turning him into a black hole. "Couldn't find you out there."

"Yeah," Iyad managed. "Sorry, I'll be right back." He was looking for something. Iyad couldn't remember what it was, but it was here. He was sure whatever he needed was in this room.

"What's that game you and Mohammad used to play back here?" Hassan suddenly asked. "When you were kids."

Iyad paused, absently tracing the old crate from where he'd set it down next to him, the wood rough beneath his fingers.

"Sorry?"

"You know... Game... something?" he prompted intently.

"Oh, Mini X-Games."

"Yes! You lot had those little finger skateboards and cars you'd race around." Hassan's eyes brightened at the memory. "And that was the winner's podium, wasn't it? Where you'd both stand up and give your champion's speeches," he smiled, waving to the box Iyad was still absentmindedly running his fingers over.

Iyad dropped his hand to his side.

"Yeah, you hated it." Iyad meant for his words to come out jokingly, but they sounded more like an accusation. He had a hard time leveling himself whenever he was uncomfortable— and he often was.

"Well, I wanted you both to know how to run the shop." Hassan chided before his smile grew distant. "Hamza loved it, though."

Iyad forced himself to concentrate on his breathing. He couldn't remember the last time he'd heard Hassan say his father's name. He couldn't remember the last time *he'd* even acknowledged his father's name.

Hassan cleared his throat when Iyad didn't respond, the sound faintly echoing from the bone-white walls around them. "How's school? You still taking those business lectures so you can be the brains when you and Mohammad take over?"

Iyad pressed the nail of his middle finger into the pad of his thumb, focusing on the sweeping ache that concentrated there. Iyad grew up to love Ahmed Azyaa, and in time, inherit it with Mo. And he did love it. Until watching what doing so did to his dad when the store began to go under.

Hassan was consistently himself then. He'd remained systematic and logical, even when Hamza began to overcompensate for their troubles while reviewing their failing expenses. That's when the chest pains started.

The last thing Iyad wanted to think about was taking over.

"You know," Hassan went on, a black hole caving in. "I've missed you, Yad."

"I've been here," he told him impassively, and an elephant settled in the room between them.

"You know what I mean."

Iyad did, but admitting to that was something better left alone.

"I enjoyed seeing you when your friends came by." Hassan was gentle with his words. His uncle was always mindful, but Iyad noticed how much more careful he'd become when they crossed paths these days. How he tiptoed. "Will they be coming back sometime?"

"Erm," Iyad mumbled, thinking slowly. The elephant blew its trunk, and the sound trumpeted through Iyad's ears. He spoke up to quiet it. "If I'm honest, probably not. Pretty sure I've upset Fatima beyond repair- the erm, the one with the braids," he clarified.

"I remember," Hassan smiled. "And I'm sure whatever you've done is repairable. If you'd like it to be, that is." Iyad didn't know if he wanted it to be. He didn't know what he wanted at all from knowing Fatima. If there was even to want, so to speak.

"I'm sure you'd think so, since they're both so *lovely*," he blurted after another awkward beat passed.

Hassan shook his head. "Farah ratted me out?"

"*You* ratted me out."

Hassan grinned. "Fair point."

Iyad raised his eyebrows. "You got Mum so excited that she was even talking about me marrying Fatima. She's mental."

Hassan nodded, "That she is, but. . ." The rest of the sentence hung in the air, and Iyad got the burning sensation that his uncle agreed with her.

And, of course, he did. Iyad knew his mom and uncle were old-fashioned. I.e., you meet a girl you even moderately like, then marry her if she lets you, and do so as soon as possible. To call a spade a spade, he understood it.

He knew that's what the Quran said, and so, he did his best to follow its guidelines himself. Maybe that was why he had trouble around Fatima sometimes. Looking at her, Iyad easily understood why the Quran reminded him to lower his gaze around women.

Still, however beautiful Fatima was to him, it didn't change the fact that even if she chose to follow Islam again, there would never be anything romantic between them. Just this dizzying warmth he felt whenever she was around that he could never understand—and her ex that she didn't seem to want to let go of.

"But nothing," Iyad contested. "It's just a project."

"Ahh, of course. Just a project," Hassan echoed airily. "Anyway, come on, nephew. You know we can't leave Mohammad in one place on his own for long."

Iyad nodded. It wasn't lost on him that this was the longest he'd spoken to his uncle in years. He didn't know what to make of that. But he couldn't help himself from thinking about it as he followed Hassan back out onto the shop floor, where he found himself face-to-face with the reason why he'd been in the stock room to begin with: the man who'd asked him for a kufi that was currently sold out on the floor.

Iyad's eyes widened. "Just a moment, sir," he gestured with a finger, swiftly retreating inside to bring the next load out.

SPACE. ONE THING FATIMA HATED WAS SPACE.

Space was for astronauts, cacti, and Iyad, who'd been ignoring her like the plague, treating her as if she were just anyone else from their class for the past week. Honestly, it shouldn't have bothered her so much. They barely knew each other, and he'd made it clear from the beginning that he hadn't even wanted them around, anyway. Plus, she had Javier. She thought.

Fatima wouldn't admit it to Sadiyah—she could barely even admit it to herself—but she was starting to wonder if she was wasting her time on him. They'd been texting for nearly two weeks, and she still didn't know what was going on between them. She wondered if maybe it was her fault that nothing was.

With Iyad, at least she could pinpoint where things had gone wrong. What she'd done. Clearly, pushing that conversation had reminded him of his dad. Even though she didn't know about that fact at the time, she should've realized something was wrong. She should've stopped.

Coulda. Shoulda. Woulda.

Now, she'd ruined any chance of them ever being amicable again at all. Did she care that they weren't amicable? A little. Did she miss talking to him? Some.

Maybe Javier could feel that she really was losing focus on an "international waters" delusion like he'd predicted. Maybe he knew, somehow, and that was why nothing between them had changed and brought them back to their previously declared relationship statuses. Yeah. Makes sense.

Fatima rolled over and felt around her bedside table for her phone before tapping it awake in the dark. 5:08 A.M. Childish Gambino's *Awaken, My Love!* album had finished playing in her

AirPods, and the left one had entirely disappeared. She sleepily searched through the covers for it, then put them both away in the case to charge.

What was it that Iyad had said?

You've got to put yourself first, and think of men afterwards, like meat. 'Cause once you go spoiling us, we get rotten.

At the time, she didn't know what to say, so she deflected. But now in the blue-black early morning, prime time for Fatima's habitual overthinking to go uninterrupted while Sadiyah snored away, she was still at a monumental loss. Where was the line between caring for someone and going too far? How do you love someone and still love yourself? Meat, at least, has the consideration of going rancid, so you know when it's gone bad. What was Fatima supposed to do in comparison? Kill herself while loving him until he finally up and told her he was rotten, too?

She rechecked the time. 5:15 A.M. That meant it was only a little past midnight back home. Maybe if she got the ball rolling herself. . .

With a wince, Fatima sat up, unlocked her phone, and opened her messages before she became lucid enough to doubt herself.

Hey, she started. *I miss*

"What are you doing?" Sadiyah whisper-hissed right before Fatima felt the impact of Sadiyah's whole body colliding on top of hers. "Give me that!"

The one thing boxing, mixed martial arts, and high school hallway fights all have in common is that they're loud. That's not something you can be at five in the morning in someone else's home. Fatima struggled piecemeal to keep her phone in hand, but she was completely caught off guard when Sadiyah jumped on her like a pro-wrestler leaping from the top ropes into a ring. She locked her phone and sucked in a breath, trying to burrow herself deeper into the blankets. Still, Sadiyah managed to wrangle the phone away from her.

Beep-beep-beep

Winded, Sadiyah flew back to her bed and quickly turned off her phone's alarm before unlocking Fatima's again. Unfortunately, they both knew one another's passcodes. Fatima cringed as her phone's bright light hung her out to dry.

"You're texting Pretty Boy at five in the morning, are you *kidding me?*" she snapped. "Why are you still texting him at all? And you're using caps and periods? Is this an essay? Is he the *President?* What are you *thinking?*"

Sadiyah's face was all screwed up and dramatic like she'd just witnessed someone die in a horror flick, when the only thing that'd been killed so far was Fatima's dignity.

Fatima sucked in a breath. "I was *thinking* you were asleep."

"It's time to pray, Tweedledee." Sadiyah waved an aggravated hand in Fatima's face. "I'm going to go make wudu. I'll be back," she sighed. "And I'm taking this." She locked and chucked Fatima's phone into her pocket, then flitted off to the bathroom.

Fatima rolled her eyes, but otherwise remained silent, her gaze fixed on the stray light glinting through the room's blinds as Sadiyah shut the door behind her to go wash up for Fajr, the dawn prayer. She was too busy checking her pulse to care that Sadiyah had taken her phone. It'd been a while since she'd moved that much. Her eyes searched around in the dark, thinking.

What was she thinking? That she could text Javier—the CEO of needing space, and also hating it—and he was going to change his mind?

Did she want him to change his mind?

Fatima laughed bitterly to herself, thinking of what she'd almost done as Sadiyah strolled back into the room. Neither said anything. Fatima fell back onto her headboard, while

Sadiyah quietly pulled her black prayer dress over her sweats, wrapped her hijab over her head, and began to pray.

Fatima hadn't prayed in over three years. Not formally, at least. There was something about watching Sadiyah's steady recitation that ignited a curious feeling in her chest, leaving her slightly confused. It reminded her that, at times, she missed it—the closeness she felt to something higher than herself, to having someone around who she knew she could always count on. Someone who didn't need space. Ugh.

"Did you know your heart has its own electrical system?" Sadiyah asked once she'd finished, taking off her prayer clothes and settling back into her bed.

Sometimes Fatima forgot how sciencey she could get. "What?"

"Your heart," she repeated softly, taking Fatima's phone out of her pocket and turning it over in her hand, "is just like your phone, when you think about it. They both need communication to work. Your heartbeats are intricate electrical signals that pump around six liters of blood per minute to keep you going. And I guess all your phone needs is a dumb text to do the same for you." She tossed Fatima the phone.

Fatima clicked her tongue and put it back on the charger. She squeezed her eyes shut and groaned, wishing she'd just stayed asleep. "I wasn't going to send it," she lied.

Sadiyah rolled her eyes. "You've got to let that boy go, Ti."

Fatima laced her fingers, her voice hoarse, almost hollow. A few seditious tears fell, and she quickly wiped them away. She was still heartbroken. She was still angry. She still felt. Everything. All the time. And didn't know where to place any of it. "I know, but this was years, Sads. I'm alone now."

"No, you're not. I'm here, ukhti," Sadiyah said, her breath was getting choppy, and her eyes were starting to close. They were both getting tired again.

"You won't always be, though," Fatima yawned, shifting uncomfortably under her duvet.

Sadiyah inched over to Fatima's bed, which was considerably better than her hawk-swoop down from before, and said, "You and me forever, inshallah. Pinky thumb."

They looped their fingers together. Bringing the action of "pinky thumb" into effect, or just saying it in general, was how they made promises to each other. Sadiyah was the one who'd introduced Fatima to the idea of strengthening a pinky promise with stamping their thumbs at the end. It meant "I'm serious," and "I trust you because it's you," and "Please, don't let me down," all at once—assurance they both needed sometimes.

"Pinky thumb."

Sadiyah hopped back to her bed. "And block him," she mumbled into her pillow.

Fatima queued up Noname's *Telefone* mixtape and slid her AirPods back into her ears, contemplating yet another boy who was sending her mixed signals. "What about Iyad, though? He didn't even look at me in class last time."

"He probably thinks you feel sorry for him," Sadiyah propped her head up on her hand to think, her black bonnet drooping down behind her.

"It's not that I felt sorry for him, it's just that I—"

"That. That right there," Sadiyah cut her off. "You both are surviving very different things, so you have to accept he may need to survive his situation in a different way than you do. I get that you're a fixer, but Iyad clearly doesn't want to be fixed. It's like this: if you see his house is crumbling, and he's not asking for help, you walk away," she ordered slowly. "Let him do his own work, or he'll just resent you later for being his handyman."

"Sometimes I feel like you just repeat your favorite parts of advice columns. What does that mean?" Fatima asked, too out of it to process Sadiyah's drawn-out metaphor.

"You don't build a man," she simplified. "Because all you're doing is building him for someone else."

"But what if—"

"No." Sadiyah shook her head and fell onto her pillow. "Just give him some time and see what happens."

"But what—"

"And if you're going to get stuck on Iyad, get. Rid. Of. Pretty Boy."

"But—"

"Good night, Ti."

CHAPTER TWELVE

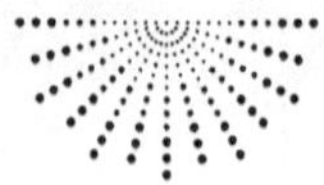

ONE THING SADIYAH MITCHELL WASN'T ABOUT TO DO WAS LAY UP crying or enable crying about a man (or two) on a rare sunny Saturday in London.

She reclined in bed, watching the morning light gently sweep across the ceiling. It was just past nine and Fatima was still asleep. Sadiyah had been intermittently awake since their last conversation and had given up on falling back asleep altogether when she caught the sunrise from their window.

For the life of her, she couldn't understand why Fatima clung so hard to those men—or any man, in general. She, herself, had tucked away memories of her father so tightly in a pocket of her mind that she imagined they'd fallen through and disappeared entirely at times. Or maybe they stuck to her like old gum on the bottom of a shoe, in the back of her mind, but graciously out of sight. Either way, she wasn't about to panhandle for his return.

When her dad left, she learned her lesson and decided never to expect anything of a man again, since they were naturally selfish, overly sensitive, and would always end up leaving her behind anyway—claustrophobic pests.

To be clear, though, Sadiyah didn't despise all men. She loved her brother, she thought Tom was great, too, and she even liked Iyad just fine. They were all fine. But knowing people like them wasn't a consistent occurrence, and Sadiyah preferred consistency above most things.

She preferred the company of more reliable men. Those who kept their promises and showed their true colors as shades that didn't fade. Outside of her father, the primary reason why she'd deserted her expectations, she'd tried her hand at trusting one other man before, and he'd ruined things between them so terribly that she decided she'd never make a mistake like that again.

In the silence, Fatima groaned and wearily lifted her hand toward Sadiyah, tapping away at an invisible remote. "You already snore like a bear, stop thinking so loudly," she groused, trying to turn down Sadiyah's mental volume.

Sadiyah chuckled, picked up a pillow from behind her, and thwacked her with it. "We're going out today," she announced cheerfully.

In a flash, Fatima jolted upright, struggling to lock eyes with Sadiyah, before she hurled the pillow back at her with tactical precision. But then, the moment quickly unflashed when Fatima fell almost immediately back onto her pillow.

"Might as well get up," Sadiyah grinned.

After a frigid moment, Fatima rasped into her pillow, "Go. . . bed. Sleep now."

SADIYAH PRIDED HERSELF ON BEING ASTUTE. WHEN THEY MOVED into their homestay, Louisa explained that she'd be offering toast and jam for breakfast every morning. She didn't explain; however, that a month later, she'd be hiding the jam and using up the bread for Artie's lunch, leaving them without the one free meal they were supposedly entitled to every day. Using that knowledge to her advantage, Sadiyah expertly coaxed Fatima into leaving their bedroom with the promise of a full plate of breakfast. Her treat.

Sadiyah slouched backward into the soft blue seating of the double-decker bus on their way to Spitalfields. It was the first time they'd been on one of the buses alone since orientation when Tom had shown them the ropes around the city. Sadiyah and Fatima were not accustomed to any such ropes. They were from the South, where riding buses was less frequent than in the city, so they thought of the double-decker bus like they did school buses back home, expecting a fixed route with stops where the driver would definitely pause to let riders on and off. However, for some reason, that wasn't the case here.

"Bro, he just skipped another one," Fatima mumbled, panicked, as the bus driver faithfully ignored what she thought was the bus route. "Should we press the button?"

There was a big red button in front of their seats that said 'STOP.' Something about everything they'd ever been told about big red buttons, especially the ones saying 'STOP,' kept making them think twice about pressing it. What if it was only meant for emergencies?

Sadiyah smoothed a hand over her skirt. She'd gotten so stupidly happy for a girls' day out and planned everything down to the letter, but all of that meant nothing if they couldn't get off of this never-ending bus.

"Yeah," Sadiyah agreed. "Push it."

"And look like some dumb tourist if that's not what it's for?" Fatima shook her head. "Nah, you do it."

Sadiyah looked down at her phone. "We're the next stop," she said.

"Then press it." Fatima doubled down.

"Fine, fine," Sadiyah reached for the button, then reasoned, "But what if we did it together?"

Fatima was quiet for what would've been the rest of their

program as she thought it over. Sadiyah knew sometimes this was how she contemplated things, carefully, as if the world stood still inside the palm of her hand. But it didn't. And the bus driver had proven since the moment they'd boarded that he was more than willing to let them keep riding along forever.

"Yallah," Sadiyah said under her breath. "You owe me if this goes wrong." She pressed the button, and what do you know? The bus driver pulled over and just. . . stopped. Heh.

Crisis averted, they headed toward the breakfast spot she'd found with a shared sense of accomplishment, as if they'd just solved world hunger. In Sadiyah's case, she had solved something. In Fatima's case, well, she didn't have one.

"I think we might be better than James Bond," Fatima said in her seat after they'd ordered their drinks, grandly brushing her sleeves down along her forearms.

Sadiyah picked up the menu with a raised eyebrow. "I think you need to seek help," she reached across the table to point at Fatima's menu. "I'm getting this."

"*That's* an English breakfast?" Fatima looked like a pigeon had just flown over her and dropped a deuce directly in front of her.

A woman at the table next to them shot Fatima an annoyed look. Sadiyah glared at the woman because she didn't do well with people mistreating her friend, and then she glared at Fatima because her friend *had* asked for it. "If you're going to be a Dino Nugget and fries-only type of girl, I'm going to need you to do so quietly."

Fatima kissed her teeth. "I can't help it if I'm in shock. I didn't know they ate baked beans and toast for real." She glanced at the menu again. "*With* eggs? "Did they come up with this before or after they got toilets?"

Sadiyah coughed, fighting to suppress a laugh. "What?"

"I just feel like that's important to know. You know, chronologically. Historically," she drew the word out slowly, and

Sadiyah tried to distract herself by rolling and unrolling the sleeves of Fatima's beige hoodie she'd borrowed for the day.

"I can't take you anywhere." She shook her head as their waitress sprang up at the table.

Sadiyah ordered as close as she could to a full English breakfast, landing on veggie sausage instead of pork, potatoes, mushrooms, tomatoes, eggs, beans, and toast. And Fatima kept it simple with just pancakes and eggs.

An hour later, they'd cleared off their plates and decided to walk off their meals at the Old Spitalfields Market. It was hectic once they'd gotten there, with the blended scents from the food stalls and the sounds of people from all corners of the globe together in one place, selling off both old and new things.

Sadiyah and Fatima tried their best to see it all, ambling through the antique stands where Fatima bought a green leather purse (using her cash finally!), and Sadiyah chose a few uniquely patterned scarves for herself.

As Sadiyah attempted to pay for them, a notification flashed on her phone, diverting her attention. Instinctively, she began to swipe it away from her screen, assuming it was either a design idea from Pinterest or some notification from Instagram. Instead, it was the alarm she'd set up to make sure they wouldn't miss their reservation at Ballie Ballerson:

Time for the ball pits.

"Dang!" she snapped, quickly wrapping up her purchase before clasping Fatima's hand in hers to guide them as they ran through the crowd. "Come on, we're going to be late."

Somehow, they made it to the bus and then to Ballie Ballerson just in time. The whole place was truly adorable, both their childhoods resuscitated with pink strobe lights and playful decorations in a way Sadiyah didn't know she was nostalgic for.

"I haven't been in a ball pit since I got too big for the play area one over at IKEA." Fatima raised her voice over the pop music flooding the speakers as she stepped into the recessed floor, filled with bubblegum-pink balls.

"I find it hard to believe you've ever been too big for anything," Sadiyah chastised, lifting a brow as she trailed behind her.

"Hush."

"No, really. I could probably lose you on Sesame Street."

"Are you saying I look like a monster?" Fatima prodded. She tilted her head to the side, arms folded, the movement jangling her gold hoop earrings as they reflected the flickering lights.

"No, you know I'm not saying that. I'm just saying you're—" Sadiyah squirmed and muttered to herself when she couldn't think of what to say back. "Whatever," she curtailed and threw a ball at her, officially declaring open season.

Fatima jerked back and shrieked, "Dirty shot!"

Fortunately for Sadiyah, there were no referees around to discern the clean shots from the dirty ones. So, she and Fatima spent their time waging a hollow, inflated plastic ball war with each other. They took pictures and sang along—badly—to the songs on the radio. But then, slowly, Fatima's voice started to fade, and since Sadiyah knew her so well, she noticed.

"Ti?" she asked softly, putting her hand out and wading across the pink sea toward Fatima like she was afraid she'd drown. "You okay?"

Fatima's eyes had ballooned, and she worked her jaw for a heartbeat, an uneasy tension seeming to emanate from every ounce of her frame. "I'm fine," she wheezed. "It's just a bit of sensory overload. I... I can't..."

Sadiyah didn't do this often. But there was a split second where she froze as Fatima clearly fell into a panic attack. She wasn't concerned with the people nosily trying to figure out what was going on, mainly because Sadiyah was more concerned with why she herself didn't know why her friend suddenly looked like a lost and terrified child at Chuck E. Cheese.

"Sads?" Fatima muttered so softly that Sadiyah was surprised she'd even heard her.

Sadiyah traced Fatima's line of sight outside to find a couple holding hands across the street. Was that it? Was the guy dipping down to kiss the girl on her forehead as they talked, sending her into a spiral? Sadiyah grimaced because, of course, it was. Knowing Fatima, it wasn't so much the sight, but the implication of it. More specifically, the implication of who she didn't have to do the same thing with her: Pretty Boy. Ugh.

"Yeah," Sadiyah shook her head, fully coming back to her senses. "Reservations ending in a few minutes, anyway. Let's head out."

OUTSIDE, SADIYAH COACHED FATIMA THROUGH DEEP BREATHING exercises until Fatima looked a little less like she was about to spontaneously combust.

"I'm sorry," Fatima panted, crouched down and flattening herself against the cement wall behind her, her head sagging in the crook between her thighs.

"Don't apologize," she gently scolded, bent down in front of her. "Breathe in." Fatima inhaled. "Out." She coughed. "What's going on?"

"I'm stupid," Fatima breathed, her words sounding rough and strained.

"I'm gonna need you to be more specific."

Fatima rolled her eyes.

Sadiyah smirked.

"I feel like I'm always making the wrong decisions," Fatima explained. "Like I'm stuck. I love Javier, and he keeps leaving me. Now he's here, but he's. . . not, at the same time."

Sadiyah sucked in a breath. "That's not love then."

"Then what is it?" Fatima snapped. "Lust?"

Sadiyah made a face, but kept whatever smart remark she had ready at bay. "It wasn't love. It wasn't lust. You've only ever described him as limerence to me."

"Limerence?"

"Yes. Keep up, English major." The corners of her mouth curved. "Limerence is a trick. It's more or less a placebo for love and lust, since it's just as intense, if not more. The difference is that it's also one-sided, so it always leaves the one experiencing it worse off."

Something Sadiyah never admitted to anyone was that she knew her father was about to desert their family the day before he did it. By now, she hardly remembered the specifics of how he'd told her—just the bare bones of the conversation. Just the way she'd felt.

Essentially, he'd said he was tired. He'd forgotten who he was years ago and deserved to recover that information. At that moment, she didn't know what he was talking about, letting him finish up his monologue so she could get back to her K-drama. The next day, after he left them out of nowhere, and as her mother sobbed on the kitchen floor for a man who hadn't said "I love you" to her, her mom, or her brother in what felt like forever, she'd figured it out. Looking at her friend now, with clouded-over red eyes, all she could see was her mother.

"I wish he'd stayed gone, if I'm honest," Fatima sighed.

Sadiyah narrowed her eyes. "You can make that happen."

"No, I can't," Fatima laughed bitterly. "He's here now. What am I supposed to do? Tell him to leave?"

"Exactly that."

Something in Fatima exploded. "Why don't you get that I can't do that? He always leaves, but he always comes back to me. And if he comes back, then I can't leave him, Sadiyah," she blinked. There were people pretending not to watch her on the sidewalk. If Fatima noticed, she didn't seem to care. "Some-times, I'm not even sure I want him," she whispered.

"Then why—"

"BECAUSE IF I DON'T TAKE HIM, THEN WHO'S GONNA TAKE ME, SADIYAH? You said it yourself this morn-ing, *I* built him. . . and I did that for me. Not for him to go and be exactly who I want for someone else."

"Has he ever been who you wanted for you, though?"

"That's not important."

"It sounds like you don't think you are, either."

Fatima laughed. Or she made a strange gurgling sound that may have been an attempt at one. "*Of course* I'm not. What-What about that isn't clicking to you? I would've been better off if I could've *at least* been more like you. I would've never even given Javier the time of day, but surprise: I. Am. Not. Like. You. It's not in me. I can't be the perfect girl, the perfect Muslim like you are, but I *can* be a good girlfriend, Sadiyah."

Sadiyah hummed a note of something, but remained other-wise quiet. It was honestly sad to her, seeing phenomenal women like Fatima and her mother beat themselves up over people who wouldn't do the same for them. Not seeing them-selves as anything further than a footnote to someone else's life story.

Sadiyah understood love as something fickle, which meant there was a slim-to-none chance of ever keeping it. So then, to her, there was no point in crying over it either. No point in Fatima amounting all of her self-worth to the little that guy clearly thought of her. No point in her being emotionally avail-able for an emotionally unavailable man.

"I don't need your smart words or your smart comments," Fatima kept up. "Or for you to *keep* calling him Pretty Boy. His name is *JAVIER*, Sadiyah. *JA-VI-ER.*"

Sadiyah didn't care if the boy's name was Rumpelstiltskin; she wasn't about to keep getting yelled at over him. "If you're so hung up on *Javier*," she shot back, scooting away. "Then why were you texting Iyad this morning?"

Fatima shot her a disgruntled look. "I didn't."

"Check your phone, then," she rolled her eyes. This, she knew, was petty of her. But this conversation was getting tedious, and if Fatima wasn't willing to listen to her, then there was a chance she'd listen to herself.

Fatima took her phone out of her purse and opened it to Javier's texts. Finding nothing, she clicked on Iyad's name:

Hey, I miss

The cursor blinked in the message box at the end of her unfinished message to Iyad. She deleted it and exited their conversation.

"Why didn't you tell me? You said 'Pretty Boy' this morning. I heard you."

"I assumed it was," Sadiyah sighed. "But then I looked at it again and saw you were about to send that text to Iyad. Look me in the eyes right now and tell me you were so sleepy and stupid that you accidentally opened Iyad's messages instead of Pret-," she caught herself, *"Javier's,* the guy you're *supposedly* so in love with."

Fatima swallowed and turned her attention to the ground. Sadiyah continued speaking when she didn't look up. "I wanted you to find out about it for yourself, so I'm sorry for bringing it up like that. But I'm not too keen on being your punching bag, Ti."

"I'm sor-" Fatima tried, reflexively.

"Save it," Sadiyah bit out, then took a breath. They weren't going to get anywhere if they both lost their heads. "Why won't you let him go? Why do you keep chasing after him?" she asked, quieter, trying to understand.

"I feel bad," Fatima answered, just as softly.

"You think he has ever even once felt bad for you, though?" They were quiet for a moment, the constant chatter of the city filling the space around them. "Did you really not know that you were texting Iyad?"

"I didn't, but it doesn't matter anyway," Fatima rationalized. "He won't talk to me."

Sadiyah shook her head. "We have the project, and he's just a little proud. I'm sure next week will be different once he's had some time to cool off," Sadiyah tried to reassure her because, as out of pocket as Fatima was, all she heard was her mom crying on the kitchen floor.

"I'm sorry," Fatima pressed, reaching out between them for Sadiyah's hands. Sadiyah rolled her eyes, but took them in hers. "I know you worked hard planning today for us, and I ruined it."

"You don't think I left some wiggle room for one of us to hyperventilate over how great a job I did?" Sadiyah scoffed. "Give me some credit."

Fatima eyed her friend, blinking bewilderedly, her mouth dry. "I'm sorry," she said again. "I've been awful and I'm sorry."

"We're good," Sadiyah said, pulling Fatima's body toward her into a hug. "Come here." A tight hug. "We're good," she repeated. "But try me like that again and I might have to lay some hands on you."

Fatima stifled a laugh. Sadiyah heard it and pulled back. "I'm serious," she told her, but was grinning as she brushed invisible lint from Fatima's shoulder.

"I'm sorry," Fatima grinned back. "I love you."

Sadiyah narrowed her eyes. "I love you, Ti. And I mean it," she punched her fist into her palm.

Fatima grinned wider, nodding.

"Just make sure you aim all that rage at the right person next time, okay?" Sadiyah smirked, putting her pinky out for Sadiyah to hook onto.

"Okay," Fatima agreed as they stamped their thumbs together.

CHAPTER THIRTEEN

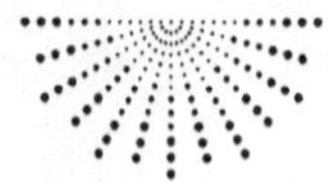

Buzz.

"You getting that, fam?" Mo asked, nodding to Iyad's phone atop his desk, as he fumbled with his controller to block Iyad from threading yet another shot past him.

They'd been in Iyad's room for the past hour playing FIFA, and Mo had been losing, rather hilariously, the whole time. Iyad didn't respond. Instead, he guided Romelu Lukaku past his cousin's defenders, shot the football to the left of Mo's goalie, and spun around in his game chair as the ball sailed off into the net. "Goallllll!" he whisper-shouted.

"Show off," Mo muttered, loudly, under his breath.

"The only thing I'm showing off is how to play," Iyad responded evenly, pausing the game and leaning over to tap at Mo's controller with his own. "You do know these buttons have purposes, right? You've been doing the same random mash technique since we were kids." His phone buzzed again. "How's that been working out for you, mate?"

"Come off it," Mo brushed Iyad aside with a grin. "I've only been letting you win 'cause you've been sulking around more than usual lately."

"I haven't been sulking," Iyad disagreed.

"Fine. Moping," Mo returned quickly.

Iyad only shook his head because there wasn't anything to say. He hadn't been sulking, moping, or whatever. He hadn't.

However.

He had been embarrassed about what'd happened with Fatima. Very. Not that he was about as protective over the memory of his father as Gollum was of the One Ring, but that he'd let that need for control over the situation cause him to be so terrible to her.

Truthfully, the state of things was simple: Iyad had read Fatima's private submission back at Kew Gardens, and instead of brushing him off when he'd asked her about it, she'd confessed something raw and painful to him. In return, he'd managed to do the same. Well, not the same. Technically, he hadn't done anything close to what could be categorized as such, but he'd done something. Something about her made him want to do something.

And that terrified him because he didn't know why.

Buzz.

Iyad's phone went off again, momentarily yanking him away from his pessimistic thoughts. "I'm fine," he muttered, then unpaused the game, returning his attention to the TV.

But then Mo, restless and likely fed up with losing, immediately stopped the game again, commandeering Iyad's phone to read the notifications. "Sadiyah?" His heavy eyebrows shot up as he shifted his attention from the phone to Iyad. "Iyad, you sly dog. Is *this* what's been having you out of sorts? Your classmate with the braids that visited the shop?" he discerned.

Mo was wrong, of course. Sadiyah wasn't the "classmate with the braids." But Iyad couldn't figure out how to explain that because he couldn't even understand why Sadiyah was messaging him to begin with. It'd been nearly a week since he'd spoken to either her or Fatima, and he was starting to wonder if he could take his streak on until class was over, they were all on their respective continents, and their project was long forgotten. But here was Sadiyah, seeking him out despite the line he'd drawn.

He jumped up from his seat and snatched the phone from his cousin. "Let me see," Iyad muttered under his breath, unlocking the device and disregarding Mo's oblivious enthusiasm.

Sadiyah:

> As-Salamu Alaykum, TG.

Iyad read over the message with a raised eye. She hadn't messaged him in their group chat. Why was she messaging him at all, then?

Sadiyah:

> If you're done pretending like we don't exist, we'll be at the South Bank today.

> You and you-know-who need to talk.

Ah. There it was. Iyad nervously scrubbed his beard at the mention of "you-know-who," struggling to unravel his thoughts over the sound of his panic-stricken chest because he wanted to talk to he-knew-who. But what do you say to someone you deserted without notice or a fair trial, especially after becoming so good at doing so for three years?

Iyad had absolutely no reason to assume the worst about what Fatima might've said back at Kew Gardens, had he given her the chance to speak. However, he knew that if she did, he would have to respond, turning their exchange into a tennis match of dead dad sentiments. He wanted no part of that. Iyad spent enough time on that in therapy, and what he knew now was no different from what he knew when he'd first started: Iyad still loved his dad. His dad was still dead. And neither of those facts kept the Earth from spinning.

He didn't see a reason in talking about his dad if it wasn't going to make the man talk back. Especially when the thought of his father's voice still made Iyad's heart do Simone Biles-level somersaults into his throat while Fatima spoke. Iyad chose to survive what could've been that conversation the way he'd survived all of his grief, his anger, and seeing his Uncle Hassan thus far: by leaving. If he wasn't there, he could convince himself that nothing bad happened or was happening. He could convince himself that he still loved his father, his father was still alive, and they still existed on this spinning Earth together.

So what about he-knew-who changed that for him after such a little bit of time? A tepid voice in his head told him not to question it. It told him to go back to playing FIFA, where things were calculable and predictable. But FIFA didn't make his nervous system go all haywire just by smiling at him.

He replied.

Iyad:

> Wa Alaykum As-Salam, I'll let you know when I'm there.

> My cousin Mo is coming with me.

"What do you mean you're not surprised?"

Iyad winced as the wind wrapped around him while they crossed the footbridge over the River Thames into the South Bank. He'd just finished his best explanation of what'd gone down between him and Fatima. Now, he was trying hard not to psych himself out of meeting up with her and Sadiyah by doing anything else that could potentially make things worse.

"I mean," Mo replied, nonchalantly. "You're good at that—ignoring people, even when they're right in front of you."

Iyad briefly snuck a glance at his cousin, who was watching a family up ahead. There were two little boys in the middle, around ten or eleven years old, counting off boats from the bridge's railing, while their parents talked around them.

"You miss that?" Mo asked, nodding their way.

Somewhere at the base of Iyad's chest, a guilty bead of anxiety began to ripple through him like a stone skipping across his bloodstream. He had no control over what happened with his dad, but he'd played a major part in the rift that took place between him and his family after. "I—"

"But this isn't about us," Mo cut him off with a sigh. His mouth curved into a slow and cautious smile, something completely unlike him. "Do you know what you're going to say to her?"

Iyad bowed his head as they descended the bridge steps and took out his phone to message Sadiyah.

Iyad:

Does Fatima know we're coming?

Sadiyah:

Would you like Fatima to know you're coming?

"No," Iyad responded to the text and Mo simultaneously, sighing as he vaguely looked at the steady flow of people moving around them. There was an acrobatic street performer busking just ahead of them. Maybe he could disappear if he ducked off into the crowd there. . . "They probably just want to corner me so we can get this project over with."

Iyad:

Where are you?

Mo blinked and then whacked Iyad on his shoulder, saying pointedly, "Her best friend. Messaged you. Alone. On a Sunday afternoon. To talk *to her*. Was school anywhere in those messages?"

"No, but—"

"Wallahi, I thought you were meant to be the smart one of us," Mo teased, smacking Iyad upside the back of his head. He wore a mocking grin, which Iyad met with a scowl as he pushed his cousin back. "Auntie Farah must've dropped you on your head as a baby."

Iyad felt the ghost of a smile trace his lips. "I *am* the smart one of us. I just had an erm- momentary lapse."

"A momentary lapse, did you? That's what we're calling it?" he smirked, and Iyad's phone vibrated in his hand. "Look, just tell her the truth."

"And if that's not good enough?"

Iyad was managing just fine at keeping things platonic between himself and Fatima. He knew she was a pretty girl, a bit brazen, and very smart. He thought she was extraordinary. But focusing on that meant he was losing focus. Iyad didn't get to do that. He didn't deserve those moments of respite that he'd finally been granted, having met Fatima.

Fatima altered something in Iyad that he couldn't quite understand. She reminded him of good times, tying him with a loose string between who he was before and who he could be now. Someone. . . happier. Someone better.

"Still," Mo continued, "Let's say for argument's sake that this is all about some project—"

"It is," Iyad insisted.

"Then this'll be a quick trip, won't it?" he shrugged casually, as another text message rolled in. This time, it was Sadiyah sending him their location. Mo looked it over. "Alright then, let's go."

Iyad took in a deep breath, holding it for a moment before exhaling slowly. He followed the directions Sadiyah sent that carried them over by the Golden Carousel, where the London Eye turned slowly just beyond them. There, they found her and Fatima sitting at a picnic table under a set of fairy lights strung up at the Underbelly Festival, sharing some chips.

Thankfully, Fatima wasn't facing the entrance, which afforded Iyad a few extra seconds to gather himself, instead of taking his chances running away. But then, Sadiyah spotted them. Iyad watched as she glanced at Fatima, who turned around and frowned just like she did the first time she saw him. He smiled cautiously at the memory. She didn't at all. With a grunt, he accepted whatever fate awaited him and followed the same loose string that had quietly tied him to her.

❈

Growing up, Fatima had always been labeled as one of the "smart kids." She was always in the smart classes with the other smart students and got the smart grades. Smart, smart, smart. She studied. She asked questions in class. She did her homework. She knew the rules, and she followed them. Smart, smart, smart.

Fatima never had a study guide for men, though. The closest she had was her dad, who was good to her, but after a point, his love didn't compare to the attention other girls were getting from the guys in school. The boys were never drawn to her the way she read about in her romance books. So, when Javier came along, a handsome and well-known track star at their high school, she folded almost instantly.

He was straight out of a movie. Holding her books. Talking on the phone well past the point of studying, and until one of them had fallen asleep. He made her laugh. He sought her out when she came to his track meets. He did everything right, up until the point where she was finally his.

As she watched Iyad and his cousin walk up to her and Sadiyah, it occurred to her that men were her kryptonite. And so Iyad, being of the variety of self-identifying men, must clearly be no different.

"Sadiyah?" Fatima turned around in a whirlwind because she was starting to put two and two together, and the only plausible solution to the equation was that she'd been set up. "Sadiyah Hanan Mitchell. What did you do?"

Sadiyah blinked, all coy and innocent as if she hadn't just stabbed Fatima in the back. "I did," she hummed, reaching for a fry because betrayal must've left her stomach empty. "What you both wouldn't."

"As-Salamu Alaykum, hello hello," Iyad's cousin—Mo, if Fatima remembered correctly—said as he stopped in front of them, brushing his waves down with the opened palm of his hand. "Fancy meeting you lot here."

"Wa Alaykum As-Salam. She knows," Sadiyah said, motioning for him and Iyad to sit down.

Mo accepted the invitation with a sigh as he dropped down beside her. "Good. I didn't know where to go from there," he grinned and pointed to the book in Fatima's hand. "Whatcha reading?"

Fatima's expression remained severe. She eyed Iyad, now seated next to her, and attempted to soften her features to answer Mo's question. It was a hard task, though. Fatima's mind had spread itself thin across all seven continents, and her nose was busy inhaling the disorienting scent wafting from Iyad that reminded her of the incense back at his store.

She was busy trying to figure out why Sadiyah, of all people, had the bright and shining idea of bringing him, of all people, here. Why she cared if it was something they both "wouldn't" do. Did it matter? They just shared a project, nothing else. They didn't have to be best friends. They didn't have to be friends at all. Even if it was nicer when she felt like they were. Maybe. Before.

Fatima lifted her chin to see Mo clearer and ignored the way her heart choked for a beat when she caught Iyad watching her closely, carefully from her peripheral vision. She nervously reached into her Foyles bag and dug out her receipt to use as a bookmark for saving her place, then waved the yellow paperback for him to see. "*Opposite of Always* by Justin A. Reynolds," she told him. "I just finished another book, and saw this one in a store a little while ago, so I thought I should pick it up."

"Oi, reading used to be a mare for me and Yaddy boy," Mo said, obviously trying his best to patch up the mother of all awkward moments with a few wads of stretched chewing gum.

"Yeah, same," Sadiyah agreed, adding a wad to the mass herself.

Iyad looked down at the book in Fatima's hand. He seemed about as off-kilter as Fatima felt. "Can we talk?" he finally asked.

Not wanting to make the situation more uncomfortable for anyone else (though she had nothing to do with its inception), Fatima just nodded and mumbled some unintelligible sound of agreement because she didn't trust her mouth not to say the wrong thing. She barely trusted her legs to keep her upright as she stood, waiting for Iyad to lead her wherever.

"You hungry?" he asked her as he stood up.

Fatima shrugged casually, as if she hadn't already been planning what to eat after finishing their fries. "I could eat."

"Okay," he flashed a winsomely crooked smile and practically sprinted ahead to the food trucks and stalls that lined the area around them. Fatima nearly had to run to keep pace with him, since one of his strides easily outmatched two of hers. "This work?" he asked, stopping at the end of the line for a Mexican food truck.

Fatima nodded. She counted that there were four people in line ahead of them, so she busied herself by thinking about what she'd order on her nachos—anything, absolutely anything to distract herself from the stupid electric excitement she felt just in being near Iyad.

"Let's play twenty questions," he prompted, seeming a bit flustered, which Fatima was grateful for because it meant to her that at least she wasn't the only one. "I'll go first. What's your favorite color?"

"Orange," she answered primly, keeping her arms folded and her eyes on the line ahead. She didn't want to see even an iota of his brown skin in the sunlight. Either as a survival instinct or due to a complete and utter lack of guts, though? She wasn't sure.

Iyad tilted his head back and made a soft whooshing sound as he blew out a breath. "Of course, it is," he smirked.

Fatima wasn't understanding him. She squinted. "What's that supposed to mean?"

"Fatima Sommers," Iyad nodded slowly. "Summer, sun. . . I would've chosen yellow, but orange would've been a close second. Plus, it's the same color as that notebook you always have with you," he outlined, smirking more.

"Alright now, Einstein," she rolled her eyes because feigning irritation felt like her only defense in the moment. "If you already know everything, then there's no point in playing."

"But I don't," Iyad disagreed calmly. "Can't you tell that's the problem I'm trying to fix now?"

Fatima sucked in a deep breath, calming herself over the way he'd so easily made her pulse pound loud in her ears. What was this boldness? And why did she like it? She shook her head, forcing herself to return to their conversation. "Sport?"

"Rugby, I guess. Used to play time ago."

Against Fatima's better judgment, she tilted her head toward him with furrowed brows, and as predicted, promptly melted at the scene. "Really?"

"I wouldn't lie to you," he said, and she turned away when his eye contact turned into laser beams. "Was that book you were talking with Mo about the same one from the bookstore I took you to?"

If Iyad were a helpful man, he wouldn't remember little things that made her heart stutter. He'd make it easier for her to push back at him, to remember the way he left her at Kew Gardens and didn't talk to her for almost a whole week after until Sadiyah intervened.

If Fatima were as smart as she thought, she'd stick to the facts: he left. He left. He left.

However.

"Yeah, it is," she replied, a little less flatly than she'd meant to, as the final customer in front of them left and they could order. "Nachos de pollo, please. And a bottled water." Fatima reached for her purse to take out her wallet when Iyad slid in front of her, all oak and misplaced sweetness.

"Don't embarrass me," he grunted. To the man behind the counter, he said, "Two bottled waters, please, chief. And I'll have the chicken nachos, too. "

They received their food quickly after ordering and sat at one of the empty picnic tables near the one where Sadiyah and Mo were playing Uno with the deck Sadiyah had brought from home. Fatima immediately took out the little container of hand sanitizer she always kept in her purse and shared some with Iyad.

"Thanks for paying," she exhaled sharply, biting back the

urge to pay him back after he'd made it clear to her he wouldn't like that. "You get an extra turn."

Iyad inhaled a few guacamole-covered chips and went, "You mad at me?"

"What do you think?" Fatima returned, popping a few chips in her mouth as well.

"Aht, aht." Iyad dipped his face low in front of hers and shook his head. "I know you, of all people, know an answer from a question."

"Don't get smart with me," she looked away, suddenly hot. "I'm just not a fan of being left."

"Fatima. . ." he started.

She shook her head, regaining her steely composure. Fatima was not about to let him turn this into a pity party. "My turn. Why'd you leave?"

"Do you know what it is?" he cocked his head to the side. "I haven't talked about my dad in such a long time. I know we barely did then, but. . . I'm just not sure I know what to say anymore."

Fatima watched him quietly. Sometimes, she felt like she'd always known him. Others, like now, she had to remember that she was still figuring him out. Fatima had learned that Iyad wasn't the type you could push at, so she resisted the urge to pry any further. "Oh, I see," she said, down to the facts because they were all she had then. "And I opened my big mouth."

"Yeah, you did, you muppet," Iyad flashed a grin.

"Muppet?" she yelped. "Like Kermit the frog?"

"No," he let out a puff of air, and she watched him suppress a laugh. "But I started it, so I'm sorry for losing my head. I think it was even a good thing in the end. You got me thinking again."

"Oh no," she grinned, because she was finding it hard to stay upset with him.

"Are we cool?" he blurted.

Fatima almost didn't hear him. She was too busy looking at

how he'd squared off his face with hers, realizing she couldn't get herself to look away from him. Or was it that she didn't want to?

"Yeah," she breathed.

"Cool, we're," he faltered, kneading at the base of his neck. "We're friends then."

"Friends." Fatima felt the word on her tongue, swallowed down the bitter aftertaste.

"Friends, Ti," he cleared his throat. "So, what's going on with you and your, erm, break—by the way?"

"Someone told me there's no such thing as a break," she sneered. For the first time, Javier was truly the last thing on her mind, and she was okay with worrying about the ramifications of that later.

"They sound smart."

"They think so."

"Why'd you frown at me that day on the pavement? The day we met."

Fatima scoffed. "You noticed that?"

He nodded.

Fatima bit her lip in thought. "Your eyes," she answered, meeting his.

His eyebrows rose to the sky. "What about them?"

"You just looked so sad to me, is all."

"Oh." Iyad leaned back.

"Yeah." Fatima did the same.

"Why'd you stop practicing religion completely?"

She was struck by how much he wanted to know about her. Or maybe just in that he was as curious about her as she was about him. "You've skipped my turn so many times now," she leaned her head to the side.

"I'm a curious person," Iyad admitted, not relenting.

Fatima glanced past him to where Sadiyah and Mo were seated. She tried to brush aside the slight tension that settled on her shoulders, searching for an answer. The weight of the entire alphabet pressed down on her, but none of the letters would form into one solid word. Finally, she realized that even after years of the same cycle, she still didn't have a clear answer—just slippery feelings.

"I didn't pray one day," Fatima confessed haltingly. "Then it was two days, then two weeks. Then I just stopped, and I couldn't figure out how to start again. That's when my—now-ex," she coughed, "stopped wanting to be friends."

"Your rotten meat." Iyad leaned in.

"Yes, my rotten meat," she half-grinned. "I forgot myself when I was with him. At first, it was on purpose, but now it's like I don't know who I am when he's not around."

"Is he still around?" he muttered.

"He—" Fatima started to lie and then caught herself. She scratched at the table, thinking of what to say next. The truth was that yes, she was still texting Javier. Javier had been her comfort zone for years. She was used to the way he loved her. Even if he couldn't admit to it sometimes.

Realizing that, Fatima decided it was best not to answer. "And now it's to the point where I can admit that sometimes I miss Islam," she continued truthfully. "I miss praying. I miss my hijab. I miss feeling. . . grounded. But I know that the day I choose Islam again is the day I can't go back to him because I can't have both." Fatima shook her head. "Now you've got me talking too much."

"I don't mind." Iyad paused. "Wa Huwa ma'akum ayna maa kuntum," he recited the Quran. She quickly realized she liked how easily he could slip into recitation. "It means, 'And He is with you wherever you are.' Not your ex, not Sadiyah, not. . . me. But God. He never left you. So you can always practice again because He never expected you to be perfect in doing so anyway. Just to try."

"Yeah?"

"Yeah," he resolved, looking her over gently. "And just so you know, the right person won't make you choose between the two."

Fatima felt a sudden heat spread across her face under his gaze. "Yeah?" she repeated.

Iyad nodded resolutely. "Yeah."

Fatima felt her breath catch on the wind. She rested her cheek on her hand to try to steady it. But after the silence lingered with no one to break it, Iyad eventually said, "Ready to head back?"

No, Fatima wanted to say. She wanted to stay there with him a little while longer. But since there was no discernible reason as to why she would have said that, Fatima nodded in agreement. Iyad placed her takeout box on top of his own and led them over to Sadiyah and Mo, this time slowing up and matching his pace with hers.

Mo put his hand of cards face down on the table when they made it back. He paused the Stormzy song he was playing on his phone, a choice that Fatima silently commended since it served as a welcome interlude from the music she'd heard all day—a mix that somehow ranged from 'Sweet Caroline' by Neil Diamond to 'Caroline' by Aminé. "We all friends now?" he grinned.

Friends. Fatima couldn't understand why the word smelled like battery acid and rotten eggs. She wrinkled her nose to ward it off. 'Friends' would have to be good for her. No. It *was* good for her. Knowing where she stood with Iyad was good. It was better, she had to admit, than not knowing the same for Javier.

"Let's play some Uno and change that right quick," Mo went on. He had the sort of smile that made Fatima think of a child who always had ice cream money and never lost in kickball, just roundabout happiness. "I'll deal," he said, and put his hand out for Sadiyah to give him her cards.

"No, you won't," Sadiyah combined her cards with the deck

in the middle of them, then held her hand out for his. The two looked like two servers waiting for someone to give them a tray. "You cheat."

"Swear down?" He screwed his eyes at her mischievously, but relented, adding his cards to hers. "I'm an *opportunist.*"

"Opportunist," she muttered under her breath and cut the deck. "If that means 'to cheat,' then sure."

Fatima took out her phone and sent a text to Sadiyah as she handed the cards out across the table.

Ti:

Why'd you ask him to come?

Sadiyah responded after a few turns.

Sads:

'Cause I knew he would.

CHAPTER FOURTEEN

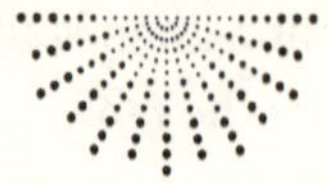

A LITTLE AFTER TEN IN THE MORNING THAT NEXT WEEKEND, Fatima found Louisa crocheting on the living room couch while she and her husband, Paul, watched a news anchor discuss Brexit on the television. Fatima quickly took a headcount of everyone else. Sadiyah was still in bed, and Artie was outside playing with a friend in their Heelys. Meaning, the bathroom should've been free for at least another hour or so.

In her two months of living at Louisa's, Fatima had drastically altered her bathroom routine. She'd explained the functionality of a washcloth for the first time after accidentally forgetting hers in the shower, and listening to Louisa have a field day explaining how unnecessary the "flannel" was. She took quick showers since Louisa didn't want her and Sadiyah in the bathroom any longer than it took to take a bird bath. And she'd only conditioned her hair so far since there was hardly ever any time to do anything more.

Louisa's hair was something out of a conventional fairytale: long, silky, and widely idealized. Fatima's was the opposite. Even in box braids, her hair was coarse, tightly coiled, and a little too needy for Louisa's comfort. Which was why it'd taken so long to convince Louisa to bend her rules so Fatima and Sadiyah could at least have one twenty-minute shower a month to wash their hair thoroughly.

"Good morning." Fatima stood just at the entrance of the living room, shifting her weight around.

True to Paul's fashion, he flicked a glance toward her, then turned back to the Brexit broadcast, running a free hand through his silver hair.

"Good morning, dear," Louisa said as she looked up from her weaving and smiled. "Can I help you with something?"

"Oh, no," Fatima smiled back and then fidgeted some more. "Just wanted to make sure now was a good time for that twenty-minute shower we talked about, since everyone is," she swallowed, looking around one last time, "away."

"Oh, pish," Louisa said, waving a saliently veined hand in the air. "I've had girls here before with hair like yours who wore those, erm, cap things like you're wearing now," Bonnets. She meant bonnets—and not the British one, either, that meant the hood of a car. "*They* never needed twenty full minutes, so I hardly think you will either, dear." The edges of her lips curled upward like the Other Mother from *Coraline.*

Fatima realized then that if Louisa regarded her as a deer, then she was no different from Bambi's mother, making Louisa no different from the hunter who shot her dead. She made a mental note to shorten her twenty minutes down to fifteen, thinking of how her parents and Sadiyah's mom, as well as Sadiyah herself, had all warned her against living in someone else's home. Somehow, Fatima convinced them otherwise because of the security in knowing they at least had someone who knew they'd made it home every night. At this point, she no longer shared her previous sentiment.

"Out in a bit, then." Fatima forced a flat-lipped nod as she backed away, returning to the bathroom where she'd already left her shower caddy with everything prepped and ready.

Fatima turned on her timer as soon as she shut the door behind her. Then she got in the shower and let her hair get wet, immediately turning the water off to add shampoo.

Standing in the silence while the morning light dipped into the tub and shimmered off the shower's glass door, Fatima let her mind drift as Erykah Badu's 'Green Eyes' filled in the gaps of languid silence.

"My eyes are green," she whispered to herself and turned the water back on, rinsing the shampoo from her scalp. *"'Cause I eat a lot of vegetables. It don't have nothing to do with your new friend. . ."*

She couldn't help it. Thinking of green eyes at all would always bring Javier to mind for her. Fatima imagined what he might be doing with his "new friend"—most likely Bea, who was more than likely sleeping on her side of his bed these days. Fatima wasn't so full of herself to act like she was the only fish in the sea, especially when it came to Javier, who was so incapable of being on his own. Still, her awareness of this didn't make the fact that where she only saw him, and he only saw her as one of many options, hurt any less.

"I don't care, I swear. I'm too through with you, I am. . ." Fatima kept singing. She poured a heap of conditioner into her hand and turned the water back off, taking some time to work her fingers through the braids. *"You don't mean nothing to me, so go ahead and be with your friend. . ."*

One time, when Fatima was in the barracks, Javier told her that a guy from work, Jacobs, had explained to him how he had married his wife young because he thought he was in love. But then he went and got her pregnant. Now, they have five kids, and he can't stand them almost as much as he can't stand his wife.

Naturally, Fatima asked Javier what he was getting at with telling her that, since they'd just been quietly playing video games together on his bed. He never answered. Not directly. Just said that while he and Jacobs were talking, Bea suggested he should date around while he's still young. See what's out there, et cetera, et cetera. She guessed that's what he was doing now.

"I'm insecure, but I can't help it. My mind says "move on," my heart lags behind. . ." Fatima sang, turning the water on again. She'd decided to actually shower first and let the conditioner sit for a bit longer, thinking about how Javier used to joke that he couldn't think straight whenever a pretty girl was around—wondering if it was even hard for Bea to take him in Fatima's absence, or if she was just there and convenient. Or if maybe, she was better.

Fatima sighed, her head dizzy from comparing herself to a girl she'd never even met, and began washing the conditioner out when someone knocked at the door.

"Yes?" she called, then absentmindedly brushed away a tear that'd escaped her. No one said anything. Another knock echoed. "Yes?" Nothing. She leaned back under the shower head, allowing her tears to flow freely. *"But I don't love you anymore, I'm so insecure. Never knew that love did this. . ."*

Since their car accident, this was the longest Fatima had been underwater without feeling like she was slowly dripping away with the droplets. London seemed to be made of water-hungry clouds, raining all the time. She thought it bothered her because they took away clear skies, but now, two months removed from the boy she'd coddled for years, she realized she was actually afraid of it too—she just didn't have the time to reach that epiphany because she was too busy focusing on his needs and throwing her feelings to the wayside. Summing them up to an unexplained loathing.

"Loving you is wrong. Is it?"

Then there was Iyad, who came back to her despite running away. And, despite his evident aversion to human contact, he'd seemed to get along with her just fine. But Fatima wasn't known for making the best decisions about men; Javier was blatant proof of this. So how could Iyad be any different?

Fatima's thoughts were broken off when the water stopped running. Why in the world had the water stopped running? Automatically, she tried turning the faucet off and on, like it was a computer on the fritz. When nothing happened, she wrung out her hair (that thankfully, she'd just finished washing) and covered it with a T-shirt.

Fatima stepped out of the shower and threw on her clothes, desperately trying to make it seem like the redness of her eyes was from lingering hair products instead of a reminder of moments with Javier that ruined the picture-perfect memories she was struggling to keep hold of. Like how she used to tell herself that those times when he'd get back from work and come onto her even if she'd already told him no, were just proof of how much he loved and needed her. Or that time she stupidly read his texts while he was in the shower...

She sighed, forcing off the idea that he was just selfish. That he'd guilted her into bed with him with stupid lines, telling her how bad she'd made him feel about himself. *"If you don't want me, just say that,"* he'd go, among other iterations. Fatima told herself that she was remembering their past wrong. She had to be. Because if she wasn't, and he wasn't as good as she'd dreamt him up to be, then what was she spending all of this time waiting on him for?

Fatima collected everything and opened the door to get back into her room when she caught the tail end of Louisa saying something to her.

"...dear?"

She was too tangled up in her own web of thoughts about Javier to understand. Fatima blinked to refocus. Once. Twice. No dice, whatever Louisa said wasn't coming to her.

"I'm sorry?"

"I said, you were in the shower for quite some time, dear," Louisa repeated, her tone shifting impatiently. "I knocked on the door, but you never turned the water off. So, I had to do it for you."

Fatima blinked again. And again. "I'm... sorry?" she sounded out because whatever she'd heard, she hadn't.

"Well, your school isn't paying us all that much for you both to be living here," she raised an eyebrow. "Really, did you think taking a shower for that long would be reasonable?"

A beat passed. Fatima forced herself to breathe as she imagined Louisa running downstairs to shut the water off, then back upstairs to laugh about it like an evil queen who didn't know any better ways to spend her time. "Do we have a problem, Louisa?" she eventually asked.

Louisa stared at Fatima, lining up her prey to shoot. "Excuse me?"

"How long was I in there for?"

Fatima was trying her hardest not to feed into the angry Black girl stereotype. She was well aware that Louisa was being ridiculous. Still, Louisa was also being ridiculous from the comfort of her own home, where she had the complete capabilities to throw Fatima out of at any moment. So, Fatima reeled every raging feeling she had back inside of herself.

"Doesn't matter." Louisa all but hissed the words out. "Just be sure it doesn't happen again," she demanded, stalking off downstairs.

Fatima stood motionless in the hallway for a moment. When she returned to her room to finish moisturizing her hair and rush to leave, her fifteen-minute alarm went off.

"I DON'T KNOW ABOUT PLOTS LIKE YOU, BUT I DO KNOW THIS IS the part of the story where the villain shows up," Sadiyah clicked her tongue as Fatima stewed beside her while they headed to Hyde Park.

"You're saying I'm the villain?" Fatima asked. Admittedly, she was only partly listening.

Sadiyah cleared her throat. "Where'd you get that from what I said?" she gawked. "I'm saying Louisa is diabolical."

"She is." Fatima glanced outside the train window at a sign sweeping by them and sighed. "And I definitely wasn't even in there for the twenty minutes we *did* agree on. I hadn't even hit fifteen before I was back in our room."

"Diabolical," Sadiyah repeated gruffly.

"Diabolical," Fatima agreed.

Fatima was still doing her best to keep her emotions from reaching a crescendo. There was no space for them in her homestay. No space for them on this train. She figured that maybe there'd be an inkling of space at the park. Fatima looked down at the directions in her lap. If they followed them correctly, they'd be there soon enough, and she could quit nearly biting off her tongue to keep herself from screaming.

Good. For medical purposes, that was very good.

"So," Sadiyah said as the train began to slow down at their stop. "Should we hit up your bodyg—"

Fatima cut a glare over her glasses and stood up.

"Your bodyguard," Sadiyah finished, unbothered, as they walked toward the doors. "Let him know Louisa's been giving you trouble?" She made a fist and cracked her knuckles.

"What's he gonna do? Come running just 'cause I'm a little irritated?" Fatima rolled her eyes as if the mere thought of said bodyguard didn't coax a tiny smile from her when the train doors opened. "Don't hold your breath."

"This station is Hyde Park Corner," the speaker announced above them.

"I would never," Sadiyah asserted satisfactorily, stepping onto the platform. "I think he's done enough to prove himself in that way already, Tweedledee."

. . .

Fatima fanned the sanitizer off her hands before digging her thumb into one of the clementines she and Sadiyah brought to the park. She settled onto her jacket, spread out behind her, and watched as swans and geese paddled by in the lake in front of them. Despite the emotional thunderclouds back at Louisa's, today was a good day. The sun was a soft yellow, the sky was a gentle blue, and the clouds were wispy and billowing above them.

She used to play soccer on and off from elementary all the way up into high school—she was never all that great at it, but always made the team after tryouts since she was small and it was convenient to have a 4'11" defender who could take a hit and steal the ball when needed.

Growing up around the sport, Fatima got used to the little snacks her mom would pack for halftime: oranges, water, and maybe some chips. Sitting on the lawn at Hyde Park, surrounded by the familiar scent of grass and orange peels, felt a lot like then. Felt a lot like back home. Fatima hadn't realized until right then that she was homesick.

Beside her, Sadiyah snored quietly after claiming she needed more time to close out her REM cycle following the morning's chaos. Fatima, being fifty percent of the aforementioned chaos, didn't object and decided to read her book, *Opposite of Always*, in the meantime.

She took her time working through the pages. The story was about a guy named Jack who was trapped in a recursive time loop that restarted every time he failed to save the life of the girl he loved. And, because Fatima turned to putty for love stories, she found it interesting that he could be so in love that he kept trying to save her, despite the repeated heartbreak every time she died anyway.

Fatima ran her tongue along the outside of her teeth as she continued reading. Thinking of Jack made Fatima think of Iyad. And thinking of Iyad made Fatima feel a little like a chocolate bar that'd been left outside in the summer heat: overly sweet and hideously melted. Made her forget all about what he'd told her back at the South Bank: that they were friends. *Friends. Friends. Friends.*

That's why they kept finding themselves together outside of class and the parameters of their project. That's why he'd come to the South Bank when she was upset. That's why he only talked to her and Sadiyah in class. That's why Sadiyah was wearing the blue hijab she got from his family's shop for free. *Friends. Friends. Friends.*

Iyad was Iyad, though. Not Jack. And this was reality. Not fiction. Iyad did nice things because he was a nice guy. Fatima liked to look at him because he was a good-looking guy. And she enjoyed talking to him because he was a guy who listened to her, who didn't make her feel like she was unbearably dull or obtuse. Iyad always gave her his undivided attention, whether she was talking about her favorite *Star Wars* plots or her favorite kinds of pens. He was good to her, and she liked *that*. Fatima didn't like *him*. They were just friends, after all. According to him.

Maybe the problem, then, was less that they were friends and more that he was a guy. The last time a good guy started as a friend to her, she ended up as nothing more than a warm body to him. Maybe the problem was that Fatima was having trouble believing that she *could* even be friends with someone like him, someone who seemed so unreasonably good. But was he good? Was Fatima the type that'd even know what that was?

Clearly, Fatima didn't know jack about Jack.

She took a deep breath and marked her page when she heard commotion ahead of her. Taking her guard status seriously while Sadiyah slept, Fatima looked up to find a bright pink-haired woman roller skating behind little orange and green traffic cones while playing 'Ain't it Fun' by Paramore on a speaker strapped to her back.

"Ain't it fun?" the song asked. *"Living in the real world."*

Sadiyah sprang up with a jolt and leveled a stare toward the source that'd woken her.

"Why can't I just have peace?" she sighed and sank back down onto her jacket.

"Ain't it good?" the song and crowd went on together. *"Being all alone."*

"Peace is overrated," Fatima said and jumped on top of Sadiyah, to which Sadiyah rolled her eyes and pushed Fatima off, grinning lightly in return.

Not long after, the growing crowd had completely hidden the skating woman from view, but the song played on. Sadiyah dug into a clementine, and a new rush of citrus sprouted around them as Fatima sang along quietly, glancing at her phone on the ground beside her when Javier sent another text.

Javi:

Wyd?

Ti:

relaxing at the park for now, thinking about how i'll bring you here one day after we're back together.

Javi:

I never said that.

Fatima stared at her phone for a few beats, trying to figure out what he was talking about.

Ti:

that you wanted to go to the park with me?

Javi:

No, that we'd get back together.

She squeezed her eyes shut, almost as if on instinct, breathing in deep. After the day she'd already had with Louisa, Fatima decided that she wasn't going to be dealing with anyone trying to ruin her mood while she was doing her best to enjoy her day. Fatima opened her eyes. The sun was still bright. There was a sweet citrus and earth scent carried by the breeze around her.

Today would be good. And if Javier didn't want to be, they didn't have to be anymore. He wouldn't have to worry about her texting him anymore. She would teach herself to be done with him. Done with talking to him. Done with trying to stitch them back together.

"Don't go crying to your mama," she sang resolutely with the song. *"'Cause you're on your own in the real world."*

CHAPTER FIFTEEN

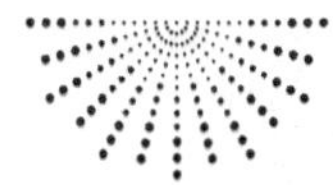

MONDAY MORNING BEFORE CLASS, FATIMA AND SADIYAH WENT TO Tom's office for their program's halfway check-in.

"Women," Tom sighed, his gaze swinging tiredly between them. Fatima and Sadiyah had been taking turns discussing the gory details of their trip, just reaching the part where Louisa turned the shower water off on Fatima. "You lot have my phone number, why don't you *use it?* You're meant to ping me if something isn't up to scratch so I can address it accordingly."

"Honestly, that never crossed my mind. Plus, I don't want to get us kicked out, wait weeks for a reassignment, and have everything be awkward in the meantime. I mean—" Fatima leaned back on his office balance ball, trying not to look too concerned, saying, "I don't want to make things harder for you."

"How kind of you," Tom snickered, then glanced at his computer. "It is a tad late for rearranging your housing assignments, but I'm sure in this situation I could. . ."

"Tom, look, it happened. It's fine. Nobody died." Fatima's smile flashed, then faded.

"I'm glad you've set the bar so high." Tom's face was a straight line.

Fatima shook her head and bounced up, her phone bobbing in her lap. "It'll be fine so long as we're barely around the place anymore."

Tom exhaled and looked to Sadiyah, sitting in a little wooden chair beside his desk. "Is Louisa like this with you, too?"

"She barely even talks to me," Sadiyah shrugged, a ghost of a smile framing her lips. "And I like it that way."

"I've just never heard of something like this," Tom muttered more to himself than to them.

"You also get like one Black person from our school a year in this program," Sadiyah smirked and picked at her fingernails. "You're really maxing out with the two of us this time around."

"Fair," he relented, closing his laptop and adjusting his argyle sweater. "Oh! I forgot to tell you guys. I've got a surprise for you all with your project that I think you'll enjoy, considering how much your little trio has been getting along lately."

Fatima leveled a glower at Sadiyah, then repeated to Tom, "'Getting along?'"

"Yes, considering the rocky start you all were off to back in January," he waved a hand. "Or did you want to talk about the gallant display at Euston Station and beyond?"

Again, Fatima directed a grimace to Sadiyah, who seemed indifferent after relaying one too many Iyad-centered stories. Then, she aimed one at Tom for good measure. He, too, appeared unfazed. How mutinous.

"He was just being nice," she explained.

"I'm sure. That's why he didn't talk in class for the entire week before you all got here, and now he's yammering on in every chance he gets." Tom observed smartly. "But only around the two of you."

"Well, we're all friends." Fatima defined them all just as Iyad had done for her. She decided to forgive the sly look Sadiyah and Tom shared, because they hadn't been there to hear him say it. And then repeat it for good measure. "We. Are. All. Friends," she enunciated.

"We definitely are," Sadiyah trailed off and wiggled her eyebrows at Tom before finishing, "friend*ly*."

Tom snorted and covered his mouth, making a noise that sounded an awful lot like stifling a laugh. Must've been a weird sneeze. Must've been allergies.

"You're supposed to be impartial, Tom," Sadiyah reminded him, mimicking the same garbled sound behind her covered mouth. Weird. Sadiyah never got allergies. Must've been the London air.

Or mutiny.

"Whatever's afoot, I'm glad." Tom gathered himself. "He's a good kid."

Fatima stared. "You both make me tired," she shook her head, resolving to let it go. Fatima knew a sinking ship when she saw one, and she could see that this one was quickly headed underwater. "Anyway, what's the surprise?"

"You'll see soon enough," he winked.

MANY PEOPLE CONSIDER MONDAY TO BE THE WORST DAY OF THE week. Iyad used to agree, but how could he now, seeing that it was the first of the only two days he was guaranteed to see Fatima?

He first realized the day was gaining his favor when he stopped going back to bed immediately after finishing his dawn prayer. Instead, Iyad got into the habit of getting up and getting dressed, making himself a cup of tea, and sifting through details of inventory spreadsheets and other ones that he'd made for Ahmed Azyaa.

He liked working on their accounts—typing in numbers and

making potential plans, just as his dad had taught him to. Sometimes, when Iyad came to class a little early and Fatima and Sadiyah hadn't arrived yet, he kept going.

Iyad sat up to shield the glare of the morning light from the window that was glinting on his computer screen as more of his classmates trickled into the classroom. Fatima and Sadiyah would typically be in class by now, planning their weekend trips and outfits, but they were nowhere to be found.

Hearing them talk about things he'd usually thought of as trivial like that was exactly the sorts of unbearable conversations Iyad had anticipated when he'd initially visited Tom's office seeking reassignment from them altogether. Every day, the two of them validated his preliminary concerns, and somehow, Iyad knew that as long as Fatima was there, he would continue to redefine the word "unbearable." He would break down its etymology to involve actual bears and things they were unable to do, rather than her and something he couldn't stand.

Something about her made him want to question everything he'd ever known. But then Iyad remembered, thanks to her incredibly raptorial ex, that there'd always be a limit to his curiosity because he could only ever go as far as the capabilities of 'friend.'

Iyad went back to his computer. He was starting to play with applying the equations he'd learned in his business lectures to his own schematics for production, sales, and new social media projects for Azyaa. He hadn't contemplated the shop like this in such a long time, so he had no plans to tell anyone that he'd started up one random Monday morning, because then there'd be questions. Then he wouldn't be able to keep believing all his work was theoretical anymore. Just lines, numbers, and theories. Theories. Theo—

His fingers tapered off, and he entered a string of gibberish as the class door languidly creaked open with Tom, followed by Fatima and Sadiyah trailing behind him.

"Tom says he's got a surprise for us," Fatima groaned, already sounding riled up as she sat down in the seat he'd saved next to him and took out her notebook.

Iyad thought she looked about as frightening as an angry duckling. He raised an eyebrow and dipped his head down to her height, catching a hint of vanilla and shea. "I'm guessing you don't like surprises," he asked, ignoring the entry he'd just typed that closely resembled a cartoon-censored profanity speech bubble. He opened a new, blank document. The cursor blinked on the first line before she spoke again.

"Hate them," she scowled and pulled her braids into a pony-tail, further emphasizing her overall angry duckling-ness.

"Steady now, killer." Iyad put his hands up. "I don't have any surprises for you, and I promise I never will if you promise no more death glares."

She rolled her eyes, but Iyad saw the gentle curve of her lips when she said, "Deal," and then went back to her notebook, dating the page with a little heart.

From the corner of his eye, he saw Sadiyah pretending to gag and Fatima quickly dismissing her with a swat. Then, she drew another one, and Iyad pushed down a strained swallow. It was just a heart. Nothing to do with him.

"Righto," Tom clapped his hands together. "Have we all done the reading on today's king, Henry VIII, or did you all just bugger off since you've known about him since primary school?" He grinned knowingly at the class, who, if they were anything like Iyad, had done exactly that. "Back to primary school then, shall we? Let's see how good those young minds are. Gemma, kick us off."

Gemma looked almost bored, tilting her head to the side to stretch out her neck, and then letting her dirty blonde hair fall with her. Returning to the center, she said swiftly, "He hates women."

"Woman hater, okay." Tom scribbled the words on the

whiteboard beside Henry's name, then pointed his pen toward her. "Some would argue that he was a victim of his circumstances just as much as his wives, even. That securing a male heir was considered more important than attending to the needs of his wives and concubines. What would you say to that?"

"That we would all be a lot better off if patriarchal law didn't dictate men's need to be so coddled."

"I agree. And the son he wanted so bad died after reining for like six years," chimed in the girl in front of her, Cat. "He was, what? *Nine?* When he came into power?"

Tom nodded, writing down *patriarchy* and *short-term son reign,* extending from *Henry VIII = woman hater* at the center. "Just a note," he said, turning to face the class again, "King Edward VI did ascend the throne, but he ruled under a regency. In practice, real authority was his appointed council, since he was too young to govern directly."

"Mm," Fatima hummed, nodding as she continued her annotations with rapt intensity.

"Yeah. Still, his daughter didn't reign for much longer either after him," the guy beside Cat said. Daniel.

"But she *reigned*—" Cat started.

"By marriage." Daniel interrupted.

"Incorrect," Tom added pointedly. "She was next in line."

"—and she's remembered even more than her father all these years later." Cat finished.

"Yes," Daniel agreed. "But as Bloody Mary, so. . . is that really a win?"

Cat rolled her eyes.

"As much as I love a good detour," Tom quipped, fanning his papers out. "I'd like to get this train back on the tracks. Let's hear from our group of friends who've been assigned today's king." He clasped his hands and gestured toward Iyad, Fatima, and Sadiyah.

Sadiyah let out a soft chuckle, and Fatima rolled her eyes before speaking up. "I'm interested in the relationships he had with his wives," she said.

"Good," Tom prompted. "What about them?"

"Well," she hedged, flipping through her notes. "I read that his first wife, Catherine of Aragon, had actually already married Henry's older brother, Arthur. But then, Arthur died, and Henry had to take his brother's place. So, I wonder if all of Henry's marriages were doomed right from the start. If his wives never had a chance because Henry never felt like he did so himself. If he felt like he had to compare to the king that he expected his brother would've become."

There was a pause just long enough for Iyad to notice a hint of something uneasy in Fatima's eyes before she blinked it away. To his left, Daniel quipped, "If she's not in his sheets, she's for the streets," earning shrapnels of laughter from some, mostly the guys, and irritated grimaces from others, primarily the girls.

The discussion lasted the rest of class without pause.

By the end of the lecture, Tom cleared his throat while everyone was collecting their things to go. "Alright," he spoke up. "As you lot know, I've been thinking of adding another location to our time together. So, surprise, surprise, to the group presenting on Henry VIII. I hope you were all paying attention today, as we'll soon be headed to Hampton Court Palace on Wednesday."

Fatima was onto something about surprises; they actually were terrible, insidious pests. Iyad couldn't see how this news could've been considered a good thing, being that *he* planned to take them to Hampton Court Palace himself. If he couldn't now, then that meant there wouldn't be any need for him anymore as their "Yank-appointed" tour guide. Worse, there wouldn't be any excuse to see them anymore outside of class. To see *her*.

Iyad felt like he'd been gut-punched. Maybe he did know the meaning of 'unbearable.'

CHAPTER SIXTEEN

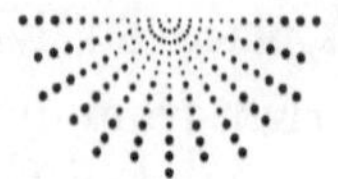

IYAD HAD A VOLUME CONTROL ON THE VOICE OF REASON IN HIS
head. For instance, when it told him to brush his teeth before he
ate in the morning, he listened. But when it told him this trip to
Hampton Court meant he would no longer be needed around
Fatima, he shut it off. Then, he took it to Currys PC World to
exchange it for a new model—one that didn't overthink as much
as he did.

"You okay?" He looked down at Fatima, who was fumbling
through her bag as their group came up on the palace's
entryway.

Iyad couldn't remember the last time he'd been to Hampton
Court. Its Tudor-style red-brick exterior, laced with Baroque-
esque details inside, as Tom had just finished describing to the
half-circle of students gathered around him, would always fasci-
nate Iyad. It made him wonder what it was like for Henry when
he'd lived in these quarters that were, in some way, big enough
to be considered their own little village.

"Yeah, the sun is just. . ." Fatima trailed off because maybe
her voice of reason needed to take a trip to Currys, too. It was
always making her forget things. Her glasses. Her pens. Him?

Reflexively, Iyad lifted his hand in front of her to block the sun so she could focus better. He'd made a mental note, not too long into knowing her, that she had a hard time with concentration. Logged it right alongside the ones saying she hated surprises and loved romance novels.

She took a deep breath and glanced over at Tom, who was still talking. "Thank you," she sighed, returning to her bag. "I can't find my glasses."

"Up top, maybe?" Impulsively, he grabbed them from her head with his other hand and passed them to her.

"Oh," she said, fitting them on her face, and then batting her lashes at him like a siren ready to tear him apart. "Thanks." At least, he told himself that she was batting her lashes at him. Really, she was probably still struggling against the sunlight.

"Someone ought to look after you," he said, losing his head just enough to make him speak his mind. Just a little.

"Are you talking about yourself?" she blinked, all coy and sinuous. This time, he couldn't blame the sun or his voice of (un)reason for all of the seismic activity he could feel shifting inside of him.

Iyad didn't answer.

"Anyway, let's be off. Our tour is just about to start," Tom was saying as Fatima closed her bag while Sadiyah took a few more pictures of the palace.

"Come on, Sads," Fatima hooked her arm with Sadiyah's, the long sleeve of her black dress fluttering slightly in the breeze as they strolled away from him.

His hand was still up from previously shading her when they left.

THE TOUR THROUGH HAMPTON COURT CONSISTED OF OBSERVING the architecture and *ooh* and *ahh*-ing whenever the docent shared a new fact. Iyad was awarded the task of blocking the girls whenever they wanted to take pictures of things they probably weren't supposed to, like King Henry's replicated crown, a deep purple velvet cap covered with gold, pearls, and different colored gems that they absolutely hadn't taken photos of.

But *if* they had, that would have been just an example.

They'd just stepped into the Great Hall and were being told how it was where most royal ceremonies were held, when the guide sidestepped into the topic of Henry's second wife, Anne Boleyn, who "lost her head" on charges of high treason.

"Why do they say she lost it like it was a set of keys?" Sadiyah muttered, folding her arms over her sweater. "They make it seem like she volunteered to be killed, not that her husband had her murdered when he couldn't get his way with her. I swear, men never surprise me."

Iyad arched an eyebrow, anticipating a touch of joy or anything to alleviate Sadiyah's sudden forlornness. Instead, after a few more historically annotated intervals, vis-à-vis the guide narrating the paintings along the walls that celebrated Henry's lineage and the achievements of the Tudor monarchy, Sadiyah just. . . sighed. Then, she rested her head on Fatima's shoulder, while Fatima clicked and double-clicked her pen between persistent notations.

Before long, they entered the kitchens—a wide room filled with rustic fireplaces and weathered stone walls that let in the light from the open windows above. In one corner, a spit roast turned slowly, cooking two pieces of already charred meat while historical reenactors meandered around, responding to tourists' questions.

Iyad peeked at Fatima's notebook as she circled the words "veritable hell" on the page, something they were told a Spanish visitor called the space because of the heat. He'd been realizing lately that he cared even less about all of this historical fuss than he'd initially thought, but he liked it when Fatima perked up after learning something new. Or, was it that he liked her?

Nope.

No.

No.

Lightly, he ducked his head down between her and Sadiyah, muttering, "I don't know what they're making, but my mum could do up a feast in here."

"Really?" Fatima asked, tilting her ear back to him.

"One hundred percent," he confirmed, squirming his pointer finger between them. "Rice and peas over there, oxtail in there, roast the chicken here," he drawled.

"Hang on," Fatima set her pen inside her notebook, closed the book, then snapped her head around. "You're Jamaican?"

Iyad blinked, trying to think through why she was asking so seriously. Had he missed the memo about her not liking Jamaicans? "Yeah?"

She opened her mouth as if to say something, then snapped it shut, making some strangled sound like a dog choking on a bone. Was she choking? Iyad made a mental note to learn CPR once he was sure she wasn't.

"What's your guys' background?" He tried to make sense of whatever gears were turning over in her head. "You Jamaican, too?"

Both of them blankly stared at him in response. "Post-slavery?" Sadiyah finally asked.

Fatima snorted, "I think they skipped over that lesson out here," she teased, laughing quietly. "Anyway, does she make escovitch? Your mom?"

Iyad gladly welcomed the return to the previous topic. "What?"

"It's fried red snapper with peppers and this kind of vinegary sauce on it," she explained.

"I know what it is." Iyad said wryly, then, "What?"

She took a breath. "What?"

"You realized I was Jamaican and the first thing you thought of was getting a plate of fish?"

"Well," she drifted her gaze back to the guide, and Iyad kicked himself because, silly as it was, he liked it when her attention was solely on him. "We were talking about food, and it *is* my favorite dish so. . ." She let the sentence hang there. Then, she turned back, letting her eyes, those dangerous pools of darkened honey, linger on his.

Iyad cleared his throat. Gathered himself. *Steady. Steady. Steady.* "So you *did* just want a plate of fish."

Sadiyah sputtered a laugh as Fatima returned to her notes.

"Maybe I just want to meet your mom," she shot back teasingly.

Iyad scoffed. Somehow, Fatima always managed to surprise him. For a moment, he thought of what his mom said about her and blurted out, "Maybe you should."

He thought he was joking with her, too, but the more the idea settled in his chest, the more he wasn't so sure.

THE LAST TIME IYAD WAS SURROUNDED BY THIS MANY FLOWERS and Fatima was at Kew Gardens, when things had gone royally kaput. Today had been a different story, though. He'd made sure of it. Something about being around Fatima made Iyad want to be better than he'd been lately.

Something about her turned his nerve endings into a dyad. Good. Bad. Happy. Sad. Being around her made him want to always choose the better alternative. He hadn't made a full one-eighty in his self-development yet by any means, but he was realizing that he needed to work something out. His dad would've wanted him to work something out. So, he decided to try.

"I didn't realize it was spring until I saw all these flowers," Fatima murmured.

Their class had been dismissed to explore the gardens that featured a myriad of tulips and soft-edged statues standing amid the hedges.

"Forgot it was March?" he asked, crunching a few rocks from the gravel underneath his trainers. "I thought the first of the month was payday?"

Fatima bit her lip, and Iyad quietly concluded that he liked that. "It is, and we were paid, bookie," she attested. "But I'm not sure. It's still as cold as when we got here most days, but that doesn't stop the fact that the seasons are still changing, and we'll have to leave soon enough. I don't think I'm ready to go yet."

Then stay.

Iyad scrubbed his beard, biting the inside of his cheek to keep from voicing his thoughts, when Sadiyah faced them, announcing profoundly, "We three should take a picture. Since Hampton Court is our spot, you know?"

"Why're you talking like that?" Fatima tilted her head.

Sadiyah tilted hers, too. "Like what?"

"Like Yad but. . . more."

"More?" Iyad spluttered. "When have I ever said something along the lines of 'We three?'"

Fatima stared at him with open fascination. "Really?" she deadpanned. "Half the time you sound like you're trying to make Shakespeare sound cool for kids."

Sadiyah's laughter spilled out almost immediately. "Couldn't have said it better myself. Now come on, Henry, put that wingspan to use." She handed her phone to him, and he snatched it warily.

"If I'm Henry, then who does that make the two of you?" Iyad asked, raising the phone above them all.

Fatima rolled her eyes, but not before Iyad distinctly saw her once him over. Twice. "Guess we'll have to find out," she told him.

AKA: He'd have to stay around to find out.

AKA: She wanted him to stay around to find out.
AKA: She *expected* him to stay around to find out.
AKA: TG was back in business, baby.

CHAPTER SEVENTEEN

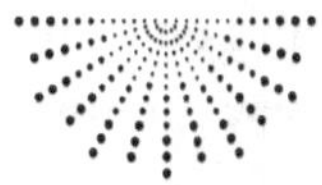

Fatima flicked her eyes to Claudette's office ceiling as Claudette continued to look through Fatima's most recent quarter of edits for *Control*. Today, they were focused on Fatima's suggestion that the book could potentially be given a happier ending. And Claudette was going out of her way to question every aspect of Fatima's idea.

"Does the ending truly have to go that way?" Claudette asked woefully, red pen poised over her manuscript copy. "Isn't a happily ever after just an exit strategy? A pandering effort for audience gratification? Is it even genuine?"

She spoke like the correct answer would be the only antidote to soothe her mental anguish, when in reality, Claudette was just cartoonishly dramatic. Still, she had a point.

Fatima thought about the differences in herself when she'd come to London and now. How she'd cried over Javier for breaking up with her and then deluded herself into believing he'd eventually want her back. How Iyad told her not to wait up.

You've got to put yourself first, and think of men afterwards, like meat. 'Cause once you go spoiling us, we get rotten.

Was it a happier occasion if Fatima continued to let go of

Javier? Was it wrong that, not so far behind the thought of putting herself first, she couldn't help but wonder what that'd mean for him?

"D: All of the above," Fatima smiled wryly. "I think stories are two-way streets for the person telling them and the one being told. So, being that this is a coming-of-age story, a happily ever after here would just be giving its agreed-upon resolution."

"Who's to say genre can't be subverted? Just because something's been done one way doesn't mean it can't be done another."

"But if there's still suffering when the whole point is to suffer *and then survive it,* then the plot is unresolved. And if it's unresolved, then either you've got a lazy writer with an incomplete story, or an incomplete story that's to be continued."

"Hmm," Claudette pressed her lips together and nodded. They'd been working on the draft for the past two hours, hovering over Claudette's conference table like helicopter moms shadowing their kids on a playground. "I wouldn't say laziness is the case here, though. For instance, maybe this story could benefit from a continuation."

Fatima shook her head. "You think Elle didn't go through enough to deserve something good by the end, yet?" There was a chance she was taking this all personally. Parallels, as Claudette had called it.

"No, I'm not saying that." Claudette huffed. "I'm just questioning if this is the time for it. Who are we to say that she doesn't get resolve for another five years, or so?"

"Then we'd recommend an epilogue for five years later," Fatima suggested. "This story doesn't need a sequel."

"Why not?"

"Because she learned her lesson." Fatima pointed out, realizing at the same time that there wasn't a chance she was taking this personally—she was.

Fatima only saw herself in Elle. She needed this character to make it through all of her bad days so Fatima could believe that she could, too. That was the reason why Fatima had fallen in love with reading to begin with. It wasn't just an escape for her; it was an answered question that she couldn't give herself. And she couldn't accept even the idea that the answer at the end of her story could also be to endure more heartache.

"But," Claudette continued to push, because it seemed she was never sated. "Are you saying it's enough because of the story being told or because of who's telling it?"

"Both." Fatima answered resolutely. "I think we tricked ourselves somewhere into believing that suffering is synonymous with artistry, and I don't think that's always helpful," she went on. "It feels like if artists aren't visibly troubled enough to cut off their ear or stick their head in an oven, then their work is somehow unworthy.

And for Black stories, it's worse because our rat race of overcoming generational trauma is overly consumed by folks who will romanticize it without ever understanding it. Which is why the major widely-marketed tropes in Black literature are really just reframed reminders of our oppression, since Black people are mostly ever constructs in the books that gain more popularity. It's like if we're shown as something that's not inherently real, then we won't think to evolve—even though we clearly do. It's not that they don't exist; we just don't have enough popularized defiances of our stereotypes. Of us just having fun, for example, because our joy can never just be an emotion if it's ultimately seen as a resistance."

"And so," Claudette wondered, "the best way to resist this resistance... is to resist?"

Fatima nodded. "Not to say the teen angst in *Control* is a bad thing, though. I still think we need that in Black fiction because we get more 'dead teen' than we need, you know? So if there's a chance to give ourselves something good, why not take it?"

For some reason, this must have been the smoking gun

Claudette was searching for; her lips parted into a smile, and her gold tooth winked at Fatima. "So then, we've got some work to do."

"What do you mean?"

"Elle's ending is still somewhat depressing in its current state. I agreed with your idea for a lighter ending, but I needed to be sure we were on the same page regarding the reasoning behind it. Considering the subject matter."

Fatima glanced out of the window; raindrops gently tapped against the glass, and a groan escaped her on impulse. She shouldn't have even been surprised that Claudette had just Jedi mind-tricked her into explaining her thought process.

"What? You don't agree?" Claudette's eyebrows knitted as she tilted her head.

"Huh?" Fatima blinked, a little disoriented from having so many thoughts colliding at once. "No, I just feel like you could've told me all of this from the get-go."

Claudette chuckled softly and jotted something down in the margins of her paper. "It's better when you have to work for it, don't you think?"

CHAPTER EIGHTEEN

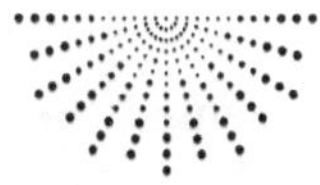

ONCE, BEFORE IYAD'S FIRST YEAR OF UNIVERSITY, HE BLEW OFF
anything to do with Azyaa in favor of hanging out with Mo in
Central London. Mo, who had just finished his A-levels, was the
more extroverted of the two. He always brought out that much-
needed social side of Iyad, who was never the biggest fan of
people, places, and things of that sort. Still, Iyad was eighteen
and wanted to have a good time. And since it was a given that
his cousin never needed to be baited into a good time, that's
exactly what the pair had dedicated themselves to: a night of
good, baseless fun.

They met up outside the Oxford Circus Underground
station, walking around as new songs like 'One Dance' by Drake
and 'Work' by Rihanna surged from the speakers of the shops
they'd passed. That was the night he'd met Layla: russet skin in
high heels that brought her right above his shoulders. Liberian.

Layla stood by the entrance of the escape room they were
heading into with her friend of a similar complexion and bone-
straight black hair by her side. Both were chatting with a
disheveled-looking man in a stained blue jacket who'd set up
camp right outside the door.

"You lot from round here?" he'd asked them, bloodshot eyes darting around like a fly dodging a good swat.

Anyone could tell how nervous both girls were, fidgeting about and such, but the man was only talking. He hadn't touched them. He hadn't yelled or done anything like that. Still, there were the optics. There was his father and uncle, who'd always told him to look out for anyone who ever seemed to need it. So, he and Mo slowed up near them. Just in case they did.

Layla must've swiftly deemed them to be the lesser of the two possible evils then, because almost immediately, she flung her arms around Iyad and greeted, "There you are! Hi, baby." She'd said it with a smile that seemed to say, *Sorry, but I'm out of options,* as she sweetly tucked a stray curl behind her ear and backed away.

Iyad glanced between her and the persistent man who repeated his question upon seeing more potential clientele. "You lot from 'round here?"

"Sod off, mate," Iyad told him crisply, because he wasn't going to pretend he didn't know the girls had already tried to get away from the man before he and Mo showed up, and that the guy was going out of his way not to take the hint.

"Listen, I've got. . ." the man trailed off, ignoring Iyad, too. He dipped his hands into his pocket and took out a little baggie with white powder that could've been cocaine as easily as it could've been baking soda.

On instinct, Iyad and Mo positioned themselves in front of the girls. They'd been getting the same "See it, say it, sorted"-type talk for years. Long before ever learning anything about birds and bees.

"Nah, nah, bruv," Mo waved him off, quite noticeably a little irritated at the prospect of having a good night ruined so early. "What'd he tell you?"

Wordlessly, the man cleared his throat, put the alleged coke-slash-baking soda back in his pocket, and with a dejected nod, left.

Iyad turned and noticed the two girls watching him and his cousin. He was just about to wish them a good night and escape into the escape room when Mo swung the door open and said, "Coming in?" This was commonplace with Mo, catching new friends wherever he went like Pokémon.

"Guess so," Layla responded, a coquettish grin accompanying her unmistakable appraisal of Iyad.

Not attempting to appear oblivious to her for a second, Iyad tipped the brim of the black New York Yankees cap Mo had insisted he wear on account of him being in desperate need of a cut. He could play ball if she wanted.

When they got inside, they all decided to try a Leonardo Da Vinci-themed escape room together. Iyad ducked off with Layla whenever there was a puzzle that required two sets of hands and hyped her up when she figured something out. Things were so different then. Having fun. Good, baseless fun.

So, when he noticed Mo leave Layla's friend (for the life of him, he couldn't remember her name) to go to the other corner of the small room to read something on his phone, Iyad focused more intently on the puzzles and Layla. He ignored the way Mo's eyes widened at the glowing screen because what good would it be knowing what suddenly flustered his unflusterable cousin?

He supposed that maybe that was why Mo came to him.

It could be argued that Iyad may have felt it coming on. Maybe there was some silent warning that went off inside of him that said, *This is your last chance. Enjoy. Enjoy. Enjoy.* Maybe Iyad never quite figured out what it was that had him so dedicated to staying so distracted, but apparently, he'd missed exactly fifteen phone calls from his mom and Uncle Hassan that night. He wasn't ignoring them—not consciously, he wanted to believe—his phone was just on vibrate. Could he really be at fault for that?

Either way, Mo ran over to Iyad just the same. And, do you want to know the best way to lose your head while solving puzzles next to a pretty girl? You find out that your usually calm, cool, and collected dad has been admitted to the hospital. It's coming up on ten at night, it's not looking good, and you and your cousin (who skipped out on your shop duties) are locked in an escape room that you haven't completely figured out yet.

Want to top it off? The game host won't let you out until you're screaming so loud that you don't even realize Layla and her friend have come to look about as scared of you as they did the man outside. Maybe more, honestly, but you can't find it in yourself to care. You just have a heart-throbbing need to get out. Get there.

Want to make it worse? You come to the best of your senses on the taxi ride over after convincing yourself that your dad will be okay once you see him. Once he knows you'll help out at the store more. Once it's not just him and Uncle Hassan. Once he knows you'll pull your weight. You'll stop buggering off. You'll do right by him. You will. You just have to see him. Tell him. Make him understand that this time will be different. This time you'll show up.

You spend the rest of the ride like that, unaware of when the rain starts or when it turns into a downpour. You're too busy muttering promises aloud and ignoring the cabbie who thinks you're drunk, telling you not to puke in the back of his car. You've long since forgotten about Layla and company. You barely remember that Mo is even there at all, his leg shaking like he's thinking of getting out and running to the hospital instead. You're focused. You're in the zone. You've made up your mind. You just have to see him.

And then you do.

But you don't.

Because that night's the night your dad dies. On your taxi ride over, he suffers the finale of his stress in the form of a heart attack at forty-one while you were out covering all of the wrong bases. Not only that, but amid the shock—or the horror, or whatever it could be called—you mistake your father's identical twin for him, for the first time in all your eighteen years alive. You tell him all of your promises. And you go absolutely feral when you realize they were all made to the wrong person, rendering them null and void.

Except. Are they? Really? Eventually, Iyad had to come to grips with the fact that he didn't have the right to throw Hassan to the wolves like that. He didn't have the right to give up altogether just because he wanted to. Just because it was easier for him. His uncle had to have been just as tired as his dad, and Mo didn't deserve to go through the same heartbreak Iyad did. So, they made unspoken amendments to the clauses Iyad created.

For instance, Iyad would let Mo continue to do whatever it was he wanted, so long as Hassan was there when Mo got home at night. Or, Iyad would be the perfect employee, so long as he didn't have to look his uncle in the eye again. He'd be a good man like his father asked of him. A praying man like his father taught him. A base-full man.

So long as he didn't have to remember that night.

Now, as Iyad stood across from Hassan at the shop counter while carefully folding a sea-green abaya to check out a customer, Iyad thought maybe he could work on extinguishing the fire still smoldering between them. For whatever reason, Mo wasn't in today. Not yet, at least. Meaning that without his cousin to act as a buffer, Iyad would have to try on his own.

First, he'd have to get his thoughts together. As Hassan cleared the queue, Iyad put his computer on the counter to work through his documents. Lately, his professor had been emphasizing the crucial role of positioning within a given project—its physical and digital placement, pricing, and other factors.

In terms of physical location, Ahmed Azyaa was doing great. So, he figured their potential for future trouble was in their digital landscape. Simply put, Ahmed Azyaa didn't have a digital landscape. They didn't have social media. They didn't have a website. He was sure that even making one hadn't occurred to his uncle, who could hardly even manage to unlock his phone on a good day.

Hassan was an analog man down to his core, so Iyad wanted to have at least one idea fully fleshed out before he brought anything to him. But maybe having some input on the ground floor was a good thing? Hassan was the one who'd initially found Azyaa's location, anyway. Maybe he had "the eye" all those articles Iyad had been reading kept talking about.

Iyad sighed while scrolling through Instagram, when Fatima's account popped up as a suggestion for him to follow: @fatimasays.jpg. He clicked it right as Hassan came up behind him.

"Well, isn't that a familiar face?" Hassan said, pretending to straighten out the stack of Qurans piled on the counter. "Guess you've repaired the unrepairable, nephew?"

Iyad never hit the back button on his browser tab faster. "No, I, erm," he started, but Hassan had already broken the rules of engagement by, well, engaging. He took a deep breath to steady himself. "I wanted to show you something, actually."

"Oh, yeah?"

"Yeah," Iyad confirmed and rubbed the back of his neck. "I was thinking in my classes of ways to improve Azyaa, and I've been working through some ideas, if you wanted to see."

Hassan nodded. "Of course."

Iyad went to Azyaa's profile page. Up to this point, he'd covered the essentials: the profile name was @ahmedazyaa with a golden calligraphed "A" as the logo set against a dark green backdrop. They had a biography detailing the shop's stock, location, and operating hours, as well as three posts showcasing the storefront, the bookshelf wall, and a display of hijabs. At best, they looked like a new account. At worst, a somewhat convincing bot.

"Mmhmm," Hassan said, after he'd finished reading the caption for the picture with their hijab display. Iyad's professor had advised him to highlight whatever he could, so the caption emphasized that most of their inventory was either handmade or imported from overseas, from places like Turkey.

Iyad scratched his head. "I know."

"You know what?"

"It's bad, innit? I should've come to you first, but I wanted to sort it out myself. I was even thinking of adding a website, but I think we'd have to pay for it, and I'm not sure if we should commission it or if I should try and code it myself. Here," he panted, taking a breath as he clicked over to one of his many spreadsheets. "I worked out the cost of production if we think of taking a website more seriously, but I figured Azyaa just needed to be on the social radar more, don't you?"

"Mm," Hassan hummed again, and Iyad had to nearly bite his tongue off to keep from filling in the silence with more of his rambling thoughts. "You sound like Hamza," he finally said.

Iyad quickly noticed that the comparison didn't sound like a good thing. "What?"

"Hamza was tough on himself, too. Everything always had to be perfect with him. That's why he—" Hassan looked at Iyad and shook his head at whatever comparison he'd just made between Iyad and his father. "Just go easy on yourself," he finished thoughtfully. "We can work this out together if you're interested? I can be as active as you'd like me to be," Hassan smiled, and Iyad felt the bubble of anxiety in his lungs burst open.

"Yeah," Iyad said, forcing himself to look at his uncle. "We should."

"We should," Hassan agreed, not breaking eye contact.

They were about four seconds into a near-staring contest, enveloped in a surprisingly easy silence, when Iyad's phone suddenly pinged.

"Excuse me." Iyad opened up their group thread, quickly forgetting his uncle was still there.

Ti:

> yad, did you know london bridge is actually in the states?

"Lon—?" Iyad narrowed his eyes at the screen, unsure of where she was headed.

Ti:

> does that mean the states have the better one, and y'all just got the leftovers? 🙃

"My days," he snorted. The corner of his mouth curved as he thought about how random she could be—and how much he looked forward to every passing idea she had. Iyad snuck a glance at Hassan, who was badly pretending to dust off the counter. Then, he messaged back.

Iyad:

> I'd say it means "y'all" got the mock-up.

> We got the finished piece.

Ti:

> agree to disagree.

> redcoat.

Iyad:

> Cute but wrong, Yank.

Sadiyah:

> 👀

Iyad's brows furrowed, trying to understand what Sadiyah was referring to, when he reread what he'd sent. Oh.

Iyad:

> The fact, I mean.

> The fact is cute.

> But wrong.

He was digging a ditch, but he couldn't stop himself. He couldn't let Sadiyah have a leg up on him.

Iyad:

> And you are a Yank.

He dug again.

Iyad:

You both are.

Ti:

lol, i'll let the fact be cute as long as we agree that i'm not wrong.

Technically, this time when he dug, it wasn't even on purpose. Iyad sent his reply at the same time that he'd received Sadiyah's. So, when she said:

Sadiyah:

You're beautiful and never wrong.

He said, literal nanoseconds later:

Iyad:

Exactly.

Iyad blinked, uncertain whether the situation needed mending at all since he technically agreed with the sentiment. Meanwhile, Hassan remained faithfully by his side, dusting the already dusted-off counter. Iyad knew almost immediately that his mother would find out about this interaction soon enough.

Ti:

i'll take the win.

oh, yad. when do you think you'll have time
to work on the project again? i've got some
ideas.

Iyad:

I'm free whenever.

Iyad looked up at the top of his screen. The chat's contact photo had been switched from that Spider-Man meme to the selfie they took together at Hampton Court. He had to squint to see it a little better. He was standing in front, his arm outstretched, with a widely smiling Fatima and Sadiyah behind him. Iyad hadn't realized until then that he and Fatima were matching that day; him in his black quarter-zip jumper, Fatima in her black dress. Sadiyah, in her own world, wearing purple.

Another text came in.

Ti:

kay, thanks yad. sads and i are shopping for
spring break, so i've gotta jet.

byeeeee

Iyad swayed some, suddenly a little lightheaded. Without giving himself any time to talk himself out of his reply, he wrote back.

Iyad:

Ciao bella.

Then, he quickly locked his phone and stashed it in his

pocket like it was covered in anthrax. Slowly, he looked up at his uncle, who didn't even last three seconds before laughing in his face.

CHAPTER NINETEEN

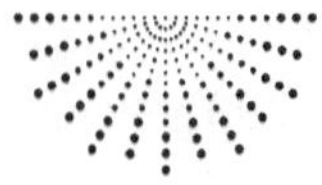

Fatima was never great at making friends—not the kind that lasted, anyway.

She did try, though. The summer before college, when Javier deserted her and she had no one to turn to, Fatima found a Facebook group for incoming first-year students at her university. She managed to get pretty close to at least five of them. But there was a big difference between online and offline personas that Fatima hadn't taken into account by the time they'd made it onto campus.

For example, Sadiyah's brother was usually a calm person, but all that went out the window when he talked about basketball, and especially when debating who was the best between greats like Kobe and Jordan. His excitement didn't mean that he wasn't being honest about his true nature; it just meant that, on a broader scale, there were always multiple facets to any one person. That, at least, should always be a basic assumption.

For Fatima, unfortunately, it wasn't. She'd learned quickly that she'd made a grave error that summer by being so active in those chats. By trying. Because, as she was so dearly told in a text message (the day after move-in when Fatima said she was too tired to hang out with the group she'd e-met immediately), that read a lot like an HR email letting her go from a job:

A friendship is a two-way street, and if you're not even willing to drive, then there was no point in buying the car. See you around! We wish you all the best. 🩶

Then, she was removed from the group chat.

She didn't have to be told that the English major had led the charge in writing that one. Fatima saw her in a lot of their classes, where she still talked almost exclusively in trite riddles. But, Fatima reasoned, at least they were kind enough to let her know they were done with her after she couldn't immediately meet their expectations. Javier just had a penchant for leaving her whenever he pleased.

Maybe that was why she clicked with Sadiyah so easily.

Sadiyah didn't have expectations of people. She didn't send wily HR text messages to so-called friends or wait around for seasonal boyfriends. And if she ever mentioned her dad, it was as the punchline to a joke. People were categorical with her.

Stay? Good. Don't? Still good.

So naturally, sometimes Fatima wondered what categories Sadiyah labeled her as. What boxes she ticked off to be filed away in her friend's mental cabinets. More than that, though, Fatima just wanted to know how Sadiyah did it—envied that she could, even. Sadiyah's innate ability to seem less breakable, less fragile, like Fatima tended to be, was a skill Fatima could only hope to learn one day.

"You're not paying attention to me." Sadiyah snapped Fatima out of her thoughts. "What's up?"

Fatima snorted. They'd just spent the day out shopping around for their spring break trip in two weeks and were finishing the day off at EL&N London café in all of its pink and rose-filled glory, after just leaving Primark. Fatima edged back in her seat and looked at Sadiyah as she sipped her cappuccino. "Why do you think we became friends? Really?"

"On second thought, I'm good with the silence," Sadiyah smirked. "I don't want to ruin your soap opera."

"The main character could never," Fatima told her, trying to look innocent. "So?"

Fatima watched as Sadiyah, wearing a pink hijab to match the cafe's decor for her pictures, grandly flung it over her shoulder and stretched across the table to cut out a piece of Fatima's chocolate cake with her fork.

"Because." Sadiyah took her time chewing her one forkful as if she'd force-fed herself the entire cake itself. Then she sighed, swallowed with great significance, and said, "Because I didn't want to be alone anymore, and I figured you didn't either."

"Mm." Fatima pressed her lips together, wary of saying the wrong thing and triggering Sadiyah's remarkable aversion to ever discussing human emotion. She knew full well she ought to be grateful for having salvaged even this much of a confession, since most sappy conversations tended to turn Sadiyah about as skittish as a raccoon under a streetlight. So she didn't push any further, though she really wanted to know what Sadiyah meant by "anymore."

Fatima knew something had happened not long after their freshman year began. Sadiyah had gone home over Thanksgiving break and came back. . . different in a way Fatima could never put into words—in a way Sadiyah would never explain. Maybe whatever happened then was what she was referring to.

"Speaking of how great we are together," Fatima said, pivoting back to the reason why they'd gone out for the day in the first place, "let's figure out our plans for spring break."

"Translation: *I* need to lock down our spring break plans." Sadiyah chided, visibly relaxing.

"Don't act like you don't enjoy it."

"I do," she admitted smugly, pulling out her phone and

maneuvering to some list she'd already made of what to do and where. "I was thinking we'd go to Paris and Barcelona."

Fatima thought over the options. Barcelona sounded good. Conversations with Javier had shown her that Fatima had developed a decent enough gauge of speaking Spanish to get around in Spain. She also knew the country was beautiful and that it had beautiful food she wanted to try. But then there was Paris, which she knew next to nothing about.

She picked up her fork and mechanically stuffed two scoops of cake into her mouth, imagining what it might be like there—*bonjour*-ing their way through Paris. A few *mercis* at the Eiffel Tower. Maybe an *excusez-moi* or two by the River Seine.

It could be fun.

It made her nervous—already being in a new country and preparing herself for two more—but it could be fun. And because that was exactly what she'd promised to commit to in Claudette's office, Fatima swallowed her doubts, put down her fork, and said, "I'm down."

CHAPTER TWENTY

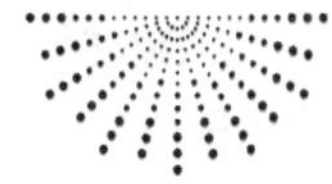

Iyad believed that hating rush hour was a worldwide phenomenon. Some things just warranted hatred. Rush hour in a hot, congested train that was getting hotter by the second, and ripe with the smell of chicken grease, seemed like as good a place as any to start.

He was only there because he'd gotten distracted earlier that afternoon, finalizing the website submission for his uncle to see. So far, Hassan liked his ideas for Azyaa so much that they'd implemented some of them into their everyday business design —and had already begun to see them gaining traction. But all Iyad could focus on was that he and his uncle were working together. That they were talking. Intentionally, even.

"Mind the gap," the train speaker's voice boomed over the crowd.

Iyad planted his feet and shifted his rucksack against his chest as he held onto the pole, bracing himself when the train lurched forward from Euston Station on its way to Azyaa. He'd been spending much of his free time working on things for the store when he wasn't there (or thinking about Fatima), building the social media platforms, researching market trends, SEO, and a lot of other things he hadn't cared about in years. But today was different because he'd worked himself into a husk *because* he was thinking about Fatima.

He was worried. Iyad was, by all accounts, a worrier. He knew this. Blame his dad for dying with no notice, for why Iyad now needed notice of everything. Worried about everything. Worried about him being on a train to Azyaa while two of the most directionally challenged people from North America to Europe were on a train to France.

Looking at it from the right angle, his worry was a good thing. It meant he had good sense. Therefore, it was as warranted as his disdain for this hot, cramped chicken grease metal box that he was currently stuck sweating inside of.

There wasn't an ounce of elbow room to take his jacket off, but there was loads of space and opportunity to pray they'd make it to their hotel, just as they were so sure they could. He knew he'd have to believe in them. But after meeting them, lost practically right in front of the building they were looking for, that was something easier said than done.

So, working on Azyaa to bide his time would have to do. He had to shoulder his stress somehow, and his family's business felt like the right place to turn to. Iyad smiled to himself. His therapist would be proud to see him now, all these years later, and he was late to work, not because he was too anxious to see his uncle, but because he was fixing something up *for* him. Wow. Sound the alarms. Bake this man a cake. Maybe the old Iyad was showing face again. Just a smidge. Just the good bits.

"Mind the gap."

The doors opened, and a lady who smelled like a cigarette came alive, slammed her bag into Iyad as she forced her way out. He couldn't even be mad. One stop to go, and she made for one less person breathing down his neck.

But then Iyad realized that this was his stop too, and, just like Miss Cigarette Smoke, he elbowed his way through the swarm of bodies onto the platform right before the doors snapped shut.

IYAD FOUND MO ARRANGING SOME BOOKS ON THE SHELVES WHEN he got to the store. He paused as the door chimed shut behind him, scanning the floor before walking over to his cousin. "It's just you?"

"Don't look so disappointed," Mo smiled expectantly. He'd been in a good mood lately. A better mood, really, if that were even possible for him.

"I'm not disappointed," Iyad countered, though a renegade part of him was. He shouldn't have been surprised that Hassan wasn't there. It wasn't like they'd planned for him to be there. Especially since Hassan was rarely ever around when Iyad was there anymore. For some reason, that fact bothered him now. "Just asking."

"'Just asking,'" Mo mocked, glancing behind him before leaning in. "You're late, by the way," he told him in a quiet voice, almost conspiratorially—no doubt delighting in the fact that, for once, he was on time when Iyad wasn't.

Normally, Iyad would've bucked back a little, reminding Mo of the many times he'd been there early and had to cover for him. However, he didn't care about that at the moment. He was currently battling a festering urge scrambling within him that made his mind keep crawling back to Fatima instead.

It was clear that Iyad had a hard time rationalizing his thoughts when it came to her, mainly because he *shouldn't* have been having thoughts of her at all. Fatima's only significance to Iyad should've fallen comfortably under one domain: their project. With a special provision for their tangential group chat on occasion, but that still would've brought them all back to square one: their project. Somehow, he felt like he'd hopscotched his way right on over to square eight hundred and seventy-nine when it came to his thoughts of her, and he had no clue where that'd landed him.

"I've been busy," Iyad sighed.

All he needed was one little text that said they'd made it. Then, maybe, he could breathe a little better. Iyad checked his phone, willing that exact message to appear, but alas, nothing.

Mo grinned. At the phone. At Iyad. He said, primly, "I bet you have been."

Suddenly, Iyad felt a bit caught. "I don't know what you're insinuating—" he started to say something, but the words wouldn't click into place the way they were meant to. It was most likely a lie, though, whatever it was that he was working toward. Actually—definitely. It was definitely a lie.

Mo grinned again. At the phone. At Iyad. Then, to the customer in their peripheral vision who was headed to the counter to check out the cream thobe he had stretched across his arm. They'd both spotted the man at the same time. Growing up at Azyaa gave them a shared sixth sense for such things.

"I'm not insinuating anything," Mo continued quickly. "Noticing? Yes. Assuming this has something to do with Fatima? Maybe. Insinuating? Not at all." Then he grinned. Again. For the third time. Iyad really hated that smug look of his sometimes. Nearly as much as he hated rush hour trains.

Iyad followed behind his cousin, who was headed to ring the man up. In the time it took him to run into the stock room, put down his jacket and rucksack, check his phone for mothballs, and come back to the floor, Mo had already finished the transaction.

"So," Mo began, a little too expectantly. "Wagwan?"

"Mohammad," Iyad answered slowly. "Fatima *and Sadiyah* are going to Paris today. I was just checking to make sure they made it."

The thing was, he knew they hadn't. They wouldn't be there

for maybe another half hour if there were no problems on the way before they were even in the city. But. What if there were problems on the way?

God. This was getting pathetic.

"As a friend?" Mo asked through narrowed eyes, clearly unconvinced.

"What else?" Iyad countered with just about as much conviction as a rock floating on water.

As far as he could tell, Iyad and Fatima were just friends. Even thinking of complicating that fact any further, while knowing she was still caught between her ex and questioning her religion, just seemed unfair to do. Especially when she'd be back in the States soon enough. And he'd still be here.

Mo snorted, not the least bit moved, but he graciously allowed Iyad the space to live in his safe bubble of delusion and believe otherwise. "Dad says you've been working on some brand things together," he cocked his head to the side in question.

"We have," Iyad nodded. "I was using Azyaa as a model to work from in class, then I just," he squinted, thinking, "kept it up, I guess."

"And now the pair of you are in cahoots?" Mo probed interestedly.

Iyad didn't know what to say. Frankly, he didn't know *what* was going on. Or, if "cahoots" was a word that'd define it. But he wasn't mad about it. Whatever "it" was. Mo didn't seem to be either.

HOURS LATER, AFTER MO AND IYAD HAD CLOSED UP SHOP AND Iyad was back in his bedroom watching TV, Iyad's phone began to buzz.

Ti:

> made it to our hotel!

> almost couldn't find our uber, lol. the station is
> confusing, and our driver spoke as much
> english as we do french—but we did it!

He found himself staring at the screen for way longer than he'd care to admit. Happy she'd actually thought to message him at all. Until then, he'd just been hoping she would.

Iyad:

> Glad to hear it. Be safe out there.

> Also, I can pick you two up from the airport.
> Where should I be and when?

Ti:

> we should be fine, but thanks for thinking
> of us.

Sadiyah:

> I'll take the free ride. Let's let Tweedledee
> figure it out for herself.

Sadiyah sent him their details: 7 April, 8 pm, at Terminal 5, Heathrow Airport. To which Fatima responded:

Ti:

Iyad:

> Dirty.

> I'll be there.

He put his phone down before it occurred to him to clarify.

Iyad:

> For both of you.

Ti:

> do you mind if i share my location then? it'll be easier for you to find us that way.

> especially if we get lost. . . again. lol.

He didn't mind. Iyad really, really didn't. Iyad replied, reminding his heart to beat steady. Steady. Steady.

Iyad:

> Of course.

> See you then, Ti.

CHAPTER TWENTY-ONE

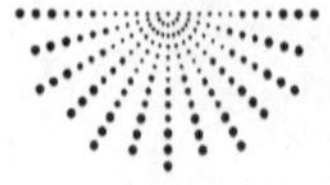

SADIYAH HAD BEEN WEARING HER HIJAB OFFICIALLY SINCE THE DAY after she'd gotten her period in her eighth-grade trigonometry class. She'd been excited to finally have her official start at wearing it, but her enthusiasm quickly waned when the stares began. When she realized she wasn't Sadiyah anymore, and had become "Scarf Girl."

In the beginning, she made a game of the way people looked at her, trying to decode what each glance her way could've meant. For instance, Sadiyah would try to theorize if they were just curious about her. More like, she was desperate for them to be. Because being curious meant being clueless, and Sadiyah's beating little scientist heart could understand that—the need for information. Welcomed it, even.

The trouble was that sometimes a look of curiosity and a look of contempt were just about the same. There was only the slightest difference in the way the face contorted. Curiosity was genuinely interested, like a child inspecting a new toy. Contempt was a bit more like someone smelling rotten fish and barely being able to conceal the fact. She'd seen them both enough times from strangers and people she'd thought of as friends to tell the difference. She'd seen the latter all day as she and Fatima traveled across Paris.

Sadiyah fixed the black and gold pashmina she'd gotten from Iyad's family shop along her face. She'd gotten used to people watching her over the years, but it still made her anxious sometimes. It still made it hard for her to breathe. To swallow. Sometimes, being watched so closely made the material of her hijab feel like a boa constrictor tightening its body around her neck. Sometimes—and she only ever admitted this quietly to herself— she wondered about taking it off. Would there be anything to stare at, then?

She let out a quiet sigh as the wind picked up around her. To her left, the Eiffel Tower was sparkling white and gold against the night sky while she and Fatima had themselves a little picnic on the grass at the Champ de Mars. It was the end of their first legitimate day out in Paris, and after tomorrow, they'd leave for a week away in Spain. So far, they'd already visited Versailles, strolled outside the Notre Dame Cathedral, and had the best fresh-squeezed orange juice Sadiyah had ever tasted in her life.

Now, they sat by the Eiffel Tower enjoying crêpes from a little kiosk they'd found not too far away, as Sadiyah proceeded to have a quiet little panic attack about something she'd already had years to get over. This was something she was supposed to be good at—ignoring people's curiosity, contempt, or whatever else it was. But she couldn't now. The way people's eyes stayed glued on her while she'd been in Paris had just felt too familiar. It made her feel like a kid again. Small. And alien.

Still, Sadiyah was desperate to enjoy her "holiday," as the British called it. So, she pushed down her feelings because they weren't helpful to what she'd planned. To her two-day itinerary. Or her carefully studied directions.

Or her work.

Her time.

Her effort.

Her silently whispered pleas for the looks from everyone around her to just

stop.

When Sadiyah came home from school in tears because her first day wearing her hijab hadn't gone as well as she'd hoped, her mom gave her a mantra: Skin and bones. The mantra wasn't to say she was better than anyone else; it was to make it clear that she was just as special in her own right. But when Sadiyah kept crying because she couldn't let go of those negatively placed stares, her mother explained it further:

A person is just a person at the end of the day, baby. Skin and bones, she'd said. Sometimes folks don't do better because they don't know better—they weren't taught it. But you were. So let them make you their business if they want to, but don't go and make them any of yours.

Skin and bones. Sadiyah never let go of that.

She bit into her crêpe, and a smidge of chocolate fudge oozed out, falling onto the lawn, just as a vendor selling miniature figurines of the Eiffel Tower tried to offer her and Fatima a pair.

"No, thank you," Fatima shook her head, then turned to Sadiyah. "Is it good?" she laughed, reaching into her purse, no doubt in search of a sanitary wipe.

"It- what?" Sadiyah blinked herself all the way back to the present, feeling the melted chocolate at the corner of her mouth. She wiped it off with the pad of her thumb. "Were you saying something?"

Fatima gave her a deeply probing look. "I was saying," she shrugged dramatically, handing Sadiyah the wipe. "If this science thing doesn't work out for you, you should seriously look into vacation planning. Or something like it, at least. You're good at putting things together."

"I am, aren't I?" Sadiyah considered that for a moment. "So

many talents, so little time," she drawled, cleaning off the sides of her mouth, then her hands.

"Now you're fishing."

"Correction: I am a fisherman. Fisher*woman*, technically. But you know, semantics."

Fatima rolled her eyes.

Sadiyah, beaming brighter than the Eiffel Tower's flickering lights, asked, "Do you think your boy—"

"My *what?*" Fatima practically squawked.

"Is alright?" Sadiyah continued. "Poor guy almost had an aneurysm when we said we were leaving London."

Fatima bit into her crêpe. "I know, he's adorable."

"*Adorable,* huh?"

"Fisher. Woman," Fatima deadpanned. "I just mean that it's nice that he thinks of us."

"You."

"*Us. We.*"

"*Oui?*" Sadiyah's mouth twitched. "Hm, then I'd have to agree. Yes, it is nice that he thinks of you."

Fatima just shook her head, very clearly trying to hide the half-smile ghosting over her lips. Despite her efforts, a soft chuckle still escaped.

"I told you I like him," Sadiyah reminded her lowly, finishing her food off. "And I have good taste, you know. It's one of my many talents. Not one of my mom's," she smirked. "But *oui,* definitely one of mine."

"I bet," Fatima agreed, her poorly covered smile still showing. "Doesn't change the fact that he's just as much of my friend as he is yours, but you're right when you're right. He is a good guy."

Sometimes Sadiyah couldn't tell whether her friend was genuinely clueless or just pretending to be. She was quiet for a moment, thinking of how best to prod at her friend's obviously growing crush. "Wanna send him a picture so he knows you're good?"

"Yeah, okay." A glimmer flickered in Fatima's eyes just before they widened. "Wait, no. But we can take a picture *of* us and *for* us only." Fatima shook her head, muttering under her breath. "You think you're so slick, don't you?"

Sadiyah tried to hold back her laughter as she opened the camera on her phone. "Almost had you. "

She took their selfie with the tower shining beautifully behind them, its light catching the gold-flecked patterns in her hijab. Photo in hand, Sadiyah looked from the picture to her friend—someone who had always seen her for who she was, not just the fabric on her head—and smiled.

CHAPTER TWENTY-TWO

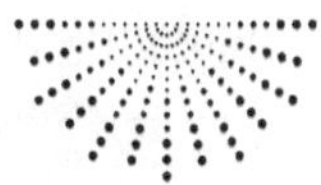

MARCH GAVE WAY TO APRIL IN SPAIN, WHERE FATIMA FOUND
herself struggling to catch her breath as she trudged her way up
the steep hill to Park Güell. She dropped her head between her
legs as she gasped for air, one hand on her thigh, the other
pressed against the wall beside her, streaked with brightly
colored graffiti. In the process, her ponytail whipped around,
nearly slapping her in the face as it swung through the empty
air in front of her.

"This is just sad," Sadiyah said as a woman walked past them
with what felt like the fifth dog Fatima had seen in the past five
minutes.

"If you must know," Fatima lashed out—or tried to, because
how effectively can one really lash out while wheezing?—"I'm
trying my best."

"If *you* must know," Sadiyah maintained. Her voice was
annoyingly even because she was annoyingly fit. She continued,
"Your best is is. . ." Sadiyah paused to take an obviously needless
breath, quickly reminding Fatima that she was also annoyingly
theatrical when she wanted to be, "sad?"

"Choke, Mitchell. Just choke."

Rather than choke, Sadiyah snorted and draped Fatima's arm across her shoulders to hold her up. "We're almost there," she encouraged her, matching Fatima's slow steps as they began to climb again, because in addition to her annoying qualities, she was also one of the best people Fatima had ever known.

Fatima shielded the sun's glare with her hands after finally cresting the hill, where she had all but begged the conveniently placed vendors to sell her a water bottle, since she'd forgotten her own and was ravenous. Finally clear-headed, she looked around her to see that Park Güell was even more beautiful than the Cheetah Girls had made her believe when she was younger. It was golden palm trees and whimsical mosaics. It was the view of the city with the morning sun's glow cast over it. It was just. . . something. If something could be everything, all at once.

Not just Park Güell, but that her current reality had stretched from living in England to hiking around Barcelona and witnessing some of the most beautiful sights she'd ever seen firsthand. It was a reality she was happy she'd never given up on.

"I'm sorry I couldn't get us in," Sadiyah said, which was true; she couldn't. They were currently standing at the park's outskirts because tickets had sold out fast, and they couldn't get their hands on any while they were in the country.

Fatima took another swig of her water, still hot and winded. "Close enough," she said as a pigeon waddled by.

"You're right," Sadiyah chuckled, "you probably never would've been able to tell if I'd never told you."

Fatima nodded, "Exactly, so stop worrying," she told her, eyeing a bench under a vine of purple wisteria flowers climbing alongside the rock columns. "Come on, let's talk for a second."

She closed her eyes once they'd sat down, breathing deeply. There'd been something scratching at the edges of her mind lately, and something about those flowers waving above her finally made Fatima want to give that feeling a voice. Or maybe it was the fact that she realized she hadn't genuinely thought of Javier in weeks, and that she loved it. Maybe it was all of that combined. "I think I want to do it," Fatima nearly whispered.

"Do what?"

"My Shahada."

Sadiyah's eyes saucered. "You- what?" It was safe to say that on the list of things Sadiyah probably thought would've sprung from Fatima's mouth, saying she was ready to be Muslim again hadn't made the cut.

Fatima just shrugged, working out what to say next. This had been a clear thought in her mind and maybe even between her ribcage, but not on her tongue. Not until now. "I know this sounds sudden, but it's not. I've been thinking about this ever since the day you had Iyad meet us over at the South Bank. We talked about Islam for a little while, and I basically told him it was too late for me to practice again."

"What'd he say?"

"Wa Huwa ma'akum ayna maa kuntum," Fatima recited. "It sounded a lot better coming from him, but it means, 'And He is with you wherever you are.' I'm the only factor that ever changed, but God's been stagnant the whole time—while I was practicing and wasn't. I hadn't lost Him like I thought I had. I wasn't. . ." she swallowed, "given up on. So I don't think I want to give up anymore, especially when most of the reason I did so in the first place was because of what people thought of me. Not what I thought of myself."

Sadiyah nodded as if Fatima had just said the most profound thing. "I knew I liked that kid."

"Kid?" Fatima masked a smile. "He's older than us."

"What's your point?" Sadiyah tilted her chin.

Fatima shook her head and took another breath before she lost her nerve. Today didn't seem to have enough oxygen for all of the physical and mental exertion she'd been putting in.

"I used to think religion at all was too stuffy," she continued. "Like, if I was doing what I wanted, then I wasn't doing anything right. And if I wasn't doing anything right, then I didn't deserve to follow anything at all, you know?" Sadiyah continued to nod her on. "But I've been thinking about how I've been doing everything I've wanted lately, and how you've always been right there with me. *You* seem fine. You seem—"

Fatima stopped herself, careful not to say the wrong thing. "I know you're not always fine. I know that's impossible. But I also don't see you constantly looking over your shoulder to be perfect—even though that's exactly what I said you were. I'm sorry for that," she amended.

"I know there's no such thing as a perfect Muslim, and I know you're just trying your best. So, I was thinking maybe I could give it a second go around without pressuring myself to be anything beyond what works best for me, too. Maybe that'll work out for the better, you know? I even brought the hijab that Iyad's uncle gave me here because I really do miss it all. And I want to try again." She met her friend's eyes to see that Sadiyah was still nodding along, fresh tears staining her cheeks.

Fatima stared, slack-jawed. "Bro," she questioned, poking at Sadiyah like she was some foreign object. "Did I break you?"

"Shhh," Sadiyah hushed her, then tilted her head back regally, and dabbed the tears away with the backs of her thumbs. "I just found out that I'm your role model, let me bask in this."

"When did I say that exactly?"

"It was between the lines."

"Between the letters, you mean?"

"So, you agree you said it, too?"

"You're unbelievable," Fatima wrinkled her nose to keep from laughing.

"I'm a delight," Sadiyah corrected, spryly.

Fatima rolled her eyes. But she was grinning. Yesterday, they visited the Arc de Triomf, where one man played 'Despacito' by Luis Fonsi on the violin, and another had set up an entire area to waft bubbles around. None of it felt real. All of the sun. The trees. The music and bubbles passing by her. It occurred to Fatima then that it'd been warm every day of their trip, and hadn't rained once in the entire time since they'd been away from London. Maybe something about a clear sky really did trigger a clear head like those mental health websites claimed.

"Mm," she agreed.

THREE DAYS LATER, FATIMA WAS DIGGING FOR SEASHELLS TO ADD to the necklaces she and Sadiyah had picked up after leaving Park Güell. Each necklace had a white circular pendant decorated with purple flowers—one engraved with a gold 'F' and the other with a gold 'S.'

She and Sadiyah were walking along the shoreline of Varador Beach in Mataró, where they were staying about an hour outside of Barcelona. It was the end of their final day in Spain, and the sun was setting, casting ebbing shades of burnt orange into the bright blue ocean waves that lapped against the sand.

Since Park Güell, Sadiyah hadn't mentioned Fatima's confession. Thankfully, she understood that these things take time. Fatima had been taking her time, though. At this rate, she could've even won an Olympic gold medal for it. Still, no developments.

Ten cuidado, her little heart beat the words out like Morse code, reminding her to be careful.

She'd been saying those two words to herself for the past three days during visits to places like the Magic Fountain of Montjuïc, the Museu Picasso, and with a belly full of papas bravas and paella. She was being so careful. But what was she being careful *about?*

Javier came to mind.

It'd been a while since she'd last heard from him. Thought of him, even. But once she got started, he was a dream—no, nightmare—stuck on repeat. Thinking of him was a problem for her. *He* was a problem for her.

He was her friend. Before. Fatima thought of him just as tenderly as she thought of Sadiyah. Before. Before they were dating. Before she was his. Before he was hers. Before. Before. Before. Back when Fatima should have known better.

She should've known to be careful when she told him she was feeling behind, left out, and like she was progressing at a snail's pace compared to everyone else their age back when they were in high school. Fatima wasn't anything close to popular then. She didn't go to parties. She didn't wear the same clothes as the girls her age. She got attention, but never the kind she wanted. So, it was Javier's idea, one day, the characteristic one-eighty.

Stop covering, that's what he'd told her. *You don't need religion. You need a man,* he said. *Get with me. I'll love you.*

He begged for all of her attention for so long that it'd become a routine between them. And once he finally got it—once he'd manipulated her into letting her guard down, into letting him in—he threw her out like garbage over and over, and always with some weak excuse that he retracted the second it was convenient for him to have her back in his life.

"What about these?" Sadiyah asked, holding two coral-toned seashells in her cupped palms.

"Let me see," Fatima reached for one, inspecting it closely. The crack inside was just big enough for the chain of her necklace. "Perfect," she took her necklace off and slipped the line through.

"I know. I found them," Sadiyah smirked, doing the same.

"You're so full of yourself," Fatima said, reaching behind her neck to clasp the necklace shut.

"I am, but in a good way."

"There's a good way?"

"Of course," she winked. "There's good and bad to everything. Pretty Boy, for instance, is the worst of *many* things."

"Stop," Fatima muttered. She'd walked straight into that one. "I mean. . . maybe you're right."

"I *know* I'm right," Sadiyah snorted. "*You* know I'm right. Who am I? 'Go to London, Ti.' 'It's fine, Ti.' 'I get it, Ti.' 'You don't love me anymore, Ti,'" she echoed some of the pitiful lines she'd overheard Javier whine to Fatima way too many times before their trip.

Fatima laughed. She actually tilted her head back and laughed. "Do you know," she was still laughing, "how traumatizing it was to love him?" *Was?* "He told me one time he wished I'd apologize for wanting to come out here."

It was one of those times when everything was so unbelievably unfunny that it was also the funniest thing in the world.

Sadiyah made a motion with her hand like she was swiping a card. "Charge it to the game, ukhti," she told her with a lopsided grin.

Fatima mirrored the gesture. Still laughing. Still in Spain. Still unbelievably happy. "I haven't texted him in so long," she breathed.

"And do you miss him?" Sadiyah asked her.

"I think I'm just used to him," Fatima answered. It'd occurred to her that she wanted to be done with Javier. For real this time. And there was only one way to prove to herself that she meant it. "Hey, let's do it."

Sadiyah blinked and cleared her throat, regrouping. She knew exactly what Fatima was talking about because she always knew exactly what Fatima was talking about. "You're sure?"

Fatima just nodded, extending her pinky.

Sadiyah wrapped hers around it, then stamped it with her thumb.

Not too long after, somewhere along the beach's coast, Fatima Sommers decided for herself. Then, she was Muslim again. And, for some strange reason, she really wanted to tell Iyad. But that was ridiculous, to think of him at all.

Much less first.

CHAPTER TWENTY-THREE

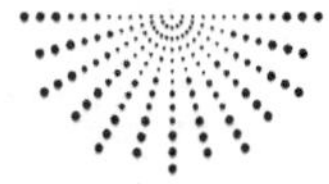

THE SEVENTH OF APRIL TOOK PRECISELY SEVEN YEARS TO COME about. Not that Iyad was counting, of course.

He was currently in his dad's old Volvo, en route to pick up the girls at the airport. Iyad couldn't remember the last time he'd sat in this car, a low, light-blue station wagon. Whenever he went home, he barely even looked at it as he passed by it in the drive. It never moved from there. His mom didn't know how to move it from there, and he didn't want to move it from there—another thing caught in the Hamza-less limbo.

Iyad drummed his thumbs against the steering wheel. Farah refused to let go of the car under the far-fetched belief that Iyad would eventually find use for it on some rainy day or other. Today had coincidentally been exactly that: a rainy day.

She'd made the biggest deal out of his coming over for the key, demanding: Where was he going? Why was he going there? With who? Who? WHO? After answering enough questions to satisfy her, Iyad sank into their living room sofa, summing everything up with, "It's not a big deal."

Although it felt like one.

Although Farah made sure he knew it was one. "Not a big

deal?" Farah crossed her arms, sounding incredibly doubtful. "You've been a hermit for all these years. Suddenly, these girls show up, and you're picking them up from the airport?" She clicked her tongue, slipping into the Patois her mother used to speak all of the time. "Yuh tink mi cyaan seet?"

Iyad held his breath, wishing the couch would come alive and swallow him whole.

"Lovely girls," she said under her breath, repeating what Hassan had called them months ago. Then, she brightened. "She is. Isn't she, Yaddy?" Farah didn't give him time enough to answer or even acknowledge her sudden change from plural to singular. "Alright now, up you get. Don't want to keep her waiting now, do we?"

Iyad sighed as the windscreen wipers scraped the rain from the car's glass. If he'd done his maths right—and he always did his maths right—then he'd waited just long enough that they should've gotten through the border by now, and were on their way outside. So, he sent a quick message to their group chat.

Iyad:

Here yet?

Ti:

you actually came?

Sadiyah:

Of course he did.

On the way out.

Iyad couldn't explain it, but there was something unnerving about how even the most minor things he did constantly seemed to shock Fatima. The way her knee-jerk reaction to every little thing he'd done for her so far was to overthink it. What did her ex do to make her doubt she deserved anything good?

He checked the back seat to make sure both umbrellas his mother had told him to bring were still there before driving up to wait near their terminal. She'd said she wanted to be sure every impression he'd made on "her" was a good one. She even packed a Tupperware box filled with fried dumplings for the ride back to the girls' homestay. He popped the lid open and snuck one for himself just as someone came and knocked on the car's window.

"Yes?" he asked, rolling it down.

It was a freckled man with red hair covered by a clear poncho. "So sorry, mate, but we need you to move if you're not picking anyone up yet."

Iyad was just about to agree and loop around when he saw them. Saw her. Saw Fatima in a black tracksuit and

hijab?

"S- sorry," he stammered, pointing behind the man. "They're right there. I see them."

The man nodded and backed away. Iyad quickly grabbed the girls' umbrellas, lifted his jacket hood, and hurried out of the car with the dumbest grin known to man on the verge of breaking out just from seeing Fatima. He took in a deep breath, swallowed it, and said to himself, *It's calm. It's calm. Be calm.*

Iyad watched as they looked around almost comically for where he was. It was clear that the pair of them might have gotten through France and Spain well enough, but he failed to believe that it was due to their attentiveness. He jogged up to them and held one of the umbrellas over their heads just as they stepped out into the rain.

They stopped for a moment, realizing that the rain hadn't touched them yet, and then turned around. Iyad found himself transfixed the moment Fatima's eyes met his.

If he'd been a betting man, he would've bet all his money that time had never moved as slowly as it did in that moment. If he'd been a gambling man, he would've gambled that when Fatima turned and looked up at him with those eyes—those eyes brimming over with amber-tinted sunlight—no eyes had ever shone like that in all of humanity.

He squinted, realizing then that it was hard to accept that he thought of her as nothing more than a friend. "As-Salamu Alaykum, you... two?"

Fatima smiled at him, and she was all he saw in that instant.

"Let's make a trade," he worked his jaw, focused on saying the right things instead of any one of the billion questions forming and reforming about what possibly could've happened on holiday for her to come back wearing a hijab. "Bags for the brolly, deal?"

Fatima seemed so caught off guard by his being there that, for once, she didn't immediately doubt him. "Deal," she accepted, handing her things over along with Sadiyah.

"So- you," Iyad was tripping, stumbling, falling over syllables. He cleared his throat, trying to make it seem like this wasn't at all overwhelming. Like it wasn't a big deal when he was pretty sure, in fact, there'd never been a deal even marginally bigger than whatever had gone on during their holiday. "You... erm, yeah? D- d- dumplings?"

Good God, the man was hopeless.

He waved the Tupperware container between the two of them, keeping his eyes on the road as he drove. "My- my mum made 'em."

Sadiyah snorted behind him, and he shot her a look in the

rearview mirror as she grabbed the box, effectively not caring about his glare one bit. But she was also quiet now as she ate, so that had to count for something.

Beside him, Fatima wasn't moving, her gaze fixed impassively out of the passenger-side window. She'd gotten incredibly still once Iyad began to drive, except for her leg that was bouncing restlessly, and it reminded him of the accident she'd told him about with her ex. That it'd been raining when it happened. Was she thinking about that? Was she thinking about him?

Iyad cleared his throat. There was a part of him, a rather large part of him, that wanted to know how on earth she was sitting next to him with a hijab on her head. He wanted to know what happened, why it happened, and what it meant. He wanted to know *if* it meant there might be a chance their friendship didn't have to end with a period anymore. Maybe a comma? Maybe. . . well, he didn't know exactly what because he didn't know words and things like that the way she did. But he wanted to. If she liked it, he wanted to learn it.

That wasn't important, though. Not now. Iyad knew sometimes Fatima got lost in her own head, but this time felt different. Bigger, somehow. She was shaking, quiet little tremors like a fault line splitting open, and it occurred to him that she was afraid.

"Ti?" he ventured, and she crossed her arms together, not saying anything. He cleared his throat. Hard. "Ti," he repeated.

She jumped a little and said, "Huh? Yeah? What's up?" Her accent was much more noticeable then, anxiety betraying how tense she must've felt.

Iyad started learning to drive with his dad when he was around fifteen. Half of those lessons had been in the rain because Hamza insisted that Iyad should know how to hold his own in case of a sudden downpour—since London was nearly entirely made of sudden downpours. So, Iyad wasn't fazed by the weather. He would've been driving the same had the sky been clear. But he didn't know how to say that to her. He didn't know how to tell her she could relax. That she was okay with him. So, he decided to change the subject.

"Remember that book you were reading back at the South Bank? The yellow one. Opposite something," he wondered. "Did you finish it?"

She tilted her head toward him. "*Opposite of Always?* Yeah, I finished it on the plane coming back here," she smiled a little, but her leg was still shaking. "Can't believe you remembered that," she whispered.

"'Course, I did. What was it about?"

Fatima didn't say anything for a full ten seconds. Iyad knew because he'd counted each one of them to stop himself from watching the rabbit thump of her leg.

"So," she started. He waited. "So there's Jack and Kate, right?" He nodded attentively. "Jack goes to a college party for a school he's planning to attend, and that's where he meets Kate, and—" she swallowed. He waited. "It's a love at first sight type of story, that's all."

"That's all?" he gaped because it couldn't be. Because her leg was still shaking. Because they weren't at their homestay yet. His GPS said there was still time to go.

"I don't want to bore you," she smiled halfheartedly. Why did she get like this with him? He once heard her ramble on to Sadiyah about a scrunchie, but telling him about a book she'd read was where she drew the line?

"Good, 'cause you can't." His nose crinkled as he picked up the Tupperware again, inviting her to try a dumpling. Fatima took one out and bit down. She smiled, and he knew she meant it because he knew what those dumplings tasted like.

"These are good," Fatima said. "Tell your *mum* thanks," she smirked, eating another.

"So Jack goes to a party. . ." Iyad prompted her, quietly

pleased that she wasn't shaking as much anymore. Maybe he'd always have a few dumplings on standby from here on out. If that's what she needed.

"Yeah, so he goes to a party and meets Kate, and you think you'll get this easy love story, but nope, Kate has sickle cell anemia and dies from it. When she dies, it starts this recurring time loop where Jack has to relive that same day up until the point where she dies again to try and save her." She looked at him, waiting, and it occurred to Iyad that she was trying to see if he was paying attention.

Seriously, what had that guy done to her to make her switch so fast from one of the most terrifyingly sure people he'd ever known to someone so insecure?

He sat up straighter, and she continued. "But I don't think the point was ever only to save her. I think she died so early in the book that you'd already expect it. So then, the story could be more about learning to accept life as it is by looking for those happy moments between the beginning and end of the story, rather than the be-all and end-all happily ever after."

"So, there wasn't a happily ever after?"

Fatima thought for a moment. Iyad noticed her leg was perfectly still now. "There was," she went in for another dumpling, then said, "I really liked it. It was just a book that happened to be about two Black kids in love, not one that existed solely *because* of them being Black, you know?"

He nodded, too scared to talk and lose their momentum.

"I might tweet him about it. I saw he responds to people sometimes," she continued.

"What would you say?" he asked.

She laughed, and it was the best sound he'd heard all day. "I don't know, we'll just have to see if I even do it."

"You should," he urged. "And then tell me about it."

"I will."

. . .

SHE DID.

The next day, Tom took the class to the Tower of London to show them the Crown Jewels and discuss their related history. All Fatima seemed to care about was the prisoners, though. Specifically, she was fixated on Anne Boleyn, Henry VIII's second wife, who was tried and convicted on fabricated charges of adultery and incest that led to her eventual beheading at the Tower.

Admittedly, Iyad hadn't put much thought into either Henry or his wives since around the time he'd first found out about the project. And especially not today. Today, he had questions. Today, he had things he needed to know. Well, at the very least, he had a ques*tion*.

What happened over their holiday?

Fatima was scribbling down notes while Tom detailed Anne's execution as they stood in front of the glass pillow scaffold that commemorated her and the others killed at the Tower. Iyad tilted his head down to her, trying not to inhale her halo of vanilla and shea because he needed to focus, but how could he when yesterday could have very well changed the entire trajectory of everything he'd understood between them?

There were knowable variables in play before yesterday: Iyad had convinced himself into believing he was keeping Fatima at a distance just like he did with everyone else. Her not being Muslim was just the cherry on top. Ergo, red line. Red tape. Red card. Red light. Red. Red. Red. It didn't matter that he'd friend-zoned her because this one variable meant there wasn't a chance between them anyway.

But what about now?

What if Iyad could acknowledge to himself that Fatima was nothing like anyone else to him? What if he could come to grips with the fact that she was Muslim now—something her ex wasn't, something he was. Did that mean he had a chance with her? Did he want a chance with her?

"You never told me about your trip, by the way," he whispered.

Fatima stopped writing, used her pen to mark her place in her book as she shut it, then looked up at him sharply. She wasn't wearing a hijab today, which wasn't surprising, since he assumed she was probably taking her time adjusting to it. He'd leave that alone. But he still had his questions. Still had his mess of a mind that was begging to be unravelled.

"It was good," she told him. "I'll show you the pictures later."

She wasn't getting it. He tried again. "Did something. . . happen?"

"Happen?" she repeated.

Was she really going to make him spell it out? Probably. Fatima had a habit of making him work. "Are you Muslim now?"

"Mus- oh!" Fatima hit her forehead with the base of her palm, and a few people looked over at her while Tom continued his monologue. She put her hands up innocently. "Sorry," she apologized, then went back to Iyad. "Yeah, I thought I told you."

"You definitely did not," he shook his head. "But I'm glad you think of me enough to have thought so." *Smooth.*

She snorted and looked down at the grass.

"And I'm glad you did it," he murmured, wondering whether he'd just made her smile. Hoping he did. "For yourself."

"Me too," she said shyly as Tom led everyone inside the castle, with Iyad, Fatima, and Sadiyah falling into step behind the rest of their group.

And that's when it happened. Iyad saw the notification just as it came through to her phone, but he didn't read it. He did, however, hear her little shriek when she did after Fatima had stopped walking and held her phone out for him and Sadiyah to see.

"Look!" She was practically exploding. "He tweeted me!"

Iyad narrowed his eyes at the screen to see the response

from the author they were talking about in the car the day before. Fatima had tweeted to him about how his story made her realize how few Black books she read that weren't centered on clichéd trauma. It was happy. It made her happy. And those facts alone made her want to help create more stories to make more people happy like that, as well.

The author's response was something to the effect of how he agreed with her. How she should do exactly what she'd said. But it was the second part of the message that, for some reason, Iyad found himself taking as a challenge. Or rather, a suggestion. Maybe even a cheat code.

He'd mentioned a lack of love stories, of adventures, and laughter in general. Iyad assumed the man had meant in books, but as he looked at Fatima, still beaming at her phone, he thought to himself, regarding her,

Yeah. I could do that.

CHAPTER TWENTY-FOUR

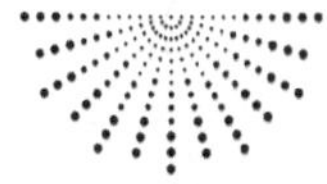

DATE: 19 Apr 2019, 10:05
SUBJECT: Crunch Time!

Hi all,

I hope you're faring well.

We're nearing the end, ladies—I'm so thankful for all of your hard work on *Control!* It has been quite a wonderful ride to watch our young protagonist's journey thus far.

As we close out, I've been speaking with our lovely author. We want to ensure that the focus on mental health is maintained throughout Elle's journey while also safeguarding the piece's critical moments of brevity. So, let's continue our correspondence on the ending.

Elle has been through so much as the story unfolds. She's learning to love and accept herself for who she is, and so on. But how do we push the ending? Before, you all were talking about happy endings. As it stands, our author hasn't agreed to the conventional happily ever after conclusion. Rather, we want the despite! For instance, despite death, there is life! Despite sadness, there is joy!

Any suggestions?

All the best,
Mia Gérard

FATIMA IMAGINED MIA CLICK-CLACKING AWAY AT HER KEYBOARD as she thought of how best to respond. Five minutes later, she'd come up with exactly nothing. Mia always wanted more than what Fatima gave. Claudette always wanted more, herself. Now, the author wanted more, and Fatima was nearing the end of her internship, so *she* wanted more as well.

More. More. More.

She pulled her braids into a ponytail to help her think better. Claudette was right back when she'd called it out. The parallels between Fatima and Elle were a key factor that tugged at her, making her feel as if it were solely up to her to fine-tune the story just enough so that *Control* could finally be published. But Mia wasn't exactly helping the process. She and Claudette shared a talent for sometimes being woefully vague regarding their intentions. What was a happy-not-happy ending? What was this "despite" she was so sure of?

"Are you trying to drill holes into the screen?" Claudette raised a questioning eyebrow at Fatima, a tinge of a smile playing at the corners of her mouth. Fatima hadn't even noticed she'd come up to her desk.

"Ha. Ha," Fatima drawled, looking away from the computer. "I'm thinking."

Claudette glanced at Mia's email on the screen and then rolled a seat over to sit down. She'd only added Fatima to the CC list a few weeks ago, telling her not to think too much of it since Claudette would be responding to all of the emails anyway. But still. She was there. Claudette trusted her to be there. To Fatima, that was big enough.

"Please share with the class what about," Claudette prompted her.

Fatima sighed. She wasn't a fan of presenting half-baked ideas. "I'd say that Elle needs. . . to get a grip."

"To sort herself out," Claudette nodded along.

Fatima accepted the correction. "Mmhmm," she pressed her lips together. "It's okay if we don't go the traditional route—bittersweet works, too. But there should be a moment that shows some level of growth, like. . ." Her eyes drifted off to the ceiling, thinking of what to say next.

She thought of herself because that's just what naturally happened whenever Fatima thought of Elle. High school was as much of a playground for Fatima as it was for Elle. The sad truth was that, like Elle, it had been Fatima's breaking point. She questioned herself. Her religion. She gave up. Gave in to a boy who lied about wanting anything good to do with her. But she was doing better now. Firming her backbone, and such.

"How about this?" Fatima studied the email again before concluding, "Despite myself, I am here."

Claudette looked like Fatima had just offered her the world. "I like it," she said, nudging Fatima's shoulder. "Now, go tell her."

Fatima stared. "You want me?" she pointed at herself. She actually took her finger and pointed it at herself. *"Me?"* she repeated, louder, because maybe Claudette had become hard of hearing in the past 0.8 seconds since she'd begun speaking. "To email. . . Mia?"

"Well," Claudette considered that for a moment, toying with her ginger hair. "It's good hands-on practice to get more active in the conversation. Plus, she's liked what you've said so far, and you've already spoken to her before, anyway."

"I guess. . ."

"Pardon?" Claudette's voice came out as a warning, sounding mildly affronted at the sentence Fatima hadn't even completed yet. "Didn't I tell you to quit all that doubting?"

"You did," Fatima confirmed.

"And yet, you are," Claudette tutted.

Fatima bowed as low as she could in her seat. "Forgive me, O valiant leader."

Claudette laughed brightly and fanned Fatima off. "You're ruining my nerves," she said, tapping a finger against the desk. "Now get this jigsaw figured out for us, will you?"

DATE: 19 Apr 2019, 11:15
SUBJECT: Re: Crunch Time!

Hi Mia,

Thanks so much for your email and kind words.

I agree that there should be a balance between mental health and hope throughout *Control.* Questioning that balance in terms of "despite" is a great way to go about it. Elle faces many obstacles: high school, love, family, friends, etc. The toughest one, though, to me, is herself. Specifically, her mind. So, what do you think of: Despite myself, I am here?

Since she's already in high school, how about heightening that? How about simply allowing her to be that high school kid she craves to be so badly, and just let her have some fun?

Cheers,
Fatima Sommers

Fatima was on her third cup of tea when Mia responded.

DATE: 19 Apr 2019, 12:16
SUBJECT: Re: Crunch Time!

Fatima,

What a fabulous despite. To build from that idea, a new question: How would you have fun. . . despite?

Looking forward to your thoughts!

Mia

What was this? *The Da Vinci Code?* What more could Mia have wanted? What, in her indomitable opinion, was the answer she needed so badly?

Fatima knew that Elle didn't see happiness as an accessible or even tangible thing. It wasn't something she deserved. It wasn't something she could grasp. It wasn't solid. But there were moments. Moments throughout the narrative where she knew that wasn't right. Moments where she let herself laugh and moments where she said what was on her mind. Moments where she allowed herself to exist, and not at someone else's expense. Those were some of Fatima's favorite beats in the book; they felt like coming up for air after being underwater for too long. They reminded her of the tweet that Justin A. Reynolds had sent her about needing more love stories and causes for adventure and laughter.

Love stories didn't always have to mean romance, though. You could fall in love with yourself. On your own adventure. Laughing at your own jokes. You could. The longer Fatima spent time in London, the more she did.

DATE: 19 Apr 2019, 13:46
SUBJECT: Re: Crunch Time!

Hi there,

I'd say that the way you have fun "despite," is to be honest about why it matters to begin with.

Elle craves acceptance and can't seem to find this relief anywhere she turns. She's a teenager, and a girl, and in love with a boy that she keeps being told she doesn't compare to enough times that she believes it herself.

So I'd say, Elle doesn't need a clichéd happy ending, but I'd hope she could be reminded that she is still young and deserves to feel alive as much as anyone else.

Fatima

The final email came right before Fatima went home for the day. From the author herself. Fatima nearly fell out of her chair when she saw it. She didn't, of course. Claudette probably wouldn't have let her live it down. But she was millimeters away from disaster.

DATE: 19 Apr 2019, 17:32
SUBJECT: Re: Crunch Time!

Hello,

I am so inspired by your insight, Fatima. Thank you for sharing.

I will take this feedback into account and work on these comments through the weekend. Hopefully, we'll have a finalized draft in the coming weeks. 😊

With love,
m

CHAPTER TWENTY-FIVE

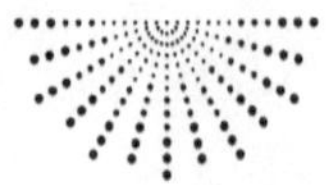

FATIMA AND SADIYAH WERE FRIENDS. BEST FRIENDS, EVEN. Sisters, more like. Apparently, she and Iyad were friends, too. Friends who were gradually getting closer. So, did that make him. . . eventually, like. . . her brother?

The thought alone was sickening.

When it came down to it, Fatima just had to up and admit (to herself, because her pride wouldn't allow the notion to persist any further) that she liked him. She knew she wasn't supposed to like him because he'd definitely stated and restated that they were friends—a ghastly word, come to think of it—but she, Fatima Sommers, liked him, Iyad Ahmed. Very much so.

Sigh.

She liked the way her name sounded when he said it (Faah-TEE-mah) and when he saved her a seat beside him in class. She liked that he got along with Sadiyah (or maybe that Sadiyah got along with him?), that he didn't seem to mind her little trips to Fatima-land, and, of course, that he was handsome (this was indisputable, since her first thought after thinking he could be a kidnapper and/or killer was not *"run,"* it was something more to the effect of *"cute"*).

She liked him. Iyad was kind and thoughtful, and he made her laugh. He listened to her stories. He thought she had good ideas. He respected her. And he was intentional. Like today, he'd invited her and Sadiyah out to work on their project, choosing somewhere he knew they'd enjoy: Notting Hill.

Notting Hill was a great choice on Iyad's part. Fatima and Sadiyah walked down Lancaster Road in front of the candy-colored terraced homes as Iyad took pictures of them with surprisingly high doses of acrobatic fanfare. Fatima was wearing her hijab—technically Sadiyah's, the blue one from Iyad's shop—and Iyad said it suited her.

Fatima liked that. Not because she needed his approval—she didn't—but because one of the last times someone commented on her hijab, it was to congratulate her for taking it off by people who'd wrongfully thought she'd been forced into wearing it. And so, returning to her hijab wasn't an easy change for Fatima. It attracted a lot of attention from strangers and demanded a level of self-awareness about herself that she hadn't had to maintain in years.

So, she was thankful when the only thing standing out between her, Sadiyah, and Iyad was his outlandish poses as he took their pictures. He bent into sideways lunges that made Fatima laugh and even sat on the ground, leaning far away from his phone so he could get their angles "just right."

It was completely uncharacteristic of Iyad to seem so goofy, but it worked to leave Fatima with no time to worry about herself. To worry if her hijab was tied right. If people were staring at her. At Sadiyah *and* her. It didn't matter then because there was a skyscraper of a man going out of his way to look ridiculous, and Fatima had a sneaking suspicion he was doing so just for her. As a friend.

Again. Sigh.

"Ti, are you still on that idea about family dynamics?" Iyad was asking as he cut into his chicken thigh.

After they'd walked around Notting Hill long enough, he said he'd treat them to Nando's for lunch. There, they could finally focus on their project since it was due in a couple of days, and they hadn't made much progress in their entire semester yet.

"Oh, um," Fatima mumbled through a mouthful of French fries. The only clear theme she'd found in all her research was how terrible Henry VIII had been as a king, husband, father, man, and, honestly, human in general, so she didn't know where to start.

"You guys know about the domino effect, right?" Sadiyah spoke up while Fatima chewed. She was more telling them they did than asking, before she continued. "We need to focus on Henry in a present-day context, so why don't we put it that simply? As in 'Henry did exactly that, so now we do this.'"

"Showing how Henry's life literally affects us now?" Fatima asked, smoothing out the creases of her dress. She'd been so excited to wear it: a powder blue smock that billowed around her whenever the wind picked up. It was probably silly to say, but it made her feel like a princess.

"Yeah."

"I like it."

"I know."

Fatima rolled her eyes and took a sip of water just as a text rolled into her phone.

Javi:

Hey stranger.

Putting it lightly, the way she choked while reading the message after what she thought was now mutual radio silence, it was a wonder Fatima managed to find her breath afterward at all. Still, she didn't mention it, because now that she knew she felt something for Iyad, talking about Javier felt unfair. Instead, she tilted her phone over to Sadiyah, who, in turn, also spluttered like a fish.

"You didn't block him?" she asked. Soft enough that Iyad most likely hadn't heard her. Bemused enough that Fatima wished she hadn't either.

Fatima just sighed because what else could she do? Lie? Suddenly, adrenaline was making her heart race a mile a minute, guilt and paranoia flooding her bloodstream. And it hurt. She turned to Iyad and asked, "Remember when you told me that meat thing at Kew Gardens? About how if you spoil a man enough, they'll get rotten?"

Iyad leaned back on his side of the booth, glancing between the two of them, and then, waywardly, at Fatima's phone. "Sure," he said, rubbing the back of his neck.

It chimed again. This time, she and Sadiyah both shifted forward to check it.

Javi:

> I miss you.

Sadiyah's eyes turned to volleyballs. *What the—?* she mouthed, then caught herself and tightened up.

Poor Iyad had no idea what was going on, and Poor Fatima was trying her hardest to press on like nothing was.

"Well, Henry was spoiled," Fatima started, "and in many ways, his rottenness manifested as toxic masculinity. I mean, I understand that especially then, especially in his position, being in love, or like, even, wasn't vital to getting married. But that doesn't mean you get to be a tyrant. That doesn't mean that you get to treat your partner any way you want just because it suits you." She wasn't sure if she was talking about Javier or Henry. "Doesn't mean he was right to kill his wives the way he did."

"Didn't he only have two of them killed?" Poor Iyad asked. "He divorced the first one."

"Abuse isn't always physical." Fatima was disappointed by his question. "And he didn't just divorce his first wife, he *created* the Church of England so he wouldn't have to deal with the Catholic Church's rules that wouldn't let him divorce her since she wasn't birthing him any sons that survived infancy. Can you imagine how painful and humiliating that must've been for her? Not being allowed to grieve one lost before the next, and having all of those eyes on her the whole time, regardless?" Fatima pressed, glancing at her phone because she couldn't help it.

"Then," she went on, "he realized a divorce would hurt him politically, so he lied on his next wife—who also didn't have any living sons—accusing her of cheating, and all sorts of other things. But really, he just wanted a new woman and literally had her killed to get one. Not once in all of that man's creativity did he ever think about making a daughter work as his heir, because why would he? When he could just trade in the car for a new model?"

Poor Iyad visibly swallowed. Fatima watched his Adam's apple bob up and back, but he didn't say anything. Which was good, because her sudden anger had surprised even her, making her not only see red, but see Iyad as the color made flesh.

Why did Javier have to show up right when she was finally starting to feel like herself again?

"Take five." Sadiyah moved closer to Fatima and said, "Breathe, ukhti. Okay? Skin and bones." Then, she handed Fatima her phone and motioned to the door. "Go outside and handle this. End it for real this time." She nudged Fatima out of their booth and started typing something on her computer. "We've got enough to work with while you're gone."

Fatima nodded and sent Iyad telepathic apologies she'd doubted he'd noticed, or would've even accepted. Then, went outside.

. . .

"Javier."

"Hey, baby." Javier coaxed, his voice was sweet velvet.

Fatima closed her eyes. "Hey, *Fatima*," she corrected, then said again, "Javier." She was doing her best to sound uninterested in him. Like the sound of his voice didn't make her feel the slightest bit weak in the head. And knees.

"I've been thinking 'bout you. Wanted to make sure you were alright?"

"And you waited until almost the end of my trip to ask me?" She rolled her eyes as she watched an older man in a kilt cross the street.

"Why're you being like that?"

"Like what?"

He didn't answer. "I miss you."

Her heart leapt a little. Annoyingly. Inevitably. Fatima fidgeted with the bow tied around her dress to get herself back in check.

"Remember prom?" Javier prodded. "You looked so good that night dancing on me. Had everyone shocked 'cause you were always reading those books till we got together," he breathed out a laugh. She didn't share it. "You even made me carry your heels around for you that night, remember that?"

"What do you want, Javier?"

"Then you made me carry you to the car since your feet hurt so bad when we left. Remember?" he persisted. "Want me to take you dancing when you get back, Princesa?"

"I don't know what to tell you, Javi." Shoot. She hadn't meant to call him that. Fatima wanted to be firm. She wanted his name to be a statement of neutrality. A formal notice that said: This is over. We are done. *I* am done.

Javier said that. Javi said, *Let's run it back.*

"You could tell me you missed me," he answered. "Tell me

you want us to get back to having fun together. Dime que lloraste por mí." *Tell me you cried for me.*

"¿Querías que llorara?" *You wanted me to cry?*

"I love it when you speak Spanish to me, baby. I think it's my favorite thing I taught you."

"Don't call me that," she rolled her eyes, fielding through her thoughts. Fatima was mad. She was so angry. Yet for some reason, she could never show it when it came to him. Never well enough, at least.

Just make sure you aim all that rage at the right person next time, okay?

Was it pathetic that she couldn't?

"Why can't I call you that?" Javier pushed, and there was the slightest hitch of hesitation in his voice before he added, "He's calling you baby already?"

"Who?"

"Eye-yad."

Eye— Wait.

"Who?" Fatima repeated.

"The newest guy following you on your private Instagram account with all of the deleted pictures of me. The one who's also in London. The one you probably stopped talking to me for."

"Things went that bad with Bea that you started watching my followers?" *And noticed I archived our pictures?*

Fatima knew that it was a Pyrrhic victory, feeling even the slightest bit of triumph that he'd resorted to such pitiful measures to know what she'd been up to. But she decided not to split hairs and take the win for what it was.

"I'm not here to talk about her."

"You want to talk about my new friend," she reminded him. "Why can't we talk about yours?"

"Because you're mine. All I'm guilty of is getting by while my girl was gone. You should be happy for me."

There was a time when Javier's possessiveness was one of Fatima's favorite things about him, but that wasn't now. Implicated ownership over her was something that she, thankfully, was no longer fascinated by.

The way she saw it now, Javier needed to know that he wasn't slick. That he'd run his course with her and wouldn't be getting any medals for letting go of Bea and coming back to Old Faithful just because Fatima would be back Stateside soon enough.

Ten cuidado. Ten cuidado. Ten cuidado, her heart whispered.

"Regardless," he continued, "we both had our fun, didn't we?" Javier asked rhetorically. "Now it's time for you to come back home to me."

Fatima swallowed, somewhat addled. *He's back,* she reasoned with herself. *This is what you wanted, for him to want you back.* But then a raindrop flicked and fell against her glasses' lenses, and she wasn't so sure of that anymore.

Ten cuidado. Ten cuidado. Ten cuidado.

"Wh- why?" she stammered, breaking out into a cold sweat. "Why do you always do this, Javier? You dropped me, remember?"

"No, baby. That's your ego talking. I asked for a break. Now, I'm not, you feel me?"

She didn't feel him. In fact, Fatima was beginning to believe she never wanted to feel him again. Break. Break up. Iyad had to be right that day at Kew Gardens when he said that made all the difference. It made sense. Sometimes, it just is what it is.

You're either on or you're off. You love or you don't. You're here or you're not, Iyad had laid out for her. Maybe it was right to have a Sith mentality when it came to Javier. To only think in absolutes. No glasses half full. Either the cup had water in it. Or it didn't.

"Fatima?"

"Is it possible to feel so close to someone and miles apart at the same time?" she asked him, holding on as tightly to her dignity as she could. But the longer the conversation went on, the more pointless that effort seemed to be.

"What do you mean?"

"I had the same question when you asked me," Fatima almost laughed. As the rain began to come down more steadily, fogging up her glasses, and Javier's voice echoed through her phone's speaker, all she felt like doing was grabbing her car door handle as they spun out and crashed into the highway's guardrail, like back when they'd gotten into their accident.

Suddenly, London wasn't just rain-soaked cigarettes and roses. It was burnt rubber against wet asphalt. It was her head throbbing. It was her vision getting blurry at the edges. Fatima crouched down to her knees, flattening her back against the glass wall behind her. Water pooled atop her dress in bunches, turning spots of the light-colored fabric into awkward, deepened shades of blue.

Javier let out a long-suffering sigh. "Listen, baby, I messed up, and I've got to take that on the chin. But just because I made a mistake doesn't mean we should forget all our time together, does it?"

Ten cuidado. Ten cuidado. Ten cuidado.

Fatima was shaking. Terribly. Awful bodily convulsions like uncontrollable little earthquakes shattering through her bones. She knew Javier was going to come back. That's why she held out waiting for him for so long, no matter how delusional it made her look. She *knew* he'd come back because he *always* came back. But why was exactly what she'd wanted somehow the worst possible thing to have been given? Why did she feel like she loved him so much that it was slowly killing her?

"I'm sorry," he urged, and she hated the way her heart began to crack at the thought that maybe, for once, he meant it.

"For what?" Fatima managed to ask. She wasn't proud of it,

but she could feel herself starting to slip. Knew she would fall entirely if he could answer this question right.

"All of it." But, of course, he didn't.

"So you don't know why you're sorry."

"I know I want us back together, isn't that enough? I know I'll never love anyone half as much as I love you."

"Do you?" she asked on impulse, reluctant because she was afraid of his answer. "Do you love me?"

If he didn't, at least everything that'd happened between them would begin to make a little more sense. Because if he did, if he really did love her and it manifested in this way—and she stayed? Grinned and bore it for all those years? How stupid did that make her?

"You alright, Ti?"

She looked up just as the rain stopped and found Iyad standing above her, watching her carefully while shielding her from the rain with his jean jacket. Fatima shrugged helplessly. Iyad didn't move.

"*'Ti?'*" Javier repeated Iyad crossly. "Is that *him?*" he bellied.

"If it is?" she snapped.

"Ti," Javier pressed.

"FATIMA," she bellowed, her volume surprising even herself. "Don't call me anything else."

"Fatima," he sighed. "Come on, Princesa. It's us."

"No. It was *supposed* to be us, Javier. But you go from this girl to this excuse, to the next. Always taking, taking, taking. And what does that leave me as, huh? The idiot you get to leave behind who waits around like Boo Boo the Fool, hoping one day you'll love her again? OR *AT ALL?* Are you even worth that? Me stressing you? Me waiting for you? Me wanting you? Me loving you? Can you name me *one* thing you've ever done to deserve any of that from me?"

Javier didn't say anything.

"You don't get to leave me anymore and expect me to let you

come back," Fatima said over the sound of her heart pounding in her chest. Her head was spinning out. In the silence, she looked up at Iyad. His worried brown eyes hadn't left hers still. She found herself hoping they never would. "I have to go," she said finally.

"Wait—"

"What?" she snapped.

"I love you, Fatima."

For the first time, she didn't know what to say to that. So she hung up instead.

CHAPTER TWENTY-SIX

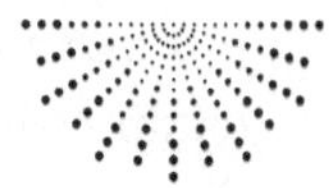

RUSH HOUR WAS COMING UP ROSES WHEN IYAD COMPARED IT TO his feelings regarding a stranger named Javier. Or, as Sadiyah seemed intent on saying, Pretty Boy.

"Why do you keep calling him that?" He wanted to know because he was aggravatingly curious about who'd wound Fatima up against him so quickly.

"Jealous?" Sadiyah tutted between diligent bites of corn on the cob. "You wanna be Pretty Boy so bad," she smirked.

"No," Iyad blurted, not understanding how Sadiyah could make jokes at a time like this when he, for one, could hardly breathe. His throat was definitely closing up. "I just wonder why that guy is." By now, Iyad had definitely made up his mind that he did, in fact, like Fatima. So, hearing that her ex was allegedly a top-tier evil Adonis wasn't exactly welcome news. He raked a hand through his beard and fell back, trying to seem nonchalant when he asked, "But is it a good thing? To be that?"

Sadiyah snorted. She was always laughing or almost laughing at him. "Not if that's the only thing he's got going for him," she said.

"Oh."

"This is their routine," she explained. "He dumps her, but keeps her on the hook just enough so that she's never sure if they're really over. Then, right when enough time passes and she finally starts to feel good without him, it's like he senses it—like some Bat-Signal goes off—and he shows up out of nowhere to ruin all my progress."

Iyad lifted a brow. "*'Your'* progress?"

Sadiyah shrugged. "You think I'm not out here suffering with her every time he pulls this Houdini trick?"

Iyad eyed Fatima out of the restaurant's window suspiciously. She looked so uneasy when he'd found her and Sadiyah at the Underground station today before they walked to Notting Hill together, squirming about in her hijab like a kid in an itchy jumper their parent made them wear.

Oh, he'd resolved. *She's uncomfortable. Let me fix that.* Which subsequently called for the next hour of him in funny-looking poses as he took their pictures, hoping that maybe she'd relax.

And then she did. And she laughed. And she was happy. And she was so beautiful.

And then Javier called.

"You like my friend, right?" Sadiyah inquired. She must've followed his gaze outside, too. Must've seen how reticent her friend had become. "Do better than Pretty Boy did."

Do better than Pretty Boy did?

Iyad decided to take in the moment of her potentially giving him her blessing to feel the way he did about her friend with all the casual confidence of a penguin learning to fly. He swallowed spasmodically. "I thought they'd cut ties," he coalesced. Carefully.

"They have *history,*" Sadiyah said, as if the word itself were toxic.

Iyad tried to make a joke. "So you think maybe she just needs a new 'Pretty Boy?'" Okay. A half-joke.

Sadiyah rolled her eyes. "You know what you look like.

Don't waste her time on you just not being ugly, 'cause her time wasted is *my* time wasted. And do you think I like having my time wasted, Ahmed?" she asked, waving a chip at him.

Before he could think of a smart reply, Iyad heard tiny little footsteps marching somewhere near him. He turned and saw that the restaurant window was starting to pile up with little troops of raindrops, slip, slip, slipping down the glass. Then, he noticed that Fatima was beginning to slide down the wall outside the same way.

Do better than Pretty Boy did.

"She'll catch a cold," he said to Sadiyah, who was also up in seconds.

Not too long after they were all back inside from the rain, Iyad watched as Sadiyah pestered Fatima to tell her exactly what'd happened. Admittedly, he was just as eager to know.

It was dizzying, the effect he was finding that Fatima had on him. Iyad didn't fully understand it yet, but when he thought of the way she'd held herself outside, like she was at risk of melting into the pavement, he realized for sure then that he wanted to be the one who held her together instead. Made sure she stayed put. Right in front of him, where she was now. Safe and miles away from Javier.

But how could he say that when Javier was probably the only one on her mind right now?

"He said *what?*" Sadiyah stared at her, open-mouthed, after finally badgering Fatima into relaying her conversation.

Fatima grinned softly, a distant, almost watery look in her eyes. "That I should be happy for him."

"For getting with another girl while you were away?" Sadiyah confirmed, incredulous.

"Exactly."

Sadiyah clasped her hands together. "I'm gonna scream if you get back with him."

Anxiety churned over in Iyad's gut. Something tight wove its way around his lungs, threading through him like the needle of his mother's sewing machine. His mouth moved to speak without his permission. "She's not gonna get back with him."

Both girls turned to him. "Because?" Fatima asked warily, as if she'd already planned to do exactly that.

Sadiyah smirked, looking between them like they were tennis balls at a Wimbledon match. "Yeah, Iyad. *'Because?'*"

Suddenly, he wasn't a fan of her knowing he liked Fatima.

"I just mean—" Iyad stopped himself. What did he mean? That she shouldn't get back with her ex because he's terrible and she deserves better? Or because he wanted her to see him as that better option? Iyad decided it would work better for him if he didn't question either for the time being. "I just mean you said you wanted to be with someone who didn't make you choose between them and Islam. And, if I understand your background with him. . ." he trailed off.

"Oh," Fatima sighed, relaxing. "I know our background isn't good, but there's—"

"History," he cut her off, repeating what Sadiyah had explained to him earlier.

"History," Fatima repeated slowly. "Someone told me to try to see how necessary he is in my life. To see if I'd be fine without him, and I have been, but—"

"But?" Iyad interjected. His mouth had become a loose faucet that he couldn't seem to turn off. "What's the problem then? You're saying good things like they're bad," he rushed.

"But what if I'm wrong?" Fatima answered weakly.

Iyad glanced at Sadiyah, who quietly shrugged in return. "Ti does fine without Pret- Javier," she corrected herself as she went on, "when he's out of the picture. But she loses herself when he's back in it."

"That's not true," Fatima said, but the tenor in her voice was all wrong, unsure.

"Then block him," Sadiyah challenged her.

There was a pause before Fatima attempted to change the subject. "Weren't we supposed to be talking about our project?"

Iyad eyed her as she hurriedly flipped open her notebook, her movements frantic and wild. "So back to the domino effect that Sads was talking—"

"Actually, yes," Sadiyah sniffed. "Back to what *I* was talking about. What do you think would happen next if you actually went through with letting him go?"

"I don't see how that has anything to do with the—"

"It does," Sadiyah kept going. "Would you be better or worse off?"

"How would I know that if I haven't done it?"

"Haven't you, though? Every time you're with him," she held out a palm, "like Henry's wives, we know it only hurts you." Sadiyah flung out her other hand. "But the second you leave him alone, you come out better for it. Every time."

"I—" Fatima squeezed her eyes shut. "I'm working on it, alright? I never said I was even getting back with him."

"Did he. . ." Iyad trailed off. He wanted specifics. He wanted her attention focused on him, and not on her ex, who was clearly focused on the nearest girl with a pulse. "Did he mention anything to make you want to go back to him?"

"He actually mentioned you."

Iyad's stomach hit the ground. "What about me?"

"He's jealous of you because he thinks we're more than friends," Fatima clarified just as Sadiyah's hand dramatically flew to cover her mouth.

Iyad responded before giving himself any time to process what she was saying. "And us being more than friends made you want to stay. . . with him?"

"Ti. . ." Sadiyah hummed, her hand still placed firmly over her mouth.

"No," Fatima shook her head, wagging a finger between them like a disappointed teacher. "No- he just- I don't know why I said that," she stammered. "He saw you followed my Instagram and came to his own conclusion. I know we're just friends, Yad."

The week before Iyad met Fatima, he was thinking about signing up for rugby again. Things were much simpler when he used to play: Have the ball? Keep the ball. Don't have the ball? Get the ball. Iyad didn't have to rely on his brain to think him through a situation because his body reacted first.

The first day he saw Fatima, his heart literally skipped a beat. Then, when they'd finally spoken and that man barged past her, his body reacted before his brain just at the idea that she could've been hurt. Almost instantly, he'd forgotten about tryouts. Instead, he was focused on when he'd see her again. For how long. What he should say. What he should wear. She took the place rugby took years to fill in an instant.

"Would it be a bad thing?" Iyad chanced aloud, his tone careful. He didn't know what he was doing or why he was doing it, but he couldn't stop himself. "Us being more than friends, I mean."

Fatima looked at him like he'd grown a third eye. He held his hand over his forehead to cover it. "What are you talking about?" she asked. "We're friends. You said we're friends."

"What if we weren't?"

"But you said we are."

You said. You said.

There was a certain cadence to Fatima's voice when she reminded him of his very thoughtless action. Somewhere between accusatory and. . . sadness? No, that couldn't be right.

But just in case, he asked her one more time, "What if we weren't?"

She froze. "If we- huh?" Fatima blinked and turned to Sadiyah, who was all but watching them with 3D glasses and a bucket of popcorn as she stuffed herself further into the inside of the booth to see them better. "Huh?" Fatima repeated.

Sadiyah didn't answer.

Iyad silently thanked her.

Something anxious and stupidly hopeful surged through him as he let his instincts take over. He palmed at the back of his neck to try and compose himself. Across the table, Fatima, though clearly at a loss, remained breathtaking the more he looked at her. She scrambled his thoughts into mush without even trying. And Iyad welcomed it.

"Fatima," Iyad worked her name out slowly, like she was a perched bird he didn't want to scare away. "Is it possible that someone could take back what they said for the bet—"

"Stop," she waved him off. "You don't get to do that. You said we were friends, so I believed you. I don't know if you're joking or what, but either way, it's not right of you to say that. To even mention taking it back. Especially now. Are you- Do you think you can get at me 'cause I'm a little sad right now? Do I seem that weak to you? Did you hang around us to- to use me?"

What? Had Javier twisted her up so bad that she immediately saw herself as a conquest instead of a prize? Iyad held his breath, thinking and rethinking of where exactly he'd gone wrong. Was it in his timing? Was it what he'd said? What should he say to fix it? Could it be fixed?

Iyad wanted to explain that he felt himself change just by being near her. That he wanted to stay there. He wanted to be something new. Someone good. For himself. For her. But how could he say any of that when everything between them was going up in flames right in front of him?

Without thinking, he slipped back into the cold version of himself he'd been before he met her, pushing back on instinct.

"Did you just compare me to your good-for-nothing ex? After I've been nothing but kind to you?"

Fatima rolled her eyes. "You want a reward? Should I clap?"

Iyad's whole body shuddered. Confusion, hurt, and fragments of anger shook his voice. "You're joking," he said, disbelieving. "When did I become the problem?"

"When you made this about yourself," Fatima snapped immediately. "You sound like you're trying to go after a grieving widow. The body isn't even cold yet."

"All I said was 'what if,' I never *actually* took what I said back!" he insisted. Even if he wanted to, which, let's be honest, he did. He didn't. He'd only posed a question to see if the answer might've been something affirmative. To see if he might have a chance with her. And now she was blowing things way out of proportion. "Why are you acting like this?"

"*Acting?*" she repeated him, rage braided through every letter. "I'm not *acting* like anything. Why—"

"Ti, wait," Sadiyah gestured her hand wildly in front of Fatima like a referee who'd missed a play. Iyad forgot she was there for a moment through all of the sudden madness. "I think this is just a misunderstanding. Iyad didn't do any—"

"No, Sadiyah. He doesn't get a pass just because he's done a few nice things. He's been using me this entire time. Getting close. Hanging out," she started listing off Iyad's actions like they were MOs for a crime, not like they were just things he'd genuinely looked forward to. "I was a game to him. I'm always a game to them." Fatima raised her voice, and Iyad caught glimpses of patrons eyeing their table as it imploded.

Sadiyah glanced at each table until they returned to their own business before continuing. "You're a game to who?" she asked.

"Men," Fatima seethed, hollow and ragged. "But I will *not* be one again. Much less twice in one day."

"Fatima, I wasn't—" Iyad attempted.

"You *are!* You're just like him."

"No good?"

"Hey, now," Sadiyah waved a hand his way, although he knew she agreed with his sentiment toward Javier. Now was clearly not the time for honesty, but he wanted so desperately for her to let go of her delusion.

"If he's no good," Fatima spoke up, "then you're no better."

Do better than Pretty Boy did.

This was not what Iyad had intended. It wasn't even close. Fatima practically spat those words at him, using the least amount of effort she'd mustered to speak the entire time. She seemed almost drained now. Exhausted after her conversation with Javier, and now with him. Was Iyad really no different? Was he really a bird of a feather with exactly who he wanted to steer her away from?

"What if I believe you?" she asked, tired and heavy. "What if you really were just speaking in hypotheticals?"

"I *was,*" Iyad couldn't help but say.

Fatima continued. "Then wouldn't it be true that you were still just playing with me? Messing with my head because you *thought* it was funny to ask me that?"

Iyad's hand instinctively reached for the back of his neck again. He clutched it so firmly that the entire area began to ache, but he couldn't stop himself. He didn't know what to do. What was right. "I was never playing with you," he lamented. "I would never play with you. Can you please trust at least that, Ti?"

"Fatima," she corrected him, practically bristling. "And no."

"Fatima," he echoed her name frantically as if it were the law itself. Iyad was losing her. And he was still trying to understand what exactly he'd done that was so bad that it didn't even warrant her at least hearing him out. "Please. I wouldn't lie to you, you know that."

"I don't need to know anything to do with you besides the fact that we need to get this project done." Fatima stood up from the booth. A language barrier. Was that what it was? Did 'what if' mean something different in the States than here? "Then we'll be done with each other for good," she turned to leave.

"Fatima—" Iyad tried, but the way she left, he knew better than to follow.

"I'm sorry." Sadiyah looked at him like he was as miserable as he felt. Then, quickly disappeared too.

Once upon a time, Iyad decided that he was so afraid to lose anyone else after losing his dad that he ran everyone off first. And then, Fatima ran away from him, and it was the first time since his dad that the idea of being left behind had struck him. Now, he'd run her away again, and he was left beyond stricken; he was shattered.

Defeated, Iyad slumped down in his seat. He ignored the clumsily concealed stares from the people around him, focusing solely on a more critical matter. All he wanted to know was how to get her back—even though he was sure he couldn't.

PART II

Watching the sun.

CHAPTER TWENTY-SEVEN

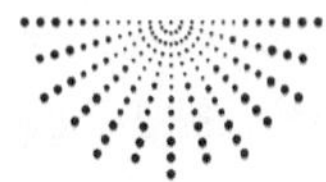

FATIMA DIDN'T RAISE HER VOICE WITH JAVIER FOR THE SIMPLE fact that the last time she had, she nearly watched him die.

It was her fault, though. Really. She'd spent the entire week leading up to when it happened, caught in her own world as she studied for her finals, barely leaving any time for him. Still, Javier spent that week wrapped in a boyish glee because of a secret date he'd planned for them. The one caveat was that it was time-specific. As in, timed specifically during Fatima's Medieval Fiction final, her hardest exam by far, right at the end of her sophomore year.

She'd gotten cocky by then. Spoiled by exams consisting solely of take-home assignments with open-book privileges, courtesy of following the English studies track. The last thing she'd expected was that this one final wouldn't be as straightforward as the rest of them. That it wouldn't have a simple writing prompt she could skirt by while rewatching *Clone Wars* episodes. Instead, she'd be tested on the intricate plots of books she'd never actually read because she'd waited until the end of the semester to begin and take her class seriously.

"You'll make it, baby," Javier told her over the phone as she ran to the auditorium where student proctors were leading test sites for the late afternoon test sessions. His voice was soft and syrupy in her ear, and she felt herself smile at his encouragement.

"Yeah," she heaved. "I'm almost there."

"To take your test?" he asked, bewildered, before breaking into a breathy laugh. "No, I mean that you'll make it in time for our reservation. If you finish in an hour—let's say an hour and a half, if you really need that much time—we'll be golden. I know you can do it, Princesa." He spoke to her with a smug confidence as if what he'd said had already come true.

Fatima focused on not tripping over her untied shoelace as she ran. "Javi, the test has a *three-hour* window. What happens if I need all three hours? Actually, I think I might," she rushed. Her mouth was dry as she climbed the stairs into the auditorium. "I keep saying that I think you should cancel it. We can go another time," she promised.

"I can't do that," he told her.

"I'll make it up to you."

"You won't have to. You'll make it."

She didn't.

And that, of course, was her fault. Really. Despite all of Javier's confidence, Fatima *did* end up needing all three designated hours to finish her exam, which meant they'd missed the date night he'd been so happy about. Something that was entirely her fault.

Fatima should've made it clearer that she couldn't make his reservation. She shouldn't have ridden the fence to make him feel better, which actually had just led him on. She should've been clearer. Fatima reminded herself of this all as she sprinted from the auditorium to Javier's sage gray Honda Civic parked out front.

Normally, when he saw her coming, Javier would get out of his car for her. He'd jog around to the passenger side and open the door for her to get in. He'd ask her something like, "Do you have a map?" And she'd fall for it when he'd followed up with, "'Cause I keep getting lost in your eyes."

Normally, then, he'd kiss her. And she'd remember why she chose him over everything and everyone else when the warmth of his lips met hers. When he reminded her why he wasn't just the moon and stars to her. That he was gravity itself, quietly tethering her heart to his.

So, she didn't know how to act that day when he wasn't normal. When he didn't get out of the car. Didn't kiss her. Touch her. Tell her some corny pick-up line. Instead, he just sat there after she'd let herself inside. Quiet and fuming.

"Sorry," she apologized impulsively. "It was harder than I expected, but thank you for waiting for me."

Javier didn't move. His eyes were sealed shut when he spoke. "I find that hard to believe."

Fatima squinted, a little drowsy after hours spent in the exam room. "Javi, I understand you're mad, but I did tell you to cancel it."

"And I told you no," he returned. Then, "It's fine."

Nothing seemed fine, though. "Are you sure?" Fatima asked. A Motown song was playing faintly on the radio. Javier always played old-school music that Fatima forced herself to learn and care about because she cared so much about him. So, it must've been her fault that she didn't take what he'd said more seriously. Didn't show up when he'd asked her. Really. "I didn't mean to—"

Javier turned the song up. "Just My Imagination" by The Temptations—she recognized immediately from all the times he'd played it—slid through the speakers. "We already missed most of it, so we'll just head back to mine." He frowned as he

turned to look at her, his sinking green eyes filled with frustration. "What took you so long?"

Sometimes, he could be so invested in his own world that he
didn't know how to welcome Fatima's. Maybe that was the
problem then. Maybe if Fatima stayed wrapped up in him, too,
nothing bad would've happened.

"I told you. I–" she started as raindrops began to sprinkle
against his windshield.

"Yeah, yeah, yeah," Javier dismissed her, turning the wipers
on and pulling out of the parking lot. "You had your little book
report to do. Three hours though, Ti? You could've just said you
didn't want to come with me."

"I did want to go," she tried as they exited her university
and veered onto the main road. She was already too defeated
to say what she wanted, which was, *I don't even know where we
were going to begin with, much less why you can't go there without
me if it was so important and on the same day as my exam. And it
wasn't just some "little" book report. How could you call it that? Why
are my things never important to you, Javier? Am I not important
to you?*

But since Fatima would never say any of that to him, she
nearly whispered, as they got onto the highway, "Don't be like
that, baby," as she reached out to touch his shoulder.

"No me tocas." *Don't touch me.* Javier recoiled, flinging her off
as if she were something vile. "You always do that when you
mess up."

Fatima sagged back in her seat in a stunned silence, staring
at him through wide eyes and furrowed brows. Then, against
herself and toward his blatant revulsion, she blurted, "I didn't
mess up."

Javier turned the wipers on their highest setting. The rain
had quickly picked up and was beginning to wash over the car
more steadily then. He huffed, clearly aggravated, letting out a
grunt through his closed mouth—a long, deeply guttural sound

that may as well have been a growl. "You're saying I'm lying? I waited for you for all that time, *and I'm lying?*"

"No," Fatima said immediately. Her mind was racing, cataloging everything she'd done up until that moment that could've been so wrong, beyond the fact that she couldn't be in two places at one time. That she couldn't care for him when she needed to care for herself. "I'm just saying that I told you I had this test and that it would probably take a while. I get that you had something tonight, too, but it's not like I stood you up on purpose. Or at all, really."

"Quit that," he raised his voice, raw and threadbare, as if he'd tugged on all his vocal cords and bungee jumped each syllable out just to speak. Or maybe the music was just too loud. Maybe the rain was. "Quit the 'I told you so' act like this is my fault. Like me telling you where we were supposed to be going would've made you any faster. Just call it what it is: you didn't want to go," he shook his head. "I'm so sick of wasting my time on you."

Fatima retreated as close as she could to the passenger door, putting as much distance between them as possible. Something about his sudden volume shook her. She believed he wouldn't put his hands on her, but when he got so loud and felt so distant, she wasn't so sure anymore. Still, she couldn't stop herself when she bit out, "You're mad at me for no reason, Javier. It's not like I could've just—"

"*No reason?*" Javier gripped the steering wheel like he was going to pull it off right there. "I asked you to do *one thing* for me."

"Fail my final?" She knew that wasn't what he meant. But that's what it felt like. "You can't be serious. You didn't even ask me how it went."

"FATIMA, WHY DON'T YOU GET THAT I DO NOT CARE ABOUT YOUR DUMB TEST? You study *English*." He sounded disgusted as the words fell from his mouth, like they were rotting right in front of him. She could've sworn they were. "That's already dumb when you *speak the language.* You went to college to waste your time, and now you want me to *care* about that?"

"Wha—" She managed to stammer out a stupid, stupid, mangled sound, "Javier, you know I hate it when you talk to me like that."

"Don't tell me how to talk, Fatima. You don't control me. I was going to take you out to the movies. You've been saying you wanted me to do something special for you, so I got us tickets to see *Infinity War.* But I guess that doesn't mean anything to you since you couldn't even manage to show up."

Fatima had to think for a moment. She didn't know what *Infinity War* was right off the top of her head because she didn't know much about comic book heroes or Batman, and whoever else he hung out with. She had actually made it very clear in the years of knowing Javier before they'd even dated that she never saw the appeal in those things. *He,* on the other hand, loved them. Fatima remembered slowly that he'd actually seen the movie already. So, she realized, this was just something truly meant to benefit him, disguised as if he'd gone out of his way for her.

Something in Fatima snapped when she put those pieces together. Came apart at the seams and unravelled her restraint in an instant. It wasn't that Fatima didn't care about Javier's interests because she did make an effort to entertain them as if they were her own, believing that was how she should conduct herself in a relationship. But why couldn't he do the same for her? Why couldn't he at least pretend? Why did he have to make it so obvious how trivial she was to him?

"This was all over a Batman movie?" she worked out.

"Batman is DC," he clarified. "*Infinity War* is a Mar—"

"Javi, I'm sorry, but you know I don't care," Fatima countered automatically. "This had nothing to do with me from the get-go, and you know that, so how dare you blame me for a decision *you* made?" She leaned in. Close enough to taste the cucumber scent of his cologne, but she couldn't bring herself to try to reach for him again. Her hair stood on end like rose thorns at the thought, frenzied repulsion bleeding out from her. "And to say what I'm studying is dumb? Javier, you know you don't have a leg to stand on when it comes to talking about school."

He stiffened. "What?"

"What do you mean 'what?'" she almost taunted him, feeling every bit as cruel as he was. "Or did you forget that I helped you through every one of your classes senior year because you were a lost cause? You're only in the Navy now because you know you wouldn't be able to make it through any more school without me."

Fatima sat back, watching the cars fade into one another along the busy highway. By then, the rain had converged into a full-on downpour. It beat on the car's hood. Skimmed down the windows. Coated the road.

"You think you're better than me or something?" he asked her, and there was an instant where Fatima felt her heart cleave as she looked at him drive through the deluge.

Her fear began to stink up the car at what she'd started, and Fatima found herself distracted by the smog. She wondered if all the hurt, anger, and desperation swirling so thick in the air, choking her, was how being in love was supposed to go. If love was meant to be this unwinnable war that she continued to fight in. Or if she was just meant to lose out instead.

The more she fixated, the more Fatima realized that she had no idea what they were even talking about anymore. Was it her lateness? His grades in high school? The fact that he'd bought tickets to a movie that he knew she never wanted to see? Fatima just knew she didn't want to be made a fool of. She didn't like feeling used. Manipulated and easy to get over.

"I think you're sick of wasting your time on me." She

parroted him because maybe if he heard how crazy he sounded, he'd take it back.

He didn't. "Maybe I am."

When Fatima spoke again, the sounds that came out were. . . off. Shaken like bees thrown around in their own hive, each word stinging as it left her. "You're a joke."

"You're a bit—"

The car slung forward like an uncontrollable rocket ship seconds away from a crash landing as it drifted across the lanes. Without thinking, Fatima instinctively grabbed the door handle, her stomach spinning as erratically as the car.

Javier reached out for her. "Ti!"

They were hydroplaning. The car had initially pulled left on its own, led by the rain-slicked road. In his overcorrection— yanking the wheel right—Javier had only made things worse. They spun out in wide, helpless circles, drifting from one edge of the highway to the other.

Fatima shut her eyes and held her breath.

"Ti, I can't stop it!"

Somewhere between the first and fourth lane they'd shot across, Fatima's mouth had been sewn shut, filled with wet cement that dried there. What was the last thing she'd said to him? *You're a joke.* Would that be the last sentence that fled her tongue before she died? If Javier survived this, would that be the depiction he remembered her as? Would he laugh at her funeral? Would he go? Would he miss her? Would he notice she was gone? Would he care?

"Ti, please!"

It was only seconds. Seconds before the car swung into the guardrail on the opposite end of the highway, leaving them facing oncoming traffic. Seconds she still saw in the hushed stillness at night whenever she couldn't fall asleep. Seconds where Javier's head had rammed into his window. His body going limp. His blood covering his T-shirt. The smell of rain and oil mixing, a thick and smoldering incense.

Fatima stared at him as he lay there, a spiderweb of glass had cut into the window around his head like a broken halo, and she didn't know what to do about it. She wasn't hurt in the crash. Not bad enough. Not like him. But her mouth still took too many of those precious seconds to work. To fit out his name. To scream. To beg for him to wake up like he'd begged her for help that she couldn't give before they'd crashed.

Javier took too many seconds to come to. Seconds Fatima spent softly whimpering that she'd never yell at him again. Never try to leave him again if he just opened his eyes. So it was only right that, once he'd finally managed to heave himself out of the car—now smashed in on the driver's side from the guardrail impact—and into the rain, that she kept her promises.

A few people pulled over to help them in the shoulder lane. One of them called an ambulance. Another assisted Javier in popping his shoulder back into its socket when he discovered it was out of alignment. Fatima heard the joint click into place like a skewed Lego. She heard those three dumb words she'd said before he lost control of the car in the seconds before he almost died.

You're a joke. You're a joke. You're a joke.

What she'd told him kicked around in her head like the offbeat rhythm of an unsteady drum, reminding her, after all, that it was her fault the accident happened. Really.

So, she spent all her time from then on hoping to make it up to him.

CHAPTER TWENTY-EIGHT

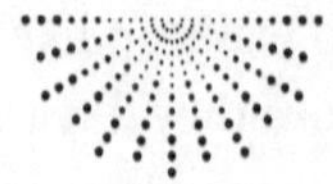

Saturday morning, Iyad decided to open Azyaa alone, telling himself that he needed the distraction to help purge Fatima from his mind. It was a shift he usually had no trouble talking Mo out of since his cousin usually hated coming in at all on most Saturday mornings. And evenings.

Iyad unlocked the storefront, flipped over the open sign for incoming customers, then walked back to his seat behind the counter, thinking of what to do next.

For all intents and purposes, Iyad was sure he couldn't stand Javier and whatever vampire-like grip he had on Fatima, but Javier hadn't torn into him at that Nando's yesterday. Fatima had been brutal with him. Still, Iyad missed her. He wanted to know how she was doing and if she missed him, too. If she slept well and was drinking enough water, because sometimes, she forgot to. But she'd made her stance on him clear enough already, so it wasn't like he was going to ask.

If he's no good, then you're no better.

Those words kept replaying in Iyad's head. He wanted to believe Fatima didn't mean it. That the steady, hardened look on her face as she spoke, something cold and dark, actually had nothing to do with him. That his impulsively suggesting taking back their friendship for something more wasn't such a bad idea. That it wasn't a bad idea to want something more with her. Because she wanted something more with him, too.

If he's no good, then you're no better.

Yesterday, Iyad had experienced a moment. A moment where he genuinely didn't care how it happened. He didn't care about her going back to the States. About anything other than the fact that somehow, someway, they ended up together on the same side of the Atlantic. He wanted to have a chance with her so badly, but then Javier called and ruined everything, and then he'd gone and gotten himself caught in the middle of it.

Or. Maybe. Maybe it wasn't all Javier's fault—Iyad hated the thought the second it manifested, but maybe he was in the wrong, too. Maybe it was selfish to ask what Iyad did to her. At that time, at least. Maybe Iyad was so over being alone that he jumped at the chance to change it. Maybe she was so new to being alone that she didn't want to. Still, that didn't change what she'd said.

If he's no good, then you're no better.

What did that even *mean?* Fatima had been with Javier for years, and in the span of the few months she'd known Iyad, she saw him in the same light? Was that fair? Did he have the right to question if it was? Iyad was in the middle of pulling at his beard in thought so tightly that it might've been at risk of falling completely off when he heard his name.

"Iyad?" Hassan's voice, hushed and tentative, brought him back to reality. "Yad, you alright?"

Iyad's old therapist used to do an exercise with him called "Switch." The goal was to force Iyad to say exactly what he thought, without any thought at all. He was probably thinking of that exercise when he responded, the word coming out rough and shifty, as if it were standing on the ledge of a high building wanting to fall. "No."

There was a pause before his uncle spoke. "Would you-Would you like to talk about it?" he probed carefully.

Iyad looked around the store. No one was inside yet apart from the two of them, but he couldn't understand why it was even the two of them when he was supposed to be there alone. "Why are you here?" Iyad interrogated instead of answering, the borders of his words coming out octaves higher than usual. He sounded like he'd been crying.

"Was in the neighborhood," Hassan sighed. "You know mornings are the best time for walking."

That was true. His dad and uncle used to love going on morning walks together, catching up. Iyad hadn't realized until right then that his uncle had been doing it alone for all these years.

"You wanna tell me what's going on?" Hassan tried again.

Without any thought at all, Iyad repeated, "No."

"Hm," Hassan hummed, and they fell into a stiff silence for a moment.

"How do you know when it's time to let go of someone you care about?" The question threw itself out of Iyad like it'd been waiting to escape.

Hassan eyed his nephew carefully. "Why let go if you care for them?"

"Because I don't think they want me to."

"To let go of them or to care for them?"

That was a good question. So good, in fact, that Iyad had absolutely no idea how to go about answering it. He weighed both sides. Fatima obviously didn't mind him letting go of her. Yesterday had made that fact abundantly clear.

In the time he'd known her, she seemed more accepting of him caring for her, though. So long as it was in a friendship capacity. The problem was that he didn't want to be her friend anymore. He wasn't so sure if he ever did. He took in a breath. "I don't know," he grunted. But he did know: Stop caring. Let go. Move on.

Easier said than done.

Hassan came behind the counter, clapping Iyad gently on the back. His hand lingered there. For some reason, Iyad didn't jerk it away. "I know that in missing him, in. . . seeing me," he faltered. "I know these years haven't been easy on you, Yad."

Wait.

Did he think Iyad was talking about his father?

"But we've loved you this whole time," Hassan continued. Iyad didn't correct him. "We never want you to feel like distancing yourself was something we wanted. We- I thought—"

"It's just easier," Iyad interrupted, straddling the fence between talking about his dad and Fatima. "Why go somewhere if my presence only complicates things?"

"Yad." Hassan's voice was as stern as it used to be when he and Mo acted out of order as kids. It made him pay attention. His uncle's eyes shone with a glint of something Iyad couldn't quite decipher. Heartache? Could you see a heart aching through someone's eyes? "Kum faya Kum," he told him. *Be, and it is.* "The nature of being alive is in its complications. That's the fun of it, that you never know what's coming next. The sooner you accept things as they are, the sooner those complications aren't as hard on you anymore."

"What if I don't deserve them to be easy? What if it's all my fault?" Iyad murmured.

"What is?"

"All of it. Everything. I'm always in the wrong place at the wrong time, saying the wrong things."

"You're always exactly where you need to be."

Hassan said this so decisively that Iyad found himself nearly believing him. But his uncle wasn't there. He hadn't seen Fatima. Hadn't felt her anger so strongly that he could smell it, heavy and acrid. She'd changed right in front of him from the person he thought he knew, the one who understood him well enough to know he'd never hurt her, and into a stranger.

But maybe his uncle was right. Maybe it was all just complicated.

"How do you know that?" Iyad's hand traveled behind him to the back of his neck, holding it in place. Not so much to change the subject, but to understand how they'd even gotten to where they were now, he asked, "And why did you keep trying with me? Keep talking to me? Aren't you angry about how I've treated you since. . . it happened?"

"You weren't so bad." Hassan smiled, playfully shooing him. "You *aren't* bad at all. You were hurt, and you were grieving, and you were doing your best to protect yourself."

It hadn't occurred to Iyad until then that this was the reason he'd acted how he did for all those years—protecting himself. Was Fatima doing the same? Did she feel so defenseless that defending herself from him felt like her only viable option?

Iyad had been so wrapped up in how her words had affected him that he hadn't once stopped to consider that his might've done the same. Might've bothered her so much because . . . maybe. . . did she. . . did Fatima want to be mo—

The door chimed just as Iyad almost completed his doomed train of thought. Both he and Hassan looked over as a customer walked in. Hassan nodded and went to assist the man, leaving Iyad alone to think. He decided then that, no matter his feelings toward Fatima, he would do exactly what his uncle had done for him: stay away. He'd give her space and see what happened after. If that meant she went back to the States and nothing changed between them, then he'd just have to accept that as his own complication.

CHAPTER TWENTY-NINE

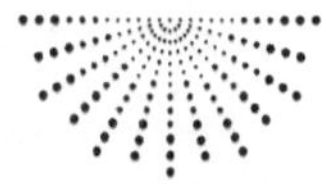

THE SUNDAY BEFORE THEIR LONDON PROGRAM HAD OFFICIALLY ended, Fatima was staring outside of the 87 bus's window as it swept over the city. Tom was hosting a "Fine Arts & Dining Day" for everyone interested from their school program. They were currently on their way to Tate Britain, and she was busy thinking about how weird it was to be on an outing without Iyad around.

Fatima's whole body was raw. Two days ago, she'd felt like it'd been sucker punched, throwing her spirit from it and leaving her forced to watch in horror as she tore into Iyad like a crazed shark who smelled blood in the water.

The singular fact remained that Fatima liked Iyad. So, when he questioned taking back their—she thought—well-established friendship, she short-circuited. She was confused. She was still processing that Javier had finally confirmed what she'd already known about Bea and combined that information with exactly what she'd been waiting to hear: him wanting her back despite that. She was still working through her feelings about both revelations. More, she was working through her confusion that she wasn't feeling much of anything at all about Javier in the tender way she always had. And that she was beginning to see Iyad in that light instead.

While he was busy being funny.

She shifted toward Sadiyah, in the seat next to her, and quickly asked before giving herself a chance to reconsider, "Should I text him?"

Sadiyah studied her. Through the window beside her, the early-May flowers hanging outside the shops looked more vibrant in the soft afternoon light. "Javier?"

Fatima couldn't decide if it was more concerning to her that Sadiyah's first instinct was to assume she was referring to Javier or that she'd called him Javier instead of Pretty Boy.

"Iyad, actually," Fatima corrected.

Sadiyah opened her mouth to respond, and just like when they'd initially left Nando's until now, promptly closed it. Her mouth made a sharp popping sound, like a bubble bursting.

"I think I might like him," Fatima admitted, hoarsely.

Sadiyah made the same open-mouthed plop. "I'm in shock," she goaded.

Fatima rolled her eyes.

The bus rolled to a stop near the museum, and Tom jumped from his seat up front. "Come along, everyone. Let's keep moving!" he called, ushering everyone outside.

Looking at Tate Britain, Fatima felt a little like she was back in fifth grade on a field trip around Washington, D.C., since the building reminded her so much of one she'd find there at first glance. Fatima was still thinking about how briefly familiar everything around her was when Sadiyah, abruptly, broke her concentration.

"Ti. Speak," she prompted impatiently, folding her arms as they headed toward the building. "You were saying you're in love with Iyad."

Fatima pursed her lips. "I was not saying that," she said hotly, fiddling an anxious hand over her hijab to make sure it wasn't out of place. She kept her hand there, confessing quietly, "But I messed up."

Sadiyah agreed. "So you want to apologize?"

Fatima nodded. "Is that a bad idea?"

"No, just—" Sadiyah stopped walking at the top of the steps and pinched her nose. Fatima held her breath. "What would you say?"

"I don't know. I don't know what came over me then."

"I do," she shrugged. "You went into survival mode. You're terrified of things you don't understand, and before you had a chance to figure out what was going on with Javier showing up from whatever evil cave he dragged himself out of, Iyad shocked you. And you got mad because you wanted him to mean what he said—because you like him."

Oh. Yeah. That was actually exactly what'd happened. So, of course, she'd have to clean the mess she'd made. Fatima thought about what she'd say to him as they walked inside the museum while Tom described Tate Britain's interior. Its "beautifully laden original Victorian architecture, high ornate ceilings, and wonderfully large windows that let in natural light for all of the work on display." She walked past Van Gogh paintings in golden frames, still thinking of Iyad. Still debating how he preferred his apologies.

Would he accept a simple, *I'm sorry, please forgive me?* Then, maybe a heart? Or, since he was English, should she sign it with an "x?" Or was it an "o?" Which one stood for hugs and which for kisses again? Now was not the time to confuse them.

Maybe she shouldn't ask for forgiveness at all because it could come across as baiting him into reciprocating. Maybe she should say more. Yeah. What about, *Hey, I'm sorry. I like you and I'm scared that I like you because I know you don't like me. I know I overreacted when you joked about us being more than friends and that it was harmless because we are friends but I like you and I was caught off guard by you. & by Javier. Actually, no—let's not talk about Javier.*

But Iyad, I'm sorry. I'm so so sooOo sooOOOoOoOoOoO so sorry. I really am. Forgive me? Unless you don't want to, of course. But it would be cool if you did.

That one was a hard pass, too. Way too telling, and the grammar wasn't winning any awards either.

Fatima kept walking around the exhibit, ending up in front of a painting featuring Jesus, Alayha as-Salam—*Peace be upon him*—when her phone buzzed. Iyad?

Javi:

> Do you forgive me yet, baby?

Ugh. Was that what she sounded like as she thought of how best to apologize to Iyad? The way Javier skulked back to her suddenly reeked of desperation in a way it never had before. She stuffed her phone in her pocket to clear the scent of him from her mind, glancing back at the painting before turning to Sadiyah with a burning question she never thought to ask until now. "Have you ever thought of stopping?"

"Stopping?" Sadiyah stared.

"Practicing Islam," Fatima choked the words out.

Sadiyah twisted the "S" pendant of her necklace. "Huh?" she almost whispered, most likely trying to figure out why Fatima had switched from boys to religion. But she recovered. "Yeah, I did. I never stopped completely, but I did question it for a while. I think it's logical to be on the fence about something sometimes rather than just mindlessly saying yes or no. Why? Are you thinking of—"

"No," Fatima said quickly. "I just wonder how you were sure which side of the fence to stand on."

Sadiyah looked back at the painting. "His mother," she decided with finality. "You know, there's always a lot of nativity scenes out during Christmastime. I saw one at the store one day and realized that Mary, Alayha as-Salam, always wore a head covering," she pursed her lips. "I just thought that was so beautiful, that everyone remembers her that way. Made me never want to take mine off."

Fatima thought about that. She grew up in church, attending Sunday school, and waking up to Kirk Franklin songs on Saturday mornings when it was time to clean. She knew the rhythms of the pews for years until her parents became Muslim and everything changed. She followed them without question. Years later, when all she had were questions and no satisfying answers, she decided to stop asking—trusting anything Javier said as the answers she needed instead.

Something about finding Iyad when Fatima was finding her religion made her feel completely different, though. Things were easy with him.

Iyad carried a patience toward Fatima that Javier always lacked. He didn't try to change her. He reminded her of Jumu'ah prayers on Fridays, sitting on the ground cross-legged in her socks and listening to the imam's khutbah while the little kids played. Waking up at five in the morning to pray, fasting during Ramadan, and the accomplishment of making it to Eid afterward, even her Eid outfits that she always felt so pretty in.

She didn't have to be careful with him. Being herself always felt like more than enough. Now, because she'd gone off the deep end, there was a good chance he'd never want her around him again at all. And she hated even the idea of that.

After a few beats of silence between them, Fatima finally said, "Thank you," because she couldn't think of any other words to explain how well Sadiyah had just untangled things for her. "You can be so smart sometimes, Sads."

Sadiyah's lip twitched. "I get by."

. . .

A FEW HOURS LATER, AFTER LEAVING THE MUSEUM AND attending a play that Fatima was too preoccupied with thoughts of Iyad to remember, Tom led everyone to a cozy Italian restaurant somewhere in Soho. Fatima and Sadiyah both had bruschetta, followed by seafood pasta.

After Tom paid for their group's tab, they all lingered outside for a little while longer, laughing as midnight approached. By then, Tom was rolling his own cigarettes like they were blunts, completely ignoring the pack's overly graphic health warnings. At the same time, Fatima and Sadiyah were eating their gelato, since they hadn't gotten any drinks. Somewhere around then, the girls realized they were the only sober ones left from their group.

"Now, are you sure you both can find your way home?" Tom asked, after drunkenly explaining their way back.

They had no business being so sure of themselves when they said yes.

CHAPTER THIRTY

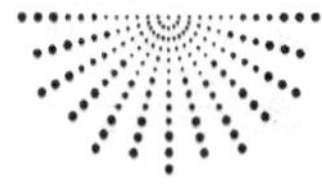

It should come as no surprise that Fatima and Sadiyah got lost almost as soon as they left Tom. In their defense, Drunk Tom gave terrible directions, Sadiyah's phone died, and Fatima's GPS wouldn't stop glitching.

"Don't you work in Soho?" Sadiyah asked, open-mouthed.

"Not after twelve in the morning," Fatima grumbled, struggling to defend herself. They were in an unfamiliar neighborhood, submerged in pools of London fog that only meant that they could've been anywhere, as far as Fatima was concerned. "Didn't Tom say we have to take the bus since the trains don't run this late?" she tried. "Here," she glanced at the map on her phone as a bus rolled to a stop in front of them. "This one has to be right."

It wasn't.

The girls ended up further in no man's land, with two no-good phones and Tom's now-useless instructions. As they began to gauge they weren't getting any closer to their homestay, Fatima decided it was time to try one last idea.

She pressed 'call' before she could lose the nerve to do so. Then, promptly began to lose it anyway on the first ring. By the third, it was definitely gone. By the fourth, she was sure she shouldn't have called in the first place, especially with the way she'd left things between them. But he answered on the fifth.

"Hello?" he murmured. His voice was slow and heavy and made her forget why she'd called him in the first place.

"Iyad," she answered, eyes locked tight on her Sambas as she tried hard to block out Sadiyah's probing stare.

"Fatima?" The word heated her up from the inside out when he said it. She wanted to hear him say it again.

"Yeah," she confirmed, working up the nerve to keep talking. "We're lost. Do you mind—"

And maybe it was the way he didn't hesitate or that he didn't ask her any questions. All Iyad responded with was a simple, "I'm coming." Still, it was the fact that he was so willing to show up, despite everything strange between them, that shredded her —simply, happily—into tiny, infinitesimal pieces.

◆ ◆ ◆

WHEN IYAD'S BEDROOM WAS NEAR-PITCH BLACK AND HE HAD SIX trails of spit trailing down from the side of his mouth and onto his pillow, his phone rang. "Hello?" He didn't know who it was, but whoever was calling him was going to get an earful for it. He'd either just been in the middle of a dream or battling a dragon and winning.

"Iyad."

Immediately, he stared at his phone screen, read her name to see if he was imagining things, then put it back to his ear, still half believing that he was. Half believing that he'd heard her voice enough times to dream up even the vowel shifts of the way she said his name perfectly. He took a breath. "Fatima?"

"Yeah." She sounded worried, which quickly worried him. "We're lost. Do you mind—"

Something in him jerked then, and Iyad was sitting up in his bed before he'd realized it, "I'm coming."

IYAD HAD INITIALLY SUSPECTED THERE WERE TOUR GUIDE DUTIES for the Fatima and Sadiyah written in invisible ink on Tom's assignment guide after they were all grouped together. Funny that, since they turned out to be nowhere near as painful as he'd initially thought them to be. Happy coincidences, he decided.

Fatima called him because she and Sadiyah had gotten lost on a random road somewhere and didn't know how to get home. He was already well acquainted with the fact that their shared sense of direction was, in a nutshell, rubbish. From knowing them over the past few months, he'd also understood their sense of pride to be, for starters, significant. So, if they called him at one in the morning, they needed him. And if they needed him, if Fatima needed him, he'd be there.

Thankfully, although things were still rocky between them, Fatima hadn't turned off her shared location yet. Iyad wanted to make a pit stop at his mom's to pick up his dad's car, but he decided against it because it would have taken him too much extra time. He threw on a pair of gray tracksuit bottoms and a hoodie, then left his room. They were about twenty minutes away by bus if he hurried.

"Sorry we put you out," Fatima's voice mumbled through his phone's receiver.

They hadn't hung up since she'd initially called. Iyad rationalized that since she had enough battery life to do so, it was better to keep her on the phone while he was on his way, just to be sure they were alright. Not for the few pencil shavings of conversation that warranted him when she wasn't talking to Sadiyah. Although he wasn't complaining about them either.

Iyad had concluded that he wouldn't talk about what happened between them before, because now clearly wasn't the time. He would play it cool. He would be her friend. He fixed his beanie over his head as the 205 bus arrived. "Shut up," he chuckled softly, stepping on and tapping his card against the reader. "Let's play Would You Rather."

"Would You Rather?" she asked, and Iyad could practically see her pupils turn to question marks. He liked how even in their more than awkward haze between the uncertainty of "Are we good or not?", she was still her. A little wobbly, but still, there was that unmistakable Fatima-ness that he gravitated to. Sweet and warm. "Like, would you rather speak any language or to any animal?"

"Exactly. And any language," he answered, his mind wandering as he considered his question for her. Iyad leaned back into the seat, closed his eyes for a moment, and yawned. "Would you rather be stranded on an island with no one to call or on Baker Street with me to call?"

He actually heard her suck in a breath. It was a solid five seconds before Fatima said anything. "The island. Definitely the island."

"Have you always been this stubborn?" Iyad opened his eyes after hearing someone cough. When he scanned around, he found that other than the driver, there was a man on the other side of the bus behind him with the first iPod Nano he'd seen in years. He turned back around.

"Would you rather me be stubborn or boring?" Fatima teased.

Iyad looked outside at the deep blue city illuminated by streetlights and office windows. "Boring," he teased back, and pressed the bell to signal his stop, making sure to thank the driver when he left.

She laughed faintly, then redirected her attention to Sadiyah, saying something about their host mom and how much she'd been enjoying their time away from her antics. As they talked,

Iyad followed his phone's directions until he found them standing over by the Baker Street tube station.

"Behind you," he cut his way into their conversation, and just like the first day he saw her, Fatima swung her head around to face him. Except this time, instead of frowning, he could've sworn he saw the corners of her mouth lift and that barely there dimple. He could've sworn...

Iyad's throat bobbed. He swallowed hard as they hung up their phones, now facing each other. "Hey, Ti," he said.

"Hey, Yad," she smiled, and there it was again. That gentle curve. That pencil shaving.

CHAPTER THIRTY-ONE

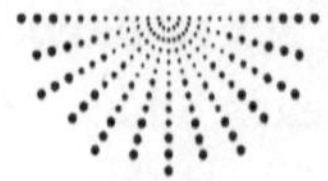

Fatima sat next to Iyad on the ride back to her homestay. They'd had to take two buses, the first of which went for about thirty stops before they transferred to their current one, where they'd have to wait for about another ten. None of them had spoken on the first bus, and as Fatima watched from the corner of her eye as Iyad's GPS bobbed on his shaking leg while he navigated their bus route, she wasn't so sure if this ride would be any different.

Iyad seemed nervous. Fatima wanted to know if she was making him nervous. If he felt as nervous as she did, herself. She took a fidgety, shallow breath, squeezed her eyes shut for a moment, and decided to bite the bullet, "Iyad?"

Iyad blinked, peaking over at her. "Yeah?"

There was an instant. A glimpse when she called him and he was on his way, that things between them felt as if they'd gone back to normal. But now, in the hollow lull amidst the steady mechanical whir of the bus's engine, things had definitely gotten weird again.

"Can we uh—" Fatima started. She sounded like a child asking for candy after their bedtime. "Can we talk?"

He nodded. "Sure."

"I'm sorry," Fatima blurted. She bit her lip, trying to figure out what to say next since those two words were the only ones she'd cemented back at the museum.

Fatima wasn't good at talking. Not when the things she needed to say were important, at least. Then, Fatima shone more on paper—and at least after her fifth draft of efforts. But Iyad had come to find them in the middle of the night with no objections. After what she'd said to him, he was still here. So, he deserved for her to at least try.

"I was out of line when I yelled at you. I know there's no excuse for it, but I just wanted you to know that it had nothing to do with you. I'm. . . working through some things."

Iyad nodded slowly, analytically like a professor assessing a thesis. "It's okay, Ti- Fatima. Things happen."

"No." She leaned toward him without thinking. "You were being my friend, and because I like—" She stopped talking, remembering the line between words she should and shouldn't say. "Like, I took it wrong," she corrected herself, "and things escalated because of it."

Fatima hesitated. When things spiraled with Iyad, she told herself it was because he was just like Javier. That he'd hung around her so she'd drop her guard around him, and she'd eventually become dependent only on him. That he was using the same demented playbook as Javier did on her. She should've known how absurd the thought was when it'd first struck her. Should've realized she was just triggered at the fact that she liked Iyad already, and that he was so solid in their friendship that he thought he could play around about it with her.

If she hadn't felt for Iyad the way she did now, things could've been as simple for her as they were for him. So, Fatima decided it'd be best if she cut down her feelings to: Iyad, boy, London, friend—because maybe then she could keep him in her life a little while longer.

"Look," she tried to start again, but her breath caught on the words she hadn't yet said. "We're just friends. Friends joke. So I just wanted to say that I'm sorry for taking things too far and I-I hope you'll forgive me."

There was a second, so quick she almost tried to convince herself she hadn't seen it, where something flashed in Iyad's eyes that she couldn't decipher, distant and unreadable. Before Fatima could make sense of it, it was gone.

"Yeah. Forgiven. Friends. Exactly," Iyad told her.

"Exactly," Fatima forced herself to agree.

"I forgive you. I—" Iyad clarified, then faltered. "Just remember I'm not him, okay. I'm not—"

"I know," Fatima couldn't stop herself from interjecting, but she needed to be sure Iyad heard her. Understood she meant what she was telling him. "I've always known that. I'm sorry."

"So, then," Iyad clapped. "We're good. We're," he swallowed hard, "friends."

Fatima smiled, but she couldn't have meant the action any less. "Great. And start calling me Ti again," she tried to joke with him. Like a friend. Because that's what friends do. Joke.

"'Kay, Ti," Iyad smiled back. It was cautious, but it was there. "Oh, and as you both know," he spoke up so Sadiyah could hear him, although Fatima was sure she and the bus driver, as the only other two people around, had heard everything already up until then. "Ramadan's coming up, and since it's your final week in London—and Ti said she wanted to try my mum's cooking— would you guys like to come by for Iftar?"

Fatima tried not to overthink what it could've meant that Iyad was inviting them to have dinner after fasting all day for Ramadan with his family, since, after all, he was inviting her *and* Sadiyah—maybe even the bus driver. She had to remember that she wasn't anyone special. Not where it counted. She was just a friend. Just platonic.

"Ti never said she wanted to try your mom's food," Sadiyah

said, deadpan as she looked up from the game she was playing on her phone. "She said she wanted to meet your mom, if I remember correctly." Her grin was more wicked than the Cheshire Cat's. "But yeah, I'm game."

Fatima glared at her friend, who shrugged innocently and went back to her phone. "We'll be there," she grumbled, attempting to sound nonchalant, though the anxious flutters inside of her were anything but. "Oh, also," she added, desperate to change the subject. "I know I left you in the dark about it—and again, my apologies—but I finished our presentation, so we should be fine for tomorrow. Just," she scrunched her face, thinking of how she'd basically used their project as an outlet to rant about how angry Javier (and Iyad, at the time) had made her, "please know I was very upset while I was working on it." Fatima managed a tight laugh that she was sure fooled absolutely no one.

"No worries," Iyad grinned, handsome as ever. "Less work for me."

"Exactly," Sadiyah agreed, and no one spoke again. Not until the bus reached their neighborhood, where Iyad walked them to their doorstep and said he wouldn't leave until he heard the front door's lock click. Another thirty minutes passed before he texted their group chat to let them know he was home.

Fatima waited up, noticing that he'd changed their chat's photo back to the Spider-Men meme she'd initially set for them, most likely because she wore hijab now and wasn't in the previous picture. How considerate.

Iyad:

Made it back.

It was a little after three in the morning at that point, and

Fatima was swooning at her phone like a world-class idiot. She wrote back.

Ti:

great. thanks for coming, tg.

And because she couldn't help herself.

Ti:

i'm glad tom made you keep us around. 

But that didn't begin to cover what she'd meant. What she'd wanted to say was something more along the lines of, *Thank you for showing up. Thank you for still being here*, and, *Please don't leave me.* But that's not what you say to a friend, so she told him goodnight and closed her phone, annoyingly remembering she still hadn't yet responded to Javier.

CHAPTER THIRTY-TWO

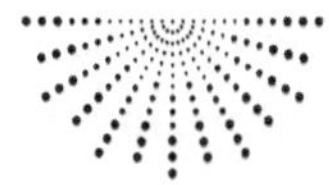

THAT NEXT DAY—ACTUALLY, THAT SAME MONDAY MORNING—
Iyad put his alarm on snooze five times before praying when
dawn came in, then six more times leading up to Tom's lecture.
On the seventh alarm right before class, Iyad opened one eye
just long enough to see that Fatima had sent him a screenshot of
Tom okaying them being late to class that morning because of
the night—same morning—before. So, he snoozed the
eighth one.

The ninth.

And tenth.

But that didn't stop them from still having to present once
they'd all arrived.

"My ever-tardy King Henry VIII troupe," Tom patted his
open palm on the desk a few times with a sneaking grin. "What
place does Tudor England have in our present day?"

Small (not-so-small) confession? Iyad hated public speaking.
It was embarrassing. His thoughts got all jumbled and came out
in knots, unlike the girls, who approached the class with a mili-
taristic precision.

Rather than reading paragraphs word-for-word from

PowerPoint slides, they led the class in a discussion focused on the binary fundamental values of personage as they pertain to patriarchal structures. It was a concept that might've taken Iyad a lifetime to come up with. But according to Fatima, it barely took her the train ride home after she'd left him at Nando's— which he quickly understood meant that the clear multitude of quips she'd come up with when referencing Henry wasn't only at Javier's expense. Iyad wondered how much of what she'd initially written down with him in mind was encased in feelings she still held.

"And so, as this relates to relationships in Tudor and contemporary times," Fatima was saying, "let's look at the family unit. Say I'm Catherine of Aragon, the first of six wives to my husband, King Henry VIII." She glanced at Iyad with those star-filled eyes, and for a quick-tempted second, Iyad was glad to take Henry's place.

He'd automatically ignored the "first of six" comment, caught up entirely on the unfettered "my" and "husband-ness" of what she'd said. Yesterday—today—Fatima had apologized to him, and Iyad was intent on making things go back to normal somehow, smoothing out their friendship as if he felt nothing for her at all.

Fatima cleared her throat. He'd completely forgotten she'd written out a list of cues for when it was his turn to speak—it currently was. Iyad looked down at the notes and said, "What is her role in my life and mine in hers?"

Traditional hunter-gatherer epithets were thrown around the classroom that Sadiyah listed on the whiteboard, where men were likened to *breadwinner* and *protector,* while women were *caregiver, nurturer,* and so on.

"Now," Sadiyah turned to the class, capping her dry-erase marker. "In Catherine and Henry's case—and we're only focusing on them because if we went through all of his marriages, we'd be here all day," she grinned, earning a few cursory laughs throughout the room. "Is it fair to say these roles are evidence of a flawed structure if there's no room for flexibility?"

"Flexibility as in?" Tom asked, his tone leading.

"Contingencies," Fatima answered nimbly, twirling the end of her hijab around her finger. Iyad noticed she'd been wearing it a lot more frequently lately. "Henry only became king because his brother died, which led to his marriage to his brother's widowed wife. That's a smooth contingency.

"However, with Catherine," she continued, "Henry had two main challenges: first, he struggled to father a male heir who survived infancy—only his daughter Mary I survived from his first marriage. Second, he failed to secure an annulment from the Pope to end that marriage after he'd most likely decided it was Catherine's fault for not giving him a healthy enough son. So, the most logical contingencies would've either been to make his succession work despite having a daughter, or to continue trying for a son."

"What if he didn't see those as options?" Tom pressed.

"Clearly, he didn't," Fatima parried. "He thought changing his people's way of life because he couldn't get his way was the better alternative."

"How exactly?" Tom continued to push.

"By breaking from the Catholic Church led by the Pope, and creating the Church of England with himself at the head of it, just so that he could grant himself his own divorce. He was greedy. He put his own needs before his people's, and a world leader whose world exists only in his mirror or in those who resemble his reflection doesn't deserve that title."

Tom conceded with a nod.

Sadiyah arched an eyebrow briefly at Fatima, probably catching the edge Iyad had in her friend's voice. She went back to the whiteboard, drawing the class's attention back to her. "If a woman's place in society is only to contribute solely to a man's comfort, we can agree that's limiting, right?" She drew a triangle with *King Henry VIII* scrawled at its center. Then, she wrote out the words *wife, mother,* and *whore* on its outlying margins.

"Especially when that man is insecure," Sadiyah continued. "Then, the supposed head of the household, of the *country* in this case, is unstable, which means that when he starts to fall, everyone behind him tumbles after like dominoes. First, his wife," she pointed to the word on the bottom left of the triangle, "is broken down as an autonomous being. Then, as a mother," she gestured toward the triangle's peak, the supposed pinnacle of womanhood inevitably collapsing in on itself. Finally, at the last word, she concluded, "Once her worth is reduced to her genitalia as a so-called 'whore,' then, as said before, all anyone thinks of her is that, 'She's for the streets.'"

Bits of laughter.

"No one cares about her as a person anymore," Sadiyah shook her head, cueing Iyad that it was just about his time to take over, "just what she can do for them. What she can *give* of herself to them."

Iyad straightened his shoulders. Dear God, he hated public speaking. He glanced down at his notes from Fatima again; her handwriting, a daintily mixed blend of cursive and print, was so cute. . . and small. Honestly, it was incredibly hard to read when he was already so preoccupied with trying not to make a fool of himself in front of the class.

"Where we see this fitting into society today," he hedged, squinting his eyes at the paper, "is in loveless partnerships built on unrealistic entitlement and unsatisfied expectations that seed resentment.

"After Henry's son Edward," Iyad went on, "from his third marriage, came to power and eventually passed, the throne passed to Mary, his daughter from his first marriage. Mary likely resented her father's break from the Catholic Church because it was directly tied to his disrespect for her mother and the faith she'd grown up in. So, like her father, she made her personal struggles a national one, executing Protestant leaders and reformers who opposed her efforts to restore Catholicism in England. That's why she's remembered as Bloody Mary today."

"Daddy issues," a voice spoke up before Iyad could pinpoint where it came from.

"I understand this is how his actions are mirrored in our society, but where does he *fit?*" Tom probed.

"Right where he's always been," Fatima spoke up. "Except when he does something unforgivable, it's still somehow forgiven. He's proof of a flawed system that's allowed for those antics to exist and for contemporary men like him to feel validated in their actions, no matter who gets hurt. Case in point: most of you might not have known or remembered why we still say Bloody Mary if you weren't in this class. Still, saying the name is commonplace. But why doesn't Henry get a nickname? Why is what he did allowed to be forgotten?"

It was something about the way she'd asked her last question —like she was pleading for an answer she still desperately needed, as if she'd already asked herself the same over and over, and came up with nothing. After she said it, the class was quiet for a few suspended moments, then moved on to the next presentation without deviating much from their usual flow, acting as if what she'd posed was rhetorical and never answering her.

Not even Iyad.

CHAPTER THIRTY-THREE

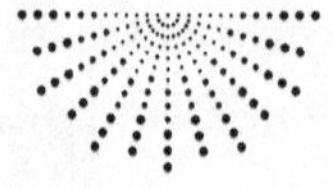

FATIMA WAS SITTING ACROSS FROM CLAUDETTE AT A FISH AND chips restaurant in Camden Market for their last lunch together, explaining the details of what had happened over the weekend and into yesterday.

Fatima liked her conversations with Claudette because Claudette always helped to make sense of things that didn't make sense to Fatima by finding the heart of stories within reality. And stories were good for Fatima because stories were fiction. Fiction was always practical when real life wasn't. And practical was good. Right now, practical was practically a godsend.

Her phone vibrated on the table, and she flipped it over to see the notification.

Javi:

Baby?

She flipped it back.

"Your ex sounds like a bare idiot," Claudette squinched,

taking a bite of her cod. "And he showed up while you were with the new guy, right? What's his name again? Eeee," she drawled the sound out with a little smirk.

Fatima pretended not to see it. "Iyad. And he's not 'the new guy,'" she repeated. "He's just my friend."

"Iyad." Claudette thought for a moment, disregarding her. "We like Iyad?"

"We do."

"But Iyad doesn't like us. . . romantically?"

"He doesn't."

She sighed dramatically, putting her fork down. "I'm going to say something crazy."

"Please don't."

Claudette half-grinned. "What if he does? What if you're creating this one-sided love narrative that, although I'm sure would work out great as a book, is maybe not what's actually happening right now?" When Fatima looked away, Claudette continued. "I get it, though, you know? When I was around your age, I moved into a flat with my first real boyfriend after knowing him for just six months, because he needed a flatmate and I was young*er* and dumb enough in love to do that for him.

"Anyway, he cheated the whole time and lied about it and everything else so often that I just got used to accepting what he said rather than challenging him. Then he broke up with me right before our lease was up a year later, because he, quote, 'wanted to experience more of the world and less of my oppressing exigencies.'"

"You're kidding," Fatima stared. It was hard for her to imagine anyone treating Claudette that way.

"He was a literary-type, too. He always had to dream up exhaustive ways to tell me I was too needy when all I ever really needed was for him to care about me," she explained, annoyed. "Want to know where he told me all of this?"

Fatima canted her head in question.

"On the tube, if you can believe it," she scoffed humorlessly, her gold tooth flickering against the light. "The class act said he didn't want me to 'make a scene,' so he did it in public, and I was so delusional then that I just convinced myself all of our drama was romantic conflicts in our developing storyline. That they could be turning points if we both cared enough to make them that. But now he's married with kids. . . to one of the girls he cheated on me with, no less."

"Poor them," Fatima laughed softly.

"I know, right?" Claudette joined in, and for a brief moment, their laughter was all there was before she continued. "It took me years to feel like myself again after all that time spent pining over a runt of a boy who never deserved me anyway."

Fatima was thoughtful for a moment before she asked, "You think I'm doing that? Pining over a runt?"

Claudette squeezed a lemon wedge across her plate. "I think you're caught between what's known and unknown to you, and you're scared. You were definitely pining for your ex when you first arrived. Now, I think you're scared that you're realizing you don't need him as much as you thought you did, and that there may be something better to have been gained from this Eeee," she drawled again.

Fatima rolled her eyes. She knew Claudette was well aware of his name by now. Still, she bit. "Iyad." She rolled her shoulders, straightening her back as she responded. "But like I told you, we're just—"

"Friends?" Claudette lifted her eyebrow. "My love, I've never met this boy, but I think you've drastically misread the situation here."

Fatima tried not to choke. "Huh?"

"'Huh?'" Claudette repeated. "If I'm not mistaken, you only know him because you and your friend were assigned to a project together. Four months ago. A project that you decided to do on your own in the end, might I add. A project that you all barely worked on all this time because you were too busy just hanging out together. A project that, even when it was over, he still made an excuse to hang out with you again—and of all ways, by inviting you out with his family?" she recounted. "As far as I can tell, he's only guilty of theorizing a relationship with you—something you immediately shot down, might I add—and giving you a pretty good idea of what it'd look like had you not."

Again. Fatima tried not to choke after Claudette's pointed observation of her current circumstance. She decided not to eat or drink anything until the topic had been changed to anything else. Like the weather. Brits loved talking about the weather. "I didn't shoot him down," she muttered.

Unless. Did she? Was she so caught up in Javier that she didn't see what she wanted right in front of her? No, that couldn't be right. Fatima was scared about what it meant that Javier had returned. That every part of her wanted to be done with him, but that she couldn't bring that desire to fruition because she didn't want to break the promise she'd made to him that day while he was passed out in the driver's seat of his car on the highway.

And besides, it wasn't like Javier was just some fling. Some random occurrence. She'd spent way too many years of her life on him, both as a friend and a girlfriend. To throw that away all cavalier and be left to grieve the memories alone just sounded crazy to her.

There was a pause before Claudette asked, "Do you think men just hang around girls because they," she swallowed, *"want to? Instead of wanting some*thing?*"

"You think Iyad wanted something? You think he was using me?"

"No. Boys who use girls don't pick them up from the airport in the pouring rain and ask about their favorite book like some pre-rehearsed romance," she shook her head. "Not. . . the sane ones. But boys who like you show so by being good to you. Boys who *want* you? Their actions are synonymous with their words. Didn't you say that's why you liked *Star Wars* so much, anyway?"

Fatima thought for a beat. "I said that back when I first got here, you remembered?"

"It'd do you well to stop forgetting so much," Claudette punctuated. "Would save you quite a lot of time."

Fatima didn't know what to say. The more she listened to Claudette, and, she supposed, even herself. . . Claudette's argument was beginning to make sense. But if it were true, if she were right, then. . . why did Iyad agree to maintain their friendship so quickly?

"You know, *Control* is almost finished with its final stages of editing," Claudette continued, switching gears. Fatima wished she could be as good as her at moving on and through things. "Once it's out, I'll get you an advanced copy straight away. Actually," she hedged. Claudette never looked nervous, and she didn't seem to be now either, but she looked something like it. Hesitant? Maybe. Unsure?

"We all loved your feedback so much that I thought you could come back here after you graduate from uni for a full-time position as my editorial assistant to start. Fully sponsored. I'll even help you find a place to stay, or you can stay with me for a while, so you won't have any more dastardly situations like the one you're in now," she cracked a quiet smile at her veiled reference to Louisa.

Fatima didn't return it. Her body was frozen, and she had to force it to kickstart when she gasped. "You're for real? You want to hire me?"

"I'll ignore that doubt I've heeded you so many times against," Claudette winked. "But yes, you deserve it. You're not the same sad girl I met when you first got here."

"Oh, really?"

"Yes, really. You're a different sort of sad girl," she teased. Fatima's brow furrowed. "Truthfully, though, I know you're way better now than when you first started here. You've just got to realize that on your own."

"Is the hijab the difference?" Fatima tried to steer the inevitable emotional turn of their conversation toward something more obvious, rather than getting caught up in something she couldn't fully understand. Couldn't see. Focusing on the exterior was always easier.

Claudette rolled her eyes. "No. It's you, you knobhead. It's that you've taken this time to work on yourself and become better for yourself, and it's showing. That's exactly why I want to make sure Aynevol snatches you up before anyone else sees in you what I do. Can't have you working on the next critic's darling somewhere else, now can we? Which brings me back to these boys," she breathed. "Just a thought: why not go somewhere your heart doesn't feel so heavy all the time?" she smiled primly, then forked a fry and bit into it before continuing.

"I understand your dilemma because I was once *in* your dilemma," Claudette went on. "I understand wanting to believe in the appeal of rose-tinted glasses to conceal one's many," she coughed, "many flaws. But, your runt never deserved you any more than mine did me, and I know you know it." Then. "Do you even want to be with him? Your ex?"

"I think I'm supposed to."

"That's not what I asked." Claudette schooled her expression in that unflinching way of hers.

Fatima fought the urge to roll her eyes. "No," she admitted sorely. "I've been good without him, and I want to keep it that way."

"Then what's the problem?"

"He came back."

"If he didn't come back, would you have sought him out?"

"Nah," Fatima shook her head. "Not anymore. Not this time." That was something she was sure of. That she was happy to be sure of.

But Claudette was a bulldozer, still digging away for the story. Still forcing Fatima to turn pages she wasn't sure she could. "Why not?"

It was about thirty seconds of Fatima's eyes darting around as she thought through how good her four months in London had been before she responded, her voice so faint as if she herself hadn't wanted to hear what she'd say next. "I think I hate him. I think I've hated him for a long time, really."

"You said Anakin's love story was your favorite," Claudette remembered. "Maybe you're just accustomed to the complications of dealing with a villain if they have a good enough sob story for you to tack onto."

Fatima's stomach pitched at the idea that she could be right. That she'd stayed with Javier for so long because she pitied him more than she'd ever pitied herself. She ate her last piece of fish slowly. "Vader's the villain."

Claudette was unchanged. "Same man. Same difference."

Fatima sighed. "I don't think Iyad's a villain, though."

"Well then, let go of the one who you know is," Claudette returned. "I saw that list you promised to finish back at the beginning of your time here. Only writing one thing up there was a bit lazy for my taste. . ." she sidebarred, musing about Fatima's solitary to-do: have fun. "Also, it was more of a result, and I thought it was obvious that I wanted what you cataloged to be more action-based than not. Still," she sighed, "mulling from one guy to the next isn't you fulfilling your word, is it?"

"I'm not mulling," Fatima told her, although she was doing exactly that.

"And I'm not your favorite boss you've ever had," Claudette chided, knowing that she definitely was. "Listen, you don't need *any* man, person, thing, or what have you, to complete you. Allowing someone into your life should complement who you already are. Focus on knowing the difference, yeah?"

Fatima nodded.

"'Kay, good. I'm sure you already know what you have to do about your little conundrum, so just do it," she scolded gently.

"Like Nike?" Fatima mused.

"You mean Nike?" Claudette challenged playfully, enunciating the brand's British pronunciation with one syllable, unlike Fatima's two. "Let's get back to work now, yeah?"

BACK ON THE TUBE TO THE OFFICE, CLAUDETTE LEANED TOWARD Fatima and spoke softly. "By the way," she posed. "What'd you get on your assignment with your friend and Igor?"

"Iyad," Fatima corrected instinctively, puffing out her cheeks. "And an A."

"And you did that work fast and spitefully," Claudette snorted, righting herself in her seat. "Yeah, Aynevol would be happy to have you."

CHAPTER THIRTY-FOUR

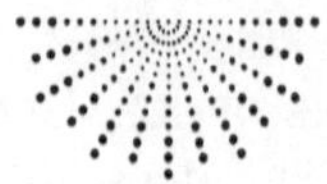

RAMADAN HAD OFFICIALLY BEGUN. WHICH MEANT THAT FATIMA had been fasting from sunup to sundown for the first time in years now. And so, Tom was kind enough to wait until the sun had set to have his (late) afternoon tea at The Gherkin so that Fatima and Sadiyah could break their fasts while they ended the semester with everyone else from their school's London program.

"I think Louisa's on a mission to make it impossible to miss her," Fatima decided, helping herself to a scone from the edge of the cake stand at the center of the table in front of her.

She looked out of the window at the city below them. London was a beautiful, hazy blue, sparkling in a way she hadn't noticed before. She looked at cars driving over Tower Bridge and people walking through the lawn at the Tower of London. Boats sailing through the River Thames and the distant skyline punctuated by a vast expanse of buildings stretching into the horizon.

The table Tom had prepared for them was also lovely. Fatima had only attended a tea party once before, years ago. Sitting here with pristinely arranged cakes, teas, and sandwiches felt like that all over again. All of the porcelain table-ware, pastel colors, and overall prettiness in a famous landmark like The Gherkin, of all places, was an excellent conclusion to her time in London. But she wouldn't be telling Tom any of that. The man's ego was probably the only one in history that could rival Sadiyah's.

"Last night at dinner," Fatima was explaining, "Louisa yelled at us *through* yelling at our host brother, because he was copying us eating pizza with our hands."

"Problem being?" Tom questioned, taking a sip from his tea.

"Apparently, all food is meant to be eaten with a utensil. No exceptions. Otherwise, you 'look like a Neanderthal'," Sadiyah recited, somehow managing to convey a deluge of eerily similar Louisa-uppityness just through the intonations in her voice.

Fatima nodded. She was well aware that her good-natured host brother, Artie, hadn't actually done anything wrong. She was also fairly sure that Artie was aware of this fact, too. However, Louisa was wonderfully passive-aggressive, and Artie was in the wrong place at the right time with a slice of pizza in hand, so there was no saving him.

"And you both were the real 'Neanderthals' in question, I'd assume?" Tom asked them.

"Your assumption would be correct," Fatima replied, spreading jam on top of her scone after she'd added butter to it.

"Oh my days," Tom went. "How you two managed with a woman as. . . tactful as that is phenomenal in and of itself."

"Well, we *are* phenomenal women." Sadiyah boasted, biting into a cucumber tea sandwich.

Tom snickered. "Would you like to know something else that's phenomenal?" he asked, eyes wide as if he himself didn't know what he'd say next. Tom picked up a scone and motioned for the table's full attention. "Eating this," he motioned to the scone on Fatima's plate, "is an atrocity."

Fatima stared in shock, suddenly flashing back to Pizzagate. "Excuse me?"

"Of course," Tom said imperiously, zoning back in on her plate. "We call this a 'Devonshire scone' when the clotted cream is spread before the jam, as Fatima has so kindly demonstrated for us, versus the 'Cornish scone'—the better traditional method —when the jam," he smeared preserve across his scone, followed by cream, "is spread *before* the cream."

"You're fighting over. . ." Fatima gave him an odd look. "Cold butter?"

"You're fighting over a slice of pizza?" Tom arched an eyebrow.

"Should I fight over butter, pizza, or Henry VIII?" she asked instead, immediately regretting it.

Fatima could be so senseless at times. She could talk about butter. She could talk about pizza. She could even make the both of them if she wanted to. Still, she couldn't talk about Henry anymore, because talking about Henry inherently meant thinking about Javier, and thinking about Javier meant she wasn't done with Javier—the last person she wanted occupying space in her mind.

"Definitely King Henry," Tom chose despite her. "Considering the group is all here now."

The group is all—

Fatima's thoughts were interrupted as she and Sadiyah followed Tom's gaze behind them to find Iyad in a black thobe, holding a plastic Tesco bag in his hand. Right then, a gossamer warmth fluttered within the walls of Fatima's chest, and she found herself smiling at the sight of him—precisely the opposite of what was expected when looking at a friend. But when she let herself think of what Claudette had said about him, Fatima was sure that "friend" wasn't the right word for how she felt when thinking of Iyad. For how on edge seeing him and thinking of spending time with him—and his family today—made her.

Those were not "friend" thoughts. Fatima didn't honestly know the last time she'd had true "friend" thoughts of Iyad at all. *If* she ever had. Or if they'd always been thinly veiled instances of "what if," shrouded by the dizzying giddiness she constantly felt around him.

Fatima wanted to know if he liked her. If there was a chance he wasn't joking when he threw out the idea of them being more than friends. She wanted to know if he could've been testing the waters to see what she thought. To know if, instead of at least throwing him a life ring, she'd left him to drown.

"Sorry, I'm late," Iyad said, holding the bag up. "My mum needed me to pick up some extras." He smiled at the table, and then, she thought, right at her.

Something about that moment made Fatima's heart swoon. Made her roiling nerves melt into puddles she'd instantly forgotten about, because he was here. And she was alright so long as he was close to her.

Oh no.

"All good, TG," Sadiyah wiped her hands on her napkin and stood up.

"Look at you all cleaned up," Fatima lilted, voicing her thoughts before she could stop herself.

Iyad tilted his head, confused, before a slight smirk of delight danced at the corner of his lips. "I look alright?"

Fatima forced her tongue in the space behind her bottom teeth, narrowing her eyes at him as she tried not to smile back. He made her head spin. And the idea that she could currently be doing the same to him was all the more disorienting.

"Not to dine and dash, Tom," Sadiyah spoke up after exchanging an annoyingly knowing look with Tom, "but we're in high demand, as you can see."

"I do see," he agreed instantly, not hiding his amusement as he looked between Fatima and Iyad. "To think, you all were so cross with one another in the beginning. Now look at the lot of you, good friends and such."

Sadiyah cleared her throat, but Fatima knew her well enough to know it was really a bad attempt to cover a laugh. "Can we get a picture with you before we go?" Sadiyah asked him.

"For a tenner," he told her with a smile.

RAMADAN HAD OFFICIALLY BEGUN. WHICH MEANT IYAD HAD BEEN fasting from sunup to sundown for what marked somewhere around a decade during this Ramadan now. And so, understanding that this was Fatima's first time back in the swing of things in a while, he wanted to be sure to do whatever he could to make things easy for her. Iftar seemed like as right an answer as any.

Iyad stood up from his seat as a pregnant woman boarded the tube to let her sit down, which left him standing in front of Fatima and Sadiyah on their way to his mom's. He held onto the grab handle above him, curling his Tesco bag with some extra bell peppers and cooking oil for his mom around his fingers with his other hand.

He'd had an extensive phone call with his family on the way to The Gherkin to pick the girls up, where he, respectfully, told them to be on their best behavior when he brought the girls over. To which they, respectfully and collectively, told him to, "Shut up."

He knew Mo's mom, his Auntie Amani, wouldn't be a problem. She was a lot like his uncle, quiet and level-headed. And, Iyad rationalized that Fatima and Sadiyah had already met his Uncle Hassan and Mo, and nothing had gone up in flames then. He'd also been around his uncle himself a lot more frequently lately, and not once had the world ended. So, really, it was just his mom who'd been anxiously awaiting her turn to meet the "lovely girls," who was the primary wild card he had to worry about. Especially after what she'd already said about Fatima.

I'd like to meet your future wife soon.

For some reason, he couldn't find it in himself to continue as if that weren't a reality that interested him.

"Mind the gap," the PA system rang out as the tube doors opened.

Iyad was trying not to ogle at her, something that, when it came to Fatima, was just about as natural as the sun not shining. He gripped the bar above him tighter as someone behind him shifted, sending the Tesco bag swinging in her direction. She flinched, then her gaze flitted up when he hadn't let the bag smack her in the face after redirecting it to his side, her eyes meeting his for a moment. Something inside of Iyad stirred, unauthorized flight patterns making their way about him.

"Mind the gap."

He smiled. A bit sheepishly. A bit excited that he had her attention. He could've stayed there all day.

"Mind the gap."

He could've. He really, really could've. But then, he realized this was their stop and remembered his dad's sage advice against staring directly into the sun. Annoyingly, he had to listen this time and look away.

"TiSadiyahOurstop," he heralded, managing to come back to earth just in time to rush them off the tube before the doors shut them all inside.

But not at all without Sadiyah, wide-eyed and gobsmacked on the platform's edge, who asked wryly, "Do you know where you're going?"

Iyad was keenly aware that what she'd said was less of a question and more of an accusation. Frankly, it was an accusation she was right to have, but why admit defeat when he didn't have to?

"I've got to keep you on your toes somehow, don't I?" he insisted loftily, striding past the busker singing 'Wonderwall' by Oasis, toward the "Way Out" sign that led them onto the street.

Sadiyah grinned derisively and followed suit, Fatima falling into step beside her.

IYAD QUICKLY LEARNED THAT FATIMA WASN'T CHATTING RUBBISH when she told him how much she enjoyed escovitch. What felt like seconds after receiving it, she'd already put back a quarter of the fish, which only made his mom fawn over her more, further complicating the fact that he was still working to prove to them that she was just his friend.

FRIEND.

He'd never been so disgusted by a word before.

"I can't believe I'm meeting you girls just now," Farah lamented, scooping from the dish of brown stew chicken she'd made at the center of the dining table onto her plate. "And you're already leaving tomorrow."

"He's embarrassed of us," Sadiyah covered her mouth as she explained, her words muffled by the food she hadn't finished plowing through yet.

"Oh really?" Auntie Amani asked, the corner of her lips curling into a faint smile.

"Not at all," Iyad eased back, sweeping a laughing glance over them all. It'd been years since they'd been able to do something as simple as eat together. He, obviously, knew that he'd been the main issue for this, if not the only one. Iyad spent so long avoiding his usual routines. His usual people and places he'd grown up with. Just the thought of sitting at this table used to terrify him, as if he were betraying his father's memory. Desecrating it, even, by never being enough to amount to how incredible a man he was. But now, he was sitting in his father's seat, at his father's home, looking at his father's identical twin, and he felt. . . oddly okay. "Just her," he nodded toward Sadiyah.

"Yeah," Mo agreed, immediately instigating. "She cheats at Uno."

"*I* cheat?" Sadiyah blinked, completely dumbfounded. "Says the 'opportunist,'" she mimicked him with air quotes.

"Can you believe this?" Mo scrambled, nearly whining. He pecked a bit of oxtail gravy from the tip of his thumb, persistent as ever. "Mum, Auntie Farah—"

Iyad turned to Fatima next to him while Mo tried hopelessly to plead his case. He grinned as she watched Mo and Sadiyah crack on, amused, but quiet. It occurred to him then, admittedly a little delayed, that she liked crowds and group settings in general about as much as he did, which was most likely why Sadiyah was doing most of the talking and Fatima was still stuffing her face.

"You alright?" he asked her in a low voice, raising an eyebrow.

Fatima set her fork down on top of her rice, which looked more like a challenge than she might've intended to let on. She glanced up at him and said, just as softly, "Yeah." Then, her eyes shifted anxiously between the table and him. "Wait," Her eyebrows lurched just above the brim of her glasses, and Iyad began to speculate that he'd never truly noticed glasses before at all. Never as anything more special than a hat or a sock. Glasses were always just glasses until that moment when he realized how adorable and animated they could make a person. Could make her. "Is me—"

"No," Iyad went, cutting her off with an impulsiveness he found himself thankful for.

"I wasn't finished," she insisted, pulling at the edge of her hijab over her shoulder to straighten it out.

"Didn't have to," he said pertly, his full attention on her. "I already knew what you were going to say."

"You read minds now?" Fatima assessed him, holding his gaze, and Iyad would've been lying if he said her nearness didn't send delighted little shockwaves trailing down his spine.

Iyad shook his head. "Just yours," he answered archly. He liked this girl more than he'd ever liked anyone before. In fact, what he felt for Fatima made him question whether he'd ever truly felt anything for anyone at all, which made it all the more painful when the reality settled in that she didn't like him back. Not in the same way, at least. "You were about to say something about why you shouldn't be here," he said, knowing she had a biting tendency to think the worst of herself. Just like he did. "Weren't you?"

Fatima didn't answer, and that only proved to Iyad that he knew her well enough by now to have been right. So he went on speaking without thinking, because if he had, his next words may never have come out.

"I could be wrong, though," he supposed. "Maybe you were about to make me beg for you to stay?" he posed, quieter this time. "Were you?"

Fatima's eyes pinched together, then bulged, and Iyad quietly liked the idea that he could get that sort of blatant reaction from her. "Maybe I should," she said, then pressed her lips together, like she was surprised she'd told him that.

He was.

Iyad sighed frustratedly, holding himself back although he was wishing he could've been closer to her. Wishing he could close every gap that separated them. "Maybe you should," he repeated the rounded vowels in her accent with a crooked smirk. "I could wait for it to rain again and go cry in a puddle with a white T-shirt on just so you'll say yes."

Fatima snorted. "You gonna take some notes from Usher?"

Iyad shook his head, trying not to laugh with her. "You think

I haven't already?" he asked, forcing himself to believe that if this was what friendship with Fatima looked like, he'd have to accept it. He was so happy to know her. Happy for how far he'd come thanks to her. "You gonna miss me when you go, Yank?" He tried to throw the thought of this ideal friendship onto her.

She didn't seem to catch it. "Not at all."

So, Iyad threw it again. "Not. At. *All?*"

Fatima glanced away from him, to the table, "Can you shut up?" she whispered, and Iyad noticed her cheeks had noticeably reddened. "You're loud."

Iyad's grin only deepened across his face. "Am I embarrassing you?"

"You—" she started, glanced at the table again, and caught herself. He'd never wanted to know the end of a sentence so badly. Fatima shook her head and looked back at the half-eaten fish on her plate. He tried to pretend he didn't notice when she bit her lip. "Do you think you could help take the head off for me?"

"You want me to decapitate your fish?" he asked incredulously.

"I want you to decapitate my fish."

His eyes danced. This was his friend. This was good. It had to be. "No,"

Fatima tilted her head slightly, and he could've sworn she was pouting, her bottom lip ballooning out, and her eyes a few degrees larger. Maybe he was imagining it. "Why not?"

"'Cause you're not gonna miss me." Still, he mockingly pouted in return, and then they were just. . . watching each other. Two friends. Not saying anything, but somehow saying everything. Speaking in languages that hadn't been written. Patterns that hadn't been seen. He could've stayed like that forever. Watching the sun.

"Please," she tried again.

Iyad couldn't help the grin that needled its way across his

face, stretching wider and wider. "Are. You. Going. To. Miss. Me. Yank?"

"You're insufferable."

"You're not answering." He scrunched up his face, then said, lower, "And you still have a fish head on your plate."

"FineI'llmissyou," she said it fast and slightly louder in that charming voice of hers than he knew she intended, because when his mom heard, looked over, and winked at her, the look she gave back was a tangled mess of mortification and a flimsy attempt to seem casual.

And for some reason, seeing her all flustered like that sent Iyad into a fit. A loud, shamelessly uninhibited stream of laughter that he didn't stop, even when the entire table was looking at him.

Meanwhile, Fatima had busied herself counting the spots in the textured ceiling above them, a sweet little smile tugging at the edges of her lips despite her obvious effort to suppress it. She really did make him feel the happiest he'd felt in a long time, somehow both lightheaded and calmed in a way he'd never experienced. It was honestly almost maddening, knowing so surely that he'd miss her the second she was out of his sight. But it'd be alright. Iyad had to force himself to believe this. That he'd be good when she left, because he was already more than accustomed to missing people.

"It's getting late," Hassan finally said when Iyad calmed down enough and was taking the fish head from Fatima's plate, placing it on the edge of his own. Iyad caught his uncle quirk a smile at that, then he popped a date into his mouth to try and hide it. "Why don't we all get ready to pray Isha for the night so the girls can get home and get ready for the airport tomorrow?"

Iyad didn't want to agree, but it was getting late, and they were still very terrible navigators. So, although he was still going to head back with them before he went to his place to make sure they'd made it, the earlier, the better. Especially since he was sure they hadn't packed so much as a speck of lint yet.

He also didn't want to agree when his family said he should lead the prayer instead of his uncle, because he was now the "man of the house." That idea had never occurred to Iyad, but he went along with it, standing in front of everyone when they moved to the living room to pray together—with Mo and Uncle Hassan in the middle row, and Auntie Amani, his mom, Fatima, and Sadiyah forming a neat line side by side at the back.

Iyad recited the prayer aloud, with everyone following his movements a few echoed moments after. Then, as he sat on the floor in that fleeting instance once he'd finished and everyone was concluding themselves, Iyad stole a glance behind him.

In that brief pause, watching Fatima recite quietly to herself, Iyad allowed himself to dream up an alternate reality. One where the word "friend" didn't exist. One where the ocean separating them was no more than a drop of water. One where she was here. Always. His.

CHAPTER THIRTY-FIVE

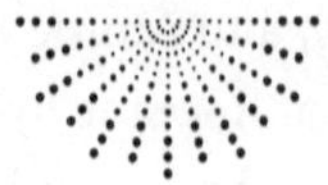

FATIMA AND SADIYAH WERE FINALLY LEAVING LOUISA'S HOUSE OF horrors, and it was safe to say their host brother was the only part of it that would be missed.

"Don't forget about us, Artie," Fatima sniffed. She'd been eager to leave her homestay ever since Louisa first greeted her, but now that the time had finally come, Fatima found herself weirdly emotional about it.

"Never," Artie guaranteed. "And I have your WhatsApps!" He held out his phone, and Fatima immediately wondered how many other exchange students' WhatsApps he also had logged in there. He was used to this: random foreigners coming and going. How long would it be until Louisa erased the memory that they'd ever even been there to begin with? A week? A day? The moment they were gone?

"Yeah," Sadiyah added. "We'll send you a picture of Spider-Man next time we see him," she said, and the tension of their impending departure seemed to loom a little less around them for a second as they remembered a conversation that felt like so long ago in their trip.

But then Louisa spoke up and effectively broke the illusion

immediately. "Oh, I can't believe the day has come!" she beamed as they all stood on the sidewalk together after the car service Tom had ordered for them arrived.

"I know, right?" Fatima sighed dramatically, as if the idea of never seeing Louisa again truly pained her.

"Those rustic accents of yours," Louisa rambled on, "and how I can hardly tell the pair of you apart ever since you both started wearing those," she made a circle gesture with her whole palm at them. "Scarves and such."

Sadiyah snorted, no doubt at Louisa's audacity. Louisa's glaring need to say something about Sadiyah's hijab and overall "Muslim-ness" had been apparent since their first day. It'd become all the more evident when Fatima fell back into wearing hers as well. No one treated Fatima any differently since she'd begun wearing her hijab again, which was nice because it made things easier for her to concentrate on herself and studying her religion, rather than anyone else's distracting opinions. But Louisa was in a category of her own. Unfortunately.

"Anyway, we've got to head out," Fatima said. "Thank you for housing us, Louisa. Bye, Artie."

"Bye, Fatima," he waved. "Goodbye, Sadiyah. Safe travels."

Fatima flashed one last "rustic" smile at them and then headed over to the car, thinking about how last night was the last time she'd ever see Iyad after he'd taken them home for the second time to make sure they'd gotten to Louisa's safely.

Fatima forced down the disappointed bubble in her throat when it was made clear to her that knowing him would end there. That their friendship would likely end right there at the doorstep of Louisa's home.

She told herself to just be satisfied with even meeting him at all. Iyad was a good man. Kindhearted and sincere. Fatima was coming to realize she'd never seen those features in a man who wasn't her dad or Javier before they'd started dating. And it was nice to remember that things could be that way.

Yesterday, while the girls were saying their goodbyes and thank yous after Iftar, and Fatima was still reeling from how beautiful Iyad's voice was reciting verses of the Quran during prayer, Iyad's mother pulled her aside. Fatima's nerves had spiked right then, thinking of the confines of being so close to someone so close to Iyad and fearing she might end up saying something she shouldn't.

"I'm so glad you came." Farah's smile was small, like the quiet, hesitant way Iyad would when he didn't want to let on how excited he was about something. Fatima found many similarities between him and his family last night, but she was most intrigued by the ones he shared with his father. The way he shone when they spoke about him. "You two are lovely," Farah lauded.

"Oh," Fatima went, relieved because this was something she could easily respond to. "Don't tell Sads that. Compliments go straight to her head."

Farah nodded. "She is, too."

"'Too?'"

Farah nodded again, her eyes flickering to Iyad, laughing about something with Mo and Sadiyah. "My Yaddy is a big guy, you know? But he's always been 'fraid of the fish heads. Used to make me and his father take them off before we could even give him his plate," she pursed her lips, regarding Fatima deeply.

Fatima held her breath.

"And then, along came you," Farah finished definitively, like those five words would've explained the cosmos. But it was now a day later, and Fatima was still at a cosmic loss about it.

SADIYAH TRIED REALLY HARD NOT TO COME ACROSS AS FULL AS herself. But Fatima and Iyad were making it hard.

Somehow, they'd spent the majority of the four months of their time together clouded in some warped delusion that they were just friends. She understood it from Fatima's point of view. Her friend was woefully defeatist when it came to herself and the things she wanted. So, of course, the idea of the boy she liked ever liking her back hadn't occurred to her, but wow—how long would it take until it did?

Iyad, on the other hand, well, Sadiyah didn't know exactly what his deal was, but it wasn't any less annoying. So, she decided to give him a little push. Her friend had the right to know there were more fish in the sea than—shudder—Pretty Boy.

That's why, yesterday, after they'd gotten back to Louisa's and Fatima was in the shower, Sadiyah decided to text him.

Sads:

You are the king of meatheads.

That got his attention within seconds.

Iyad:

Pardon?

Sads:

Meathead. As in bonehead. Blockhead. Idiot.

Iyad:

I know what it is, but how am I one? I literally just took both of you home.

Sads:

Why didn't you tell her?

Then, because he was a meathead and thereby prone to grossly misunderstanding what was going on, she explained further.

Sads:

That you like her.

Iyad:

Fatima? Not sure what you're on about. I like her fine as a friend, though. She knows this.

More than you, though, admittedly.

Sads:

I can only PRAY that you like her more than me, bonehead.

Iyad, come on, let's drop the act. I'm tired.

It felt like years before he responded, but Sadiyah still heard the shower water running, so it couldn't have been that long.

Iyad:

Go to bed then, blockhead.

I'm respecting her wishes.

Sadiyah snorted. He was just as hopeless as her. Perfect.

Sads:

Very honorable, but I wouldn't be telling you this if it weren't right to.

Iyad:

What do you mean?

Sads:

What do you think I mean?

Iyad:

She likes me, too?

Sadiyah tried to think of how best to go about what she'd say next. He sounded like a third grader picking off the petals of a daisy, saying, *She loves me, She loves me not.* Still, he was right to be a little wary after all the things Fatima had said to him. But Sadiyah knew Fatima was just—as he'd say—chatting rubbish.

Sadiyah knew her friend. She knew that Fatima liked him. Tender, delicate, and real. And, above all, she knew Fatima deserved to know that feeling was reciprocated. But Sadiyah also wasn't going to completely sell Fatima out by giving away all that information, either.

Sads:

Figure it out, meathead.

Sadiyah swallowed as she and Fatima checked into their flight now, happy they'd be on the same return flight after being separated by winter break plans for their trips into London four months ago. Yesterday, she'd told Iyad when they'd be heading to the airport and exactly where to find them. But now, they were nearly finished signing in, and the kid was still nowhere to be seen.

"Looklooklook!" Fatima was pointing at the check-in kiosk so intensely that she might've broken it had she made contact. "Sads, you're my witness. We got here five hours early, and I *still* barely made the flight."

"Remind me where you got your tickets from, so I never do." Sadiyah stared at the screen in disbelief.

"Aht, aht." Fatima tutted superciliously. "Not a ticket. I bought a *reservation,*" she corrected, selecting one of the last two available seats on the plane diagram before she was truly stranded in London. "Remind me never to go third-party again."

Sadiyah muffled a laugh, shaking her head before she turned around to scan over their surroundings, a bit shocked that Iyad hadn't shown up yet. She was honestly surprised about it. Sadiyah had wanted to believe that Iyad was different from what she'd already thought of most men, which was why she'd gone out of her way to meddle between them, but it hadn't worked.

But maybe that was for the best. Maybe Iyad could serve as a fond memory for Fatima as the years went on. Not everything needed to turn into a romance.

"You good?" Fatima asked, leaning on the handle of her suitcase, looking in the same scattered direction Sadiyah had been.

Sadiyah raised her hands. "Of course," she answered, "I—"

Fatima's eyes widened almost impossibly at something behind Sadiyah, before she whispered in arrested disbelief. "Iyad?"

Sadiyah laughed softly to herself, surprised but happy that he was here. She moved aside, glad to see the moment they finally realized that "just friends" was never all they were.

FATIMA FOUND HERSELF FROZEN, EYES FIXED SOLELY ON IYAD'S, half-unbelieving that he was even there—until he said, "This is exactly why I said someone ought to look after you."

He gave her an anxious smile, apprehension tempering his voice, then reached behind him to grip the back of his neck. Fatima had gathered a while back that him doing so was the biggest tell when he was nervous about something.

What did he have to be nervous about?

"If you miss your flight, you might really have to stay here with me," he told her, but all Fatima could do was stare.

She knew he was waiting for her to respond. To say something. Anything. But Fatima was too busy trying to understand why he was even there to begin with and why she could feel her heart racing at the sight of him.

Thump, thump, thump.

There was that rabbit hop inside of her again. Curious and tempted. Not at all careful.

CHAPTER THIRTY-SIX

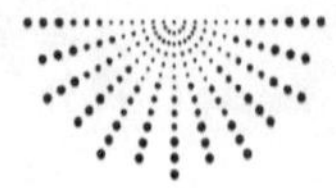

Iyad needed to get a grip, or a clue, or whatever that silver thing that you hold onto on a roller coaster was called—a safety bar, yeah. He needed several of those because telling Fatima how he felt was a lot more complicated than his initial plan to let her go back home without ever saying a word. It wasn't just a simple "I like you, do you like me?" he'd have to say. In Islam, it was "I like you, will you marry me?" And was that a question that he was even ready to ask?

More, was a proposal something Fatima was ready to hear? This morning, Iyad dissected his messages with Sadiyah the night before for way longer than he'd care to admit. He'd yanked them wide open like they used to do frogs in biology courses because he needed to know the anatomy of every letter, every word, every pause between their messages.

Then, for a second opinion, he had Mo come and review them as well, just to see what conclusion his cousin would come to. Surprisingly, Mo had landed in an entirely different galaxy from Iyad, agreeing that Sadiyah had made it "bare obvious" that Fatima was into him in the way he'd hoped. According to

Iyad, Sadiyah was elaborately setting him up for failure. But what if she wasn't?

In the end, it was the "what-if" of it all that was the reason Iyad was currently on his way to the airport in his dad's car with a little gift in the passenger seat that he thought Fatima might like. He hadn't thought through what he'd say to her yet, though. He was still debating if he'd let himself get there to say anything at all since talking himself out of things was an activity he thrived so well at. But then again, there was that sneaky "what-if."

Iyad turned into the car park once he'd reached the airport, cutting the ignition after he'd found a spot. In the stillness, the reality of what was meant to come next locked both his legs in place, holding him down by the shoulders and pressing into his chest. He was overheating. He was panicking. He'd done this enough times to know exactly what his symptoms meant. It'd been a while since Iyad had a panic attack, but he knew what to do.

Breathe, he told himself. *Breathe. Breathe. Breathe.*

He reached for a bottle of water from the center console without looking and came up empty. Oh. Right. It was Ramadan. He was fasting. He opened his mouth wide. *Breathe. Breathe. Breathe.* He thought of Fatima. By the time he was eating again this evening, she'd already be hundreds of miles away from him. Would it have mattered if he'd said anything then?

Iyad turned the car back on so he could roll the windows down for a moment to feel the breeze outside, then glanced at the time on his phone. He was cutting it close to missing her if she went through the security line right after checking into her flight, but Iyad wasn't going anywhere in his current state.

Breathe. Breathe. Breathe, he reminded himself, realizing that the more he thought of her, not his nerves, not his efforts to find the right words. Just her. Just the girl who brought so much light into his life after he'd spent so many years trapped in shadow and misery—the more he felt himself come together again. So, he leaned into it.

Not too long ago, they'd gone on a trip to the Clink Prison Museum in Bankside with Tom. The museum was quite literally the original Clink prison, restored (and dramatized) as close to its former nauseating glory as possible. It was the site of countless brutal punishments and horrific conditions, which often led to its prisoners' demises, and were now proudly displayed in graphic detail. Not a place for Fatima Sommers.

Fatima was the kid who was off catching butterflies on the field during football matches. She was the type of girl who used hand sanitizer like it was the cure for mortality, wondered if army ants had military drafts, and if some birds were afraid of heights. Not, by any means, someone you took to a prison museum. The sickened grimace stuck on her face for most of their tour was as good an indication of this as any.

Iyad remembered trying not to stare at that grimace, biting back his smile at how she pulled her bag close to her as if one of the wax figures in there would've come alive and nicked it. Looking at her, Iyad thought of his mom. This one time, when he was about eight and on a day trip to Bath with his parents, he convinced himself that he'd get superpowers if he could touch the water in the Roman Baths since it was so old and green.

He almost got away with it, too. If it weren't for his meddling dad, who'd caught hold of him by the back of his shirt like he was a basketball. If it weren't for his mom getting so angry that she stopped talking altogether. Upset about his health, safety, and other useless things that kept Iyad from fulfilling his destiny.

It was so hard for him to understand when his dad whispered something in his mom's ear that made her laugh. So hard for Iyad to wrap his mind around why that made his dad look so accomplished. So fulfilled. So happy. But he got it now.

Looking at Fatima made him understand a lot of things he hadn't before.

"How's the book coming?" Iyad asked her as they continued walking around the museum. She was staring open-mouthed at a figurine of a man being stretched to death.

Fatima glanced at Iyad, her face was tightened in a way that didn't make it clear if it was in response to anything around her or to his presence. "What?" she'd asked him as if what she was seeing was simultaneously keeping her from hearing clearly. Iyad wanted to laugh at that, how theatrical she could be. He wanted to thank her for it as well. For how easy being around her made him feel.

"The book," he pushed with a newly contented ease about him, "that you said you were editing for work?"

"You want to know about the book I'm working on?" She said it so slowly, as if it were impossible for him to be even remotely interested in the things that interested her. This wasn't a new fact. Still, it disappointed him for a second. But then he brightened, deciding to double down on making sure she understood there was a fine line distinction between himself and Javier.

Iyad cocked his head to the side and teased in question.

"Are you gonna keep me waiting, or are you gonna tell me?"

Sadiyah snickered, not-so-quietly, beside Fatima. She, it seemed, had no qualms with being inside a dank prison that smelled like wet feet.

Fatima looked up sharply, but her eyes were dancing. "It's going good," she smiled, and the stretched-to-death man seemed to fade into oblivion. "I think I'm only going to be able to get one full pass through editing, but everyone seems to like what I've done so far."

"When you're editing, are you looking for missing periods and things, or are you basically rewriting it?" he asked, genuinely curious.

Fatima was quiet for a moment. "Neither," she shrugged. "I mean, of course, I'm looking for typos, but it's more than that. It's like I'm trying to polish a diamond, if that makes sense. Like, the book is already good, but some parts are better than others. My goal is to make sure every page is just as good as the last."

"Like Sherlock Holmes?"

"Call me Sherlock Homegirl," she told him. And although it was so incredibly corny, something about her saying that made Iyad laugh. Then Fatima joined in, and soon they were both snickering in the middle of a dungeon like wayward prisoners.

Iyad remembered feeling like it was just the two of them there, not worried about anything or anyone around them. Not worried about his fears of getting close to Fatima while knowing she'd ultimately leave. He was just enjoying her company. And he realized then, truly apprehended as he sat in his father's old car, that he hoped to continue doing so for a long, long time.

Coming to that realization, Iyad's anxiety subsided from a tidal wave into a gentle swell lapping against the shore as he sat in the car. Iyad's lips curved without warning as he rolled the windows back up and quickly got out of the car, his feet carrying him exactly where he needed to be.

Minutes later, Iyad had gone to where Sadiyah told him they'd be checking into their flight, finding Fatima nearly bashing the screen in with her finger. He remembered her saying she'd almost missed her first flight into the city, which was why she felt the need to be so many hours early today. He guessed the same thing was happening again.

Iyad leaned into the wall behind him, letting people pass by as he stood there trying to focus on what to say. When he came up empty, just a restless need to be next to her, he decided it'd be better to follow his instincts and walked over to her.

"Iyad?" Fatima stared at him so shocked that it would've been funny had Iyad's bumbling heart not currently been in danger of beating straight out of his chest.

Set on following his instincts, Iyad tried to make her laugh. "This is exactly why I said someone ought to look after you," he said, concentrating only on her and not the deeply satisfied grin spread wide across Sadiyah's face. "If you miss your flight, you might really have to stay here with me."

Fatima just stared at him, though. Big brown eyes, soft as silk, locked on his.

He tried again. "Hey, Ti. As-Salamu Alaykum."

"Wa Alaykum As-Salam," she continued to stare. "What are you doing here?"

Fatima had that wild look about her, like when she had too many thoughts colliding in her head at once, wavering back and forth from him to Sadiyah as she sporadically put two and two together. Iyad wished, for a moment, that he could gather each of those thoughts, then find a way to stop time so they could discuss them all. Understand each one. Understand her. In detail.

Iyad wanted a moment. Moments, really, to sit and talk to her for hours. He wanted to know everything. To know that what he was about to say was right. That she'd be okay if she heard it. Iyad thought about the project she'd completed for them, driven by frustration after too many repeated cycles from a man who'd let her down too many times. He thought about the question she'd asked during their presentation, *"Why is what he did allowed to be forgotten?"*

Iyad had been thinking about that question a lot afterwards, realizing that if they were okay by then, then she must've been talking about Javier. At least, he'd *hoped* she was talking about Javier. About all of the things she'd gone through in loving him, someone who didn't know how to love her back. . . About how she was still reeling from it.

Fatima still needed time to come to terms with what she'd been through, so Iyad decided he'd do his best not to say anything that might make her feel rushed about anything to do with him at all. But he just needed to know one thing in the meantime.

"I have to ask you something quickly," he worked out.

"Right now?" she asked him.

"Can only be now," he winked. Then breathed. Then breathed again for good measure. "If I told you I—" Iyad looked down at his palms as if anything that could help him were written down on the lines there. He ran a hand over the back of his neck. Iyad promised her no surprises. This would have to be his one exception to the rule.

He tried again. "You like *Star Wars*, right?"

"Yes," she said, almost as if on instinct.

"So. . ." He swallowed. "You like Anakin?"

"Yes."

"And you also like Vader?"

"Yes."

Iyad took in the deepest breath known to man. "You like me?"

"Yes- wait. I—" Fatima blinked. Fast. Hard.

But he heard her. Loud and clear. Iyad could feel a lopsided, sloppy smile already spreading across his face. He said aloud, finally and for the first time, "I like you too, Ti." *And I know you've been through a lot and are still going through it now, but you have a good heart. I hope you know I'll protect it.*

Instead, he only said, "I um- I got you something actually." He handed her the bag he'd nearly forgotten he was holding.

Fatima eyed him suspiciously, taking the bag and reaching inside of it to find a pen and notebook modeled to look like a VHS tape for the third episode of *Star Wars: Revenge of the Sith*. She slapped her hand over her mouth and squealed.

Iyad lit up even more, feeling the planet begin to climb back on its axis. "I saw that you filled up the one you were always writing in from class. Thought you could use a new one."

"Thank you, Vader," she gasped, still smiling.

"Of course," he told her. "I've gotta tell you one more thing," he said, glancing at the notebook as she began to tuck it away.

"Yes?"

Suddenly, Sadiyah's smug face came into view, and Iyad remembered they weren't alone. He clicked his tongue. "Can I actually see the notebook for a sec?" he asked. She passed it over and he took it, careful not to brush his fingers against hers. Forcing himself to keep some distance between them, even though all he felt now was that there was too much of it. "And the pen?" She dug it out from the bag, too.

Iyad flipped the notebook to its last page, dated it, wrote a secret message just for her to see, signed it for formalities' sake, and then passed it back like a primary school note that he didn't want the teacher (Sadiyah) to see.

Fatima opened it, and the way that she smiled as her eyes scanned over the page was all the reassurance he would ever need. "Are you serious?" she peeked at him, nodding dizzily before he could even fix his mouth to answer.

And it was so stupid a passing thought, but Iyad wanted to pinch himself right then because how could any of this be real?

This girl.

Fatima.

She had brought light itself back into his life after all these years, and Iyad would always be thankful to her for that. So, of course, his answer was automatic. "Wallahi."

PART III

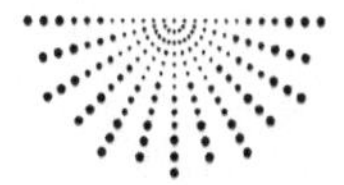

7 May 2019
When you're ready, will you marry me?
- Iyad Isa ibn Hamza Ahmed

CHAPTER THIRTY-SEVEN

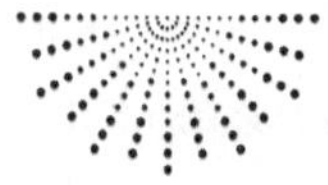

Fatima bit her lip as the FaceTime call rang. She was nervous, adjusting herself in front of the camera to make sure she'd fit squarely in the frame once he'd answered. It felt like a lifetime since they'd last spoken, even though she'd only been back home from London for two weeks now, so really it hadn't been all that long. Not in the grand scheme of things. Still, it didn't feel like enough time had passed. Not nearly enough to forget what'd happened between them. To forget what he'd said to her. But for once, she'd have to face it—face him—without losing her nerve.

"Fatima?" he groused into the phone, sleepy eyes meeting her own.

She hadn't heard his voice in almost a month. She swallowed tightly, then quickly fitted his name out before giving herself a chance to hesitate anymore. "Javier? Got a minute?"

Javier eyed her suspiciously. Fatima hadn't told him she was going to call, which was already out of character considering where they'd last left things off. She'd honestly barely given herself any notice before tapping his contact ID to call him.

Fatima had stopped acknowledging Javier's attempts to contact her after their last conversation to give herself some time to think. By now, Fatima had thought long enough about Javier to write entire dissertations on their relationship. Things she felt and didn't anymore.

She'd been reading the Quran a lot more recently, too. Something that stood out to her was the notion of predetermination, which essentially dictates that everything happens for a reason. Fatima finally understood that concept, with delightful finality, to mean that she was meant to meet Javier and experience what she did with him so that she could become the person she'd grown into today. And for that, she'd always be grateful for the time they'd spent together.

"I was beginning to think I'd never hear from you again," he sniffed and raked a hand through his hair, a matted mess of curls whirling at the top of his head.

If Fatima were there, she'd already be spraying his hair down with the water bottle she'd gotten him—the one he never seemed to use on his own—and sectioning it to comb through. But she wasn't there. Fatima reminded herself that he'd have to take care of himself from now on.

"I know. I'm sorry." She meant that. Fatima knew it was wrong to leave him in the dark for so long—especially knowing how it felt to be on the other end. "But I'm here now and I wanted to—" she shook her head. No. She needed to be decisive. "Javier, we have to end this."

Javier blinked, confusion etching his frame. She'd been on the receiving end of this conversation with him before. But never him. "End. . . what, exactly?"

"You know."

"Us?"

Fatima nodded.

Javier froze. "Never."

"Excuse me?"

"I just got clearance to come home for a while. I was going to surprise you," he told her quietly, sounding almost embarrassed about it. "Is this about him? I see you're wearing that," he waved a hand at her like he was conducting an orchestra, before correcting himself. "You're wearing your hijab. He made you do that? You know you could've just come to me if things were getting that bad again."

Fatima sighed. For a moment, she wished she'd carried out her initial plan of sending him this information over a quick text, blocking him on everything, and being done with him for good. But she'd talked herself out of that because she felt like he deserved more. He was always deserving of something from her at her expense.

She looked at the notebook Iyad got her on the table behind her phone and felt her eyes brighten, thinking of him. That notebook was easily better than anything Javier had ever gotten her because it showed how well he'd actually taken the time to get to know her. How much he'd cared to.

Still, as great as it was, it didn't top the fact that he'd shown up at the airport that day. That he'd told her he had feelings for her despite how terribly she'd misread him before. That he didn't make her feel pressured into making any decisions before she was ready. Iyad was always making her feel safe, and she loved that about him.

"This isn't about anyone," Fatima told him truthfully. Iyad had become a major question mark for Fatima after he'd written that earth-shattering message in her now-favorite notebook. Despite their time difference, he'd been texting the group chat every day since the airport, but he hadn't once mentioned what he'd said to her, leaving Fatima feeling like she was on less than equal footing with him.

Sadiyah suspected he was trying to be respectful so Fatima could figure things out for herself while Ramadan was still going on. Keep things as halal as possible, and such, which was why he'd only been texting their group chat and never Fatima on her own.

"Finding a man isn't hard," Sadiyah had reassured her over the phone one night. "Finding a good one is, though. Iyad is good, Ti." It was already summer break before their senior year once they'd returned from London, so the two had mainly been subjected to phone calls until August, since they lived three hours apart. "He's definitely down bad and a bit weird, but then again, so are you, Tweedledee," she added, still vouching for Iyad as plainly as she'd done since the beginning.

"Things also didn't get bad for me to start practicing Islam again. I wanted to," Fatima continued to tell Javier, speaking as evenly as she could manage. She sidestepped his belief that she needed him to save her from herself and his warped idea that Islam erased her autonomy and turned her into a shell of who she was. As if that wasn't exactly what he'd done to her for years. "I decided this for myself. Not him. Just like I'm deciding that it's time for us to be on the same page about where we are right now."

"We're not." Fatima watched as the last remnants of sleep left Javier's face, and an angry realization set in. His jaw clenched, and she could almost count the uneven twitches ticking at his temples. "I know you, and I know you don't mean this. You- You couldn't. You need me. You love me."

This was the Javier that Fatima knew disturbingly well. The one who decided for her that she didn't know what she was talking about. What she needed. For the first time in a long time —probably ever—Fatima forced herself to pay proper attention to what Javier said. How he conducted himself with her. No feelings. Just the analytics. Just the words. Just the fact that he told her she loved him. Not that he loved her. Or that he was sorry for the way he'd treated her. For Bea and whoever else. That he'd change. That he'd do better. Be better.

"You're so selfish," Fatima snapped, way louder than she'd

intended, glancing at the notebook from Iyad again. How could she have ever compared Iyad to him?

"And you aren't?" he shouted erratically.

Immediately, Fatima remembered the screeching sound of Javier's car skidding across the waterlogged road during their accident. Usually, whenever she found herself transported back to that moment, she forgave him. She let whatever was wrong be her fault—even when, most times, it wasn't. She let him be okay even when she wasn't. But not this time.

"No," she went, just as stiff as he was. "I'm not. I've been your scapegoat for too long because you don't know how to take care of yourself, and I'm *tired of it.* I am tired of *you,* Javier."

He just stared at her. She hadn't raised her voice at him in so long. The last time—

"You could've died," she went on. "When we got in that accident. When you lost control, not because of the rain, but because you were so busy being mad at me. Because you can't get anything done without me—or with those girls you get with whenever I'm not around, for that matter. I am exhausted, Javier. But I stayed because I thought I had to. I thought I almost killed you, so I convinced myself that leaving you would be like I actually did, but I'm not in the wrong here. This is not my fault."

Just make sure you aim all that rage at the right person next time, okay?

This was it. Fatima knew this had to be her turning point— the moment she finally killed the memory of that day and its hold on her. *His* hold on her. She had to kill it dead, sever its tie to her, and free herself from its agony—from its memory, its heartbeat. From him.

"And Javier, I could've died too," she finished.

Time dragged on, silent and drawn out, like a rubber band being stretched to its limit, before Javier said anything. When he responded, he said exactly what Fatima needed to hear to know she was making the right decision.

"I wish you did."

Then he hung up. And she let him.

TWO WEEKS LATER, THE MONTH OF RAMADAN WAS ENDING, AND Fatima's mom was braiding her hair as they prepared for Eid al-Fitr.

"Fatima," Nadia flicked the top of her daughter's head with the back of the rat tail comb she'd been using to part Fatima's hair.

Fatima jumped up from her seat cushion. "Ah- wha- why?"

"You've been tender-headed your whole life, but haven't made a sound till now. What's up?"

"What do you mean?"

Nadia poised the comb as if she might swat it again. So again, Fatima scrambled away from her. Her father, Tony, spoke up from the couch next to Nadia, laughing, "Nadi, will you give the child a break?"

Fatima was thankful for the distraction.

"Not at all," she affirmed. "Something's up. I know it, Tone."

"You sure it's not just the sky?" He winked.

"Comedy has never been one of your strong suits, my love."

"Yet and still, you love me."

"Mm," she hummed, returning to Fatima's hair after Fatima sat back down.

My love.

Love me.

Love, love, love.

Iyad said he wanted to marry her. Did that mean he loved her, too? Did Fatima love him? Did she even know what love was? Truly?

"Fa. Tuh. Ma." Nadia called again, this time hitting Fatima's shoulder with her open palm at each syllable.

"Wh- *What?*" Fatima all but wailed, leaving her seat to avoid hearing (really, feeling) her name again.

"I just pulled a knot out," Nadia informed her, rolling a hairball between her fingertips.

Fatima stared at the evidence in question. "Do you *want* me to scream?"

"I *want* you to tell me what's going on," Nadia answered, sounding genuinely on edge.

Now this was a weird development. Nadia never insisted on information from Fatima so overtly—neither of her parents did, which was how she'd managed to spend her time on a different continent without telling them about every little detail of what'd happened.

So what was this? Suddenly, her mother had become a hammer and turned Fatima into the nail she rapidly thwacked at until said hammer got what she wanted. More, what was this desire Fatima had to give in?

"My boyfriend and I broke up," Fatima said the first thing that came to mind. Which, now that it was out there, was the lowest matter on the hierarchy of Fatima's endless list of thoughts. She wasn't bothered about Javier and his whereabouts at all. Fatima was sussing out that her feelings for Javier had turned to pity a long time ago, and she'd spent too long mistaking it for a, she thought, necessary love. She'd gotten confused and lost herself in him.

"When?" Nadia asked.

"Um," Fatima started, counting the time out on her fingers. "A few mont- wait. *When?* You mean who?"

"I assume you mean your smooth-talking friend, right? The one with the curly hair?"

Tony paused the TV. "Smooth?" he thought. "Oh, Nadi. You mean the study buddy?"

She nodded.

Fatima blinked. "The stu- oh." She remembered Javier coming over and helping her study for their Spanish tests at the kitchen table before they started dating. "Y'all knew? That was years ago."

"It was hard not to know," Nadia sighed.

"Sometimes, we wished we didn't," Tony confessed. "We know what we taught you, but how you live your life isn't up to us, you know that. You make your own decisions and see what sticks."

"Still," Fatima shook her head, calculating the incalculable. "Why didn't you say anything?"

"Why didn't you?" he volleyed.

Nadia stayed quiet, studying Fatima as if she were a sample in a petri dish. Fatima had many strengths, but direct eye contact was never one of them. She looked away almost immediately. "This isn't about him, though, is it?" Nadia pressed. "If it were, you wouldn't have come back. . ." she trailed off, but Fatima knew exactly where she was headed.

Muslim, Fatima pieced the rest of the sentence together herself.

She knew that's what her mother meant without having to hear any more because she'd seen her parents' faces when she finally met them at the airport. First, there was the confusion—Fatima had never told them about it while she was away in London because she didn't want them to know if she changed her mind. Then, there was only their acceptance.

All her dad said was, "Yeah?" while framing her face so happily she thought he might burst.

"Yeah," Fatima replied softly. She hadn't thought out what she'd say to them, but 'yeah' seemed to sum it all up. So what was going on now?

Nadia clapped her hands and said thoughtfully, "You, who at twenty, still cries when you brush your hair—"

"'Kay now, crying is a stretch."

"—haven't even so much as flinched once—"

"Again, do you want me to scream?"

"—because of your *friend?*" she narrowed her eyes. Fatima rolled hers. "You know you're not a good liar."

Being a good liar probably wasn't something good to wish for, but Fatima, really, *really* wished she were one. Or, she actually could've at least been a bit more heartbroken over her breakup with him. That was an emotion she knew would be easier to understand and rationalize, instead of the truth: she really didn't care about him at all anymore.

"I met a boy when I was in London," Fatima conceded.

"Mm," Nadia muttered, finally seeming pleased after excavating this new information. "What does Sads think of him?"

"She likes him," Fatima said. She knew how much her parents trusted Sadiyah's judgment alongside her own. "He worked with us in our history class for the whole semester, and we all got pretty close, but then. . ." she said, reaching for the notebook Iyad had gotten her. Fatima flipped to the last page, showing them his surprisingly neat handwriting, since she still had difficulty saying his message out loud.

"Oh," Nadia murmured.

Tony cleared his throat. Then again. And a third time. "Iyad. Muslim name," he scratched behind his ear.

Fatima nodded. "I like him. A lot, actually," she went on. "His mom even sent abayas to me and Sadiyah from their shop as Eid presents. And, before we even knew each other all that well, he almost beat up a guy for hitting me."

"'*Hitting?*'" Tony repeated. Fatima forgot she'd made the creative decision to leave that colorful tidbit out of her storytimes.

"Well, what had happened was—"

"Later," he interrupted sternly. Translation: Let me get my mind right to hear about it first.

"My point is, he's good," Fatima finished, not giving everything, but giving what she hoped would be enough.

Nadia still wasn't having it. "And?" she coaxed.

Fatima broke immediately. "And what if he doesn't stay that way?" she choked out, thinking of how quickly Javier didn't.

Nadia regarded her for a long moment, watching her with those same careful amber eyes Fatima was constantly told she had herself, before she resolved, "He might not."

"What?"

"'What if' is the thief of what is. What *is* true is that you loved that boy, and you learned what it looked like when you didn't get that same love back in return. What *is* true is that you can't change what happened—nor should you, because you *are* stronger now than when you left here. So *if* this Iyad is the same as him, you'd know by now. And I didn't raise you dumb enough to make the same mistake again. Did I?"

Fatima shook her head, but she wasn't sure if she meant her denial. She wanted to believe that she was doing okay. That she truly was better now than she'd been before. But what if she wasn't? What if, despite her wanting Iyad, her doomsday predictions of how she'd inevitably ruin them were right?

What if Javier was never the problem? The mistake. What if she was?

"You deserve good things," her mom persisted. "You deserve to be happy. I don't know where you got it in that big head of yours that you don't. But," she squinted, "do you *even* want another relationship now? Don't you need time to yourself?"

Not even a beat later, Tony spoke up. "You love this boy?"

Inhale. There were too many questions. Fatima needed to breathe. She needed to think. *Exhale.* "I could."

Those two words seemed to sum up everything. *I could* want another relationship. I'm finally over my last one. *I could* need time to myself. I haven't had any in a long time. *I could* love him. But does he love me? Could he?

Neither of them pressed for confirmation as to which question she'd responded to. Fatima didn't know which one she'd choose if they had. All she knew was that she needed space. From all of it. Just a bit more time to clear her head. This wasn't just any relationship she was thinking about. This was Iyad. This was forever. Maybe.

"He wants to marry you?" Tony continued.

"He does."

"And you want to marry him?"

Fatima felt her breath catch and nodded. She did. Not just yet, but she'd marry him, and she wanted to make that fact clear.

"Well," he declared. "Why hasn't he contacted me yet?"

Fatima glanced back at the notebook. "He's waiting for me," she told him, feeling a glimmer of sunshine ready to break through her chest at the thought. She picked up her phone, unsure of what would come next, but sure enough, because it was him.

CHAPTER THIRTY-EIGHT

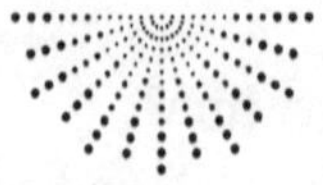

HE CONVINCED HIMSELF THAT IT'D BE EASY: CALLING HIM.

But as Iyad repeated to his cousin and uncle what he'd told (or rather, written) Fatima at the airport, he realized he had no idea what he was doing—specifically, what he'd do after Fatima gave him the green light that she was ready for more with him.

"I knew you liked her, but you told her. . . what?" Mo looked like he'd seen a ghost, Bigfoot, and the Loch Ness Monster, all at the same time. He leaned back, dramatically, against the stock room's door frame for support. They were all huddled in there after finishing the clean-up from the Pre-Eid crowd, like they were planning some elaborate heist. Well, in some offbeat way, they were.

"Again, I wrote it down," Iyad corrected.

Mo clicked his tongue. "Does it matter?"

"Did you mean it?" Hassan crossed his arms. He'd been so quiet while Iyad explained what he'd done, letting Iyad work through his thoughts the way he used to before everything went south between them. Mo, nearly hyperventilating with a million thoughts a minute, the way his father would.

"I did," Iyad answered, although he hadn't spoken about this at all to anyone since he'd written that question down in that notebook—not even to Fatima—but he'd been thinking about it to himself nonstop. "I do," he asserted. He'd asked her to marry him. But *how* could he marry her a whole ocean away? "I love…" he couldn't say it. Not in front of them. Not yet. Not with that dumb look plastered across Mo's face. "I love the way we met."

"What are you on about?" Mo muttered aloud at the same time Hassan asked, "What do you mean?"

"That I got to be her friend first," Iyad explained. "Someone she could trust without expectations. I got to learn things about her, and things about myself that I don't think I would've ever entertained again if we had never met."

He knew he wouldn't have, actually. Iyad planned to go the rest of his life with his uncle cast off to the side and his dad in his rearview. Both there, but just barely. Just enough. Things weren't like that anymore, though, and Iyad knew that change was all thanks to meeting Fatima.

After a moment, Hassan said airily, like he was caught between sometime then and before, "My brother was a scoundrel back in our early days. You couldn't trust the man as far as you could throw him," he sniffed.

Iyad stood there stock-still, listening like he was trying to break down a rocket science equation. He rarely ever heard his uncle speak about his father after he'd passed, hadn't given the man the chance, to be fair. Still, he never would've imagined the keyword when they'd finally, truly, gotten around to it would've been "scoundrel."

"He- he was always lying, going back on what he'd said. Hamza was selfish. He was a con man in every sense of the word, always going on and on about this and that so much that you'd forget how full of it he was because you wanted to be around him. You wanted to trust him. You wanted to forgive him. My brother and I always looked alike, but Hamz was always the best of us—even when he wasn't." Hassan grinned wistfully, with love as evident as hearts themselves in his eyes.

"He was never a bad man, but it was impressive, all of the bad decisions he could make. One after the other," Hassan went on. "But even the most off-the-wall of us can get turned around, yeah? 'Cause it felt like we met your mother out of nowhere somewhere around then, and your father was never the same.

He convinced me to go in with him on buying Azyaa. On trusting him. On believing in us. . . We never talked about how quickly he'd changed from who he used to be into the man you may remember, but we all knew it was thanks to her being put in his life that he'd gone and righted himself."

"What are you getting at?" Iyad asked, although he was sure he knew already.

"Wa khalaqnakum azwaja," Hassan recited. "The Quran says, 'And We created you in pairs.' What if Fatima is yours?"

Iyad couldn't move. Couldn't speak. Hassan kept going.

"I have no way of knowing that, of course, Allahu a'alam." *God knows best.* "What I do know is that your father was one stubborn yute, and meeting Farah completely changed that about him. I see that same stubbornness in you, and the way you've changed after meeting Fatima. . . it makes me think of him."

Oh. He saw it, too? How all the good things that had come into his life had aligned at one shared coordinate: her. How she was the good thing about him. How she was exactly who he'd never known he'd spent years waiting for. Missing. Needing.

"He loved her first, too, you know?" Hassan said. Wait—

"You knew?" Iyad murmured.

"The fish head," he offered gently.

"The fish head!" Mo jumped in. He was grinning teeth at that, clapping his hands together like a seal after a well-executed circus trick. "I was gonna say I saw it back at the South Bank, or after all that laughing you did with her at Iftar, or- or when you asked me to read Sadiyah's texts, but the fish head!" he snapped his fingers loudly. "I used to chase you around the house with them, but you turned big man for your girl," he quipped.

My girl, Iyad thought. *My girl.* He liked that. 'My wife' would've sounded better, but 'my girl.' For now. If she wanted. He'd face all his fears for her without a second thought if it meant he could have her around.

Still, Iyad rolled his eyes, not wanting to give his cousin a leg up on him. "Do you ever shut up?"

"Don't chat to me," Mo continued to laugh. "You should be paying me for not clowning you right then."

"So, here's where we are," Hassan scratched his head, bypassing Mo. "Eid is in three days. You graduate next month. She graduates next year. If you're going to do this right, Yaddy, you know who you've got to talk to next. But even before that, I know my brother would've wanted me to tell you what your grandad told us before we got married ourselves.

"You need to be sure of yourself on your own before taking any next steps with someone else because this is not a decision you can run from. This is something that changes everything, and you've got to be ready for that. Not just for you, but for her, too. You need to be the man I know you are—the man I know Hamza would be so proud to see today—for both of you. "

Iyad almost collapsed to the ground beneath him. Would he? Would his dad have seen how he'd acted over these past few years and still be proud of him? Still smile at him the way he used to?

He wiped at his eyes, refusing to cry in front of Mo, of all people, and whispered, "But what if her dad doesn't think I am? What if he doesn't like me?" he breathed. "What if I'm not good enough. What if he thinks I'm terrible for her? What if Fatima agrees? Wha- What if she doesn't even want me? What if she changed her mind?" *What if I was right that I'm meant to stay alone?*

Mo hit him from behind.

"Mohammad!" Iyad spun around.

Mo sucked in a breath, smirking roguishly. "You really aren't that smart. Are you, brudda? Allahu a'alam," he repeated Hassan. "You'll have so much more peace in life if you stop always trying to control every little thing. Say bismillah"—In the name of God—"and let things sort themselves out, yeah?"

Iyad sighed, caught off guard by Mo making sense, when he heard a notification ping on his phone. There was a moment, a flash of a second, where Iyad thought to ignore the message completely. For some reason, he couldn't. He sighed, taking it out of his pocket to check, and just as Mo had said, things were already sorting themselves out.

Ti:

> hey, yad.

> would you like my dad's number?

Sads:

> FINALLYYYYYYYY

He quickly took the number and messaged her dad before he could talk himself out of it. Everything would come together. For her? He'd make sure of it.

Iyad:

> As-Salamu Alaykum. Hello, sir. My name is Iyad Ahmed.

I'm messaging you to speak about marrying your daughter.

FATIMA WAS THROWN, CATAPULTED—NO—TELEPORTED FROM HER bedroom to her parents' when she heard her dad's computer ring.

When Iyad told her he'd be speaking with her dad on Eid, three days after she'd given him his number, she'd jokingly-not-so-jokingly asked if he was sure about this. About her. He'd followed up and said he'd been sure ever since that day in the train station when the man pushed her—he just didn't know it yet.

It shouldn't have come as such a surprise to Fatima that he'd felt so strongly about her for that long in light of the whole "Will you marry me?"-ness of their current situation. But still, that day at the station was so long ago. They'd barely known each other then... and he was sure?

The realization struck her like a hurricane, flooding the flowers that bloomed from her toes to the space beneath her ribcage as she took in what he'd told her. It was why she was currently army crawling in the sapphire-blue abaya his mom had sent her, holding the notebook Iyad had given her to document what she heard for her debrief with Sadiyah later on.

"So," her dad started off strong. "You'd like to marry my daughter."

"I- I would, sir?" Iyad answered quickly. Fatima couldn't see him through the little crack in the door she was straining to watch through, but Iyad sounded incredibly more English than usual. Was that a good sign?

Tony cocked his head to the side. "You sure?"

Iyad cleared his throat. "Of course, Mr. Sommers. I think she's incredible."

"That she is," Tony nodded decisively. "I understand it's, what, around one in the afternoon over there?"

"Yes, sir. Quarter past."

"How's your Eid been? Did you go to service?" Tony probed, sitting up straighter in his seat. Fatima edged in a bit closer to the door, the wood now just a hair away from her forehead.

"Yes, sir," Iyad answered. Fatima knew Iyad could be polite, but she'd never heard so many 'sirs' before on his account. This side of him was interesting, new. She wanted to keep finding new things about him. "I went this morning and left early so we could speak."

"This must be important to you, then," Tony observed. "Yeah, we're about to head out ourselves. But you know Ti and time..." he trailed off, laughing softly.

And then they both were. And it truly would've been a lovely sound to hear had Fatima not been lulled into submission by that same false security blanket for the past twenty years already.

"Did she tell you how we met?" Iyad asked.

"Nah," Tony shook his head.

And for good reason, Fatima thought to herself.

"She and Sadiyah were late to class their first day," Iyad responded naively, utterly unaware that he was bunny hopping all the way into a trap. "And lost."

"So you were late too, I assume," Tony interrogated. He was baiting Iyad. Setting him up for failure, only to mess with his head and see if he'd fold. If he'd choke and give up. Fatima and her father hadn't discussed this less-than-sparing tactic that he was going about with Iyad, but she'd lost to him enough times in Spades to know that her dad was trying to get in his head.

The awkward silence that followed told her that he had. She held her breath.

"Iyad," Tony went on.

"Yes, sir."

"How is your deen?" *Your deen. Your faith.*

"It's strong, sir," Iyad told him, sounding slightly more at ease with the change of subject.

Tony crossed his arms. Fatima, against her better judgment, crept in closer. "Did you fast for Ramadan?" he asked.

"Yes, sir."

"Every day?"

"Yes, sir."

"Do you pray every day?"

"Yes, sir."

"Five times a day?"

"Yes, sir."

"My Fatima," Tony relaxed in his chair. Fatima imagined him crossing his hands over his belly the way he did after he finished eating, contented and full. "She's the type of girl who's happy to let someone else have the spotlight. You're not the type to take it from her, are you?"

"Of course not," Iyad insisted. "Stealing her spotlight is like. . . stealing light from the sun," he mumbled.

This time, Tony was quiet. "Hm," he said. "You must really love my Fatima to come up with something as sappy as that." There was an obvious mirth to his voice that Fatima caught onto immediately.

"I've missed her every day since she left," Iyad started, not agreeing to what Tony said but not outright denying it either. She pulled herself closer to the door, just barely closing the gap between herself and the panel to hear Iyad better. "I lo—"

Tony cut him off before she got to hear those three golden words. Fatima slid back.

"Wouldn't it be easier if you were with a girl who's already in London, though?"

Excuse me? Was her dad trying to ruin everything? Of course, it would've been easier. He could probably get any girl in London if he wanted. All anyone had to do was look at him. Or talk. Or. . . come to think of it, the man was actually a wonder to the senses and should therefore be locked away forever. With her. Was that possible?

"It would," Iyad attested, evidently forgetting the purpose of the entire phone call in the first place. "But it wouldn't be her, so I wouldn't see a point."

"Good answer," Tony nodded in approval. "I also understand you were protective of her when I couldn't be there. Thank you for that."

"Of course."

"And you're ready to discuss her dowry as well?"

"Absolutely."

Stupidly. So, so, stupidly, Fatima inched forward again. Not a measured, calculated centimeter of space, but the last tick of the ruler that she didn't have to give, causing her forehead to bang against the door she was trying her hardest to avoid. When she looked up, the door had swung all the way open, and two sets of eyes were now planted squarely on her.

Fatima smiled sheepishly, taking her time to stand up. "Hey, Yad," she waved.

"Hi, Ti." Iyad waved back on the screen, immediately sounding more familiar than he had the entire time. Did she do that? Make him comfortable? The thought had just barely had time to register in her head when Iyad spoke up again. "And to answer your question from before, sir," he started, now focusing his gaze on Fatima's. She nearly combusted just under the steadiness of his stare. "I love you."

No. Self-combustion is precisely what happened. This was the first time Fatima had explicitly heard him say that. She didn't know until then that it was exactly what she was waiting to hear until the words were written so clearly across the ocean walls that separated them.

I love you.

Right then. Right there. Scared as she was of everything she didn't know about what was to come of them, it was the safety of those three little words and the knowledge of all his actions combined that struck her.

I love you.

Or maybe it was the immediate realization that she was in love with him, too.

EPILOGUE

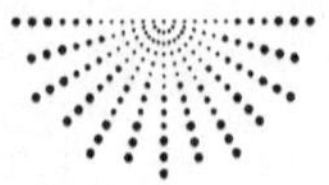

Two Years Later

Iyad had never been so nervous in all his twenty-four years of life. But then again, he'd also never seen his wife in that time either.

Wife. He couldn't think of four letters stacked together in the English dictionary that sounded better than those.

Iyad hastily rubbed his hands together and blew into them like he was trying to light a fire before glancing up to check the plane arrival times. He hadn't been to Heathrow Airport since he'd last dropped Fatima and Sadiyah off for the States in 2019.

That wasn't the plan, of course. Iyad meant to fly out to see Fatima after waiting nine months for her to decide she was finally ready to marry him. He was going to come for a short visit during her spring break in March. They were going to have a nikah wedding ceremony and everything, but the year 2020 didn't go as planned for anyone.

Instead, Fatima finished her senior year, graduated, and they got married from their respective countries all over Zoom video calls. And Iyad bided his time during the COVID lock-down, waiting for the day he'd see her again.

For starters, he spent more time at the shop. The pandemic hadn't been easy on Ahmed Azyaa in the slightest, specifically, on his Uncle Hassan. The store was forced to go almost completely digital, which was a complete and total nightmare for him. But it was good in other ways. It forced Iyad to take the media-based plans he'd already been working on more seri-ously, giving him something to focus on besides missing Fatima.

Iyad had also graduated by then, so he was at Azyaa with Hassan full-time, strategizing ways to keep Azyaa afloat and ensure its success while safeguarding his uncle from burning out, like his dad had. He even decided to go back to therapy—and somehow convinced Fatima to start going for herself as well—to stay in check with both himself and everyone else. Like his uncle. They'd been seeing a lot more of each other recently, steadily falling back into their old routine. Mo even came around the shop more often (and on time). He also went by Mohammad now. Everyone liked that more.

Iyad had learned that he felt better when he was busy. So, he stayed busy making sure he was ready for Fatima's return to London. They needed things. A home. A bed. Matching mugs and house slippers, too, apparently. According to her.

He stayed patient for those two years as well. Loving her from his side of the Atlantic. Even more patient during that second year when they were actually married. When she was finally his. And still so far away. But now, as he spotted a blur of green skittering past him, he was just happy he didn't have to be patient and wait anymore. That he didn't have to hold his breath any longer.

Seeing Fatima pinballing around the arrivals hall because she refused to wear her glasses, despite obviously needing them, felt a lot like finally being able to breathe. It reminded him of when his dad used to tell him to, "Ask God for what you need, and wallahi, the blessings will come."

They'd come. Ten-fold. His uncle was still standing, and he was just about to take his wife to the flat she'd picked out as his dowry gift to her.

Iyad stood from his seat to follow after her, picking up the bouquet of daisies that he'd gotten for his new favorite Londoner, along with the dumplings he had his mom make for her.

"Fatima," he called, jogging after her. Several people turned around, but none of them was the girl he'd been waiting what felt like his whole life for. He jogged a little faster and tapped her shoulder. "Ti."

Fatima turned around, and Iyad was eviscerated at the spot. That was his wife looking at him.

Wife. Wife. Wife.

"Vader?" Fatima said, pulling down her facemask with a wide grin. He slid his off as well.

Iyad swallowed, drinking her in. It was surreal, to say the least, seeing her for the first time in years right in the place where he'd seen her last. He couldn't stop staring. Scared she wasn't real. Terrified she was just some extremely high-tech software, and if he blinked, the computer's illusion would glitch and she'd disappear. He didn't know if he could handle her disappearing again. He needed her. Here. Now. Forever. His.

Wife. Wife. Wife.

Iyad couldn't believe it'd been two whole years since he'd seen her face apart from his phone's screen.

"I'll call you when we make it back, Sads," she muttered, pulling an AirPod out from underneath the fabric of her hijab as she hung up her call and put the bud back in its case. Her eyes flitted back and forth between him and the ground, seeming as nervous as he felt. "As-Salamu Alaykum, you found me." That sweet half-dimpled grin shone his way. "And uh, Sads says hey."

Iyad nodded. His smile in return to her was operatic. "Wa Alaykum As-Salam. I wouldn't have to look for you at all, though," he said, taking her glasses from the top of her head and fitting them over her eyes, "if you ever wore these."

Fatima scowled at him as she adjusted the lenses. And, because she was beautiful even when glaring, and because she was his, and because he couldn't help himself, he dipped down and kissed her on the cheek.

Then, realizing these were their first moments of physical contact, Iyad hesitated, unsure if his impulses were welcomed just yet. His uncertainty only deepened when he noticed Fatima's blank expression directed back at him. Iyad rubbed his free hand at the base of his neck, trying to settle himself, and determined not to make any more missteps. He reached down to collect her bags, wordlessly exchanging them with the bouquet, when she finally spoke.

"Do that again," he heard her say, cradling the flowers like a newborn.

Only, he hadn't heard her say that because he talked to this woman nearly every day since he'd last seen her, and she hadn't once said or sounded anything like that. Surely, he'd misheard her. He thought they'd gotten used to each other's accents. Surely not.

"What?"

But then Fatima Sommers, incredible woman that she was, reached up on her tippy toes and spoke clearly, directly, into Iyad's ear, "Do. That. Again," she dared him with wanton eyes, then sank gently back down to the ground.

Wife. Wife. Wife.

If love were a sound, one unmistakable to Iyad's ears, he would've sworn it was her voice in that moment. He looked her over, her satin brown skin and honey-speckled gaze. This woman had to be the personification of love made flesh.

And she loved him.

Was in love with him.

Iyad was shocked and delighted by that fact every day, so he would always do his best to make sure her love was a fact that never changed.

Wife. Wife. Wife.

Growing up, Iyad was always told he didn't follow instructions well. But with Fatima, he knew for sure that he wouldn't be having those same problems. He skirted a glance around them. "Come here," he breathed, holding her hand and pulling her over to a narrow opening that hid her between a support column and his body.

Iyad wiggled his brows at her blatant surprise as she pressed her back into the wall behind her. He gently cradled her cheek, his thumb tracing her features, watching her for a few seconds in absolute awe that a project about a man who was terrible to his wives had led him to loving his own.

Wife. Wife. Wife.

Doing as told, Iyad Ahmed bent down, and this time, truly kissed his wife.

MAYBE IT WAS THE JET LAG. MAYBE IT WAS THAT IYAD HAD NEVER touched her before, and Fatima spent half their time apart imagining what it'd be like once he finally had. Maybe it was that she spent the other half talking his ears off about every possible thing she could think of, but Fatima suddenly couldn't speak at all. Not English. Not Spanish. Not gibberish.

The man had just kissed entire dictionaries out of her.

"I love you," he whispered finally, leaving her heart pounding as he pulled back.

So this was why airports were so popular in the rom-coms. With twenty-two years of entertaining herself with the genre under her belt, Fatima thought she'd at least be a little unbothered when she'd finally reconnected with Iyad. But if seeing him was enough to do her in. . . how could she have known that his kiss would completely unravel her? How could she have known she'd fall so quickly into one of those giddy, loose-limbed, might-burst-with-happiness-at-any-moment reflexes, just like in the movies, immediately wanting more?

"Again," she worked the word out, heady.

Iyad made an awful attempt at hiding a wolfish grin as he adjusted the strap of her book bag against his shoulder. *"Again?"* His eyes widened, amused.

Fatima didn't know what it was about him. Ever since their nikah was settled a little over a year ago, it was like she could see this switch turn on in Iyad's head that told him he could finally step off the cliff's edge of everything he wanted to say to her and dive straight in.

He made sure to tell her he loved her every day and gave little weather forecasts on London's indecisive skies. He read the Quran with her. He sent her flowers. Hijabs. Handwritten letters. He even sent her a Darth Vader plushie as his temporary stand-in since he couldn't send himself on account of the pandemic. But they were back now, picking up right in the place where they'd left off, and that's what mattered. So. Yes. Again.

"You missed a spot," Fatima pointed to her cheek, feigning distressed concern. "Here. If you leave it, I'll be uneven all day," she tilted her head, wagged her body around loosely as if gravity were only weighing half of her down, and closed her eyes.

After a few seconds of nothing happening, Fatima peeked out of one eye to find Iyad taking a picture of her. He was beaming, just like she had when Claudette fulfilled her promise by sending her a signed copy of *Control* along with an official job offer.

"My wife is beautiful," he explained a little too loudly.

Fatima laughed and shushed him, assuming people could hear him, but his frame shielded her completely, so it wasn't like she could tell, regardless. Still, she felt herself blush brightly at the thought.

"Now," he whispered gently, nudging forward to kiss her cheek, his beard softly brushing against her skin as he did so. "You all evened out now, love?"

Love. Iyad told her he loved her, and she immediately asked for more kisses like a touch-starved gremlin. Fatima thought she'd spent long enough as a virtual wife, saying "I love you" over the phone, that she thought telling him it had become second nature. But the words felt different now that she was face-to-face with him.

I love you, she wanted to say.

I love you. She knew she did.

I love you.

Affection and romance surprisingly seemed to come easily to Iyad. Whereas with Fatima, she had the inconvenient obstacle of still doubting herself with him. Not all of the time, thankfully, just random little instances where she'd freeze up before being as sweet to him as he was to her.

She'd become a lot more hesitant than she used to be, getting so caught up in her lingering fear that everything happening now was too good to be true that sometimes, she tricked herself into believing it really was.

And that was no good. Fatima was so deeply in love with Iyad, and all he did was give her that love back multiplied. So, she really had no choice but to reciprocate him just as surely if she wanted them to work out. There was nothing coveted about her cautiousness. Not now. Not with him.

I love you. I love you. I love you.

Those three words were etched, she knew this, firmly on her heartstrings and wedged deep in the spaces underneath her fingertips. But did any of that matter if she hadn't actually said them? Now?

"I love you," she let loose, before any more pointless doubts could seep their way further into her bloodstream.

And Iyad, on account of being a waffling muppet of a man (Fatima was steadily picking up on his lingo, although she was never sure if she ever used it at the right times or in the right ways), pretended not to hear.

"Hm?" he arched his eyebrows.

But she was sure he'd heard her. Iyad always heard her. Still, if this was the game he wanted to play, she'd play it. Forever.

"I said," she cleared her throat daintily, speaking up. "I love you."

Iyad looked like he'd just won a medal. Fatima wanted to make sure he knew it was golden.

"I love you," she went on. "I love you. I love you."

"I love you," he responded, still gleaming. He put a hand out in the space between them. To which Fatima, without hesitation, put her own inside of. Although it was technically the second time today, and ever, that they'd held hands, it still felt as charged as the first. She looked down at them, laced together. Iyad's were so much bigger than hers. He said, "You know you're stuck with me now, right? I put super glue on my palm so there's no going anywhere."

Fatima laughed, jokingly trying to disentangle herself, and Iyad only held on tighter. "See," he said, stage-gasping but smug. "Stuck."

"You're a clown," she snorted, biting her lip.

"You're a clown's wife, then," he mused. "One sec," Iyad let go of her to take his facemask from around his arm and fit it back over his mouth.

Fatima did the same. Then, because there was something inside of her that missed him every day they were apart, she quickly reached out for his palm again. "Stuck," she explained resolutely, once they'd reconnected.

"Of course," his eyes lit up like a streetlight as she reached for the container of his mom's dumplings he had in his other hand, and popped one in her mouth—they tasted just as good as she'd remembered. "Ready to go home?"

"Oh, right," Fatima gasped, feeling the weight of her jet lag settle back into her limbs. She forgot they were still in the terminal for a moment. "Let's go," she told him, squeezing his hand.

He squeezed back. "Let's go."

A slow, easy smile washed over Fatima as Iyad led them from the airport. She decided then that this must be what love was. It wasn't guarded or careful. It was sure. Sure of herself. Sure of holding his hand and trusting he wouldn't let hers go. Rain or shine. She prayed things would stay this way. Forever and ever. Always.

Ameen.

ACKNOWLEDGMENTS

Bismillah.

This book was both a headache and made my head spin so much that I'm surprised it's still attached to my neck. The process of writing, then ultimately deciding to self-publish Fatima's story, was my most intimate deep dive into myself that taught me so much about who I am as I continued to learn more about her. Then again, that's the true nature of creation, isn't it? To discover? To tie a red string from your fingertip to someone else's, so life feels even the slightest bit less lonely?

I've always written, but I knew I needed *Sommers* in 2019, when I was in London and couldn't find a single book that mirrored my experience of studying abroad as a Black girl. I believe we Black and Muslim girls need to see ourselves in print. I believe we all need examples of being loved, loved loudly, and can only hope that Fatima and Iyad proved to be an example of this.

I want to thank my mama first (and not just because of the earful I'd get if I didn't) for being my first reader, listener, and believer. For going to Barnes & Noble with me for years and years and years. For sitting in those cafés between me, those piles of books, and a tomato caprese sandwich. For Highlights magazines and making Schoolastic book fairs more than somewhere I just highlighted what I wanted. For having me play hide-and-seek with the typos in newspapers and for hearing out all of my many story ideas. For asking sixth grade me what I wanted to be and not ending the conversation until I said a writer. For telling me that I already was. For everything. Shukran.

To Khadijah, I hope I can make you proud, bestie.

To Leem, for reintroducing me to anime with the cinema that is *Attack on Titan,* and for reading and rereading this book as many times as you did. Your insight. Your care. Your love of Fatima (but really of Mo) made me so incredibly happy to feel that someone else could love this world as much as I do. I hope life gives you as many green emoji checks to look forward to as you gave me.

To Bre, thank you for hearing out my hundreds of cover ideas, helping to keep my head on straight when I think too far, for our word game sessions, and endless talks (that only ever really end because my phone is rarely charged). I'm glad that tuxedo-wearing mouse gave me you.

To Saf, for showing me my first K-drama, for answering my questions, and for being as much my girl a whole continent away as you were when we practically lived together.

To Zion, for not falling asleep on the first chapter.

To heartbreak, who tried but never won. Thank you for giving me something to ~~dwell on~~ write about.

To those whose stories are attempted at being starved and bled from them, I see you. I pray for you, your freedom, the warmth of the sun to hold you, and the light of the moon to guide you.

To me, for sticking it out.

To you, for reading. Thank you. Thank you. Thank you.

And finally, to anyone who needs the reminder that they, themselves, are enough—

Wa Huwa ma'akum ayna maa kuntum. (Quran 57:4)
And He is with you wherever you are.

AN EXCERPT FROM MEENAH'S NEXT NOVEL

You didn't think we were done yet. . . did you?
It's Sadiyah's turn next!

Read on for a sneak peek of *Y ILY*—a second-chance, childhood friends-to-lovers, and marriage of convenience romance filled with banter, healing from old wounds, and, of course, tons of yearning.

❤

1

DEADWEIGHT

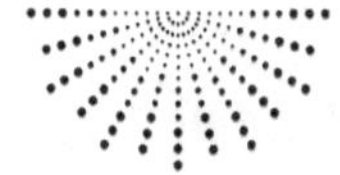

Sadiyah Mitchell wasn't afraid to die. Naturally, she didn't look forward to the occasion, but had long since accepted this impending corollary as the inevitable price she'd pay for being alive. She just didn't expect to pay up in front of her boss. In light of recent events, though, "ex-boss" was now a more fitting description of Leah Tooley.

That morning, Sadiyah had been prey let loose in a wolf's den, disgracefully unaware of what was coming for her when she walked into Leah's office. The room always struck Sadiyah as distinctly adolescent in some way. The composition of anatomy charts taped to the walls and the big blue exercise ball sitting in the corner seemed less like it belonged to the direct manager of a cardiology biotech startup and more to a middle school PE teacher, which made Sadiyah a kid in detention as she sat in the gray armchair across from Leah's desk.

"Morning glory," Leah said, her usual smile spread wide across her face.

Sadiyah smiled back. "Morning, Leah." She glanced down at the fitness tracker on her wrist. It was a welcome present from about three years ago when she started at the office as a Clinical

Research Assistant. "Am I early?" She checked the time. Not long after she'd gotten into the office for the day, Leah sent her an e-vite titled 'Business Update' with no further information.

Leah was getting in her "morning steppers" on the little treadmill underneath her desk, the rhythmic thud of her footsteps making no effort to stop. "Not at all, dear. It's about time we had this little chat."

Absolutely no warning bell went off in Sadiyah's head. In fact, she was sure she was about to be promoted to coordinator status when she leaned in, asking, "About?"

"I have to let you go," Leah replied, rushing out her words, quickly trading in her merriment for a plastered-on look of despair—one she'd probably spent the entire night before perfecting in front of her bathroom mirror.

Sadiyah didn't pick up on that, though. She was busy mentally preparing how surprised she'd pretend to be once Leah finally broke the news, unaware that she already had. "Where?"

Leah squinted her eyes, quietly bobbing her head as she waited for Sadiyah to catch on. Something Sadiyah had already done, but she couldn't show Leah her Oscar-worthy blend of shock and confusion if Leah didn't officially give the green light to do so.

So Sadiyah, playing along, rechecked her watch. "Oh! Go home for the day?" she asked, since she typically left a little early on Fridays to make it to Jumu'ah service at the masjid. "I'm alright for now, so I can hang back a little longer. Just need to finish up on my report."

"Abi can do it." Leah tied her hair up in a ponytail, the bunch of it whipping to either side like a pendulum as she walked. "You don't need to finish your shift, especially since you're almost done today. Don't worry—it'll be as if you never left early, and I'll make sure your severance pay is sent to you ASAP," she nodded.

Severance?

Just then, Sadiyah felt something in her chest slip, almost comically, like a cartoon character over a banana peel. "Wait," she blinked as the dots finally began to connect the way they should've already minutes ago. Her pulse quickened. "Hold up."

Almost on cue, Sadiyah's head spun from where she'd spend her extra cash from her promotion to how idiotically she'd spent her last paycheck. She thought about her impending rent increase, gas money, phone bill, and the fact that she couldn't remember the last time she'd bought groceries instead of takeout.

And then there was the vacuum.

That stupid hybrid cross between a vacuum and a mop that she'd been so excited to buy last month. Also, there were her student loans, her car note, and whatever else was escaping her mind in the moment, as she gathered, all at once, how expensive it was to breathe.

Sadiyah's gut pulled. She felt her heart ramming itself against her ribcage, nauseating her as she thought of what to say. "You let me work for almost an entire shift *knowing* you were going to fire me right before my out time, Leah?" she worked out, choosing to ditch the charade of the agreeable code-switching she'd granted Leah as the only Black colleague in an otherwise entirely white office.

Leah went to speak, but she hesitated, the whir of the treadmill becoming the loudest sound in the room between them. "I thought you'd want to finish the week off as strong as you started it," she said at last, her joyful mask now jeering in Sadiyah's face.

It was cruel, really. That was the only way Sadiyah could understand Leah's belief that she was somehow doing Sadiyah a favor by allowing her to complete her forty-hour workweek. In reality, the blonde wench was just milking her dry for every last minute she could with a clear-ish conscience.

"As I've been relaying," the wench went on, "our funding has been a bit dodgy lately. Which, unfortunately, has resulted in hard choices like where we are now."

"Where *I* am now," Sadiyah corrected, lowly.

"Sorry?"

"You said where we are, but you're fine."

"I—"

Sadiyah cut her off, regurgitating the words that'd felt so ridiculously important to her after so many job application rejections before she'd landed her position there. "You said I was an invaluable asset when you hired me," she panted, suddenly struggling to breathe. "What happened?" What Sadiyah really meant to ask was, *Why me?*

Leah sighed. "I'm sorry, dear."

"Yeah," Sadiyah breathed out a laugh, but her face had fallen. Then her body followed behind, slumped into her chair like the limbs of a rag doll, "It's not you, it's me, right?"

"But," Leah offered, not answering, "I'm sure you'll have a new home in no time. With a resume like yours, especially. And of course, I'd write you glowing letters of recommendation if the need arose."

At the mention of home, Sadiyah couldn't help but think of her rent again. Home wasn't just some hypothetical concept. It was an apartment she paid for by herself with the salary she fought so hard to maintain. It was the apartment she loved. That she was beginning to realize was potentially being stripped away from her.

Sadiyah tried to think through Leah's reasoning. It wasn't like the breadcrumbs hadn't been there for her to follow. Like she said, Leah had mentioned that she was worried about the company's revenue and whether they'd eventually lose their funding altogether. They were a small enterprise, still finding their footing in the medical research industry.

Leah had voiced the same concerns two years prior, so

Sadiyah wrote them off as paranoia. But then, Monday, there was her unusually short and oddly critical one-on-one meeting. And now, here Sadiyah was, an "invaluable asset," trying to stop the boulder from falling off the mountain as one anxious idea rammed into the next.

Could her leaving early on Fridays have been the reason she was in this seat now, rather than someone else? It was the main difference she could think of between herself and her coworkers, although she always made up for it. Although this exception had been approved by the HR team shortly after Sadiyah was hired. But now, as she thought about it, she wasn't sure if her absence made the most logistical sense. Maybe they resented their decision.

Maybe they resented her for it.

Maybe she was being discriminated against.

Maybe she had a case.

Maybe she could sue.

Maybe she should breathe first.

"Breathe, Sadiyah." Leah had materialized in front of her. She was holding this little pink fan in Sadiyah's face. These days, the fan had made so many appearances that Sadiyah secretly denoted it as Leah's menopausal fan. She would've never imagined it'd be used on her mid-panic attack. "Breathe, sweet. It'll be alright. You'll be alright."

Sadiyah didn't have enough air in her lungs at the moment to tell Leah to shut up. To finally admit that she always hated being called that half-finished pet name. Instead, she was more focused on her rapidly growing fit of breathlessness that'd sent her fitness tracker into a blaring frenzy. It beeped away the erratic inclines of her heart rate like the high-pitched siren of an EMT truck as she processed the news that she'd actually been let go. The irony of Sadiyah's heart rate skyrocketing in a cardiology research office was not lost on her.

"I'm fine," she eventually managed to croak out, waving Leah off. Sadiyah had spent all her time at her desk before this meeting working on a report about how well a series of pacemakers had been for the patients who had opted to use them. And now all that work would go to Abi? Abigale "Can't Get Anything Done Right" Williams? She got to keep her job, and Sadiyah didn't?

Leah cut her fan off and moved back a step, not completely leaving Sadiyah's side. Sadiyah noticed that her knee was jutted out and her hand was still somewhat reaching toward her, as if she were afraid her actions would lead to a dead body in the middle of her office.

"I'm fine," Sadiyah repeated, avoiding Leah's gaze. She glared at the treadmill instead as an odd pressure began to build behind her eyes. Sadiyah ignored the sensation, refusing to add crying to her list of transgressions for the day. "I'm good."

"You're swaying," Leah responded.

It was five more awkward minutes between Sadiyah's labored breaths and Leah's quick-draw fan before Sadiyah had gotten her wits about her and left the office, then the company, behind for good.

2

THE BOY NEXT DOOR

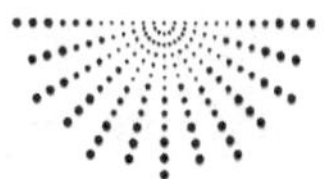

WHEN KAREEM CARTER WAS NINE YEARS OLD, HE DECIDED HE'D become a superhero. Specifically, he'd seen *Spider-Man 3* and coincidentally had a weirdly large bug bite on his wrist. Which, at the time, was only further confirmation that a radioactive spider had righteously imbued him with unknown superhuman capabilities.

Not long after, Kareem and his folks moved into a new house. It was a pale green, two-story house on a cul-de-sac, with neat front and backyards and a room all to himself. Kareem didn't care about that, though. He didn't mind his old room in his old brick apartment with the deep green awning at its entrance, the too-old playground, and the cracked sidewalks.

Truthfully, Kareem hated his new house because he knew moving there wasn't for anything good. It was an overblown effort to try and forget a terrible accident—otherwise known as his mother's sudden miscarriage—that didn't work. Just added more space for him and his parents to know exactly what they were missing.

So, they all retreated to their own corners, apart from one another. Kareem's mother, Layla, rarely left her room. His father, Amir, was hardly ever around, always busy with work. And Kareem would go to the field of trees just outside their backyard fence. He'd hang out there, climbing on the trees, lifting rocks, and doing whatever else he'd read about in his comic books, so long as he wasn't in that house.

Admittedly, Kareem was a weird kid, so he was used to dealing with his imagination alone. But after seeing what happens when a loved one dies, his ideation grew wings, and he convinced himself that everything he did from then on was in preparation. That if he could just become like one of the characters from his books, then he could stop anything bad from ever happening again. He could protect everyone. He would protect everyone.

That's when he met Sadiyah.

Sadiyah had a way of attracting Kareem's attention just by being around him. In the few weeks since he'd moved next door to her on Wisteria Street, he'd quickly learned that he was always immediately aware of her. He thought she was pretty, with brown skin covered in freckles he could've counted out like constellations, and thick, curly black hair, which made him too nervous to speak each time he'd tried to introduce himself to her in class.

"What are you doing?" Sadiyah asked him from behind one afternoon after school. She'd found him headed to the woods behind their houses then, the one place he'd thought he could hide alone. This was the first set of words either of them had ever said to the other, and it surprised him how normal it felt to have her voice directed at him.

Kareem didn't know how to respond to it, though. He looked down and saw that her shadow was practically holding his hand, and he didn't know what to do with that information, either. So he didn't do anything.

"Hey!" She called. "I know you know hear me."

Kareem took a breath, then stopped walking and slowly

turned around. Thinking about talking to her was one thing. Actually talking to her was another entirely, especially given that he knew how pitiful he'd quickly made himself look to her in school, crying on his first day of fourth grade as the resident new kid. He was terrible at hiding his efforts not to remember what had happened to his mother. At trying not to cry because he couldn't help her. Which was why he hid in his comics so often.

"I do," he finally said.

Sadiyah shoved her hands in her pockets, looking over him steadily before responding. Her eyes were the color of root beer, and she smelled like flowers. It was an exciting combination. "You hiding bodies out here, or something? You gonna kill me, too?" she pointed to the trees, "I promise you I know this place a lot better than you do."

He sputtered on a laugh. Then he kicked at a rock, in an effort to hide his nervousness and look cool, feigning truly contemplating her question. "Maybe," he shrugged, then turned back around.

Kareem didn't kill her, of course. First of all, how could a burgeoning superhero even think of that? Second, Kareem wasn't used to having company around him yet, especially her. Meaning third, for lack of a better explanation, he was curious about the girl who'd made her way to him without any invitation. Specifically, why he didn't want her to leave. Before it hit him. Literally.

"It" was Sadiyah's hot pink JanSport she'd catapulted at his head from behind him. She'd missed, thankfully, and it landed with a thumping sound against Kareem's back. He fell face forward onto the grass.

"Hey!" Kareem rolled over to find that Sadiyah was already standing over him.

She hovered there, the sun's light blocked out by her silhouette. "See?"

Kareem squeezed his eyes shut for a moment, slightly disappointed that no amount of spidey senses had alerted him to her motives. He picked up his glasses beside him, fit them back on his face, and asked, "See what?"

Sadiyah was still shading him from the sun when he stood up. That was last year she was taller than him. "That you need me to help you with surprise attacks like that."

"You were the surprise attack." Kareem countered.

"I was a warning," Sadiyah corrected, picking up her bookbag.

"You are insane," he muttered. Louder, he asked, "Is there a difference?"

"Yeah," Sadiyah smiled. "One is a warning. One is not."

Kareem just stared at her.

Sadiyah, who he'd only ever seen as exceptionally confident and definitely popular in school, suddenly looked shy. She folded her arms over her Bobby Jack shirt, not meeting him in the eyes then. "You read all those superhero books," she shrugged. "Don't you think you're one of them?"

"No," he denied. At least, not yet.

"I saw you do the Spider-Man thing when you finished Minute Math this morning." She fixed her hands and motioned like a web would've shot out and landed on one of the trees from them.

Kareem opened his mouth as if to speak and then closed it when he couldn't think of anything to say that'd save him from the truth. This girl had pinned him, embarrassingly, too many times for comfort. Had he known she'd been watching him, he would've made an effort to be much more discreet and thwipped under his desk, rather than celebrating on top of it. Kareem made a mental note to put a stop to his careless thwipping, when he decided to finally ask the question that'd been echoing over in his head.

"Why're you here?"

They were a little beyond the outskirts of the woods then. Kareem never thought it was too smart to go much further. He leaned his back against a tree and propped his leg up on it.

Sadiyah interlocked her fingers, cracking her knuckles, and just in that simple move, she was infinitely cooler than he was. "I knew you hung out here," she said, turning and pointing to her house. "I can see you from my window. Plus, my mom told me I should hang out with you."

Whatever joy Kareem had felt quickly diminished along with her final admission. Briefly, he wondered if she'd gotten his powers instead. If she'd somehow gained the ability to mind control and mindscrew before he'd even acquired anything. He tried not to be jealous. "Pfft. I can be by myself."

"I know, that's why I'm here," she nodded, then gestured to herself, "Captain Wonder."

"Captain. . . ?" Kareem thought it over. "Like Captain America and Wonder Woman?"

Sadiyah shook her head, confused. "I thought it was just Captain Wonder."

Kareem couldn't help but laugh. He was surprised by how her lack of working knowledge of something he loved so much delighted him. He put his foot back down, and it landed on top of one of the tree's roots, immediately throwing him off balance. "So your mom told you to be friends with the loser new kid?"

"The loser new kid *and* next door neighbor," she clarified.

"You really don't know how to sugarcoat things, do you?"

She waved her hand. "Why should I?"

Kareem laughed again. "I have some. . . Captain Wonder books back at home. Want to see them?"

Sadiyah adjusted the shoulder straps of her bookbag. "Let's go, Spider-Man."

He was right behind her. "At your six, Captain Wonder."

That night, Kareem and Sadiyah read Captain America and

Wonder Woman comics on Sadiyah's front porch until the streetlights came on. There, Kareem forgot about his wish for powers altogether, concluding that it would be alright with him so long as he was enough to save her if she ever needed it. Sadiyah Mitchell, his first non-fictional friend. His eventual best friend, who, thanks to her mother's coercion, saved him from his loneliness.

If only things stayed that simple as they grew up. But elementary school eventually ended, then middle school, and high school after that. Kareem stopped waiting for powers, forgot which wrist that bug bite had ever even been on, and then everything changed for good.

He sighed now. Kareem was only ever reminded of that memory for two reasons. Either he needed to remember how stupid he was as a kid to think of trading Spider-Man powers for anything to do with Sadiyah Mitchell, or he was face-to-face with her already.

"Yo," he called, caught somewhere in the middle.

They were currently outside of their masjid, him on the sidewalk and Sadiyah sitting in her car, beating her steering wheel like she was trying to snap it off its column. Usually, they pretended not to see each other whenever they crossed paths these days, since most of their interactions almost inevitably ended in long-winded arguments. But now, as he walked by her, beating her hands against her steering wheel, his mouth continued to run off before he could get it to stop.

"Aye, ma. You good?"

Kareem could see the moment when recognition tunneled its way through Sadiyah. Her fingers, curled into tight little angry balls, quit slamming against the leather as she turned his way. Sadiyah shifted her gaze to Kareem. She did not look happy to see him.

"Do I look good?" she snapped, then kissed her teeth as if he needed a clearer indication of her not wanting him around.

Kareem cleared his throat. Her hijab, wine-like violet, had fallen in part over her left eye, and her skin had been flushed moderately red. "Nah, you look a mess," he shrugged, straightening his T-shirt tucked into his trousers. "Having that pity party all loud for everyone to hear."

"Go away," Sadiyah shooed him before yanking down her vanity mirror.

There was this habit Sadiyah had since they were kids, where she'd hiccup after she'd finished crying. Not just once, but a series of strung-together spasms that she always had a hard time controlling. She hiccupped now, three of them fixed together like paper chains as she fixed her hijab in the mirror. When she glanced over to him, most likely to see if he heard, since she knew they were both well aware of what it meant, he saw that her eyes were watery.

Then, she hiccuped again. Four times.

Kareem, unlike his mouth, did not move. He didn't like who he became around Sadiyah. She had a way of aggravating him into becoming a petty version of himself who felt a lot like an overgrown toddler. Pubescent. But he didn't care. She started it.

"If I don't?" he pressed.

Sadiyah shot him a look that he was sure she'd intended to come off a lot more menacing than it did with swollen-over eyes.

Kareem squinted his own. "You gonna beat the steering wheel up some more?"

"You rather I beat you?"

His face soured. "Huh?"

"Are you dumb? I said—" Kareem was just about to cut her off, but then Sadiyah hiccuped again, and again, and he lost his train of thought. "Kareem," she said tightly.

"What's up, Sadiyah?" Kareem dipped his head down, inviting her to continue. Sadiyah's little brother, Syed, had asked him to practice basketball with him after service today. Kareem planned to meet Syed at his house after he changed and closed his office for the day, which shouldn't be a problem if Kareem made sure to leave the house nearly as soon as he got there, hopeful not to run into Sadiyah twice in one day. "As-Salamu Alaykum," he added.

"Wa Alaykum As-Salam," she returned. "Now I'm not about to get out of character for you on Jumu'ah. So go." Sadiyah pointed to the masjid behind them, then rolled her window up, creating a temporary wall of defense against him, just as he went,

"Aw, here you go with the self-righteous routine."

Sadiyah turned off the car and opened her door. The green checkered pillow he'd given her to sit on so she could see above the dashboard better fell into the space between them. She bent down to pick it up and hurriedly tossed it back into the car.

"Bro, what do you want?" she looked up at him under heavy lids. Her eyes were redder than he thought they'd be up close.

Kareem furrowed his eyebrows and scratched his goatee. "You look high," he shrugged.

Sadiyah rolled her eyes, redirecting her attention back to her reflection on the side of her gray sedan. "You know what that looks like?" she threw, but didn't hiccup.

"You know what?" He waited to see if she'd hiccup again. With each passing moment, Kareem found himself increasingly more blindsided by how childishly angry Sadiyah made him. How she was still holding onto that singular bad day, that fight they'd had all these years later.

He turned toward the sidewalk, no longer concerned with her hiccups, or now lack thereof, and bit out, "You really are miserable." Then, he strode off toward the masjid. Refusing to waver, turn around, or take it back.

3

MOTHER KNOWS BE$T

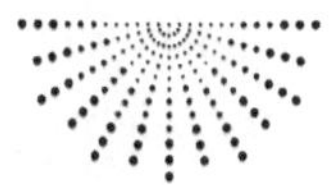

SADIYAH TURNED ONTO WISTERIA STREET AND PARKED IN FRONT of her mom's house. She hadn't originally planned to come here, but between sobbing the entire drive to the masjid and pretending she hadn't when Kareem found her, Sadiyah was desperate not to find out what happened once she was left alone again.

A million years ago, Sadiyah and Kareem would play rock, paper, scissors when they couldn't agree on what to do, and Kareem would win the fair majority of their matches. He used to say he could read her better than he could read his comics, which was saying something, since he read them so often.

Sadiyah remembered a lot of her childhood spent staring into his brown eyes that picked her apart almost clinically. He'd done that today, seen right through her effort to seem unaffected by the news she'd received this morning. So it shouldn't have surprised her much when he called her miserable, too.

Since she could remember, Sadiyah never took well to being overwhelmed. Her role in life was to be the calm one. To see everyone else's problems and find a way to fix them. She was, by extension, not supposed to have problems of her own. At the very least, not this one.

"Fired?" she muttered to herself, indignant, getting out of the car and walking toward the front porch of the white-clad house she grew up in. "I don't get fired or laid off. I quit." She angrily fished her keys out of her purse and opened the front door, murmuring again. *"I quit."*

Sadiyah slipped off her shoes by the front door after walking inside and found her mother, Zahra, in the kitchen. If Zahra sensed anything off about Sadiyah's fixation on socializing, she didn't bring any immediate attention to it. There was only the slightest twitch in her brows that made it evident she may have caught wind of something as she washed off cuts of lamb in the sink. Her skin, as rich as a chestnut, glowed under the light streaming in through the window she faced, delineated by her black hijab. She was, to Sadiyah, what it meant to be kissed by the sun.

Sadiyah sat in front of the island in the middle of the room, about to take off her hijab, when her mother spoke up after exchanging salams.

"Keep it on," Zahra told her. "Sy has company upstairs."

"Oh, who?"

Zahra didn't answer, moving on to another topic instead. "You want lamb stew tonight?"

Sadiyah was sure her mother heard her, but she didn't care enough to ask again. "Yeah," she nodded.

Somehow, being in the kitchen as Zahra now marinated the cuts of lamb, time seemed to ease up for her. It slowed, allowing Sadiyah to continue processing the news from the morning. To input the simplest change of data into her mind: She had a job when she woke up. Now, she didn't.

Sadiyah had never been fired before. Coincidentally, she'd never quit a job either since this was the first and only position she'd held since undergrad. She had graduated from college in the early chaos of the coronavirus pandemic of 2020, right at the juncture when no one was taking the pandemic seriously, and countrywide curfews had been set in place. By the time the brunt of the craziness had simmered down enough for toilet paper to last on the shelves of the grocery stores longer than fifteen seconds, Sadiyah managed to snag a job helping with studies on heart diseases. And now, after faithfully following the script of grade school, college, and career, she was being let go?

"Wash the rice," Zahra instructed, taking vegetables from the fridge and placing them down on the cutting board she'd put onto the island.

Sadiyah was distracted by the low underwater hum she heard when she pressed down on her tragi. On dampening the illusory click-clacking of her hands against a keyboard she'd never see again. On softening the blow of Leah's news. Of Leah's treadmill. That good-for-nothing treadmill. She could still hear it whirring forward in the back of her mind.

"Sads," Zahra said louder this time, the red onion she'd begun to cut was now fully chopped in front of her. Sadiyah removed her fingers from her ears. She'd hoped that since memories weren't as easily forgotten, she could manipulate them by tricking her senses—killing off the sound. But they were still there, despite her. "You want to talk about it?"

"What?"

Zahra sighed. "I can only pretend like I don't see those puppy dog eyes for so long."

Sadiyah bit her lip. It wasn't about whether she wanted to talk or not; it was that she knew she wouldn't be any good at it. Talking about her issues would both sound dumb and make her feel dumber, especially when they were hardly even fleshed out.

She'd already gotten her lease renewal offer and had maybe a month before she needed to know for sure whether or not she was staying in her apartment for another year. With her savings, she figured she could be unemployed for a little while. But the emphasis was on "little." And there was no security in "little." So, she had to know past her next steps and into the ones that followed. And if she couldn't figure that out for herself yet, it was even harder for Sadiyah to say any of that to her mom. Which meant she stayed quiet.

"Fine," Zahra conceded, raising both hands. "Rice, then."

"You're serious?" Sadiyah asked because, as far as she'd known for twenty-five years, her mother couldn't stand "helpful" hands in the kitchen.

Because of it, Sadiyah wasn't much of a chef. Back at hers, she made the minute rice that was almost impossible to ruin—and still, sometimes did. But Zahra was different. Zahra had to feel every grain under the faucet before it reached the rice cooker.

"You're right," Zahra nodded, sliding the onion bits into a bowl and moving a red and green pepper into the sink, "You'll find a way to mess that up. How 'bout you just clean these off, then cut them? We should start getting your skills down now anyway."

Sadiyah's head pulled back reflexively. "'Skills' for what?" she asked, rounding the island to wash off the peppers after her mother sat down.

"Sadiyah," Zahra said her name deliberately, like a president greeting the audience at a conference. "Do you like living alone?"

"No," Sadiyah groaned, chopping the peppers a little too roughly.

"Really? I—"

"No, Ma. I mean, 'no' as in, let's not do this."

"Do what?" Zahra asked innocently, as if they hadn't already had this conversation enough times to know exactly how it went verbatim.

"You're gonna ask if I'm ready to finally get a. . . roommate."

"A man, Sadiyah," Zahra corrected. "A man."

"That's what I said." Sadiyah ignored her. "But that's not what I need."

"What do you need then, Sads?"

Sadiyah took in a deep breath.

Back in college, when she was forced to choose between taking a physical education course and graduating, she enrolled in two semesters of yoga. She did so to avoid spending her days smelling like a rank gym sock after courses like kickboxing or rock climbing. As a result, Sadiyah found that on the (very) rare occasions where corpse pose hadn't sent her straight to sleep for the better majority of the class, yoga possessed a series of useful breathing tactics that relaxed her.

Deep breathing had surprisingly become her favorite technique because, although it came naturally, it was something she needed the biggest reminder of whenever she was anxious. It consisted of two absurdly uncomplicated steps. One, breathe in through your nose. Two, breathe out through your mouth. The mindfulness of something supposedly so simple had reliably done a good job of calming her down in the years since.

She pushed a deeper breath out.

If Sadiyah were a more innately honest person, which now was as good a time as any to become one, she would've said her real reason for coming over today was more than not to mope alone. She would've bucked up and said that while the imam was speaking about the sin of pride during service, she was trying to figure out how she'd follow suit and ask her mom if she could move back in. At the very least, confirm she had the option to.

But yet again, Sadiyah froze up. To say she might need to move back in meant acknowledging that she'd been fired. Which meant admitting she was (1) perceived as a failure, (2) deemed a failure, and (3) thereby a failure. Zahra most likely wouldn't have agreed. But Sadiyah didn't want to take that chance and find out.

"Exactly," Zahra continued when Sadiyah couldn't seem to. "And anyway, I've got some news. I was going to wait, but you know me," she smiled, "impatient as ever. So look, Sister Malika wanted to know if you'd like to meet her son."

Sadiyah sliced her palm open instead of the pepper. She pulled her hand back and held it to her chest, pushing down on the cut with her thumb. "And what did you say?" she winced.

Zahra shook her head. "This is what I mean by you having no skills," she muttered, motioning to the sink so Sadiyah would run her hand under the water as she got up. "I said I'd speak with you about it," she answered, walking into the bathroom and returning with the first aid kit. "We need your permission, of course. Now, go sit down."

Sadiyah turned off the water once her blood stopped spilling and sat next to her mother on one of the island stools. She watched as Zahra opened the kit and took out the antiseptic wipes to clean the cut. "Wouldn't it be nice to have someone to take care of you?" Zahra questioned, covering the area with a bandaid.

Sadiyah decided in that moment that she wouldn't tell her mother about being laid off because Zahra wouldn't get it. Zahra had always been traditional in a way that made Sadiyah sick. She would've asked why Sadiyah was treating losing a job like losing a man, and then would've told her that if she had one, it wouldn't have hurt so badly because she'd had someone she could immediately depend on.

Then, Sadiyah would say something about how, by her own logic, Zahra didn't have anyone to rely on either after her dad split seven years before. And because that would've just been taking it too far, Sadiyah chose not to take it anywhere.

"Ma," Sadiyah relented. "What did you tell Sister Malika? For real. You know how she is."

"Look at you getting all worked up," Zahra scoffed, but Sadiyah knew it was in part because she agreed. Sister Malika was a very vocal woman who was often hard to say no to, which was why Sadiyah had a hard time believing her mom had even tried.

Zahra cupped Sadiyah's shoulders, making sure they were eye to eye. There was a faint smell of rubbing alcohol and vegetables around them. "That *is* what I told her," she protested, shaking Sadiyah. "Mmm'n I tol er nex Fri. . ."

Sadiyah stared. She always held a deep admiration for how very Southern her mother could get, but sometimes her accent was way too strong, and her speed was way too fast, and so her words collided in a way that sometimes made no sense. "What?"

"I told her next Friday," Zahra enunciated, removing her hands from Sadiyah's shoulders, although the spiced medicinal scent still lingered on.

Sadiyah took her time, allowing herself to truly hear that her mother had finally gone full throttle and set her up on a blind date without her knowledge. Then. "MA!"

"WHAT?"

"What happened to *my* permission?"

"I'm *asking* for your permission," Zahra smiled sweetly, like she had no idea what she'd done.

"No, you're not," Sadiyah muttered.

When her dad left, Zahra took over everything as if he were just away on a vacation. It was all so seamless after the dust had settled and they were sure he wouldn't be spinning the block back to them. Sadiyah decided then that if her mother could do that without any notice, then the least she could do was to take care of herself. So it was a shame that her mother didn't think the same of her. Even more so that she was beginning to doubt in her ability herself.

"I keep telling you I don't need to get married," she pleaded, her heart knotting. "What I need is a—" *job,* she caught herself just before the word slipped out, asking instead, "What if I don't want it? Marriage."

Zahra let out a deep sigh. Her voice was soft but carried an unmistakable sense of authority. "You do," she asserted.

Still, Sadiyah found herself asking, "Why?"

"Because it's good to have someone looking after you."

"You look after yourself and you're fine, Ma." Her words came out hoarse. "I'm just like you."

"Sadiyah."

"Yes?"

"Don't ever say no dumb mess to me like that again."

Sadiyah snorted. "You mad?"

"I'm saying," Zahra cleared her throat, and Sadiyah watched the crease that swam along her mother's forehead whenever she was too far lost in thought. "I don't want you to end up like me. You're my girl, but you're better than me, so I need better for you. For Sy and for you."

"How about you focus on Sy for now, then?" she grumbled. She sounded like a kindergartner trying to get out of time out. Which, actually, wasn't too far off from what was happening right then.

"I'll focus on your brother when it's time to focus on your brother. Now is your turn," she announced, standing up and brushing off her lap before returning the first aid kit to the bathroom and rewashing her hands. "You want this," she insisted before going back to cutting the rest of the vegetables.

"No, *you* want this," Sadiyah felt her body heat over. "You want grandkids. You want me to stay in the house with the picket fence and tire swing, supporting someone else. Their life, their dreams. Raise their child. Do their housework. Be *their* woman—"

"What if I sweetened the pot?" Zahra cut Sadiyah's rant short, finished cutting the peppers, and took out the rice to clean herself.

"Huh?"

"I'd pay you."

"*Pay* me?" Sadiyah scoffed. "You're getting so desperate that you're gonna pimp out your kid for a man? Isn't that a bit too far?"

"Nobody's pimping anybody," Zahra smiled, pausing before her next words. "The first time I asked and the fiftieth time I'll ask it, it'll be your choice—"

"How many times until you're done asking?"

"—because marriage is your own commitment to make. But I'm not giving up because I know it's the right decision for you."

"How much, then?" Sadiyah was curious.

Zahra regarded her for a long moment. "Ten?" she suggested. "For help buying somewhere to live, a nikah wedding ceremony, or whatever. Starting expenses, you know? I think that'd be a good wedding gift, don't you?"

Sadiyah squinted. "Ten dollars?"

"Ten thousand, Sads," Zahra corrected, calmly. Sadiyah was usually a lot quicker to understand what was going on around her, but today. . . today was an anomaly. "Just *try* to find a good man and fall in love. You don't always have to be the man of the house."

"Ten *thou*—?"

Sadiyah couldn't even be offended by how outdated her mother was. All she heard was ten thousand dollars. This was the most rich folk dilemma she'd ever found herself in, simply by denying her mother's marriage offers for years already. Now, considering nuptials had made themselves entirely more convincing. With that much money, she'd be set. For now, at least.

Sadiyah had a decision to make. The way she saw it, marriage didn't have to be a be-all and end-all affair for her. Instead, it could be the first rung of a ladder. She could make all of this work out for her. All she needed was a man who understood that she wasn't in it for the long haul with him. She needed a convincing show and a compelling string of moments that got her to where she needed to be.

It would be fine. She would be fine. She'd work it all out and would never have to admit to ever losing her job. Things would go back to normal. She'd get a new job, maybe even a cat, and she'd be fine.

"You're sure about this?" she asked, still somewhat wary.

Zahra tilted her head back to laugh, "You forget my daddy's business does alright, baby."

"Alright" was a bit of a stretch from the truth that her grandad's construction business did really, really well. Hearing stories of her mother's upbringing was always like listening to the plot of one of the K-dramas Sadiyah watched, where Zahra, the have, married her dad, the have-not. It wasn't that she was rich, but still, as her mother put it, she was alright. She got all the Eid presents on her list, so to speak.

Unfortunately, in the burdening spirit of letting her dad feel like a man, Sadiyah often felt like she was in the "have-not" storyline. Not so much in the sense of her father's poor pockets, but his poor mindset, which she discovered the hard way, was infinitely worse.

Remembering that distinction, Sadiyah reasoned it wouldn't be the worst thing to cash in on her mother's blatant need for her daughter to get married because at least she'd get something out of the deal, too. The way she saw it, both of them seemed to win in the end. "I'll do it," Sadiyah accepted her mother's conditions before she could take them back.

"Yeah?" Zahra gasped, mouth wide open.

"I'll do you one better. I'll do my best to get married by Eid al-Adha next month, or at least secure a proposal, if you make good on your end."

"For ten thousand dollars?" Zahra confirmed, then tilted her head as if realizing the absurdity of her offer, and said, "You know I'm joking, right?"

Sadiyah sniffed. "I'm not."

Silence swung between them as impatient as a pendulum. Finally, Zahra leaned in. "Sadiyah Hanan Mitchell, what's going on? You need money or something?"

"No," Sadiyah shook her head.

Zahra carried on, fixated. "I'm your mother, you know?" she reminded her. "I'm here to help. I can just—"

"No," Sadiyah raised her voice, hoping it sounded steadier than she felt. She took a breath. Swallowed. Smiled. "No, it's not that."

"Then please, by all means, tell me what it is. Because wallahi," she swore to God, "I've brought this up more times than I can count and you've never said yes until I added a price tag."

"It's just that you're right," Sadiyah shrugged casually, hoping she acted better than she felt. "I'm ready."

". . . For a roommate?"

"For a man," she corrected, repeating her mother's words just as Zahra had done before. "For someone to take care of me."

Zahra's eyebrows raised, assessing her daughter unbelievingly. Under the cutting heat of her mother's stare, Sadiyah felt so overwhelmingly small, as if Zahra could see straight through her and knew Sadiyah was wasting both of their time with her childish charade. She wanted to give in, admit that she needed help for once, and see what happened. But her stubborn tongue got stuck on the words.

"I can do this," Sadiyah admitted finally.

"Mm, I know you can do anything." Zahra rounded the island's corner and rested her hand dotingly against her daughter's cheek. Sadiyah just about fell apart again when she heard her mother mumble, "And I'm sorry for going above you like I did." Louder, she said, "Okay, if you're down, I am too. Inshallah"—God willing—"you'll find the love that was written for you."

ABOUT THE AUTHOR

Meenah is a Black, Muslim author who's always been known for having a book in one hand and a pen in the other. She plans to rock with this persona until the wheels fall off—that is to say, she hopes they never do. Meenah earned her B.A. in English, focusing on Creative Writing and Multicultural U.S. Literature, from Hollins University in 2020, and has a minor in watching one too many dramas and anime. She writes selfishly for her younger self, who rarely ever saw girls who looked like her in books—much less as the main character. Her interests include her bed, her couch, good food, cute trinkets, and overthinking disguised as self-guided meditation.

You can find her online at meenahwrites.com.

goodreads.com/meenah
pinterest.com/meenahwritess
youtube.com/@meenahwrites
tiktok.com/@meenahwrites
instagram.com/meenahwrites.jpg

9 798999 494016